Image/art disclaimer: Licensed material is being used for illustrative purposes only. Any person depicted in the licensed material is a model.

Editor: Erin Toland

Proofreader: Roxane Leblanc

Published in the United States of America

JEM Publishing

This is a work of fiction. While reference might be made to actual historical events or existing locations, the names, characters, businesses, places, and incidents are either the product of the author's imagination or are used fictitiously, and any resemblance to actual persons, living or dead, business establishments, events, or locales is entirely coincidental.

ISBN: 978-1-952625-37-4

Warning

This book is for sale to adults ONLY, as defined by the laws of the country where you made your purchase. Please store your files wisely and where they cannot be accessed by underage readers.

Dedication

This book is dedicated to my one and only—my amazing and wonderful husband.

Without your care and support, my writing would not have made it this far.

You pushed me when I needed to be pushed.

You supported me when I felt discouraged.

You believed in me when I didn't believe in myself.

If it weren't for you, this book never would have come to life.

Also by Ellie Masters

The LIGHTER SIDE

Ellie Masters is the lighter side of the Jet & Ellie Masters writing duo! You will find Contemporary Romance, Military Romance, Romantic Suspense, Billionaire Romance, and Rock Star Romance in Ellie's Works.

YOU CAN FIND ELLIE'S BOOKS HERE: ELLIEMASTERS.COM/BOOKS

Military Romance

Guardian Hostage Rescue Specialists

Rescuing Melissa

*(*Get a FREE copy of Rescuing Melissa

when you join Ellie's Newsletter*)*

Alpha Team

Rescuing Zoe

Rescuing Moira

Rescuing Eve

Rescuing Lily

Rescuing Jinx

Rescuing Maria

Bravo Team

Rescuing Angie

Rescuing Isabelle

Rescuing Carmen

Contemporary Romance

Firestorm

(KRISTY BROMBERG'S EVERYDAY HEROES WORLD)

Billionaire Romance

Billionaire Boys Club

Hawke

Richard

Brody

Contemporary Romance

Cocky Captain

(VI KEELAND & PENELOPE WARD'S COCKY HERO WORLD)

Romantic Suspense

EACH BOOK IS A STANDALONE NOVEL.

The Starling

~AND~

Science Fiction

Ellie Masters writing as L.A. Warren
Vendel Rising: a Science Fiction Serialized Novel

ONE

Jinx

JINX

"Jinx, are you okay? What happened?" Lily follows me into my room, concerned and worried for my sanity. Not that I blame her. Wolfe and I demolished the living room.

I live with Lily and Knox and moved to the bedroom farthest from their love nest. I swear they bang each other fifty-thousand times a day. Honestly, the two of them are shameless, going at it like rabbits day and night.

Meanwhile, my sex life is as dry as the Sahara. That's the fault of the frustrating man who knows exactly what buttons to push to get me riled up.

"I'm fine." I stomp into my room, arms folded across my chest, heat rising in my cheeks. It's not anger.

I'm hot, bothered, and aroused—turned on by the only physical contact I allow myself with the wolfish Wolfe.

What an appropriate name.

The man is a mangy half-breed—if we're calling a mangy half-breed the sexiest man alive. The bastard is good-looking, and he knows it. Like, drool-worthy good. Lord knows I've spent far too many nights salivating over the bastard.

"You don't look fine." Lily looks tiny in Knox's robe.

No doubt that little spat between Wolfe and I broke up another of Lily and Knox's sex-capades.

I turn on my best friend in the whole universe, needing an outlet for my anger. Not that she deserves to bear the brunt of this messy situation.

"Really?" I pointedly check out her attire. "You couldn't wait for the party to be over before fucking each other's brains out?"

"Jinx, that's not …"

"Not true? Or not fair?" I give her an out, but she won't deny the truth to my face.

"It's not fair." As expected, Lily's cheeks flush, moving toward bright crimson as I point to her boobs, which are trying their hardest to escape the terry cloth robe.

"I knew it."

"We *were* fucking each other's brains out when you and Wolfe started World War III in the living room. What's up with the two of you, anyway?"

"Nothing." I stomp over to the window and pull back the drape.

I keep it closed as much as possible, opening it only to drive Wolfe crazy. Fucking perv likes to jack off while watching me undress, and I get off on him getting off on me.

It's some fucked up twisted shit. Lily's not wrong about that.

How many nights have I resorted to yanking out my vibrator after watching him shamelessly jerk off in front of me?

Too many.

That's the long and the short of it—and talking about long …

I hate how I ache for him, but I'm not some bimbo to use and throw away. He did that once, and he's never doing it to me again.

Never.

"Nothing, my ass." Lily closes the gap in the robe with a sharp yank and plops down on my bed. "You two are going to have to work things out."

"Not happening."

"But if you're placed on Alpha's tech team, you're going to see a whole lot more of him."

"I'm not getting assigned to Alpha."

"You're not?" Lily's mouth gapes. "I thought …"

"You're not on Alpha. Why would I work with them when you and I are a package deal?"

"You know why." Lily cocks her head. "They're getting close to cracking the cipher in those ledgers. You have to be on that team. No one knows about that kind of shit like you."

"The only way I'll work with Alpha team is if they put you on that team. Then, I'll consider it. But no way—no how—am I getting any closer to that asshole." I jerk my thumb over my shoulder, pointing toward Wolfe's house.

He and Knox are neighbors, a stone's throw away from each other, and my bedroom window happens to face Wolfe's master bedroom. It's annoying as fuck, because I can't keep my eyes off of him when he thinks I'm not looking. My view looks right into his bedroom. Directly at his bed.

Where he sleeps.

Where he tosses and turns.

Where he stays up late reading on his phone.

The only time I can't see him is when he leaves the lights off. When he does, all I see is the reflection of my window in his.

Wolfe rarely leaves a light off.

He enjoys me watching him.

Lily picks at nonexistent lint on my comforter. She curls her legs up under her bottom and breathes out a sigh. "Knox won't have it. He knows I can take care of myself but says it would be too much of a distraction for him and the rest of the team."

"Fuckers. So where are they going to place you? Delta?" That's the only Guardian team with women on it. Jenny is Delta-One and a firecracker of a woman. Charlene is Delta-six.

"You've got the filthiest mouth on the planet." Lily loves my colorful language.

"I'm not the only one who knows how to swear like a sailor." I prop my fists on my hips and give her the eye. "Especially when you fuck."

"Jinx!" Lily grabs one of my pillows and throws it at me.

I dodge it without thinking. I've got the reflexes of a cat, and I always land on my feet.

"Don't deny it."

"I'm not denying it, and if you would get your head out of your ass, you'd be doing the nasty with Wolfe." Lily shakes her head, tired of the same discussion we've been having since we moved here from New Orleans. "That man wants you."

"He wants a quick fuck, and that's all."

"You're kidding, right?" Lily makes a show of rolling her eyes, showing her growing frustration. "He devours you every time he looks at you. *De-Vow-Ers*." She emphasizes each syllable.

"Does not."

"Girl, the air ignites when the two of you are in the same room."

"Does not."

"Does so." Lily blows out an exaggerated sigh. "We're all just waiting for the two of you to get your heads out of your respective asses and fuck each other's brains out already. The tension is that thick."

"Is not."

"Just jump his bones, already." Lily flops back on my bed. She peeks up at me. "Seriously, just fuck him."

"No."

"You're insufferable." Lily scoots to the edge of the bed. "I've never seen you this obsessed with a man before. One of you has to give the first inch. It's inevitable. Might as well be you."

"Not happening." I turn away because it's my turn for my cheeks to flush crimson.

"If you do, you can set the ground rules." Lily gives an exaggerated huff of frustration. "You seriously don't want him setting them."

She's not wrong about that. It's something to think about.

But how?

How do I set ground rules?

I hate how the thought of having sex with Wolfe turns me on. That deep-seated ache returns. It pulses within me. Flushes my cheeks. Makes my pussy throb. My nipples tighten into heartless betrayers. I've lost control of my body.

Because of a man.

Because of him.

Fucker.

We didn't do nearly as much as I would've liked in Callie's bar. After I ran up to Lily's place to put myself back together and checked Callie's apartment to make sure it wasn't a complete disaster, I headed back downstairs to collect Wolfe.

The plan was to bring him upstairs where we could do the nasty all night long. I was really looking forward to it because a man like him doesn't just have sex.

He has crazy monkey sex.

I just know it. And it's driving me crazy *not knowing* it.

But when I returned to the bar, I found him cozying up to another chick, minutes after I gave him a blow job in the bathroom. A jealous rage boiled up inside of me. Righteous anger followed right on the heels of that rage until I couldn't see anything but red.

"Wolfe's an asshole." I stomp my foot, emphasizing my point. I will not budge.

"He may be, but you're stuck on stupid if you don't march over there right now and take what you want from him."

"He's a straight-up A-S-S-Hole." I turn to Lily like she's crazy.

With his cocky walk, that roguish grin, and those dark, mesmerizing eyes, he's sex on a stick, and the man is most definitely a wolf out on the prowl.

"So? When have you ever been against a little casual sex? Just because you fuck him doesn't mean you have to like him. You most definitely don't have to keep him." She slips off the bed and gathers the robe around her slim body. With a tug, she cinches the robe tight and gives me a shake of her head. "Use him for sex. He won't be the first guy you've used to scratch that itch."

"You just don't get it." My shoulders slump.

The problem with Wolfe is there won't be anything casual about it. He's the kind of man who fucks with his whole soul, burning the memory of him into a girl's body, leaving all other men feeling less than as a result.

We haven't fucked. I gave him a blowjob, and he finger-fucked me into oblivion, but I already know it'll be true. Honestly, it terrifies me. If I'm this obsessed after a bit of heavy petting and a blow job, what kind of crazed lunatic will I turn into once he fucks me with that monster cock of his. The man is hung. I've seen the whole package, choked on him as he rammed his cock down my throat and held his balls in my hand.

"What I get," Lily says, "is the insane chemistry you two share. You're still butt-hurt from New Orleans. You don't know if he actually fucked that girl."

"I know what I saw."

"So why don't you call him out on it?"

"Because."

"Because you're too chicken shit to talk about it?" She heads for my door. "It's called communication for a reason, Jinx. Tell him what you saw. See what he says. Verify before jumping to conclusions."

I'm not against casual sex.

I'm not against wild monkey sex in the back of a bar.

I'm not against getting finger banged and giving a blow job to a virtual stranger as a warm-up to some of that crazy monkey sex.

What I'm not is a girl a man fucks and leaves—stranger or not —for another chick.

That's why I detest him as much as I do.

Not five minutes after we hooked up in Callie's bar, he found another chick to seduce and fuck. When I came down, he'd already moved on, cozying up with some bitch.

The man has no shame.

No shame at all.

And he wonders why I can't stand him?

Like he doesn't know I saw him trailing that chick when she went to the bathroom? The very same bathroom where he blew my mind with the deft skill of some extremely talented fingers?

I had a mind to go after him then and show him exactly what I thought of his whorish ways, but I stomped out of the bar and headed home before the tears pooling in my eyes had a chance to fall. I haven't been with another man since.

No kissing. No petting. No fingering. No nothing.

Fucking putz.

And he keeps getting under my skin.

Each time I tell myself I'm done, he does something to piss me off. As my temper flares, I lose all sense of self-preservation, going after him like a cat in heat, only to be pissed at my lack of control later.

That's my biggest issue right now.

I.

Can't.

Resist.

Him.

And I hate that. I hate that my defenses crumble. That I'm the one yelling at him, and then my hands are all over him. That I kiss him like a deranged lunatic. All that does is make the cocksure asshole even more frustratingly annoying.

I bet he does it on purpose.

He gets me hot under the collar and waits for that heat to boil over. I don't even want to continue down this vein of thought. So, what do I do?

I do what I always do. I head to the window and draw back the drapes, hoping for a chance to see him.

He's not in his bedroom. I've got the best view of that, but there's movement on his deck. He catches me spying on him, turning to look at me through the window. How does he do that? Invariably, he catches me every damn time.

But I'm not backing down now. I'm too pissed to run and hide.

And what does he do?

The fucker stands, takes off his shirt, and kicks off his shoes. Then he pulls out his phone and sends me a text.

My eyes widen at the blatant invitation, then my cheeks heat as desire sweeps through me. I'm going to regret it, but I can't help myself.

This needs to end.

My grip on the phone is tight enough to turn my knuckles white. I storm out of my room, rage down the hall, and stomp over to his place. With my fist raised to bang on the front door, I stop.

His text. The arrogance. I'm so hot, I'm livid. I turn toward the camera guarding his front door and give him the finger. Then I turn about and march right back to my room.

Lily's right about one thing. I need to get laid. It's just not going to be Wolfe, even if the thought of sleeping with any other man seems like settling for a whole lot less.

Back in my room, I close the drapes, dress in my sluttiest outfit, grab my keys, and head to the closest bar I can find. Let's see what Wolfe thinks when he sees another man's hands on my skin. Another man's lips on mine. Another man taking what Wolfe almost had.

Two can very well play at this game.

TWO

Wolfe

A FIERY SPIRIT, JINX IS HOT AS SIN AND AS SEDUCTIVE AS A SIREN. She's a Grecian goddess sent by the gods to torment unsuspecting men who can't help but fall to their knees in reverent adoration.

She's a tantalizing temptress and a total cock tease, sending mixed signals until my head feels like it's going to explode.

Both heads.

She kissed me in New Orleans, dragged me to the bathroom, where she climbed my body like a cat in heat. I fingered her to an ear-splitting release, then she blew my mind with her hot mouth, talented tongue, and hands that took me to the brink and beyond.

Those kinds of things make a guy think a chick's into him.

I'm not wrong about that.

But ever since she and her best friend, Lily, moved to California and joined forces with the Guardians, she acts like none of that happened.

As if she didn't hump my leg.

As if she didn't shamelessly grind against me and come all over my fingers.

As if she didn't wrap her silky lips around my cock to suck me like the temptress she is.

For some reason, she's pissed, yet I've done nothing wrong.

Perfect angel here. I've treated her with nothing but respect.

Her explosive temper should drive me away, but fuck if it's not a goddamn siren's call, drawing me in, heating me up, making my mind spin, and my body come alive.

When I catch her looking at me, I'm instantly hard. Each and every time, without fail, the moment she realizes I've caught her staring, she turns away with a dismissive snort, leaving me aching.

She desperately fights her attraction. I don't mind watching that battle unfold because I know something she's yet to accept.

Jinx wants me with desperate hunger. She can be angry, pissed, and annoyed, but that's a war she's doomed to lose.

I have the best weapon in my arsenal, and I'll shamelessly use it in my quest to claim her as my own. I feed that volatile temper of hers until she's boiling hot, primed to explode, then, I kiss her. I did that in Knox's kitchen.

I love the way she fights her natural instincts.

How she refuses to accept the inevitable.

Even as she twirls, flowing in that lethal Brazilian fighting dance of hers, getting in three hits to my one, the girl can't help herself.

She always kisses me back.

Always.

She rises on tiptoe, hands lifting until she cups my face. Eyes simmering, she presses her silky lips against mine. Her kiss silences my protests, steals my breath, and sends my heart into overdrive. Adrenaline spikes, racing around my body, making me take notice even as I get lost in the tenderness of the kiss.

My heart skips a beat. My fingers curl around her tiny waist. I devour her intoxicating essence like a man starving for what he can't have. She ignites a firestorm that burns like the sun, turning everything to ash as it sweeps through me.

Then the space between us explodes. Jinx pulls back, anger building as if I'm responsible for the kiss. She slaps me and storms off in a huff.

We tore up Knox's living room. Destroying bookcases and

shattering his glass table. Fixing that is going to put a major dent in my wallet, but the kiss was worth every penny.

I've kissed before, but those kisses were weak, empty things. They didn't burn through me like Jinx's tantalizing teases.

I'd love to end one of our fights by tossing her over my shoulder, loudly proclaiming, *"You. Me. Bed. Now."* But to do that, I need to win one of our fights.

So far, I'm zero for two.

I meander back to my home, frustrated and aroused.

My house is literally a stone's throw from Knox's place. Although, it's not as big or as nice. I've got something of a '70s bungalow perched on the side of the cliff. It has two bedrooms. Perfect for a bachelor to call home.

Once through the front door, I head outside to watch the sun go down. It's my favorite time of day.

Grabbing a cold one from the fridge, I lounge in a chair and stare out over the glittering sea.

It's a calm, cloudless day, which means the sunset won't be nearly as spectacular. Not that I mind. A light breeze blows off the ocean, ruffling my hair. Down below, the slow, steady rhythm of waves hitting the beach syncs with the beating of my heart.

Not one to meditate, I've been told there's power in such a thing. My eyes drift closed as I hone in on the sounds around me.

Seabirds call overhead, screeching to one another as they hunt their next meal. Light gusts ruffle the sparse foliage clinging to the cliff wall beneath me. The wind chimes on my deck tinkle, adding randomness to the world around me. The surf below rolls relentlessly onward, churning the rocky coast into grains of sand one powerful surge at a time.

Out on the water, a solitary surfer bobs in the water beyond the breakwater. The surf along this part of the coast is deadly, but this isn't the first time I've seen that particular surfer brave the waves.

One of our nearby neighbors, Noodles, plays keyboard for Angel Fire: one of my favorite bands. His Zen-esque lifestyle is one I don't understand, and if the rumors are true, he's not out there to surf. He's there to talk to Old Joe, a great white shark who hunts these waters and happens to be Noodles's friend.

My eyes snap open as I fail, yet again, to meditate.

That Zen state eludes me with the distractions around me. I tip the bottle to my lips and swallow down the cold brew. To my left, a window opens next door. I turn, instinctually feeling her eyes on me.

When Lily and Jinx joined the Guardians, they moved in with Knox. Jinx's window faces my bedroom, which complicates things as much as it enhances the crazy attraction pushing and pulling us apart.

She leans out of the window. Her long, dark hair blows back from her angelic face as she tilts her head back and closes her eyes. Her honeyed skin takes to the California sun, deepening her tan to a golden brown. Long, black lashes frame her face, highlighting the sculpting of her cheeks and her tiny, upturned nose. Her pillowy lips, soft as sin, sexy as silk, curve upward into the most serene smile I've ever seen.

She knows I'm out back on my porch. The girl watches my every move. She also knows I've got an unobstructed view of her bedroom. It's something she uses to tease and torment me, a nightly ritual we began the first night she moved in.

Lily and Knox know nothing of the games we play. They're blissfully unaware, too wrapped up in themselves to take notice of what happens beneath their own roof.

Jinx's eyes slowly open. Her head turns until our gazes connect and instantly clash. Less than an hour ago, I held her in my arms, stealing a kiss, which prompted a fight in Knox's kitchen. That fight extended to the living room, where mayhem and destruction followed.

I still taste her on my lips.

With her eyes on me, I place the beer down on the table beside me. Then I stand and slowly turn toward her. She doesn't turn away as I peel my shirt over my head, tossing it to the deck. I eye her, waiting for her to retreat, but Jinx won't. She takes my challenge and stands firm.

Pressing my fingers to my lips, it's a reminder of that kiss in the kitchen. Her eyes flare, widening momentarily, and her pert lips part. I make a show of kicking off my shoes.

She knows what comes next. We've danced this dance for weeks.

The first time she stripped for me, Jinx didn't know I could see right into her room. Our bedroom windows face each other. She didn't know because the lights were off in mine. When I came home after sparring practice with the guys, I froze when I realized I could see everything.

I remember that day vividly, as does my cock. Already, the fucker wakes up, lengthening and hardening as it weeps for her. That first night, not wanting her to think I was a perv, I turned on the lights, letting her know our bedrooms faced each other.

Okay, I'm a little bit of a perv because I waited until she slipped out of her pants before I flicked on the lights. Her head snapped up as I stepped to the window. Our gazes locked, much as they do now.

She didn't try to hide from me. There was no shock. No anger. No indignation. Instead, she held my gaze, almost as a challenge. That night, I closed the curtains like any gentleman would, then fucked my hand with her tantalizing image filling my mind and all kinds of filthy thoughts.

For the next week, she kept her drapes closed. Then one night, when I again came home late, I walked into my bedroom and came to a sudden halt. She was in her room, light on, facing me.

I turned on my lights, letting her know I was there. If she was going to undress in full view, then I would watch. I made several concessions for her, holding back my advances, but there was no way I was going to keep my drapes pulled out of respect for her privacy.

I was here first. This is my home. And I sleep with the windows and doors open.

What happened next will remain between us forever. I slowly took off my shirt, letting my muscles ripple and flex. Then I dropped it on the floor and waited.

Half a beat later, Jinx grabbed the bottom of her shirt and drew it over her head. I kicked off my shoes, much as I just did, then slid free of the constraint of my pants.

Hard and aroused, I waited to see what she would do next.

Pull the curtains? Turn off her light? Would she sneer at me in disgust? Or was this yet another tease?

She removed her jeans as my heart lodged in my throat, beating like a stallion in the last leg of a race. I gripped the waistband of my briefs, lifted it over my engorged cock, and stepped free. With no shame, I fisted my cock, letting her see how hard I was for her.

Jinx watched me glide my hand from root to tip, leaving her bra and panties in place. I stared at her half-naked state with fantasies spilling through my mind. Jinx on her knees blowing me. Jinx bent over the side of the bed as I rutted into her from behind. Jinx in my arms, back braced against the wall, as I buried myself deep into her wet heat.

I masturbated while she watched, turning to the side as my release slammed into me. My hips bucked and jerked with my release. When I turned back, the corners of her lips turned up into a smirk. She reached behind her to unfasten her bra strap. Before letting it drop, she closed her curtains, bringing a strangled moan of frustration to my lips.

The next morning, I looked out my window. There, taped to the glass, were two numbers with a slash between them. She gave me a 4 out of 10.

Bitch.

Each night, thereafter, I've upped the stakes, eager to improve my score. I'm up to 7 out of 10, but I want more.

And I've been preparing my revenge.

Picking up my phone, I tap out a simple text.

COME OVER IF YOU DARE.

WITH THAT, I SAUNTER INSIDE, FULLY EXPECTING HER TO IGNORE ME.

But that's not the point.

There's a chip on Jinx's shoulder, which means she rarely backs down from a dare.

It'll be fun to see which way she jumps.

THREE

Wolfe

THINKING ABOUT GETTING UNDER JINX'S SKIN—I'M GOING FOR shock and awe—I strip out of my clothes and wait for her by the front door. Just as expected, she runs right over.

Jinx won't let a dare get the better of her. Not that we'll have crazy monkey sex, but who knows. I haven't given up hope. At some point, the sexual tension between us will explode.

With a shrug, I plant my feet. Hard and very much aroused, my dick stands at attention. I fist my cock and wait.

Not two minutes later, the camera at the top of my drive pings with movement. A quick check on my phone and I watch her tight ass strut toward my door. Her fist lifts, as if to knock, but then she hesitates.

Quickly switching to the camera monitoring the front door, my eyes widen and my jaw drops when she gives me the finger and storms away.

What the hell are you doing, my fiery Jinx?

An hour passes with no sign of her. As soon as she leaves, I race to my room and turn off all the lights. Her drapes are closed, denying me a view inside, but the light flicks on. Then it goes out.

My girl is a night owl. It's odd for her to turn in this early. The sun just set. What is she up to? I'm curious as a fox to find out. Almost enough to head over and check on her.

What would Knox think if I came over?

He'd probably be pissed. No doubt he and Lily are ensconced in their room, fucking like rabbits. Those two cannot keep their hands off one another. I debate for some time what to do and come up with no solution.

Jinx didn't take the bait.

How frustratingly disappointing.

Unlike her to ignore a dare. Although, what I texted was basically an invitation to fuck. Knox isn't the only one with an overly active sex drive. Unlike him, however, I'm in a major dry spell.

The last woman I touched was Jinx, and that was weeks ago. I thought we might have done more, that night in Callie's bar, but she ran off so fast, I wasn't sure what was on her mind.

I settled down at the bar, waiting for her to come back, but nothing happened. A pretty blonde sat next to me, hoping to get lucky.

Polite, but firm, I let her down easy. The blonde left. I took a piss then returned to the bar. After another twenty minutes, with no Jinx, I gave up and went back to the house the team rented empty-handed.

To say I was more than a little confused is the understatement of the century. I still don't understand what went wrong. I'm never that bad at reading signals. Jinx and I definitely connected—until we didn't.

Pulling on a pair of black boxer briefs, I settle into bed to read a book. I'm a sci-fi fanatic and love reading late at night. The guys think I scroll through porn on my phone because I always read before bed. I let them think what they will. They won't tease me for watching porn.

Reading?

I'll catch flack for that.

An hour passes and I glance out the window for the hundredth time. Jinx's room remains frustratingly dark. It's well past eleven, three hours since the sun set, and she's not home.

I blow out a breath and flip to the next chapter. I scroll right back to the chapter I just finished because I can't for the life of me remember what I read. My thoughts churn about Jinx and what I'm going to do about her. I can't focus worth shit.

After rereading the same chapter three times, I decide to throw in the towel and give up. The phone goes down. The screen turns dark. I stand and stretch, head to the bathroom, then return with my head hanging with frustration.

The light flicks on in Jinx's room. I stop and hold my breath. A few seconds later, the drapes move. Not opening all at once, but rather shifting as if something behind the drapes moves.

I step to my window and brace my hands on my back. If I'm lucky, she'll yank open the drapes and tease and torment me as I rub another one out. It doesn't feel much like masturbating considering she watches my every move. My dick wakes up, eager for the show to begin. I lower my boxers to my thighs.

Right on cue, the moment my fingers wrap around my dick, the curtains open, and I get a view of Jinx and another man with his hands on her tits.

What the fuck?

My hand drops, and I yank up my shorts. I take a step until my nose practically touches the window. That guy is all over her like an ape. Arms wrap. Hands grope. He touches what belongs to me. The guy pulls at his shirt, getting his head stuck, as Jinx coyly looks toward me.

She knows I'm watching. I *always* watch. Slowly, deliberately, she gives me the finger. My girl turns to the gorilla and works to free his head from a simple cotton shirt.

Oh, hell no.

This is not happening.

As outrage builds to overflowing, I race out of my house and sprint to Knox's front door. Knox gave all of us our own security codes to his home, and I punch that in with fury boiling within me.

Once the door unlocks, I stomp down the hall and slam open the door to her room.

Jinx gasps. The man gives a girly-assed shriek as I barrel right into him.

"Get your fucking hands off my girl." My shout rattles the roof, and I'm two seconds from committing murder.

"Wolfe, get your hands off him." Jinx tries to get between me and whoever this asshole is, but I'm not having it.

I spin him around then bodily shove him out of Jinx's room. I keep on shoving him, and he doesn't resist. The rat bastard actually turns tail and sprints out the front door. Chest heaving, I stand in the hallway as Knox and Lily race out of their room.

Like the last time, they do it in style, guns raised, ready for action. I ignore them and glare at Jinx.

"You. Me. Your bedroom. Now." It's nearly what I fantasized earlier, but unlike then, I have no intention of taking her to bed. I'm simply going to explain the basics to her; things like who she belongs to and why.

Knox and Lily lower their guns. They exchange a look and shake their heads. I get the feeling they're getting tired of the constant bickering between me and Jinx. Knox gives me a look like I'm a fucking idiot, then follows his girl back to bed.

"What the hell do you think you're doing?" Jinx props her tiny fists on her hips. "You have no right coming in here, all caveman-like, kicking out my date." Jinx shakes her finger at me. "Correction, you scared the shit out of him, and for what?"

"First off, that man wasn't your date."

"Was too."

"No. He was your revenge." I close the distance between us.

Like most Guardians, I'm a big man. Jinx isn't exactly short, but she's tiny compared to me.

"What I do is ..."

"Every bit my business." I lean in, letting her know I'm serious. "You can either turn around and walk back to your room, or I can sling you over my shoulder and carry you all *'caveman-like'*." I use air quotes, tossing her words back at her. "And I'll do it. It's not an idle threat."

"You wouldn't dare." Her shoulders roll back, indignant and growing more so by the second.

"I'm serious." The menace in my tone sinks in and gets her attention.

Jinx looks over my shoulder, perhaps hoping Lily will provide reinforcement, but Lily won't be coming. Knox has my back. He knows I'm here to sort this shit out between me and Jinx.

"The last time you tried that, you wound up flat on your back." She's not wrong.

Jinx is a fierce fighter and an expert in Capoeira. I didn't give her enough credit, but she's lethal when she fights. Her ability to react quickly and dodge incoming blows makes her a force of nature. The kicks and sweeping trips easily take down an opponent. Follow that up with any number of nasty blows using her head, elbows, and knees; she's especially violent. She's knocked me to the ground twice. Once in New Orleans and, a second time, earlier today.

But if I can get my hands on her, she loses the advantage of her flowing moves. Honestly, it's entrancing to watch her work out. Sam asked her to teach Capoeira to a few of the Guardians. Now, we're all supposed to learn.

It's effective but only from a distance.

"We can '*talk*' but not in my room." Her eyes pinch, daring me to push back.

While an angry fuck sounds all kinds of awesome, we have some shit to sort out first. One of those things is establishing ground rules.

I gesture down the hall and shift back, giving her room to pass.

Jinx sniffs with indignation, then squeezes by me. I let her get just far enough, but then I grab her at the waist and haul her over my shoulder.

"I said …" I draw out my words. "We'll talk in your room."

"Fucking asshole." She pummels my back. "Put me down."

Jinx alternates from punching with her fists to pushing up with her arms. Her feet kick, but she's not getting free. Not while I have her in my arms.

I storm toward her room, slam the door behind me, then toss her ass on the bed. Standing at the foot of her bed, I force my breathing to slow. I'm worked into a frenzy. Lingering rage from whoever that asshole was and what he was doing in her room mixes with my general frustration with Jinx.

She scrambles back on her bed, huddling by the headboard. Jinx grabs a pillow, placing it between us like a shield.

"Calm down. I'm not going to hurt you." I run my fingers through my hair, frustrated, annoyed, and having not one clue what I'm going to do next.

"Then get out." She points toward the door.

I casually turn toward the door, with no intention of leaving any time soon. The moment my back is turned, she throws the pillow at me. I snatch it out of the air and toss it to the side. Jinx is up, rummaging around in her bedside drawer.

"Seriously? You're going to draw your weapon on me? Is that where we are?"

Jinx suddenly stops. Slowly, she closes the drawer. To my relief, there's no weapon in her hand. Her arms cross over her perky tits, drawing my eye. It's precisely the distraction I don't need.

"Where exactly are we, Wolfe?" Her brow arches. "You don't want me, and I definitely don't want a whoring man-whore."

"A what?" I choke back a laugh. "A whoring man-whore? That's not even a thing."

"Is so."

"Is totally not."

I take two steps to the left, pivot, and take six steps to the opposite side of the room. Whatever this is between us, it's fucked ten ways to Sunday.

"What the hell were you doing with that guy?" I point to her open drapes. "You knew I'd be watching. Is that what you wanted? You wanted to prove a point? You won't fuck me, but you'll grab the first Joe in a bar and bring him home? Fuck him in front of me?" My voice rises until I'm shouting.

"It's none of your business who I fuck."

"It is when you involve me."

"I didn't involve you."

I storm over to the drapes and yank them apart. "When you open the curtains and turn on the light, you involve me. What the hell do you think we've been doing?"

"We're not *doing* anything." She yells right back, meeting me with vitriol and venom. "We're definitely not dating."

"And why is that?" My voice rises.

"Because you're an ass. You're a fucking ass. A prick. A jerk. A dickhead, and a ..."

"You going to spit out every word? If you are, at least take a breath. Your cheeks are cherry red, luv."

Her hands fly to her cheeks. "Don't call me that."

"What?" I think back on what I just said, then stop my pacing. "Luv? That's what's got your panties twisted?"

"Just don't call me that. I'm not your girl. I'm not your *luv*. I'm not *your* anything."

"I beg to differ. After that night ..."

"The night you finger-banged me then went for chick number two? Were you upset because that blowjob didn't do it for you? Had to move on to the next chick who would put out? How many women did you intend to fuck that night?"

"Whoa! What the fuck are you talking about?"

"I'm talking about the night we met. I came back down to get you and you were running after that blonde with your tongue hanging out."

"No, I wasn't."

"I saw you. I fucking saw you."

"What the hell do you think you saw?"

"I saw you at the bar, nuzzling her neck, and ..." Her eyes turn shiny.

Is Jinx about to cry?

Her words hit me hard and fast, slamming into me too fast to process all at once. But then it hits, and everything makes sense. I close the distance before she can react and fold her into my arms.

She resists. Jinx pushes against my chest, but there's no way I'm letting her go.

"I had to take a piss. That blonde was trying to pick me up. Not the other way around. The music was so loud, I had to shout in her ear and tell her I was waiting for someone. Shit, Jinx, I was waiting for you. I thought you were done with me. When you never came back, I left."

"What?" Her voice is so soft, I barely hear her whisper. "That's not what I saw."

"I don't care what you think you saw; I'm telling you the truth. I have no reason to lie to you."

Jinx sniffs and pushes against my chest again. Against my better judgment, I let her go. It feels like the right thing to do, even if everything inside of me tells me to hold on and never let go.

My hands fall to my side, and I take a step back, letting her push me away, giving her room. She's pinned between her bed and her nightstand. I turn around and walk to the door. Digging my fingers through my hair, I can't believe it.

"Is that why you're so mad at me?" I rub at the scruff on my jaw, confused as shit, but piecing things together.

"What other reason would I have?"

"You were plenty pissed when we weren't going to let you come with us to save Lily."

"Lily is everything to me. You bet I was pissed. All you guys, with your badass bodies, your SEAL this, and SEAL that, you think the rest of us can't take care of ourselves."

"You most certainly showed us that you could."

"I'm not helpless."

"I've never once thought that, but you sure laid into me."

"Because you fucked me and moved on."

"We never technically fucked." I lean against her door and think about all the time we've wasted. How can I fix this?

Jinx takes in a deep breath. I follow suit. Silence falls between us. My hand goes to the doorknob as an idea forms in my head.

"You're leaving?" Anger flares in her eyes.

"I'm not leaving."

"Then why is your hand on the doorknob?" Fear lurks in her eyes, and then it hits me.

It's something I should've realized, or would've if I'd known what she thought she saw. Like Lily, Jinx was abandoned at birth. They were both adopted by the same family and grew up as sisters. Their bond is tight. It's scary tight. They're close because they fear being abandoned again.

"I'm going to amend my statement."

"Whatever." She dismisses me with a flick of her lashes.

"Jinx, so help me, if you do that one more time, I really am going to paddle your ass."

"I'm not like Lily. I'm not into that kind of shit."

"Never say never, but what I was going to say is that, yes, I'm leaving, but I'm not going anywhere."

"Same thing."

"No. Very different things." I try to reason with her, hoping she'll listen to what I want to say.

"Then go."

"Luv, the only reason I'm leaving is because if I don't, I'm going to do something we'll both regret in the morning."

"And what's that?"

"You know exactly what *that* is."

"Fine by me. If you don't want to fuck me, then don't. No skin off my chin."

"For the love of all things holy, will you shut up and listen?"

"Fine." Her arms cross over her chest, drawing my attention, distracting me, and making it very hard to leave here a gentleman.

"If I stay, I'll be buried so deep inside of you, I'll never leave. You and I, we got off on the wrong foot. What you saw, isn't what happened, and you obviously have a lot of shit to sort out in your head."

"You playing shrink now?"

"No. I'm trying to be a goddamn gentleman here and leave while I still can."

"Then leave."

"Not until you listen to what I have to say."

"Then spit it out. Stop wasting my time."

"You need to sort things out in your head. I didn't do what you think I did. Which means ..."

"Means, what?"

"We need a do-over."

"A what?"

"A do-over." It's insane, what I propose, but how else are we going to erase the colossal fuck up that started this madness. "We pretend New Orleans never happened. You accept that I didn't fuck that blonde chick, and I accept that you didn't stand me up."

"A do-over?" Her brows pinch together, deep in thought. "I don't know if I can do that."

"Look, there's obviously chemistry between us. The air buzzes with the energy we share. I can stay. We can fuck. But wouldn't you rather start fresh? No hurt feelings? No trying to one-up the other?"

"No more watching you from my window?"

"Well, I'm not a saint." My attention flicks over to the paper taped in the lower-left corner of her window. "And I'm aiming for a ten."

"No need. You're a ten, ten times over. A hundred really. I just did that to fuck with you."

"Gave me something to strive for."

"Geez, if you're that easy ..." Her words trail off, and I can't help but smile.

This is what it was like in New Orleans before she dragged me to the back. We have insane chemistry. Whether angry taunts or cheesy lines, there's something about us that works.

"Let me take you out on a date."

"A date?"

"Yeah, an honest to goodness date. We'll dress up. Go to a fancy restaurant. Have some wine and see where things go from there."

I'm trying my hardest to set things right between us, but I'm smart enough to know Jinx's feelings aren't going to magically disappear. Her feelings of abandonment run deep. Those feelings shifted to me.

That's never happening again.

She's uncomfortably silent.

"What do you say? Can I pick you up at seven?"

"When?"

"Tomorrow night."

"I don't know." She nibbles at her lower lip and her brows pinch together.

"You're seriously going to turn me down?"

"I don't want to, but Mitzy and I are getting together to work on the cipher."

"Can't it wait?"

"Even one day is one day too many." Jinx tilts her head and stares at the ceiling. "Look, I'm sorry for assuming. I just …"

"There's no reason to explain."

"I'd like to start over." She turns her attention back to me. "But I need a few days to …" She waves her fingers in a circle by her ear. "To sort through my feelings. It's not a switch I can turn on and off."

"That's fair. I don't like it, but it's fair. So not tomorrow?" I still hope she'll reconsider, but it doesn't look like Jinx is going to bite.

"Not tomorrow." Her attention shifts to the window. With her lights on, she can't see outside. The window of my room is black as black can get with the lights out. "I promised I'd work on it with her after work."

"Friday? Saturday?" I shake my head and stretch out my arms. "Don't leave me hanging here."

"I'm not." She takes in a deep breath. "How about Saturday night?"

"Saturday it is." I twist the knob, knowing if I stay any longer, I won't be leaving. It's going to be hard enough as it is. "A date."

"Yes. It's a date." I open the door when she speaks again. "And I'm sorry, Wolfe. I should've said something."

I'm not sure if that's true. If I had been in her shoes, would I have jumped to the same conclusions? I think I would, and since that's the case, I'm not going to judge.

"We're going to forget all about that night. A do-over is just that. We'll pretend we never met."

"That's going to be awfully hard."

"Don't I know it." Already, my dick stirs, eager and hungry for her. I grit my teeth and control my body's reactions.

I take a step back, exiting her room, and gently shut her door. With Jinx on the other side, all I want is to rush back, claim her like I need to, but if this is going to last—and it will—we're going to do things right.

I tread lightly as I move down the hall and slip around the corner of the living room. Knox is there, waiting for me. Or maybe he's there to protect Jinx.

"Did you two sort things out?" He stands and stretches, leaning back with his hands pressed against his hips.

"Mostly."

"And?"

"Well, you don't have to worry about us fighting anymore."

"Right, you willing to take that bet?"

"No." I shake my head. "But we're good now."

"Good." Knox gives me a look. "Next time you barge over here at O-dark thirty, throw on some pants." He gestures to the boxer briefs I wear. I didn't even consider my state of dress when I ran over here.

"Copy that."

"You're such an asshole." Knox huffs a soft laugh. "I'm glad the two of you *figured* shit out." He turns and disappears into his room, leaving me standing in his living room.

He and Lily cleaned up the mess of shattered glass and hauled out the broken bookcases. That's going to cost me, but I think Lily was already looking to redecorate anyway. I'm always up for focusing on the positive.

As for the bright side of this mess, just because Jinx and I cleared the air doesn't mean her fiery temper is suddenly gone. It's a part of who she is, written into her genes. I'll simply have to tread lightly.

With a bounce to my step, I cross the short distance back to my place. In my bedroom, I pause. Jinx pulled her drapes closed.

FOUR

Jinx

THREE DAYS LATER, MITZY AND I ARE BOTH PULLING OUR HAIR OUT.

"It's gotta be something obvious." Mitzy's signature psychedelic hair shimmers from a fresh application of glitter. "You know, stupid simple."

She's a pretty thing, crazy, impulsive, and beyond brilliant. When she asked if I could help her break the cipher on the ledger Alpha team recovered from a rotten asshole of a man, I pinched myself.

Cryptology is kind of my jam, but Mitzy's so far beyond me. It's a struggle to keep up with her, and while I'm working on only this one project, she's multitasking like it's nothing.

"I know." I rub my eyes, blink, and yawn, trying to wake myself up.

We've been going at this for hours, and I need a break. Only, I can't take a break until Mitzy does. Or rather I could, but she's kind of my boss now. If the boss is working, I'm working. It's something my parents drilled into my head. They also said never quit.

"We're looking at it wrong."

Guardian HRS, among many things, owns a massive supercomputer lovingly referred to as *Jacen*. Forest Summers financed and then tinkered with the impressive computational power of the machine. He needs something gargantuan to crunch through all the data his special projects require. From cutting-edge VR simulations to Mitzy's artificial intelligence demands, which run her drone swarm, I'm surprised the supercomputer hasn't cracked the cipher on its own. Of course, there's his new robotics division as well. *Jacen* handles all the demands handed it like a champ.

"We've looked at it from every angle." Mitzy leans back and pouts.

Or maybe she's pissed? It's hard to tell. The craziness of her hair makes interpreting her expressions challenging.

When Sam and CJ recruited me to the Guardians, they wanted me to join the Guardian branch of their operation. That's what Lily's doing. She's integrating into their protocols and procedures, building on her DEA field operative expertise.

My bestie is a badass.

As for me, I was flattered to be asked to join the Guardians.

They took note of my Capoeira fighting skills, but my true love is intelligence work. That interest blooms from my childhood pastime of writing and breaking coded messages. As a kid, I always wanted to be a super-secret spy.

I love solving puzzles. One mention of that and Mitzy recruited me onto her Benefield Cipher Breaking gang. It's a gang of two; Mitzy and me.

"Maybe we should circle back to the beginning?" Mitzy leans back, blowing out her breath in frustration. "I've never been this stumped before." She runs her fingers through her hair, tugging at the psychedelic strands. "Benefield can't win."

Mitzy internalizes breaking Benefield's cipher, pitting her intellect against that of a human sex trafficker.

"Haven't we done that ten times already? I don't disagree that we need a fresh perspective, but …"

"I've been going down this rabbit hole of multilayered ciphers …" She twirls a fidget spinner in frustration.

"And?" I rub at my temples. All this screen time makes my eyes hurt.

"Benefield doesn't seem that sophisticated to me." Mitzy's frustration is palpable. "He was a rich bastard, with the morals of Satan himself, but he's not smarter than me."

Her irritation makes me smile. Mitzy's competitive and hates to lose, especially to a dead man.

"I agree. He was running a business." I choke on the words, as if running drugs and slaves is a viable business. We've been over this a dozen times. "It needs to be simple enough to make on the fly. Something he doesn't have to think about."

"Quick, easy, and specific." Mitzy twists her short spiky hair.

"Exactly." We at least agree on this. "One cipher, maybe two. We're simply missing the key phrase that unlocks everything."

"It has to be something he knows well."

Breaking a cipher is far more complicated than finding a key phrase. There are thousands upon thousands of codes developed by mankind, stretching all the way back before the time of Caesar. I can roll off a dozen or more without having to think about it: the Beale Cipher, the Bifid Cipher, the Spiral Cipher, the Book Cipher … The list goes on.

"From what Max and Knox told me about Benefield, and after I sat with Eve, I get an impression of an amoral, rich as sin bastard who cares more about hedonistic pursuits than crafting the world's best cipher."

"We're going to figure this out." Enthusiasm is my greatest weapon.

"That's what I told Forest when Max and Knox recovered Benefield's ledgers. It's been over a month. A month!" Mitzy leans back, frustrated. "From what Eve says, each month a dozen or more girls were funneled through The Retreat. How many girls are going to disappear because I can't crack this?"

Yeah, this is personal. Mitzy's frustration is easily understood. This isn't a simple job. We're talking about lives that were taken and destroyed.

"Knock one down, and another one takes its place. Benefield is gone, but the trade in slaves continues. Now that we know about the special-order side of things …we *have* to figure this out before the next snake takes his place."

A chill works its way down my spine. It's impossible to go far within Guardian HRS without hearing about the story of Moira, a rescued slave who was targeted by name to fulfill a buyer's purchase order. It happened to Zoe as well. The first time, her abduction was a thing of chance. A target that fit the general bill; young and pretty. She too was rescued, but that buyer put in another order, specifically to finish what he started: a snuff piece.

Disgusting.

It's all a fucked-up, twisted mess.

"What if it's as simple as a book cipher?"

"There's nothing simple about that." Mitzy blows out a breath, puffing her purple bangs out of her eyes. "Which book? We're dead in the water without the source code."

"Is there any way to go back and see if we can find something?"

"You mean send a team of Guardians back to the Retreat and search Benefield's office?"

"Didn't the Colombian government take control of the property?"

"Ri-ight." Mitzy rolls her eyes. "Like none of them are corrupt or involved."

"I just meant …"

"Benefield had his hands deep in the pockets of the local police, the reigning cartels, and all the way to the top of the government. They'll play nice, but if he did have a book there, the basis of this cipher, it's not there any longer. Consider that a non-starter."

"Then it's going to suck if that's what it is. There's no way to break it then."

"Not *no way*." Mitzy peers at her computer. "Just a lot of work for *Jacen*." She pronounces the initials, JCN, as *Jacen*.

It's a play on the movie "2001: a Space Odyssey," the space movie with the self-aware computer, HAL, that went rogue. The makers of that film took the letters IBM and moved them one lower in the alphabet. 'I' became 'H', 'B' became 'A', and 'M' became 'L'. Thus, HAL was born. Mitzy did the same, except she moved the letters one forward. 'I' became 'J', 'B' became 'C', and 'M' became 'N'.

Thus JCN—*Jacen*—was born.

Jacen has the computational power of several supercomputers, but even he will take time to pour through the hundreds of millions of books published to find the one key Benefield may, or may not, have used.

Needle in a haystack comes to mind.

"So …" Mitzy props her elbow on the table and cups her cheek in her hand. "I hear things have changed." Her brow arches, inquisitively.

"Things?" I play dumb, pretending I don't know what she's asking.

I'm not used to my personal business being everyone's daily topic of conversation. Although, it's no secret things between me and Wolfe have been tense. From the moment I slammed him to the floor in Callie's bar, people watch us. Personally, I don't see what's so damn interesting.

As for Wolfe, he texts me each and every day, wanting to make sure we're still on for our official put-the-past-behind-us date.

Honestly, all I want is to crawl into a hole and die. I know how to be angry at Wolfe. I've got that down to a science. I know which buttons to push and how hard to smash them to get the rise I want out of him. Since that night in the bar, all I've focused on is making him suffer.

Now?

I don't know what the fuck I'm doing. I don't even know how to act around him.

Everything's *different.*

Our nightly voyeur events?

My drapes have been closed since he tossed out Nameless Jo, my poor pickup date from the bar.

Teasing Wolfe.

Making him suffer.

I can do that in my sleep.

Our nightly ritual?

Him struggling to reach that perfect 10?

Damn if my blood doesn't run lava hot thinking about him stroking one out with thoughts of me on the brain.

But in person?

Sitting across from him over dinner?

Acting normal?

What are we going to talk about?

Hey, Wolfe, jerked off to me lately? Was it as good for you as it was for me?

My cheeks heat. No doubt they turn crimson, especially with Mitzy eying me the whole time these damaging thoughts race through my mind.

"You've got it sooooooo bad." Mitzy clasps her hands together, pleased with herself. I'm irritated. I'm embarrassed. I'm terribly turned on.

This "first" date with Wolfe? It's going to end only one way.

Explosive comes to mind.

"Well …" Mitzy's fingers tap with excitement. "Speak of the devil." Her gaze flicks over my shoulder, which has me turning around.

Sure as shit, Wolfe prowls toward me. There's no other way to describe the deliciousness that is the warrior he is. Eyes locked, he devours the ground between us, one mission on his mind.

Me.

The butterflies in my belly take flight, fluttering and buzzing until I'm nearly sick to my stomach. My heart kicks into overdrive, pushing blood through my body until it roars past my ears.

Mitzy pushes back from the table. Her chair spins and her toes touch the ground. I reach out, grabbing her wrist.

"Don't you dare."

"Don't, what?"

"Don't you dare leave me alone with him."

FIVE

Jinx

———

I'm not ready to face Wolfe in person. The last time we were in the same place, he tossed me over his shoulder. Carried me caveman-style to my room. Deposited me on my bed. And blew my mind.

There's no other way to describe it. I was ready to rip into him. Tear him apart piece by piece. My anger ran that deep. Instead, we paused. We took a break. We communicated.

It's exactly what Lily went on and on about.

Communication.

That should be a commercial.

Communication, it does the world good.

Wolfe and I could've bypassed all the anger, heartbreak, and misunderstanding if we'd only talked to each other.

I regret not doing that sooner, but was I really in a place to listen?

I can only shrug.

Abandonment and I have a difficult and complicated past. I'm much like Lily—at least the way she used to be.

Sex meant nothing to either of us. We never connected with the men we slept with. Why bother with an emotional investment? Our motto was to leave them before they left us. As a result, we tended to sleep around. Both of us still craved that connection to another person. Sex filled that hole within, momentarily at least.

We hated that men got to sleep around while chicks got labeled whores for doing the same thing. It became our personal mission to turn that mindset around.

Sex used to be nothing other than a physical release.

That was the beginning and end of it.

But then, Lily found herself a Guardian.

I found myself a man who devalued me and moved on like I was nothing. Or so I thought.

Damn, I hate the time we wasted.

"What are you ladies up to?" Wolfe on the prowl is the kind of kick in your gut that steals your breath.

At least for me.

Mitzy's immune, but then she married a rock star who has his own personal pet shark.

Yeah, a shark.

I've yet to meet Noodles, keyboardist of the mega rock band that is Angel Fire, but I'm curious about the Zen-esque lifestyle he leads.

I don't have any pets, but if I did, I'd go for a dragon. Noodles has a pet shark. I want a dragon.

"Still trying to crack this code." Wolfe pulls back the chair beside me and takes a seat. The heady essence that is him floods my senses. Dark, warm, and yummy, I can't help but close my eyes and breathe him in. "Can I help?"

"You?" Mitzy snorts. "You do know what we're trying to do?"

I don't like the tone Mitzy takes with Wolfe. There's rivalry between the tech guys and the Guardians, but just because they're the muscle doesn't mean they're dumb. Wolfe, in particular, strikes me as a man holding back.

"Yes, pixie, I'm very well aware of what you're *trying* to do."

"Don't call me that," Mitzy grumps as she pushes away from the table.

We've got four screens going at once. Different code-breaking programs work in the background, doing what we can do, but at superspeed. All we do is input the parameters of the different ciphers and let *Jacen* do the heavy lifting.

On the table, Benefield's ledger taunts us. Wolfe leans across me, pointedly brushing his massive bicep across my arm, and flips open the ledger to the front page.

"How hard can it be?" His brows bunch together as he skims the first page.

"Have you ever broken a cipher?" Mitzy's being prickly.

I get it, though it's fun to watch. She doesn't like other people touching her stuff. Not to mention, she does her best work alone and takes it as a challenge when others try to help. Or at least interject themselves into one of her projects.

Mitzy and I get along great, but she invited me to help. Wolfe didn't get that invitation; therefore, Mitzy's having a snit.

Wolfe continues to flip the pages, scanning line after line of indecipherable letters, squiggles, and doodles scrawled all over the page, spilling into the margins.

His eyes flicker back and forth, as if he's reading the entries. Watching close, he's doing more than that. He scans top to bottom, left to right, then travels back up the margins, meanders over the top and bottom, then flips to the other page.

Wolfe stops, flips back a page. Flips back another. The scrunching of his brows softens. He glances up after flipping through the first third of the ledger.

"Mitz, have you looked into Benefield's family?"

"His business associates and immediate family. Standard procedure," she replies.

"Are any of those people blind?"

"Blind?" Mitzy leans forward. "Why?"

"It could be nothing, but what do you make of this?" He places the ledger on the table, finger pointing to some of the squiggles in the margin.

"We've scanned everything into *Jacen*, but that didn't flag."

"It looks like braille to me." He shrugs while my brain goes into overdrive. "I mean, if you ignore the squiggly shit written over it and the fact it's not raised."

"Lemme see." I rip the ledger from Wolfe's hand and cradle it in my lap. "This?" I point to what I think he is trying to show Mitzy.

"Yeah." He gently takes the ledger out of my hands and flips a few more pages back. "There are similar things on some of these other pages. Not all of them are braille, but this one is." He shows me more squiggles. "This one isn't."

"You sure about this?" Mitzy jumps out of her chair and comes to stand behind me. Looking over my shoulder, she stretches between us. "This is braille?"

"Definitely." Wolfe shifts the ledger and flips a few pages forward. "Here's another one."

"How do you know this?"

"My sister's blind." Wolfe's lips press firmly together. "We all learned."

"We?" Mitzy asks.

I'm happy for her to pump Wolfe for information. After all the time we've been at each other's throats, we spent zero time learning anything about the other person.

"Who's we?" Mitzy continues to probe.

"Don't act like you don't know. You've researched everyone here, looking for anything that could potentially be used against us." Wolfe gives a shake of his head, answering without answering.

I want to know what that answer might be.

"Is that true?" I turn toward Mitzy. My expectation when coming to work here was some degree of a background check, but how deep does Mitzy's investigation go?

"Yes, I investigate everyone," Mitzy prattles on, "but it's not like you're so damn important that I keep the tiny details of your life front and center in my brain. You could just answer." Mitzy places her hand on my shoulder.

I can't believe how little I know about Wolfe. My shoulders curl in as my back hunches. Things like this, tiny things, remind me how much of an outsider I am.

Mitzy's a great boss and is becoming a really good friend. I get what she's doing. Knowing her, she not only knows every detail about Wolfe but can recite it from memory. Her question is for my benefit.

"Tell me more about this braille?" I peer at the ledger, seeing the random distribution of dots in a new light. "Okay, if this is braille, it's a part of the cipher, but how?" I hastily flip through the ledger, trying to count, hoping to get to twenty-six. Which would, or might, make this easier. Only, the dots are distributed randomly from page to page, and I'm not really sure if I'm seeing them right.

"Mitzy, have *Jacen* run a program on the scanned pages." Not sure if Wolfe stumbled on anything actionable, this could very well be the thing that cracks the code.

Wolfe leans over, closer than he needs to, and whispers in my ear. "You're fucking hot when you're working."

A shiver runs down my spine as the heat of his breath on my neck makes all the fine hairs on my body stand on edge. He takes the ledger and casually leans back in his chair.

"I'll be interested to see what your supercomputer comes up with." Wolfe turns a page, intent on the ledger. "This is odd." His thumb presses over another set of wavy lines in the margins.

"What's that?" It's my turn to lean in closer than I should. When my breast accidentally rubs against his arm, his entire body grows still. I move away, not meaning to be *that* suggestive. All I want is to inhale the heavenly scent that is Wolfe.

Wolfe?

I don't even know the man's last name. What the hell?

No way am I asking. I'm not going to look like a fool in front of him. Sounds like something to ask Mitzy when we're alone. Better yet, I can dig around and find the file she keeps on him.

"You're familiar with Morse code, right?"

"Isn't everyone?"

"Lots of people know about it. Hardly anyone knows it." Wolfe taps the page.

"Well, I do." I tap out a string of dots and dashes on the tabletop. It says, *You're an asshole.*

"You really like your codes, don't you?" The corner of Wolfe's mouth ticks up in a smirk.

"My life's dream was to be a superspy. Codes and ciphers are my thing."

"Really?" His brow arches. "That's so interesting, not to mention super sexy."

Heat builds on my neck. That's my anger rising, and for some ungodly reason, I'm getting more and more aroused. There's just something about going toe to toe with Wolfe that gets my juices flowing.

"Morse code is the first code I learned as a kid." For some weird reason, I feel like I need to explain myself.

"The first?"

"Of many."

"Is that so?"

"Yes. Ask Lily."

"Why, when I can ask you?"

"Don't be an ass, Wolfe." Mitzy looks up from her brief coding session for *Jacen*, crafting a query for the supercomputer to identify any instances of braille in Benefield's ledger.

"Well?" Wolfe ignores Mitzy, turning toward me.

"This is how much I love codes."

"I'm listening." Wolfe leans back, threading his fingers behind his head.

"I forced Lily to learn Morse code when we were in third grade."

"You forced her?"

"I had to."

"Why is that?"

"Because I liked a boy in our class, and our teacher had eagle eyes for any notes we passed. Lily and I were always passing notes and always getting in trouble for it."

"You crushed on a boy in third grade?" His brow arches with amusement. "That's young."

"Didn't you?"

"Never on the boys." He shakes his head and laughs.

"You know what I meant." I roll my eyes. "And Tommy wasn't my first crush." That came later.

"In this day and age, I assume nothing. But for the record, I like chicks." He leans toward me. "And I'm way more fun in person."

He delivers that last line deadpan, but there's a twinkle in his eye. Wolfe's referring to our nightly sex-capades. I say *our*, but I've only watched him jerk off. I never gave him a show myself. Taking care of my sexual frustrations came later; me and my vibrator with filthy fantasies of all the ways I want Wolfe to fuck me, running through my head.

"Well—proof's in the pudding, isn't it?" I return a volley of my own. "You know, all talk? No action?"

"Oh, for God's sake," Mitzy says with a huff, "will the two of you get a room and fuck already?" Mitzy turns her attention back to the computer. "Or at least give me a head's up so I can leave."

"Where's the fun in that?" Wolfe snickers.

It's a wonderful sound—his laughter—like liquid pleasure pulsing through me. I want more of that. Wolfe kicking back.

Laughing.

Smiling.

The fighting is hot as shit, but this easy back and forth is pretty damn fun as well. One is lava hot. The other is a slow, simmering burn. I have to say, I look forward to both.

"How old were you when you first crushed on a girl?" I can't help but ask. This feels like a safe question, something relatively innocuous.

"Kindergarten." He doesn't miss a beat.

"Kindergarten? You had a crush in kindergarten?"

"A crush and my first kiss." He crosses his arms over his broad chest and smirks. "While you're at it, wanna ask me when I lost my virginity?"

"You better not say kindergarten."

"Definitely not. Kissing Susie was like locking lips with a fish. She turned me off the whole kissing thing for years."

I can imagine the little boy Wolfe was, confident even then, kissing a girl. The image plays out in my head, two kids on the playground, maybe on the monkey bars or under the slide. A quick lip lock that ruined kissing for years.

"Okay, kids." Mitzy puts up a hand. "We are not going down that path."

"Why not?" Wolfe's eyes pinch as he looks at her. "When did Miss Mitzy have her first crush? Was it on a boy? Or a girl? These are the questions which keep me up at night."

"You're such an ass. And for the record, I'm not answering." Mitzy gives a derisive snort. Her mind isn't on us. With the insight Wolfe shared, she's hot on the trail of a potential solution. We are merely an annoyance buzzing at the edge of her consciousness.

"Your call." Wolfe gives Mitzy a pass with a wave of his hand. "How about my fiery Jinx? When was your first kiss? Was it with that boy in third grade? Or was that just an excuse to pass coded notes?"

"No passing of notes. That was the point, but Morse code was never fast enough."

"Oh my!" Wolfe exclaims and presses his palms to his cheeks, looking horrified. "What did you do?"

"Well, despite Lily grumbling, I forced her to learn the Prisoner's code. I'm sure you're familiar with it?"

Developed by American POWs during the Vietnam war, it's far more complicated, but once mastered, quite easy, and way faster than the ponderous dots and dashes of Morse Code.

"Yeah, babe. Know that one well. It's required knowledge in BUDS." He lowers his hands, a bit more serious. "But you didn't answer my question."

"About my first kiss?"

"When you lost your virginity." He's not letting that go.

I press my lips together, debating whether to tell him or have a bit of fun. Easy going Wolfe is hot as sin and sexy as fuck, but Wolfe riled up? That's mind-blowing and tons of fun.

I enjoy our bit of teasing back and forth, but Wolfe isn't just cocky. He's arrogant and damned sure of himself.

I can have fun with this.

"Oh, no, you don't." Wolfe wags his finger in front of my face.

"Do what?" I play innocent, but we both know I'm full of it.

"You're not going to spin this." Wolfe gives me a look, serious and determined to get the answers to his questions.

"Spin?"

"For the love of all that's holy, just tell me." His frustration is fun to watch. It's too easy, and too fun, to rile him up.

"Tell you how old I was when I had my first kiss or when I lost my virginity? You can only pick one."

"One?"

"One."

"Oh, for fucks sake." Wolfe launches out of his chair.

Before I know what's happening, he lifts me up and off my feet. With my feet swinging in the air, he plants his lips on mine. The heat of his mouth burns me from the inside out.

Our lips smash together. His tongue slips between my lips as my fingers claw at his neck, dig into his shoulders, and hold on for dear life. His mouth bruises mine, teeth clash, tongues duel. It's wild and unhinged. Everything a kiss should be.

Soul-shattering.

Molten heat flows in my veins, burning me from the inside out.

I find rapture with a simple kiss. A fluttery sensation in my belly makes me swoon. My nipples harden, tightening, as a needy pulsation makes me squeeze my thighs together.

Wolfe knows how to kiss. He puts his whole soul into the act, melding my lips with his.

Taking. Demanding.

He's dangerous.

If I have sex with him, it won't be just sex. It'll be overwhelming. After one kiss, I already feel an unstoppable force building between us.

I love it. I fear it.

His kiss blows my mind as the connection between us sparks and builds. It's overwhelming and consuming, a pressure building between me, highjacking my pulse, and making me believe *more* might be possible.

Dammit, but it terrifies me as well. I'm scared because I want everything this kiss promises. I want to believe such a connection can exist between two people. I want to fight for it, oddly possessive of it. But that fear inside of me doesn't go away. At some point, Wolfe will leave me. Which means I'll have to be the first to walk away.

As for the kiss, it leaves me breathless, aching, and wanting more.

But it's dangerous.

I pull away and push against Wolfe's chest. He slowly lowers me to the floor with a pensive look on his face. His brows tug together with a question, but he doesn't voice whatever it is.

"You're going to be the death of me, my fiery Jinx." He makes a crude adjustment of his pants.

Behind us, Mitzy tunes us out, oblivious to anything but her work.

"I, um …" I press my palms to my pants and glance at Mitzy. "I need to …"

Wolfe reaches out, tucks a strand of my hair behind my ear, and gives me a soft smile. "It's different now, isn't it?"

"Huh?"

"Kissing without anger. It feels different." His expression softens.

"I don't …" Wolfe silences me, pressing the pad of his finger over my lips.

"Don't overthink it."

"I wasn't …"

"The gears in your head are spinning so fast, I can see it." He glances at Mitzy and cups my chin. Leaning in, his lips brush lightly against mine.

I don't know that I'd call it a kiss. It's more of a promise.

"I've got to go meet the guys at the range. We're shooting today. Don't think too hard about that kiss. Remember, we're starting over."

And with that, Wolfe leaves me with the chaos of my thoughts. There's a lot to think about. Most concerning is that it's his tenderness that will cause me the most harm. It makes me want to believe in a future with him in it. I find that terrifying.

SIX

Wolfe

KISSING JINX PUTS A HOP IN MY STEP AND A GRIN ON MY FACE. I practically skip over to the range to meet the guys like a goddamn fool who kissed his first girl.

It feels like that.

Breathtaking. Heart-thundering. Soul-filling.

Fucking awesome.

All the women I kissed before pale next to holding Jinx in my arms. I'm still reeling beneath the thrill of her lips pressed against mine, the heat of her mouth, and the devastation she wrecked on my body.

Nothing compares.

Nothing.

Before I hit the range, I head into Guardian home base. Each team has our own space, affectionately called the *bullpen*, which contains each individual team member's gear locker: basically, a huge cage with our personalized gear and weapons locked inside.

The four bullpens surround one large conference room: a centralized meeting space, which we use for pre-mission briefings, education, or training debriefs.

We do a lot of training debriefs.

The Guardians, as a whole, stay busy, but we're not active in the field 24/7. Our missions are planned down to the most minuscule detail. It's a combined effort between us and the tech guys.

"Hey, Wolfe!" Jenny, leader of Delta team, raises her hand in greeting as I pass through the central briefing room. "How's it hanging?"

"A little to the left. All good." I answer with a smirk in my voice. "How about you?"

"Tits up, the gals are holding strong. Nothing to worry about." Jenny approaches, which means she wants a conversation. "You got a minute?"

"I'm meeting the guys for range time. What's up?" It's my not-so-sly way of telling her I don't have time for a prolonged conversation. Although Jenny's not much of a talker.

"It's about Jinx."

"Yeah?" I pull up short, suddenly wary. A fierce protectiveness rises within me.

"I hear Jinx is signing up with tech." She says it like a statement, but her quizzical expression flips it into a question.

"That's my understanding." I'm actually not sure which way Jinx's preference leans. Although, after seeing Jinx work with Mitzy, I have a feeling Jenny's statement is a fact.

"Do you have any pull?" She arches a brow and waits for my response.

"What do you mean?"

"The girl has mad skills. I could use her on Delta."

"I have zero pull with Jinx."

"That's not what I've heard." Jenny arches a brow and folds her arms over her chest.

"Well, it's the truth. I just came from seeing her."

"Is that so?" Jenny shifts her weight forward, propping a hand on her hip. "I hear things are—*complicated* between the two of you."

"We're ironing things out." One kiss at a time, it seems. "But she's with Mitzy. I'm afraid Mitzy wrested Jinx to the dark side."

"Any chance she'll reconsider?"

Why is Jenny trying to recruit my girl?

"Doubtful."

"Such a waste. She'd be great for my new team." Jenny doesn't like what I have to say. "At least she's willing to share her fighting skills."

"What new team?"

"Oh, something Forest has me looking into. You heard he's starting up the Guardian Protectors."

"I heard rumors."

"Not a rumor. Fact."

"And you're running the Protectors?"

Jenny would be great for the job. She's fucking badass and a natural leader.

"Not the Protectors. The rumor mill says he's recruiting Knox for that."

"Knox?"

"That's what I hear."

"Knox will never leave Alpha."

"And I thought I'd never leave Delta."

Jenny's leaving Delta? Now, this is news.

"If not a Protector, what does he have in mind?"

"Guardian Angels. Like the Protectors, but female only." Jenny's lips screw up in a knot. "You know Forest."

"Truth." I edge back, not wanting this conversation with Jenny to circle back around to anything involving Jinx becoming a Guardian, Protector, or an Angel.

She's mine. I saw Jinx first. I kissed her, which means she belongs to me.

"Well, thanks. Can't say I'm not disappointed. Was just wondering if you could put in a plug and win her over from the dark side."

"I'll see what I can do." The words spill out of my mouth without conviction. "Catch you on the flip side."

I move away from Jenny before she can ask any more favors I'm not interested in giving.

Honestly, I don't know how Knox handles it. His gal, Lily, is more than likely joining up with Delta, which puts her in the thick of domestic hostage rescue negotiations and extraction. If not Delta, Lily's likely to join Forest's new branch of Guardian Angels—at least if Jenny has any say.

Personal protection specialists, the Protectors, will be dedicated to providing VIP bodyguard services for not only those rescues who need it, but clientele willing to pay for the privilege of personal protection. I'm not sure what these Angels will be doing.

The idea of Jinx putting herself in harm's way rubs me wrong. It may be old school. I may not be up with the times, and while I think women can, and should, do whatever they want, it feels all kinds of wrong putting Jinx in a position where I can't protect her.

That's not something I can live with.

Saving others, protecting them from harm, that's my calling in life, and as far as that goes, I'm going to be late if I don't pick up the pace.

Time to get my head in the game. Stop thinking about kissing Jinx and focus on more practical matters.

In between missions, our days are filled with training. Whether that's PT, range practice, or updates on whatever new tech or gear the tech guys have for us, we rise at dawn and work way past a typical eight-hour day.

Today happens to be a day on the range, which can mean any number of things. From sniper practice to close-range pistol engagement, we're as likely to go through any of half a dozen modular units perfecting our door kicking techniques.

This job isn't for those who aren't passionate about it. The pay is good. Hell, it's better than good, but the work is exhausting.

I double-step it to Alpha's bullpen.

"Where the fuck have you been?" Liam spins around at my entrance. He's alone inside Alpha's bullpen.

I'm usually the first to any of our many briefings, but Liam beat me. That's unusual because he's usually the last to show up.

"Nowhere." I rock back on my heels and let a smile fill my face. No way am I telling these fuckers anything about that amazing and mind-blowing kiss.

It's the first time Jinx didn't slap me on the face or put me on the ground. It was everything I imagined and more.

And I definitely want more.

Liam takes me in from head to toe. "You look like a cat who finally caught the canary. What's up?"

"Nothing."

"Nothing, my ass. I'm guessing that smirk on your face has everything to do with a gorgeous as fuck Latina beauty."

"Careful." My voice comes out a possessive growl.

"Stand down." Liam lifts his hands and backs away. "I'm not interested in your chick. I don't know what the rest of you are doing, tying yourselves down. I'm living the high life."

No doubt he is. Liam's Hollywood handsome, with a face more likely to grace the cover of GQ than Soldier of Fortune. He's far too pretty for this line of work, but damn, is he one resilient fucker. The man doesn't know how to stop.

As for his comments about Jinx, he's kidding, but I'm cautious. Not much around here remains a secret, but I want to hold onto the magic of that kiss for a few more minutes.

I want to hold onto it forever, and I don't want to share it.

"What are we doing today?" I head over to my gear locker where my personal arsenal of weapons awaits.

"No idea. Max was kind of tight-lipped about it." Liam's locker sits across from mine. It's open, like mine, and he checks the readiness of his gear.

Alpha team's bullpen looks exactly the same as Bravo's, Charlie's, and Delta's. Large cages secure our personal gear and hold everything we need for a mission. The cages remain locked when we're not in the room. The door to the bullpen stays locked when none of us are inside. Security is a constant concern. Constant vigilance is our motto, bound together by the rigid protocols we maintain.

A few minutes later, Axel and Griff saunter in. They're five minutes early, which is pushing it. We tend to be the kind of guys who believe being on time is late.

"Yo." Axel gives a chin lift in greeting. "Anyone know what's on the docket today?"

"Not a clue." Liam shoves his foot into a combat boot and ties up the laces.

I follow suit, removing my sneakers for more protective footwear. Ready for anything, I wore my black tactical trousers to work. Axel and Griff head to their cages, where they kick off their shoes and change out of their jeans. They switch to tactical trousers and lace up their boots as well.

Knox wanders in next, already kitted out for a day of working in the field. The range is hot and sweaty work. In the summer, California heat can be miserable. I grab an extra set of hydration bottles and add them to my tactical belt.

"You know what we're doing today?" Liam wanders over to the massive prep table that sits between the two rows of our cages.

"Haven't talked to Max." Knox rolls his shoulders and stretches his neck side to side. "I just got here."

"Hey." I slap him on the back. "What's this about you leaving us?"

"Huh?"

"Leading the Protectors?"

"Nothing." Knox's expression darkens.

"What?" Liam pauses, looking between me and Knox.

"It's nothing," Knox says. "Forget it. I'm not leaving Alpha."

That's a statement which rings true. Max and Knox are tighter than tight. Two men who became brothers after surviving the grind of BUDS, they later went on to face the brutality of survival in the field.

Neither of them talk about it, but we all know the story and the choices they were forced to make. That kind of thing sticks with a person for life. It forms an unbreakable bond.

The clock at the far end of the room says Max is officially late. It's one minute past the hour. Knox follows the direction of my gaze. No need to ask what he's thinking.

And it's not like we're sticklers about the time. It's more that we're highly in tune with one another.

We notice when things are off.

Five minutes after the hour, we're kitted out in tactical dress: boots, belts, body armor, and comm gear. Still no Max.

"Anybody know where our fearless leader might be?" Liam rolls his neck in a slow circle and shrugs his shoulders, limbering up.

"I'm here." The door slams open, and Max walks in. "Strap on your armor. Small arms only. We're headed to B-Town."

"Another fun day in the sun." Liam doesn't look happy.

I get it. B-Town drills suck.

On Max's heels is none other than Forest Summers, co-founder of Guardian HRS. He's the only man who ever makes me feel small. I'm six-four. The rest of the guys are within an inch or two of me. We're all brawn, massively built, and men to be wary about. Forest, however, is formidable, topping our height by several inches. He's a Guardian on steroids, like a Norse god plucked out of myth and legend.

If I didn't know him as well as I do, that glacial gaze combined with his Nordic features, would have me shaking in my boots. It did the first time we met, but I've seen the softer, gentler side of Forest since then. I've seen him laugh and watched him smile. I've seen his kindness and joy for life.

He's a good soul with a heart of gold.

Tragedy fills his past, but it doesn't define him. What it did was set him on a lifelong mission to free those who've been taken. He has a soft spot for kids, specifically those forced into the foster system and placed into abusive homes, and as someone who narrowly avoided becoming a slave, he goes above and beyond to save those who've been taken.

He's a rescuer. A savior. To all of us, he's the original: the first Guardian.

We admire him, but the man is a bit quirky.

"What's up, guys?" Forest's gaze sweeps the room. "I've got something special planned today."

"Told ya." Axel slaps Griff on the arm. "Pay up."

"Damn. You and your hunches." Griff digs into his back pocket and retrieves a worn button. He flicks it toward Axel, who catches it mid-air.

Bets with buttons are an Alpha team thing. We bet on anything and everything, but instead of cash, we use buttons. It started because of Max.

The story we were told was that he's a recovering gambler. Betting with cash is a total no-go. So, we bet with buttons instead. Turns out, there is a totally different reason why the man doesn't gamble, and it's nothing I would've ever guessed.

"What does *special* mean?" I turn from Axel and brace for whatever Forest has to say.

"Nothing too fancy," Forest says.

"Tell them …" Max turns to Forest. "I'm sure as shit not telling them."

"Shit." Knox presses his lips into a firm line, and the muscles of his jaw tick with suspicion. "What the fuck kind of games are we playing?"

Range practice, in any one of the four modular towns located on Guardian HRS property, combines door kicking, close-range munitions, and hostage rescue into intense mind fuck exercises.

We all hate them, but damn if it doesn't keep us on our toes, reinforcing the training we received in the Navy to become SEALs and combines it with the unique fighting techniques that Guardian HRS developed for its hostage rescue missions.

"I'm testing a new prototype." Forest rocks back on his heels, providing nothing more than that by way of explanation.

"And …" Max eggs him on, urging him to continue. "Tell them what you told me."

Liam shifts to stand beside me. Axel and Griff close in tight. Knox takes a step back, pitting the five of us against whatever the fuck might come out of Forest's mouth.

We're used to Forest's crazy schemes. From the VR suite, which mocks up our missions, providing invaluable simulation runs before we head out, to modular towns where we brush up on our urban fighting and munitions work, we live and operate on the cutting edge of technology.

"It's nothing much." Forest glances at Max like he explained enough. That's the problem with Forest. He thinks on a different plane from us mere mortals. He expects us to know what he's thinking, like we can read his mind.

Liam and I exchange a shared look of pain. Whatever we're doing, it's not going to be fun.

"I'm testing Rufus." Forest gives a shrug.

"Who the fuck is Rufus?"

"It's not a who." Max gives a shake of his head. "Rufus is most definitely a *what*."

"As in?" Knox shifts in front of me. "This is where a little more info might be helpful."

"It's a Robotic Ultra Functional Utility Specialist. Rufus is one of Forest's automated robots: an AI dog." Max explains when it's clear Forest won't.

"You're kidding." I want to laugh, but I know better.

Never laugh at Forest. Whatever craziness he proposes, however far-fetched it seems, Forest only brings it to us for testing after it's been vetted by his tech team.

SEVEN

Wolfe

AN AI DOG SOUNDS FUCKING HILARIOUS, BUT IT'S NO JOKE. THE one thing Forest isn't good with is humor. Or, if he does joke around, I'm far too stupid to understand what he finds funny.

"Rufus is a robotic sentry dog," Forest explains. "He'll be patrolling B-town, with orders to prevent you from rescuing your hostage." Forest breaks it down for us mortals.

"Who the hell on this planet has a robotic dog on sentry duty? This is a joke, right?" Liam should know better than to say things like that to Forest.

Forest's a forward thinker, a creative genius beyond the cutting edge when it comes to pretty much everything.

"No joke. I need to know how Rufus will respond. To do that, I need trained operatives to put him through his paces."

"His?" I glance at the guys. "Why is Rufus a dude? It should be a badass bitch." My joke gets a few chuckles from the guys, but nothing other than a stony glare from Forest.

"The first phase of Rufus's testing is perimeter defense." Max gives us a look to cut the chatter.

No doubt, his initial reaction mirrored ours, but Max is the lead of Alpha team. As Alpha One, once orders are given, it's his responsibility to ensure we follow through.

"First phase? I hate to ask what the second phase might be." I mean it tongue in cheek, but Forest steamrolls over my blasé comment.

"Integration with the teams, obviously." Forest doesn't blink.

He's fucking serious, and just as I don't understand his brand of humor, he doesn't get mine. His statement makes all our jaws drop.

No fucking way.

Four hours later, I have other, more colorful expletives to lob at our fearless leader. I hate Forest and his damn AI robotic monster.

"Never been so humiliated in my life." Liam stalks over to his gear locker and makes the chain link fence of his gear locker rattle as he yanks aggressively on the lock.

All of our lockers remain locked unless we're physically in the room, and rather than old school combination locks, ours are bio-locked to our unique thumbprints and retina scans.

Alpha team dresses down in the bullpen, locking up our weapons and gear in silence.

Well—silent only for the space of a heartbeat. It begins with Griff. Spreads to Axel. Knox snorts while Max turns away.

"Go ahead. Laugh it up, fuzz balls." Liam slams his gear locker closed. "I'm not the only one who got my ass handed to me by a fucking robotic dog."

I can't help but cough. It's the only way of holding back the laughter. "We all got our asses handed to us by Rufus, but you're the only one Rufus fucked."

"Asshole." Liam throws his sweat-soaked shirt at my head. It's rank, drenched, and lands right over my face.

"Who knew Rufus would be a horny AI dog?" Griff chuckles beside me.

"Thought for a moment we needed to give the two of you a bit of alone time." Axel grins like a loon.

"You fuckers suck." Liam isn't happy with our ribbing.

Rufus took us all down. Systematic as fuck, that AI monstrosity never tired. Never stopped. It ran down Liam, launching at Liam's back, where it shoved him face-first in the dirt.

The rest of us had already been taken out by Forest's robot, but Rufus not only knocked Liam to the ground, but it engaged in questionable behavior. It was supposed to sit on top of Liam—subduing him—but every time it tried to sit, it raised its rear up again. Then tried to sit again. Then its rear went back up. Then down. Up. Down. Up. Down. Two mechanical paws on Liam's back while it basically humped him.

We can't help ourselves and break out laughing at the image of Liam getting a bit of love action from Rufus.

"Don't think this is over." Liam points to each of us in turn. "I will get each of you …" His words cut off when the door to our bullpen slams open.

Jinx runs in, lifting a sheaf of papers over her head. She scans the room, locates me, and launches at me with a shriek. I catch her mid-air as she wraps her legs around my waist and kisses me right on the lips in full view of the guys.

Before I can react, she hops down, waving the papers in the air.

"We did it! We fucking did it!"

"Did, what?" Max looks at Jinx like she lost her mind.

She slaps the papers against my chest. I grab them as she lets go.

"Wolfe helped us break the code."

"He did, what?" Liam turns his attention from Jinx to me.

"You broke it?" I glance down at the papers but reel from that kiss. Not that it was the best kiss of my life, but because not only did Jinx initiate, she did it in full view of the guys.

My heart swells with hope for the first time since we met. We might just have a chance to make this crazy chemistry between us turn into something real.

The rest of the team gapes.

"Sure as shit he did." Jinx turns in a circle, taking each of the guys in, one by one. "He's fucking brilliant." She ends her slow spin facing me. Eyes bright. Smile a mile wide. Hands clasped in front of her chest. She balances on the tips of her toes, practically bouncing with excitement. "You did. You really did."

"Um …" I glance around at the guys, thankful none of them react to Jinx barging into the bullpen.

It's kind of a sacred space—each team's bullpen—meaning only team members are allowed inside. Jinx committed a major faux pas, but none of the guys seem to care.

Max closes the distance and takes the papers from me. He scans the content, brows tugging together. "I'm not sure I understand."

"Wolfe noticed braille in the gutters of the ledger. We let *Jacen* crunch through some algorithms, and Mitzy did a little digging. Seems Benefield had a daughter, and guess what?"

"What?" Max shrugs, but I know exactly what Mitzy found.

"She was blind." An upwelling of pride rises within me. I still have it.

I used to work intel, way back in the day, but gave it up for a greater good. I thought that kind of work was behind me, but it looks like I still have some of it left in me.

"Benefield didn't have any family. No wives. No kids." Max's brows nearly kiss as they pinch together.

"Well …" Jinx looks at me and nibbles at her lower lip. It makes me want to yank her close and do indecent things. "That's what Benefield wanted everyone to believe."

I get Max's confusion. The intelligence we ran on Benefield hinted at no familial contacts. As Max and Knox entered Benefield's establishment undercover, it complicated the mission as we had nothing to use for leverage if their covers were blown.

The mission went ahead. Deverough's daughter, Eve, was rescued, and because of Eve, we obtained the ledgers. The news of a child is new and important information.

"He *had* a daughter," Jinx explains. "She died when she was twelve and was blind. We didn't break the code until we discovered her existence."

"Discovered?" Max still looks confused.

"Yes. Gabriella Gomez. Her name, birthdate, and the day of her death were the key."

I give a little shake of my head. How the hell did she and Mitzy, even with the help of *Jacen*, figure all of that out in a matter of hours.

While I was getting my ass handed to me by Rufus, the robotic dog, she cracked the code in an afternoon.

Holy hell.

That's my girl.

And if there's any question as to whether she is, that flying leap into my arms says it all. Jinx is most definitely mine. My heart skips a beat, and I feel a little light-headed.

"Holy shit." Knox takes another look at the papers. "Eve was right." His gaze flicks to Max. "Your woman deserves a fucking medal. This is a total game changer." Knox's attention shifts to Jinx, then swings to me. "Yours too."

"Huh?" Jinx's gaze bounces between me and them.

"When we were trying to get Eve out of The Retreat, she demanded we backtrack to Benefield's office." Max explains what we already know. None of this is new information, but sometimes he likes to think out loud. "I said no, but Eve was adamant. Said we had to get Benefield's ledger. She spent months watching him detail every transaction in that damn thing. We thought we hit gold, but when Mitzy couldn't crack the code, we lost hope. Do you have any idea what you've done cracking it?"

"I do." Jinx looks at me. "But it was Wolfe who gave us what we needed to do that. If anyone deserves the credit, it's him. All I'm going to do is translate it." Her gaze drops to the floor, and she draws a circle on the concrete with her toe. "But it's going to take some time, and I need help." Jinx bites at her lower lip and looks up at me through the dark fringe of her lashes.

"We'll do whatever it takes," Max says. "What do you need?"

We're all thinking the same thing; the sooner the better. No need to break it down more than that. In the time it takes us to translate the ledger, and then have the intel team come up with an actionable mission, more lives will be stolen.

More girls will be taken.

"I need Wolfe." The way Jinx nibbles on her lower lip is like a punch to the gut, taking my breath away.

Or maybe, it's the way she said it. *I need Wolfe.*

I need her like I need air to breathe, but her ask of Alpha team confuses me.

"Why me?" I point to myself, certain my confusion is scrawled all over my face.

Not that I'm against spending more time with Jinx but spending time with her isn't the same as working side by side.

I want alone time.

Personal time.

I want Jinx time in the worst possible way.

What I don't want is to share Jinx time with Mitzy.

"Mitzy said so." Jinx gives a tiny shrug, almost as if she couldn't care less if I worked with her or not.

That kind of pisses me off. We still have a couple of days until our first official starting-over date. The way she says *"Mitzy said so"* makes me think she doesn't want to work with me.

But what's with the flinging herself into my arms?

"I'm not sure what kind of help I can be. I'm sure Mitzy's supercomputer freak, *Jacen,* can read braille way faster than me."

"Yes and no." She looks up at me beneath a fringe of dark lashes, fluttering them in that sexy way of hers.

The longer Jinx nibbles on her lip, the more my cock takes notice. I've fantasized about her lips wrapping around me, her tongue stroking me, her …

Fuck.

I shift to the side, hoping nobody notices my current state of sexual frustration.

"What's that mean?" Max continues with his questions.

"It's not quite braille." Fuck if the way Jinx's nose scrunches isn't the sexiest thing in the world.

Everything about her is a turn-on. From her long, straight hair that swishes at the rise of her ass to those thick black lashes that send my heart into a tailspin, I've got it bad for my girl.

"I don't know how I can help." I spin around, close up my locker, and snap the lock shut.

The last thing I want is to look like a goddamn fool in front of Jinx. I'm good with the He-Man, macho stuff. I'm a Guardian after all, but sitting down with brainiacs? Been there, done that, left it far behind. So far behind, it's officially outside my comfort zone. I'm not sure I can dust off the cobwebs to that part of my brain.

When I joined the military, so many years ago, I was recruited to be an intelligence officer in the Navy. I used to be freakishly good at digging through data and putting together seemingly unrelated pieces of information into a coherent picture. Maybe that's why the braille and Morse code in the ledgers popped out at me?

Some say my talent was wasted when I decided to become a SEAL, but I struggled with a crisis of faith. I couldn't stand being separated from the action that my intelligence resulted in. If my work was going to send men into danger, I wanted to be right by their side. I couldn't live with myself knowing I was safe because I worked behind a desk.

That's not the kind of man I was raised to be. It's not who I am.

"Wolfe, you're the one who cracked the code." Jinx gives a huff of frustration. "You understand braille, and you know Morse code. It'll be a whole lot faster working together to decipher this."

"All I did was notice two things that didn't belong together. Cracking it belongs to you, Mitzy, and her mega computer."

"Don't do that."

"Do, what?"

"Minimize what you did." Anger simmers in her eyes as the air between us electrifies and sparks.

"Sounds like it might be a good use of your skillset." Max comes to stand in front of me and taps right between my eyes. "Dust off some of that Navy Intel training …"

"His what?" Jinx looks between me and Max, confused.

There's so much we don't know about each other.

"That's right." Liam slaps my back. "Your boy used to be an Intel officer before joining the rest of us in the mud."

"Is that true?" She turns to me, eyes wide, mouth parting, wonder growing deep in those dark, mesmerizing eyes of hers.

"It's true." Max's attention swings from me to Jinx and back again.

A smile spreads upwards until it beams off my face. This is the first the rest of the team is seeing of the thaw between me and Jinx. They're used to watching us go at it, tearing into each other every chance we get. While the shift between us is wonderful, I'm ready to move on. I'm not ready to share Jinx with the team.

"Wolfe switched from Navy Intelligence to become a frogman." Knox takes a step forward, arms crossing over his broad chest.

"He did?"

This is what I want to avoid. These are the things I should be sharing with Jinx, not the guys.

"Yeah, one of the very few officers selected by Naval Special Warfare Command to attend BUDS."

"Officer?" She glances at me, mouth parted in surprise. "I thought you were all prior enlisted?" She looks around the room, as if seeing us with different eyes. "Anyone else prior officer?"

"Nope, just Wolfe." Liam snickers because he caught me cupping my hands over my crotch.

He knows what Jinx does to me. He also knows I don't like standing out from the crowd. Bastard is having fun with me.

"I didn't know that."

"Yeah, your beau submitted his name, along with thousands of others. Competition's fierce, but more so for officers."

"Wow …" Jinx's eyes widen.

"Yeah, they train a thousand enlisted each year, but less than ninety officers." Liam is up to no good. "Your man is truly the cream of the crop. He's got brains *and* brawn. You should shower affection on him when you get a chance to be alone."

"Fucker." I ball up my fingers and clench my fists.

"Just tossing you a bone." Liam grins, baring his teeth, while the other guys chuckle.

That's it.

I launch at Liam, popping him in the jaw. The rest of the guys take a step back. Max grabs hold of Jinx's arm, pulling her to safety while Liam and I trade blows. It's not a real fight, but I tap him hard enough to get my point across. Fucker needs to tone it down.

Tossing me a bone?

Fucker deserved that clock to the jaw.

He's right in what he says. Competition is fierce for selection for BUDS, more so for officers than enlisted. Many people don't realize SEALs have officers. Those who do generally don't know we go through BUDS with no distinction between officer and enlisted.

No special treatment.

It's hell for us all.

Barely ten percent make it through the grueling training. For officers, that percentage is far lower.

"That's enough. Break it up." Max barks an order.

Liam and I break apart, breathing hard but smiling. I'm not mad at him in the slightest. Just needed him to shut up.

"Do you really need Wolfe?" Max redirects, coming back around to why Jinx barged into Alpha's bullpen.

"Definitely." Jinx's eyes simmer with latent sexual heat. The air between us crackles and buzzes, building an electric charge that will someday ignite this craziness between us.

"Do you want to do that?" Max turns to me. He won't make me do it. That'll only happen if CJ insists.

"No, but—" I blow out a breath, not sure why I'm hesitating.

Jinx gasps. "You don't?"

"You didn't let me finish. I was going to say, if it means more time with you, then I'm all aboard." I can play suave hero. It's my go-to move with the chicks. There's only one difference. With those nameless chicks, I play like a pro. With Jinx, I'm a bundle of nerves.

She gets under my skin, makes me do things I wouldn't normally do. Feel things I don't normally feel.

Her eyes close, and her cheeks turn the loveliest shade of crimson.

"Get a room." Liam coughs into his fist.

Jinx pivots. It's a slow, calculated movement. While she does, a Cheshire grin fills her face. "I put Wolfe on the ground twice. I'm pretty sure you'll be flat on your back in no time, and I know for a fact Rufus picked his favorite Guardian to hump."

Holy shit.

Laughter rips out of me. The rest of the guys follow suit, laughing and slapping their thighs as Jinx steals Liam's voice. It's so unexpected, he's still processing.

As the guys make rude movements, teasing Liam about Rufus's humping episode, I grab Jinx's hand and escape.

Once we're outside the building, I spin her around, cup her cheeks, and plant a sloppy kiss on her lips.

"How did you know about Rufus?"

"Eww …" Jinx wipes her mouth. "I know you can do better than that. As far as Liam? I was with Mitzy, of course."

"I thought the two of you were working with *Jacen* on the ledger?"

"I was … still am, but you know how she multitasks. We watched the whole thing."

"Damn. That wasn't Alpha's finest hour."

"The deck was stacked against you. Rufus mapped the entire area. He already knew the most likely spots you would attempt a rescue. It'll be different in real life." She cocks her head. "Are you okay working with me on this project?" Jinx glances at the ground, toes the dirt in front of her. "I sensed hesitation, and I don't want to make you do something you don't want to do."

"Not in the slightest." I take her hand in mine, turning it over to trace the fine lines of her palm. "I didn't think work would come first for us."

"What does that mean?" The alarm in her voice gives me pause.

"Only that I wish it was time for our date. I don't know if I can survive working beside you for that long. I'm dying over here."

My woody is almost gone and thinking about our date doesn't help.

"Ledger first. Date night later. It has to be that way." Jinx does that nibbling thing to her lip, which drives me insane.

"If you insist." I don't care what she says, I'm going to do everything in my power to move our date up to tonight. I need Jinx in my bed.

And if I can't get that, then I've got another idea in my head. It's something unexpected. Something perfect for the very odd way our relationship started. If I can pull it off, it'll be epic.

But first—first we have to do the work that will save lives.

A Guardian's job is never done.

EIGHT

Jinx

Benefield was fucking brilliant. I don't care what Mitzy says.

"You going to tell me how you broke the code?" Wolfe takes my hand, threading our fingers together as we walk back to the main building.

"You can't imagine how amazing it is." Elation continues to flow through me. It's a familiar high, a lightness to my step that always occurs after breaking through a case.

"Try me." The soft undertones of his voice roll over me like a lover's caress. I grip his hand a little tighter, eager and waiting for when we can finally be alone.

"It's both simple and complex." Pressing my lips together, I work through how to explain as simplistically as possible.

Not that Wolfe needs me to dumb it down for him. I'm learning there's far more to him than meets the eye. He's rough and rugged on the outside, but there's so much buried beneath the surface.

This isn't something I want to screw up. Which means, I take my time formulating an answer.

"Explain."

Wolfe's no-nonsense tone reminds me I'm speaking to a

Guardian rather than the man I want to shamelessly hump as I climb his muscular body like a cat in heat.

If he can be professional about this, then I need to mind myself.

Cat in heat indeed.

Very unprofessional, but it's hard. It's hard being so close and not able to do what I want.

We said we were going to wait until date night, but damn if I don't want to move that date up.

Be professional, Jinx.

Yeah, yeah. My inner voice is annoying at times.

"It's elegant in its simplicity." A lightness fills my step and infuses me with hope. "I'm super excited about the progress we made today."

"I'm going to need more than that." He looks down at me, the biggest smile on his face, eyes bright, flickering with laughter. "Elegant and simple because …?"

His look stops me in my tracks because it's unexpected. It speaks to the truth of the man I'm only now able to see. Wolfe is more than the muscle that gets things done. There's a fierce intellect behind those eyes.

That blows me away. It seems as if each time I look at him, I see a whole other side that I admire. I love everything about that.

The chaos swirling around us, that constant friction, the bickering and fighting, it all lifted away after our little talk. Like a fog thinning to reveal a clear view before us, there's a path forward I can't wait to travel.

With him.

Side by side.

"When you asked if he had a child who was blind," I say, "I thought you were crazy. How did you see that?"

"It was a pattern that stood out." His lips press together, and his gaze shifts away. It's a humbling gesture, as if what he did made no difference. "Honestly, if I didn't know braille myself, I wouldn't have given it a second thought."

He pulls me to his side and releases my hand. But it's only so that he can sling his powerful arm over my shoulder. I love walking with him this way.

"Well, it sent Mitzy digging. She found a daughter and that broke the cipher on the braille code."

"I'm sure you helped with that."

I shrug. "I helped a little, but it was really Mitzy. She's pretty incredible."

"I think *you're* pretty damn incredible." He kisses the top of my head. It's such a natural gesture, as if he's done it thousands of times before. My stomach does a little flip and a dive, turning about with giddy excitement.

I've never had a boyfriend before. Or rather, I've had lots of short-term, superficial relationships. None of them went more than skin deep. Somehow, Wolfe's dug in and wrapped himself around my heart in a way I've never experienced before.

"What about the Morse code? Was that a red herring?" He continues asking questions, unaware of the profoundness of my thoughts.

Maybe I'm moving too fast, too quickly. We still know very little about each other. Should I slow things down? Tell my racing heart to put on the brakes? Is that even possible?

I've heard of people falling head over heels for a stranger, and everyone's heard about people falling madly in love at first sight. That's not us. We're more of the lust at first sight followed by unsubstantiated anger kind of a couple. Now, we're headed into uncharted territory.

As far as his question goes, red herrings are not uncommon in ciphers. It's a way to make them harder to break, sending would-be codebreakers down fruitless paths.

"That's what we thought at first, but it was really a second cipher, layered on top. It not only translated the braille into a substitute code but formed the basis for the randomization."

"Luv, it almost sounds as if you're speaking English, but I don't think I understood that last bit." He huffs a laugh. That last bit was the contribution I made, but I'm too humble to make a point of saying it. "Randomization?" His brow lifts with interest. "Sounds complicated."

"Kind of." I shrug because it is complicated and yet makes perfect sense to me.

Wolfe noticed the braille. Mitzy found the girl. I pieced together the Morse code and discovered the randomization which made the code indecipherable. That's why *Jacen* couldn't crack it. Given enough time, the supercomputer would've eventually cracked the cipher, but that's what we don't have.

"You amaze me." He releases my shoulders and takes my hand in his again. We continue toward Guardian HQ's main building.

There's no way to stop the instant heating of my cheeks. Praise from Wolfe hits all my buttons. I can almost feel myself unfurling like a flower opening to bask in the sun. He makes me feel like more when I'm with him.

Less alone.

Unfortunately, an excess of time is not ours. Each day that passes is one day too many. It's one more day innocents are at risk.

"It's an iterative twist." I grip his forearm and glance up at him. The smile he returns melts my heart and lightens my step. "I can show you, if you want."

I found that little bit.

Not *Jacen*.

Not Mitzy.

Me.

I'm still preening with my discovery.

"Want to know a secret?" I lower my voice to a whisper.

"If it has anything to do with you, I do." The timbre of his voice changes, becoming dark and delicious. "I want to know everything about you."

His words scare me, but they give me hope as well.

Lily and I left everything we knew behind in New Orleans. We left our sister and dearest friend, Callie. Not that we don't check in several times a day, but that's a lot to leave behind. We did it because Lily fell in love with Knox, and Lily and I come as a package deal. I can't imagine a world without her in it.

I take in a deep breath and reveal one of my fears. "For the first time, it feels as if I might actually fit in here."

"First time?"

"Yeah." My gaze cuts to the ground. "I've felt like an interloper. Like the only reason I'm here is because of Lily, but working on this case is the first time where I feel like I'm earning my keep. Like, I can really be a valuable member of the team."

"Jinx, you're more than you can ever imagine. Don't think for a minute that Forest and Sam hired you because they wanted someone else and had to settle for you. They saw your potential. The one thing I know about those men is they have an eye for spotting greatness. You earned your place with Guardian HRS based upon your merits. Not because they had to take you if they wanted Lily."

"Thank you." I glance up at him, a smile fixed to my face. It's more praise than I know how to process. "I'm used to fighting for every scrap of recognition. Having others see it in me, and reward me with a job like this one, it's difficult to accept."

"I understand that."

"I bet you never doubted yourself." It's silly, but I need Wolfe to be flawed. It doesn't have to be something major. Maybe just a little teeny-tiny bit of insecurity.

"I wouldn't call it doubt, more of not knowing which direction to jump. I always knew what I wanted and went after it with a tenacity that my parents, honestly, found a bit overwhelming at times."

"How is that?"

"Well, growing up, I had two distinct groups of friends. I had my smart friends and my jock friends. Neither group liked the other. I always felt pulled between them. The jocks teased me for hanging out with the smart kids. The smart kids resented me for hanging out with the jocks. They were more popular than the smart kids, and my smart friends never fully accepted me. The same could be said of the jocks, which left me swinging in the middle, never sure where I belonged. Despite that, I made it work."

"Why?"

"Because I knew there were benefits to both sides of that coin. I needed the smart kids to push me academically. I'm highly competitive. That worked in my favor. I also needed to learn the value of teamwork. That came from playing sports. It never occurred to me that I couldn't have the best of both worlds. After a time, it didn't matter."

"I'm having a really hard time visualizing that."

"Everybody's life looks shiny from the outside, but we all struggle. We all want to belong. I fit in both groups, for obvious reasons, but because of that, I fit in none."

"Most people would say you live a charmed life."

"No one's life is that perfect."

He's the embodiment of the perfect trifecta. He's intelligent, handsome, and has the body of a Grecian god. It's almost too much to take in. I feel as if one day I'm going to wake up and realize Wolfe was nothing but a dream.

"I suppose." My gaze cuts to my feet as I kick a stray rock out of the way. "The guys said you were a Naval Intelligence officer. Is that why you became a Guardian? Is this the way to have the best of both worlds?"

"It's why I became a SEAL."

"How so?"

"The thought of sending men into danger based upon my intelligence work never sat well with me. But as a SEAL, and eventually a Guardian, I go where others send me. It's because of my intelligence background that I have a better understanding of why particular missions are chosen over others."

"I never thought of it that way."

"I know how to handle myself when a mission turns sour because I have that other viewpoint." He scratches his head and draws his hand down his jaw. "I don't know how to explain it better than that."

"I wish I didn't doubt myself as much as I do. I'm talented. I have skills. I'm good at my job. What I'm not is confident."

"Insecurity affects everyone at some point in time."

"Well, do you have any tips on how not to feel insecure?"

"Believe in yourself, and for the record, everyone around here thinks you're badass. The only one questioning your abilities is you. The rest of us know you belong."

"That's easier said than done."

"You don't give yourself the credit you deserve. Look at what you did today. Your work, your insight, is going to save lives. Let that settle on your shoulders for a moment. Allow yourself to feel good about your contribution."

"I'm going to try."

"Do or do not; there is no try."

"Are you giving me Yoda wisdom?" I stop and it takes Wolfe half a second before he halts. One of his heart-warming smiles fills his face.

"No, but if it works …" He chuckles. "Be a doer. Commit and follow through. If you try, you've already given yourself permission to fail. Be the force of change. Trying is lying to yourself."

"You're a philosopher."

"I'm a realist with a great deal of life experience."

"Well, I think you're wonderful."

"And I think you're amazing."

As for Wolfe's words, they warm my heart, more so because this easy back and forth is still so new. I feel as if we're finally on the same page. I love walking beside him. Although, he makes me feel tiny.

"As for your job, I take it this means you're choosing tech over joining a Guardian team?"

"I think so. The talent Mitzy's acquired to work on her team is beyond compare."

"Agree."

"She amazes me."

"Mitzy amazes us all. We call her Mitzy the Pixie with Mitzy Magic, which she totally hates."

"I bet, and I bet you guys say it even more as a result."

"I'm not confirming or denying that statement."

"Well, I agree with you. Some of the stuff she does looks like magic. She's definitely the heavy lifter doing the intelligence work, letting her geniuses spin out her concepts into working prototypes."

"That is a very accurate description of Mitzy, but have you worked with Forest yet?"

"Not really."

"He makes Mitzy Magic look like a kid coloring with crayons. Those two work well together. They're like this massive Think Tank, coming up with cool ideas and finding just the right people to manifest their ideas and make them real. You're a part of that machine now."

"I see that now."

"Are you feeling better about fitting in?"

I didn't realize this was a counseling session, but Wolfe definitely ferreted out my issues, laid out my insecurities, and systematically tore them down.

"Yes."

"And?"

"And, what?"

"How do you fit within Guardian HRS?"

His question takes me aback, forcing me to really think about how I can contribute to the organization. I screw my lips up, thinking, but the answer pops into my head.

"The hole I fill—the place I excel—is in the intricacies of deep dives into the abyss, which is the global computing power of a world of interconnected 1's and 0's. This is a place where I see myself thriving."

"Sounds like you've got it figured out."

"Only because of you." I lift up on tiptoe to kiss his cheek. It works only because he dips down so I can reach.

"Tell me more about the ledger."

"Well, as far as Benefield's ledger is concerned, his method is meticulous, yet simple."

"You mentioned that."

"Well, it's simple because once he memorized the substitutions, he basically created a new language for himself. Once he learned his code forward and backward, it took no time for him to write it down in his ledger. Took no time for him to decipher. Everything he needed was literally at his fingertips. I wouldn't be surprised if he could read it out loud, translating on the fly."

"Wow, that's impressive."

"He was a very paranoid man, but ultimately had to bow to the demands of running a business in real time. He didn't have time for elaborate and sophisticated encoding and decoding of his clients' needs."

"I can see that."

"There's far more to it, and I'm still a bit in awe. The multilayered cipher is unbreakable without *the* key phrase. From what I can tell, none of his associates knew about the daughter he secreted away. We wouldn't have known to look for a child if not for you. It all fell into place after that."

Wolfe really deserves all the credit for the work we're about to embark on. Not that he'll take it. Wolfe seems, at least to me, to be a man graced with the physique of a Greek god, the intellect of a genius, each tempered by the careful deliberation of a philosopher. He's much more comfortable kicking doors and rescuing hostages than he is in accepting credit for the brilliant work he does with his mind.

I love that about him.

As for Benefield's daughter, Mitzy found the girl based solely on a search for blind children in Colombia. The girl grew up in a convent and died at the tender age of twelve. That's where Mitzy had to get creative. The only thing connecting Benefield to the girl was a series of tithes, significant sums required to care for a blind child, which began suddenly and stopped just as suddenly. Mitzy found the name of a female benefactor who happened to have delivered a child days before the tithes began. She was a poor woman who suddenly had significant funds to donate.

That's what told us we found the key; a girl no one knew about, a death no one mourned, a trail of money which started and then stopped.

My instructor at the DEA always taught us to follow the money.

It never failed to uncover uncomfortable truths our adversaries would rather keep buried.

No one would've thought to use the girl's name and birth date to break the code, because for all intents and purposes, she never existed.

Fucking brilliant.

If I didn't know the kind of man Benefield was when alive, I'd study his life's work. I'm that in awe of what he did.

I'm far more in awe of Mitzy. She's a genius when it comes to uncovering information people never want found. There's much I can learn from her, and I'm eager to begin.

We now have irrefutable proof that every transaction, each client, all the girls trained and sold, are penned in his ledger.

And now, we can read it. Or will.

"So, my fiery Jinx, what do you need me to do?"

He reminds me that I basically pulled him away from his team, appropriating him for my needs. It takes a millisecond to turn that thought deliciously dirty. Once again, I can't wait for date night.

"Due to the iterative cipher he used, which is not something we can model for *Jacen* to pick apart, that piece of the job needs to be done by hand. Fortunately, Mitzy has me, and I have you."

"So, we're translating the journal?" His warm gaze simmers with banked heat.

"One line at a time." I really can't wait to begin.

"Let's do this then."

I'm right there with him.

"What do you think the next step will be once we know the names of his clients?" I think out loud. If we know the clients, we can find the women they bought.

"I hope we find far more than that." Wolfe's words come out nearly a growl, making me wonder if he's not thinking the same thing as me.

Freeing those women is the reason Guardian HRS exists.

"How's that?"

"Obviously, we'll free as many of the women as we can, but we need to know how the network was set up. As for clients, we're interested in the one who kills the women who are taken." Wolfe confirms what I think about Guardian HRS. The most important thing is to free those who've been taken, but then the rest of what he says sinks in.

"You mean the man who almost killed Zoe Lancaster?" A shiver runs down my spine, making my skin crawl as revulsion fills me. One of their clients was into snuff, a repulsive and unforgivable act.

"Exactly." His jaw tightens when I mention Zoe. Alpha team rescued her, only to have her taken from them again. "That's the man everyone wants."

"Well, that's our job. Soon, we'll know the names of Benefield's clients: the orders placed, the girls who were taken, and the man who snuffed out lives for pleasure."

Those girls disappeared from the world, silent victims of a heinous crime, but they're only a computation away as the code unravels and the ledger spills its secrets.

But that takes time.

NINE

Jinx

Two days later, Wolfe sits with me going through the tedious process of decoding the ledger. He's been silent for some time, which I've come to learn means he's thinking hard.

"You're settling in well with the Guardians." Wolfe looks up from the page he double-checks for me.

Jacen initially decodes each page of the ledger. Wolfe and I check those, tabulating all the information into a form we use to track down each and every sale. There's one set of entries *Jacen* is unable to decipher. I work on that now.

Wolfe's comment takes a moment to break through to my mind.

The man overwhelms me, making it impossible to think. I glance up and wait for his words to process. When my gaze hits those smoldering eyes of his, my stomach does a little flip. I can get lost in those eyes of his for days if I don't calm down the fluttering in my belly. With a deliberate swallow, I force my attention back to my work.

Ever since we talked, I can't help but smile when I'm with him. The air feels fresher. My steps are lighter. My heart races and skips along. The world shines brighter.

I feel happy.

I'm not used to that.

Those first couple of weeks, after Lily and I moved to California, permanent frown lines dug deep grooves into my forehead from all the scowling I did.

Because of him.

Things are different now.

Easier.

Relaxed.

"I am." I answer his question before too much time passes from when he asked. "This is an amazing organization."

"Pays better than the DEA." He closes out the file he's working on, turning the weight of his attention to me. "Do you regret leaving the DEA?" His concern catches me by surprise.

"Maybe?" I can't help but shrug. "I had a lot of doubts at first. It didn't seem a place like this could be real. I was concerned about its permanence."

"Permanence?"

"Yeah. My parents taught me to always think to the future. Don't skimp on retirement. The DEA is federal. Once you're in, you're in. The pay is fair, and the benefits are good. The retirement is dependable. I didn't know if that would be the case with Guardian HRS."

"And now?"

"I'm blown away." I speak the truth and it rings within me with a sense of rightness that fills me with pride.

This place is amazing. I wish I'd known about it before jumping through all those hoops to become a DEA agent.

"I'm glad you're here." He reaches across the table to place his hand over mine. The pad of his thumb traces circles over my skin while the heat of his gaze sends sparks of electricity dancing up and down my frazzled nerves.

He does that. The man knows how to get under my skin.

Molten.

That's the only word to describe the way he looks at me. Or maybe, I should call it ravenous?

Wolfe is an apt name for a man who looks at me like he can't wait to devour me. I'm not used to that kind of focused attention. I'm certainly not used to being exposed to it day after day.

I've always gone for the quick and easy fuck. Scratch an itch and say goodbye. I don't know how to act around him, it's like I'm afraid I'm going to fuck something up.

"Thanks."

That's something else I'm not used to; I'm not used to a man wanting to spend time with me.

"How are you getting along with those last pages?" Those mesmerizing eyes of his shift, focusing on the entries I've been working on for the past hour.

While the code is broken, that doesn't mean the translation is a piece of cake. That's the problem with an iterative code. Every other line, I have to stop and figure out what comes next.

I glance down at what I'm supposed to be working on. Mitzy left us alone. She's attending any one of her hundreds of pet projects and leaves this tedious part of the work to us.

"It's going. I'm resolving dates right now."

"That's good."

"Names will be next."

"Girls or clients?"

"Girls." The client names are much more difficult.

Previously, I remember marveling at the simplistic elegance of Benefield's code. My thoughts turned on that matter. The man did not want anyone breaking his code. That elegance is the bane of my existence, but the ledger is being decoded, albeit slowly. In the past two days, we've made incredible progress.

Wolfe releases my hand. The moment I lose contact, it feels like a great loss. Which is silly. He stands and stretches, leaning back with his hands on his hips.

I pause to admire the perfection which is a Guardian in the prime of his life. There's simply so much to absorb, and unlike our nighttime games, I get an up-close and personal view of his broad chest, washboard abs, and seriously confident stance.

As for those nighttime games, they're on hiatus. After Wolfe kicked Nameless Joe out of my room, and we had our little talk, I've kept my drapes closed. The temptation to reengage in that voyeuristic activity grows with each passing day, but it's not good for us.

Definitely not good for me.

"You're staring." He winks at me. "I hope you're ready for tomorrow night."

We have one night before our first date. My thoughts of moving that day up got buried by the work in front of us. It's a lot to go through. Our work will save lives and is far more important than Wolfe and me hooking up.

If we know who the buyers are, then Mitzy's tech team, of which I'm now a member, can track those men down. Forest, CJ, Sam, and Mitzy are going over possible scenarios about what that operation will look like.

It amazes me how thoroughly they think things through.

I assumed they would start going down the list as it was uncovered and liberate the stolen women one by one.

That's what they initially discussed, but Sam voiced concerns about word spreading about those rescues. If the clients became aware of an organization out to reclaim the women they stole, it wouldn't take much to dispose of those women, or squirrel them away to a place they can't be reached.

Sam's more in favor of a laser-targeted operation, something occurring over the span of days rather than the months it would otherwise take.

An all-out assault and recovery operation.

Sam calls it the Big Bang.

We go in hot, free as many women as we can in the shortest period of time, then wipe up the stragglers. Already, surveillance has begun on the buyers we've uncovered to date, but I'm worried. There aren't nearly as many names as I expected to find.

Either most of those men are repeat buyers, or we're missing something.

"Jinx?" Wolfe places the tips of his fingers down on the table and leans over it, getting close.

His intoxicating, and unique, scent floods my nostrils. I shamelessly take in a long, slow breath. My eyes close as his essence penetrates my senses and settles deep inside with the feeling of coming home.

"What?"

"Are you ready for tomorrow night?"

I feel foolish for leaving his question hanging like that. It seems, while I should focus on him, that my mind drifts to the task at hand. Not that it should surprise me. I've always been laser-focused on work. For Wolfe, however, I'll take a momentary break.

"I'm terrified."

Leaning in, his presence is too much. I push back from the table and gather my hair at my nape. As my fingers thread through the strands, I force myself to look at him.

"Of me?"

"Of us."

There I said it. I'm scared to death to be alone with Wolfe.

We're alone right now, but we're at work. It's not the same. Tomorrow night, I won't be watching him from my room with two panes of glass, and open space, between us.

My bravery, watching him all those nights, was only because he couldn't touch me. He couldn't hurt me. I could shut him down when I felt like it.

Tomorrow?

Tomorrow is when things get real.

"We're not going to do anything you don't want to do. Dinner? Dancing? A movie? That's all it has to be."

It had better be a whole hell of a lot more than that. I'm tired of settling for my vibrator late at night.

"What do you have planned?"

"I was thinking about surprising you. Or are you the kind of girl who needs to know so you can plan what you're wearing?"

"I'm very low maintenance, but if I need a slinky, black dress, you might want to mention that."

"Damn, the idea of you in a slinky, black dress makes me want to skip the date and head directly to the after-hours party."

"I'm not against that."

His lids draw back, exposing the whites of his eyes. Wolfe's mouth works, but no sound comes out. I can't help but smile.

"Did I just leave you speechless?"

He clears his throat and reaches down to his crotch. The man is unashamed of his sexuality and doesn't mind letting me know how I affect him.

"Speechless and hard." He takes a step back, a wicked gleam in his eyes. "I need to excuse myself for a moment."

"Just a moment?"

"With the fantasies running through my mind, it won't take long."

He's shameless.

"Fantasies?"

"Damn straight." He adjusts the tenting in his pants, but there's no hiding his hunger.

"Like what?" I can't help but encourage him.

Part of me wants to secret myself away with him and turn some of those fantasies into reality. Another part just loves getting him all hot and bothered, especially when he's not in a position to do anything about it.

"Luv, you're not ready to face the fantasies in my head."

"Is that what you think?" I can't help it.

I reach up to unbutton the top button of my shirt. In the workplace, I wear modest clothing. Always have. Anything racy or sexy is a no-go for the office. Anything blatantly feminine is also not on the list. Pop a button, or two, on this blouse, and I go from uptight to quite loose.

His Adam's apple bobs as my fingers reach for the second button.

"I have fantasies too."

He swallows and his voice comes out hoarse and thick.

"You do?"

"I do."

His eyes pinch together. "How about a trade?"

"A trade?"

"You tell me yours, and I'll tell you mine."

"Hmm, that sounds fair." I squirm in my seat because this conversation is getting me hot under the collar.

"You first," he says.

"Me?"

"Yes, the lady always goes first."

"Is that true?"

"When you're with me, it is, first and last, and many times in between if we have time for it."

I will find the time. Damn, but I can't wait for tomorrow night. I'm thinking date night should begin and end in his bed.

"All right, I'll bite, but don't back out when it comes time to tell me yours."

"I never back down on a dare."

"You might when you know what I fantasize about."

"And what's that?"

"Are you familiar with Magic Mike? Thunder from Down Under?"

"Male strip shows? Is that what you want? Have me take you to one of those?" His brows bounce with amusement. "I have no problem escorting you to one of those shows, just as long as you stay by my side, touch no one but me, and show your appreciation in bed afterward."

"As exciting as that sounds …" I lift a finger because I don't want to lose my train of thought.

Forcing him to take me to a male dance review sounds like a whole lot of fun. Although, I know how to spice it up. It'd be fun to make it an Alpha Team Girl's night out. All of us with our Guardian men, attending a male stripper's club, is perfect for ammunition when I need something later on down the line.

"You don't think that's exciting?"

"Oh, you have me thinking about it, but I was more interested in something between just you and me."

"You want me to hire a male stripper?" He gives a slow shake of his head. "Luv, inviting another man into our bed is on my very short list of never in a million years."

"That's not what I'm thinking."

"Then please, enlighten me."

"I was thinking it might be nice to see you put on a real show for me." My lashes flutter suggestively. "I've watched you strip." My gaze cuts to his crotch and the very prominent erection tenting his pants. "I've watched you …well, I've watched *that* multiple times. What I've never seen is you work for it."

"Work for it?"

"Yeah, my fantasy is to watch you really put on a show for me."

"Is that so?"

"Yup." I smile and pop the 'p,' thoroughly pleased with myself. Wolfe's cheeks turn cherry red. "You're blushing."

"Am not." He cups his cheek and narrows his gaze.

"You totally are." I stand and kick back my chair. While his eyes practically pop out of his head, I roll my hips in a sinuous figure eight. His eyes grow to the size of saucers. It's a sexy Brazilian dance move, sultry, seductive, and does exactly what it's meant to do.

Wolfe's jaw drops.

"Fuck me." He palms the front of his face, dragging his fingers slowly down as my body undulates.

"I plan to." My body slows, then stills, pleased with the effect I have on him. "What do you think?"

"I think we need to move up date night."

"No can do." I make a sweeping gesture of the table. "Work first, play later."

"Well, there's no way in hell I'm getting any work done." He thrusts a finger out at me. "I want more of that."

"We'll see about it."

"No *see* about anything." He spins around and heads for the door.

"Wolfe …" I call out.

He stops and pivots.

"Yes?"

"I told you mine …" I let my words hang in the air between us.

"Oh, mine is easy."

"What is it?"

"That for one night, you do whatever I want."

"I don't see how that's going to be a problem."

There's no doubt in my mind we're sexually compatible. We may not have done the deed, but what we did do in the bathroom of Callie's bar hints at explosive chemistry.

"We'll see about that."

"What does that mean?" My arms cross over my chest. The tone of his voice puts me on alert.

"Have you ever surrendered before?" That molten heat returns to his eyes. "I'm not talking about casual sex, giving as good as you get. I'm talking about truly letting go."

"No."

"That's what I want. One night where you belong solely to me."

A shiver races down my back, collects at the base of my spine, where icy tendrils turn to deliciously hot and erotic embers of raw desire.

Control isn't something I've ever relinquished.

"I don't know if I can do that."

"Never said you had to do anything, luv. We're simply exchanging fantasies, and that's mine. A sultan in his harem, maybe with a little bit more of that dance move you just showed."

Yeah, but I have a feeling Wolfe's the kind of man who takes what he wants. The room suddenly feels ten sizes too small as my throat closes in and my breaths turn shallow and rapid.

His head cocks to the side. Those eyes of his take me in, assessing, weighing, and driving me insane. With another precise pivot, he says nothing and marches away. Headed to the men's room, no doubt, to take care of that hard-on he packs for me.

My mouth feels as dry as the Sahara as his words circle in my head. No doubt I'll be replaying this same conversation in my head later tonight: me, my vibrator, and myself.

The door to the hallway bangs shut, leaving me to my own devices. All I can say is that I wish I was as shameless as him. I'd never rub one out while at work.

I don't have the guts for that.

To get my mind off of Wolfe, I turn back to the page of entries I'm working on. Two minutes later, I stare at the page and clasp my midsection as one particular entry strikes fear in my heart.

It's not a name, but it's him. Or rather, it's an oblique reference pointing to the man responsible for killing so many.

Wolfe

It's truly getting embarrassing how many times I squirrel away in the bathrooms at Guardian HQ, fisting my cock with thoughts of Jinx running through my head.

The more I do it, the filthier my fantasies become.

Working with her is nothing short of torture. I exist in a constant state of arousal because my entire body tunes in to her every movement, aware of her on a molecular level I can't explain.

While I take the edge off, my thoughts go to the fantasy she described, and an idea forms in my mind. It's going to take time to figure it all out. If I pull it off, it's going to be epic.

While the fighting between us was hot, it's nothing like this easy back and forth we now share. Still no sex, but that'll change.

In a little more than twenty-four hours, I'll be picking her up and taking her on a date I hope will blow her mind.

It's all I've thought about, and with everything Jinx spinning through my mind, I return to the conference room, which has become our personal workspace and my personal hell.

Her sinful body leans over the table. Her luxurious, dark brown hair spills over her shoulders and falls to her elbow, where it pools on the table. She nibbles delicately on her lower lip, a habit she's blissfully unaware of and completely unaware of the effect it has on me. And the way she stands … her blouse gapes with a tantalizing view of the black lace of her bra.

Fuck me. I almost turn around, headed back for round two, but then I take a second look at my girl.

Papers litter the top of the conference table. Large monitors fill the far end of the wall, and my girl leans over the table with her mouth gaping, eyes wide, and gaze shifting furiously between two pieces of paper.

So engrossed in what she's doing, Jinx doesn't notice my return. Slowly, I shut the door and move stealthy, entranced by her ethereal presence, not wanting to break her concentration. My quiet approach, however, is overtaken by the door behind me banging open and slamming closed.

Jinx glances up. The sweep of her gaze takes me in, then jumps behind me.

"Are you sure?" Mitzy blows past me, pushing me to the side, as she races to the table.

Jinx gives Mitzy a sheet of paper, hands shaking as she does.

"I went over it twice. It's him."

"Him?" I close the distance, curious about what Jinx discovered while I was stroking myself into oblivion in the men's restroom.

"I found the man who put in the order for Zoe." Jinx turns her gaze to me. "Or at least a reference to him."

Her words stop me in my tracks.

It's been months since Zoe's abduction on the streets of Cancun. She, along with twelve other young women, were shoved into a transport container and shipped to Colombia. There, the girls were divided into two trucks. One truck transported Eve Deverough, along with five other girls, into Benefield's hands at The Retreat. The other vehicle transported Zoe, and six more girls, to a building where the most heinous of crimes was committed.

Zoe still suffers from the trauma of that place—a place she was taken against her will, not once, but twice.

"You found the snuff asshole?" Anger boils within me thinking about the depravity of the man who purchased seven girls for the sole purpose of brutally murdering them while he got off behind the privacy of a computer screen.

As if that wasn't bad enough, after Alpha team rescued Zoe, that Grade-A asshole put out a specific hit on Zoe by name. He didn't like that we rescued Zoe and the arrogant asshole tried to finish his disgusting masterpiece.

We've been searching for him ever since, but the man is a ghost. Mitzy and her team searched for months before giving up.

The door behind me bangs open and slams closed a second time. I slowly spin around and take a step back as Forest and Sam charge into the room.

Fury fills Forest's features, a storm of vengeance in the making. Sam's tight-lipped, his expression hardens with barely contained rage.

"You found him?" Forest's low rumble makes the air vibrate. I feel his anger deep in my chest, a vibration fueled by his dark, dangerous, and deadly tone.

Jinx flinches at Forest's words. She looks to Mitzy and then to me, unsure what to say or do. Without thinking about it, I navigate my way around the table to stand by her side while Forest and Sam scan the ledger entry Jinx translated.

"You okay?" I lower my voice and place a hand on her shoulder, giving her a squeeze for support.

Forest is intimidating on the best of days. Sam is no less daunting on his own, but everything pales next to Forest's fury.

Jinx reaches up and places her hand over mine. "I'm good." Her fingers tremble slightly.

A jolt shoots through me with the realization Jinx accepts my show of support.

"How certain are you?" Forest turns his icy gaze on Jinx.

She gulps and takes half a step back, where she rubs up against me. Her shoulder blades hit my chest. Before she can bounce away and place distance between us, I wrap my hand around her midsection and hold her tight.

Forest doesn't mean to be overbearing and frightening, but

there's nothing subtle about Forest Summers. His booming voice fills a room.

"It's not a name." She clears her throat. "It's a reference. The only one I've found."

"Doesn't matter." Mitzy pulls up a chair then sends her fingers flying over the keyboard. "It's more than we had a minute ago." Mitzy cranes her neck to look at Forest. "I'll find him. It's not much, but I've done more with far less before."

"I want all hands on deck." Forest clasps his hands behind his back and begins to pace. "The moment we have something actionable, we're going in. Sam, get your team in here."

"Copy that." Sam pulls out his phone and sends out a text. The room becomes silent, filled only with the fierce tapping of Mitzy's fingers on the keys.

Mitzy Magic is something the Guardians came up with to describe the amazing things Mitzy and her team accomplish. If not cutting-edge tech, their intelligence work is second to none.

I continue standing behind Jinx, no longer touching her as she leans forward to show Sam the page she was working on.

"This is great work." Sam taps the page, skimming his fingers across the entries Jinx decoded.

"There are still a few more lines to go," Jinx taps the lines still needing work, "but it's right there."

As I was out of the room, taking care of a pressing need, I didn't get to see what Jinx found.

"There are three orders. Each has a specific request." Jinx explains what she found to the room. "Right here; Zoe Lancaster and Moira Stone. The orders were placed two weeks before they were abducted."

"Interesting."

"I'll be able to tell you more after I dig into it, but that tells us something."

"How so?" Sam's body stiffens with Jinx's comment.

"At a minimum, it tells us the period of time they require from when an order is placed to when they execute it." Jinx pulls the paper back across the table. "I haven't found the names of the girls the Guardians rescued in that shipping container in New Orleans, but this process is getting faster as I go through it."

Jinx mentioned the simplistic elegance of Benefield's system. There's no doubt she's learning his cipher as she goes. Soon, she'll be able to read it rather than struggle through several layers of decryption.

"Once I find the names of those girls in the ledger, I want to take a look at when their orders were placed and when they were collected."

"That would be good to know, but it may not help." Sam nods, but he contradicts what Jinx says.

"Why?"

"They abducted those women within the span of twenty-four hours and placed them in that container for shipping." Sam rubs at his jaw. "I don't want to make any assumptions that confuse things."

"I don't get it." I pull out the chair beside Mitzy.

"If I were running that operation, I'd collect the orders until I had enough to make the payout worth the risk," Sam speaks to the group.

"Right, that makes sense." I see where he's coming from. "Collect a dozen orders, plan the abductions over the span of a day, then arrange transport the following day."

"Right. Not that we don't need that info." Sam turns his attention back to Jinx. "I want everything we can get out of those ledgers. I just don't think we'll get what you're hoping for."

"What you say makes sense," Jinx agrees. "If we assume that's how they set everything up, all I'd need to do is look at when the last order was placed for the last girl, then sync that up with the day those girls were taken."

"We'll look at everything." Sam pulls out a chair on the opposite side of the table. "As for our next steps." He glances over at Forest. "There are several ways to play this."

The door to the conference room swings open. CJ enters with Max and Jenny on his heels.

"What's going on?" CJ surveils the room, catches my eye, then shifts his focus to the conference table.

"Jinx found him." Sam only says three words, but there's no need to elaborate. Everyone in the room knows which *he* this is; there is only one.

Guardian HRS has been on the hunt for the man who ordered the murders of six innocent girls and who nearly got away with murdering Zoe, not just once, but twice.

He's been untraceable until today.

When Zoe was first rescued, Alpha team recovered a tablet. We thought *that* would crack open the entire operation like an egg.

It did not.

Mitzy ran down every lead linked to that tablet and, if we extend the egg analogy, got the proverbial goose egg.

Nothing. Nada. Zilch.

When Alpha team apprehended Julian Townsend, the rich, entitled prick who placed his special order for Moira, we thought we'd crack open the entire operation.

We did not.

But Townsend led us to Tomas Benefield.

Benefield kidnapped Eve Deverough. When we rescued Eve, we obtained the ledger. Which we *thought* would crack the case wide open …

But then we encountered the cipher.

This is an emotional moment.

With the arrival of Max and Jenny, Alpha and Delta team leaders, it's obvious CJ called in a meeting of the minds. Not surprisingly, Brady and Tex join us a few minutes later.

I lean down to whisper into Jinx's ear. "You definitely got their attention." I point to the latest arrivals. "CJ gathered all the team leaders. Brady is Bravo One, and Tex is Charlie One." No need to explain who Jenny is to Jinx.

They know each other well. While Jinx's unique fighting style is gender indistinct, the female Guardians seem to be taking to it much faster than the men. As for Max, she knows him well.

"Wow." Jinx lifts her brows with nervous energy. "You guys don't waste any time."

"Not *you guys*, luv. You're one of us now." I place my hand over her knee and give a tiny squeeze. As Alpha Six, I'm sorely outranked in this room, but I have a place here. "You nervous?"

"Just surprised by how quickly they gathered everyone together. At my old job, we'd still be drafting the first email to send back and forth before deciding whether we had enough new data to even hold a meeting."

"Forest doesn't believe in wasting time. But there's still intel to gather, and we're not done with these ledgers." I gather up the sheets she's working on and move us to the end of the table.

Max, Jenny, Tex, and Brady take over the side of the table we were on. Opposite them, CJ, Sam, and Forest pull out chairs. Mitzy is at the head, scanning the internet, dark web, and the hidden nebulous web trying to identify our killer.

"Jinx …" Mitzy doesn't look up from her screen. Her voice cuts through the chatter, silencing the room.

"Yes?" Jinx clasps my hand under the table.

"How close are you to decoding the clients who placed the orders for the New Orleans job?"

ELEVEN

Wolfe

____

IN MANY WAYS, MITZY IS AN INTERESTING CHARACTER. SHE'S BUBBLY, sometimes obnoxious, generally quirky, and a genius.

I've never heard her in boss mode, demanding progress on a job. It takes me aback because it doesn't match my image of Mitzy. I've always pictured her hyperactive to a fault.

Jinx, however, rolls with it.

"Not done yet, boss, but it won't take too long." Jinx glances at me and her entire being lights up. "Especially with Wolfe helping."

It's a kind statement, inclusive, but not needed. The accolades for this belong to Jinx, not me. Not even as a part-owner. Jinx did all the heavy lifting. I simply dotted the I's and crossed the T's.

"I need you to get on that ASAP." Mitzy barks another order, and Jinx jumps to comply.

"Copy that." Jinx releases my hand and spreads the papers out in front of her.

I can't help but smile at the way she integrates the way the Guardians communicate into her speech patterns. She would make a great operative. It's almost a shame to shackle her to a desk.

Not that Jinx sees it that way. I've seen her fight. She laid me on the ground more times than I'm willing to admit, but watching her work this case is a whole other experience. Her intelligence lights up the room, and enthusiasm pours out of her with this intense energy.

Jinx is intelligent, fearless, and dedicated. Knox has issues with Lily operating, especially on Alpha team, but I don't share his concern when it comes to my girl. I thought I did, but I don't anymore. Jinx is more than capable of taking care of herself.

She and I get to work while the team leads start talking potential strategies they could employ. Even though they don't know who they're going after, or where he is, they'll still toss out potential scenarios and chew through them.

The room settles into a state of agitated chaos as the team leaders propose scenarios, which get picked apart by the rest of the room. At the end of the table, Jinx and I occupy a tiny bubble of solitude, working side by side, shoulder to shoulder, and hip to hip.

No one speaks to us, and we barely speak to each other. I've never felt more comfortable with another person in my life.

Or so scared.

"How're you doing?" It's been nearly two hours since the others joined us. I keep my voice low so as not to interrupt the others.

"I could use a break." Jinx rolls her neck and blinks several times as she peers down at her work. The strain in her voice betrays the depth of her fatigue.

"Let's do it." My protectiveness rises, needing to take care of my woman. I take her hand in mine, folding my massive finger around her tiny hand, but she resists.

"I can't leave." She tugs free of my grip and places her hand on the back of her neck. Looking up at the ceiling, she blows out a deep breath and rolls her neck again.

I'd give her a neck rub, but I'm afraid I won't be able to keep something like that PG-13. My body's primed for tomorrow night, ready to take that final step with Jinx by my side.

"You've been at this for hours. A short break is more likely to help than hurt. Give your brain a rest and things will be clearer when we come back."

"We're almost done."

It's late in the afternoon, and from the way the others are still going, this will last late into the night.

"They aren't." I point to the top brass of Guardian HRS embroiled in a strategy session with no end in sight. "Trust me. Take a moment to clear your head, get a breath of fresh air. When we come back, maybe you'll see something new. Or maybe it'll simply be that much easier to continue. They're going nowhere, which means we're stuck here until they're done. Trust me, this is a good time for a break."

As far as being nearly done, it's a true statement. We're uncovering truths Benefield never wanted the world to see. It's meticulous work and requires intense focus. My eyes hurt from straining too hard, and I'm not doing the heavy lifting.

That's Jinx's job.

She decodes.

I come behind, proofing her work. Although *proofing* isn't the right word for what I do. Nor is double-checking. I'm poring through her work, looking for context, areas where the code wanders off, and checking the accuracy of the information against what Guardian HRS knows to be true.

Benefield was a sneaky-assed bastard. It's not possible, but I hate him even more.

"Come."

The strain in her eyes, that slight pinching of pain, decides the matter. I take her hand and give a tug to get her moving.

When she follows without arguing, I'm thrilled. Once we leave the room, I pause. An overwhelming sensation overcomes me. I'm transported back fifteen years when I ditched class to play hooky with a girl and engage in a bit of heavy petting beneath the bleachers.

An evil grin curls the corners of my lips.

Jinx places her hand on my bicep. "Why does it look like you're the cat who just caught the mouse?" Her lips part and her lashes flutter. Her olive skin turns the prettiest shade of pink I've ever seen.

Her gaze bounces back and forth between my eyes and my lips. Eventually, it settles on my eyes. We stare at each other with silence stretching between us for a few seconds too long.

Heat builds.

Desire pulses.

My mind travels decadent paths.

"How adventurous do you feel?"

I arch a brow, suggesting mischief, not the fun kind, but something to distract her and give her mind a break. A smile tickles my lips with thoughts of all the fun we can have, but Jinx doesn't need that kind of distraction.

It's with great difficulty that I resist the urge to slam her against the wall and kiss her until she can't breathe. I consider myself a saint for not doing that right now.

Jinx continues to stare, her expression hooded, unreadable, and confusing. That flush rises from her neck to fan across her cheeks.

"Adventurous enough for this ..." Jinx grabs the fabric of my shirt and yanks me toward her as she lifts on her toes.

Before I know what's happening, her breasts press against my chest, followed in short order by her full, pillowed lips locking to mine.

I meet her soft kiss with the firmness of my lips, the solidness of my body, and the hard length of my eager cock rising to the occasion.

Holy fuck, but I forget how wonderful it feels to kiss her. And this time, there won't be a knock-down-drag-out fight following.

This is our first *real* kiss. I'm not counting the one in the bullpen.

One thing I remember from our far too short of a stint in Callie's bar is Jinx doesn't shy away from sex.

She's aggressive and determined, driven by the needs of her body, and not ashamed to go after what she wants.

If I'm not careful, she'll dominate this kiss.

While I don't mind an aggressive lover, I draw the line at who's in control. I wrap one arm around her waist, pressing my palm against the curvature of her spine. My other hand rises and my fingers thread through the silky hair at her nape.

I shift the dynamic of this kiss, driving my lips savagely against hers and turning my tongue into a weapon with only one goal in mind.

Her lips part and I thrust my tongue into her mouth, tasting, claiming, and owning.

I miss this.

Ever since that first night, this is what I crave. It's what I desperately desire. Holding her like this, dominating her like I did in that bathroom at the bar, I think of nothing but that.

The few kisses I took from her afterward pale in comparison to this.

I catch her nape and haul her close, pressing our bodies together until I can barely tell where mine ends and hers begins.

The heat of her mouth is like a firestorm blowing through me, fanning the flames of my desire until my conscious brain takes a backseat to my primal nature.

Her tiny moans rip through me. My nostrils flare, breathing her in as she claws at me with desperate hunger.

Then something amazing happens. Her fingers twitch and the desperate clawing stops. The pads of her fingers press lightly against my nape, caressing, stroking, as a sigh escapes her mouth.

All the tension in her body releases. Jinx breathes out and surrenders control. She lets me set the pace.

No longer taking.

No longer demanding.

A gasp escapes her as I redouble my efforts, firmly taking the lead. Her tiny moans fuel my hunger and ignite my need.

With my fingers twined in her hair, I control her head. Breaking our kiss, she clutches at me, then gasps as my lips press against her neck.

I kiss and lick my way up and down the soft curve of her neck. My breath flutters against her skin as my lips devour and claim.

Her chest rises and falls, pulling in air between one gasp and the next as I take my time to fully explore the sweep of her neck. On a mission to discover her erogenous zones, and master them, I take my time.

I slide my thumb along her jaw, press it against her lips, and force them to open. She gulps as I press inward with my thumb.

I lift from the sweetness of her neck and allow our gazes to connect and weave together. Standing over her, I slowly rock my thumb in and out of her mouth as I stare deeply into her eyes.

I want to kiss her again, but more than that, I want to peel away the layers between us and climb inside where I intend to make myself comfortable and stay forever.

I want to fuck Jinx and join our bodies until we're one and she firmly belongs to me.

I drink in her features, unhurried in my exploration, as my thumb pulls out of her mouth. My cock aches, wanting to feel her tantalizing mouth and talented tongue again. It's been far too long.

"You have no idea how amazing you are. You shine with the brilliance of a thousand suns. Fiery, passionate …" I tap her lips with my thumb, then lean down until my lips barely press against hers. My voice lowers to a whisper. "But when you let go—when you surrender—you're a firestorm raging through me."

My lips press against hers, harder, demanding, hopeful that my words don't scare her. Jinx isn't the kind of woman to surrender control. I'm not sure she realizes she did, and I brace for her to tell me otherwise.

But when her arms loop over my shoulders and her hands clasp around my neck, Jinx doesn't fight.

She doesn't resist.

She doesn't correct what I said.

She lifts on tiptoe, tilts her head, offers her mouth, and silently surrenders her will.

She lets me take the lead, which I do with wonder and awe.

I cup her jaw, with reverent admiration, as emotions flow through me. Her warm eyes pull my gaze, drawing me to them with the irresistible magnetism we share.

This thing between us is getting heavy. Our attraction is a force of nature. Like gravity, it's inevitable.

Unstoppable.

Undeniable.

My heart skips on a beat when I realize what Jinx is telling me. She's no longer fighting the insane chemistry between us.

"Fuck …" The word comes out low and throaty.

She releases her grip at my nape and allows her hands to trail down my biceps. Her fingers flutter over my skin, a butterfly light sensation sending pulses of heat licking along my skin and sparks dancing through my nervous system.

I can't look away. I can barely breathe. Her fingers float up, touching my face, caressing my skin. They dance along my jawline, fluttering and sparking. Her eyes capture mine, holding me captive with her surrender.

But she's wary.

She's afraid.

Jinx has trust issues, as if these are uncharted waters for her. Gracing me with her trust is a treasured gift, which slams into me, stealing my breath and rocking my world.

"You have no idea what this means to me." My voice comes out raw, a hoarse whisper sawing through the space between us.

Her brows pinch with hesitation as her gaze flickers from one of my eyes to the other and back again.

"This isn't easy for me," she says. "Don't mess with me. I won't survive it."

I'm attuned enough to her thoughts to understand she's not ready. More than that, I'm thrilled she voiced her concerns out loud.

We're breaking down the walls that separate us, but I don't mind moving as slow as we need to go.

I'm in this for the long haul.

I press my lips against hers, letting her take a moment to process her thoughts.

I pull back, still in awe, and brush the hair away from her face.

"There's no need to think too hard about it. We'll find our way one step at a time. This doesn't need to mean anything."

"But … I've never …"

"I absolutely adore you, my fiery Jinx. For now, this is just a kiss."

"You and I both know it's far more than that." Her anger

returns, a manifestation of fear against surrendering control. "Don't fuck this up. Don't hurt me."

"Never."

I make it a solemn vow.

My gaze dips to her mouth as my desire rises, obliterating all thought. I have to have her.

Now.

Kiss her.

Touch her.

Fuck her.

I never needed anything more. I've never wanted another person the way I need Jinx.

As if the same thought goes through her head, our lips crash together. Our tongues touch, sliding and stabbing, too frantic with our need to devour the other. Our arms wrap around the other, entwining as the heat between us builds. Escalating with raw desire and ravenous need.

The door to the conference room bangs open and a deep voice vibrates the air, interrupting the world's best kiss.

"Unlock those lips and get your asses back inside. Mitzy found something."

Jinx breaks our kiss and pushes against my chest. Her lower lip rolls inward between her teeth as she straightens her shirt and tugs up her jeans.

I didn't realize what I was doing, practically mauling her during that kiss. Given a few more seconds, I would've had us both naked.

As it is, the kiss is over. I yank down my shirt and tug on the waistband of my jeans. A quick adjustment ensures I won't be making a fool of myself when I reenter that room.

I give Jinx space to similarly put herself together, unable to keep from smiling at getting caught kissing my girl in the hall.

Although, I wish we were anywhere else. If we were, there's only one way that kiss would have ended.

Forest's glacial gaze sweeps between us, sparkling with mirth. A smile tickles the corners of his mouth as he holds the door open and jambs a thumb inside.

"They're coming. Give them a second to unlock their lips." With that comment, Forest slips back inside the room.

Then it hits me.

What he said.

It registers with Jinx at the same time. Her jaw drops, and she reaches for me.

"Wolfe …"

"I know …" I take her hand in mine and lead her back into the conference room.

Jinx frees herself from my grip, which bums me out for a second, thinking she doesn't want the others to see us together. But then her hand drifts up my arm until she's hugging my bicep.

"You found him?" Her voice is light and tenuous, cautious but hopeful.

Mitzy looks up from her computer screen. With a flick of her fingers, a name lights up all the monitors in the room.

"Not yet. I found something better."

"Better?"

"A brokerage firm that takes the orders. It's a shell organization, obviously, but once we figure out who runs it …" There's no reason for Mitzy to finish that thought. We all understand.

"Brokerage house?" Jinx looks at me, brows tugged tight, confused.

"What does that mean exactly?" I echo Jinx's confusion.

"It's how the clients place their orders and a clearing house for all the transactions. I'm working on a way in."

It's one step closer.

Possibly a huge leap. If Mitzy can hack into their servers and find out who's taking the orders, we can take them out. If she gets the client list, we can go after them individually. The client ordering the snuff films is still out there, but we're closing in.

"Asses in those chairs." Forest claps his meaty hands, making the room shake like thunder. "I want recommendations by morning. Tomorrow we ship out."

Tomorrow?

Jinx and I exchange a look.

We sit at the foot of the table, and as the others get to work while my knee bounces with agitation.

Tomorrow is supposed to be our night.

Will we ever get a break?

TWELVE

Jinx

MANY HOURS LATER, I FIGHT FATIGUE, BLINKING AND YAWNING behind my hand.

"Forest doesn't kid around when he says asses in seats." I bump shoulders with Wolfe, seeking physical contact.

We're right where we started, but there's a different vibe in the air. I dub the conference room War Room Central and keep my voice whisper quiet.

It's been well over eight hours since Forest bellowed his orders, locking all of us in a room to plan strategy and put an operation together.

"That's Forest." Wolfe affectionately squeezes my upper thigh. "Once he decides to do something, he won't stop until it's done. This entire place ..." Wolfe makes a vague gesture, taking in the whole room and, by extension, all of Guardian HQ. "It's all his vision. Because of him, we not only rescue people, we show them how to go from victim to survivor. If you haven't been to The Facility yet, you should stop in. Alpha team goes one week a month to teach self-defense. Actually, it would be great if you taught Capoeira to the rescues."

"You teach self-defense?"

"Yeah, it's one of my favorite parts of this job. All the teams rotate through, and it's awesome to see those we've rescued transform over time. The Facility is nothing short of incredible."

"Wow."

I lean back, profoundly affected by Wolfe's words. I see him as a Guardian: a warrior and a fighter. To know there's this other side of him, a trainer, a teacher, and a healer. He makes me appreciate his dedication to this life even more. It makes me want to do more for the Guardians.

Things between us are different now. Centered. If that's the right word to describe the flow of energy surging between us.

It's strange to think as little as eight hours ago, Wolfe had his tongue shoved halfway down my throat. I acted like a cat in heat, clawing at him with desperate hunger.

Now?

We're relaxed. As if we needed to get that little bit of sexual energy out and spent. Now, we can sit beside each other, letting it simmer and build. The chemistry between us is no less intense, but it's muted and manageable.

I no longer feel the mad rush to do the deed because I know, deep inside, Wolfe is here for the long haul. I've never had that before. Not once in my life has a man stuck around after the sun came up.

Hell, I was usually the one kicking them out after the fucking was done.

"Eight hours." I keep my voice low, complaining. "No food breaks. No water breaks. No bathroom breaks." I rub the back of my neck, desperate to work out the kinks hours of poor posture have wrecked on my body. "He's a slave driver."

"He's definitely focused."

"When we pulled all-nighters with the DEA, someone was out on a pizza run. Someone else smuggled in booze. We had coffee flowing like there was no tomorrow, and the rising of the sun brought doughnuts of every flavor to whet our appetites. You Guardians need to step it up."

"Ah, luv, remember ..."

"Remember, what?"

"You're one of us now."

"Well, I'm not technically a Guardian."

"No, but you're one badass bitch."

"Bitch?" I give him the eye as a smile bounces on my lips.

"Badass broad?" His eyes crinkle with mirth, playing with me.

This! This is what I could fall in love with, a connection with an easy flow of banter back and forth.

"That's worse." I scrunch up my nose and playfully slug him in the arm, and when I say *playful,* I mean super light and super soft. His biceps are as hard as granite and I'm not keen on hurting myself.

"Whatever." He makes a show of rolling his eyes. "You're fucking badass no matter how I say it."

"If you insist." I give a flick of my lashes because I don't disagree.

"You know I'm right." There's a wicked gleam in his eyes which speaks to the heat of our hallway kiss.

"Good thing I haven't had a sip to drink, or I'd be needing that pee break." I squirm next to Wolfe as he traces lazy circles over the top of my thigh. "Stop that."

"Stop, what?" He glances down the table, all innocence and lies, like he's not driving me crazy with his touch.

"You know what." I grip his wrist and try removing his hand from my thigh.

He's been slowly inching it up from my knee and is now less than a finger's width away from making me jump.

Although, it seems as if we're not going to get that date we've *both* been looking forward to this past week. My sexual frustration is at an all-time high.

Wolfe and I sit somewhat apart from the others, but we're still all in the same room. We're seated at what's effectively the foot of a long conference table.

Mitzy occupies the head. She's the brains of this operation. I might say Forest is the brainiest of the brains, but he's more of the innovative visionary. He dreams up incredible things, then selects the right people who can figure out how to take his idea and manifest it in this world.

Mitzy is a doer. Sharp, wickedly brilliant, she's tenacious and driven, leaving no stone unturned in her quest to solve a mystery. Sam, CJ, and the Guardian team leaders, Max, Tex, Brady, and Jenny are the muscle that gets things done.

They're far more than that. I've been listening in on their conversation during the eight hours I've been denied food, drink, pizza, coffee, doughnuts, and a bathroom break.

They're brilliant tacticians.

I've worked enough operations with the DEA to appreciate the forward-thinking, can-do attitudes of Guardian HRS's leaders. It almost makes me want to work on one of their teams as an operator instead of an intelligence specialist.

Almost.

As for me, my work remains unfinished. I'm not done decoding the ledger, but I'm tired and getting crankier by the minute.

Each time I stand, stretch, or make a break for the bathroom, Forest's pacing magically brings him front and center to the one door leading out of the room. His glacial glare sends me scurrying back to my seat, where I resume the tedious task of translation.

As if I haven't spent the last ungodly number of hours doing exactly that. At least Wolfe is with me. He pats my chair with laughter sparkling in his eyes.

This may be my first strategy session with the Guardians, but it's not his. I take my lead from him and return to my chair, shuffling my feet while glancing longingly at the door which leads to the freedom Forest denies me.

Beneath Forest's watchful gaze, I get back to work. When I drift off, Wolfe's comforting touch brings me back to the task at hand. My eyes may cross, and my vision might blur, but damn if Wolfe's touch doesn't make my heart race, sending an adrenaline surge whipping through my body.

It's perhaps *the best* pick me up on the planet.

Concerning my work, it's way more challenging with a gazillion other people in the room.

I need quiet to focus. Every little cough, each indrawn breath, and the frustrated sighs filling the room tear my attention away from the work at hand.

As for our quarry, Mitzy sniffs down the brokerage house—an innocuous term for a firm that destroys lives and trades in human lives—scouring the internet landscape for evidence of the clients they serve.

It's another puzzle as I work beside Mitzy to learn everything we can about this new lead. We've narrowed down the possibilities, spanning the criminal gamut from crime bosses in Chicago to cartel kingpins in Colombia. Undeterred, Mitzy meticulously tracks the movement of scores of potentials through the cyber landscape.

Meanwhile, I continue slaving away.

"Wolfe—" I nudge him in the arm.

"What's up?"

"Do you have the list of the girls taken in New Orleans?"

"I do." He leans toward me and lowers his voice. "FYI, we prefer not to focus on being taken."

"Huh?"

"It's not the girls who were taken, but rather the girls we saved." He glances over at Forest and my gaze follows. "Forest says words carry power. Those girls don't need us thinking of them as victims, but rather as survivors. It's the central philosophy around everything we do."

"Really?" My brows tug together. "I wouldn't think it would matter."

"Someone would've eventually corrected you, but now you know."

"Do you think it matters?" I'm quite surprised, and despite the slight surge of annoyance at his correction, I'm more curious about what he thinks than him correcting me.

"I didn't at first." His voice changes in pitch and fills with emotion. "But then I taught some of those we rescued at The Facility. It matters. They wear their survivor badge with pride as they slowly work through what happened to them. They were victims, some horribly so, and if we did nothing to help, they'd wallow in the past, remaining victims for life. For many of those kids, knowing they can take back control is the only positive they have. It's not a quick fix. Some stay at The Facility for years."

"Oh, okay, that makes sense." I never would've thought words would matter that much, but he explains it perfectly.

He places his hand on my knee. "No need to be sorry. Just didn't want you getting called out for saying the wrong thing in front of the others."

"Well, thanks." I may think it's a weird philosophy, but I'm happy Wolfe took the time to correct me, privately. If I'd made that blunder, unknowingly or not, in front of the others, I would've felt really bad.

"Here you go." He finds the right file on the tablet he's been using to double-check me.

"That's all of them?"

"It is."

"Good." I have him send me the file, then set it to display side by side with the entries on my device.

The decoding is much faster, getting easier and easier the deeper I get into Benefield's ledger. I'm learning his secret language.

A pattern reveals itself. I flip back to the list of girls the Guardians rescued back in New Orleans, matching up the entries.

There's a discrepancy.

"Wolfe …" I tug on his shirtsleeve.

"What's up?"

"There are six more names in the ledger than on this list."

"Six?" His entire body tenses as that sinks in.

"Yes." I point to the ledger.

There are only three pages left to decipher. From what I've learned, those will be transaction IDs and instructions about wire transfers and the rest.

"Benefield took orders on six more girls. This one …" I point to my translation. "Her entry is two weeks after the order which came in for the last girl rescued in New Orleans. This one is nearly a month. This last one is two weeks after that. It looks like Benefield collected names, then batched them when he hit a dozen.

These are orders for a new batch of women, taken before his death."

No need to elaborate. The Guardian's takedown of Benefield's operation put a wrench in the fulfillment phase of those orders.

"Benefield's clients have been sitting in limbo waiting for their slaves to be delivered. How long will they sit before demanding delivery?" It's not a difficult question, although Wolfe jumps in with the obvious answer.

"Not this long."

"That's what I'm thinking."

I flip back to the twelve girls the Guardians saved, looking at the time between when the first order for the first girl came in to when the Guardians rescued them.

The assumptions I make don't sit well with me. As an intelligence expert, I deal best with cold, hard facts, rather than leaping too soon to conclusions which can be more harmful in the long run.

My gut says Benefield was in the process of compiling a new batch of slave orders. A dozen seems to be the magic number he deals with, but there's no way to confirm that.

He's dead.

Who moved in to fill the gap?

Nature abhors a vacuum.

Someone stepped up, or stepped down, to handle this side of operations. They had to. Those clients initiated wire transfers for significant deposits. They'll either want their money back, with interest, or the slave they were promised.

I'm aware the Guardians feel Benefield was the head of that operation, which he may very well have been. I have no data to dispute that, and a whole lot of circumstantial evidence brings me to the same conclusions the Guardians made, but I'm an expert in how drug cartels operate; specifically, in how they're structured and the hundreds of creative avenues they use to move their money around, cleaning it as it goes.

There's always another layer higher up.

Always.

And that's what my gut tells me now. There's no reason to think this is the only copy of Benefield's transactions.

That's what the Guardians assume.

I see something else.

"Meticulous bookkeeping," I whisper under my breath.

"What's that, luv?" Wolfe leans close.

"Nobody keeps books this clean." I barely register Wolfe's words as I think this through, challenging all my assumptions and questioning the premise behind every conclusion reached thus far.

"What are you getting at?" He arches a brow.

"I don't care how OCD someone is ..." My gaze naturally travels to Mitzy, well known for her OCD tendencies. "Nobody keeps books *this* clean."

"I beg to differ. These aren't just clean, they're meticulous and coded into gibberish. Benefield didn't want anyone getting their hands on his information."

"QTP." The letters roll off the tip of my tongue

"What?"

"Question the Premise. It's something my father used to teach me." I pivot in my chair, facing him directly. "QTP. Question the Premise. He told me never jump to conclusions because once you do, it's a very long swim back."

"How so?"

"The moment you jump, whatever conclusion you jump to gets cemented in your head where it becomes fact—even if untrue. Once that happens, it's incredibly difficult to rework that belief. Assumptions cloud objectivity."

"Okay, so we question the premise. What exactly are we questioning?" His brow arches. From his body language, he doesn't believe me, but he's willing to hear me out.

"Benefield loved his ledger. He's meticulous in entering the data. Every girl. Every client. Every transaction. Why would he do that?"

"OCD?"

"That's the premise, but is it reality?"

Wolfe used to do intelligence work in the Navy before applying for, and becoming, a SEAL officer. He knows the value of taking a step back and using a new perspective to see things differently.

"If Benefield wasn't OCD, and didn't fill out his ledgers because of his compulsive tendencies, why would he?" I like how Wolfe is willing to work through my thought process with me. It's nice having a partner.

"Because he was responsible for answering to someone higher up," I state my assumption as fact, rather than as a question. Which is the wrong thing to do, but this assumption, as dangerous as it can be, feels right.

It makes sense.

"If that's the case, then he transmitted his data to the brokerage house." Wolfe blows out a breath and leans back in his chair.

"Exactly, and that's what scares me. If that's the case, those girls are in terrible danger."

"Shit." He runs his fingers through his wavy black hair and glances at the screen with the translations.

"There's no way to know for sure, but those clients put down deposits."

Those are transactions I'll track down. Wolfe has it only partially correct. I'm a tenacious badass bitch when it comes to my job.

"It's been months since the deposits," I say. "They're going to want delivery. They'll demand it."

With the way cash bounces around, needing to be cleaned several times in the process, returning that cash is highly dangerous. The return process isn't nearly as neat as the initial laundering. That opens their clients up to connections and links to an organization they don't want any association with.

Benefield's clients are among the uber-wealthy. They're accustomed to being waited on hand and foot. What they're not accustomed to is getting shafted. There will be tremendous pressure to deliver the orders.

We need to discover who's in charge, and quickly.

"Twelve seems to be the magic number when it comes to order fulfillment." I scratch my neck and pull my hand through my hair. "They're going to be under a lot of pressure to deliver on these last six orders. It wouldn't surprise me if they close up shop for a bit, once that's done."

"Why would they do that?"

"The Guardians are breathing down their necks. They'll want that heat to blow over."

"Fuck." Wolfe blows out a breath.

"After Benefield's operation blew up, who took over? I doubt they're still taking orders, but those six girls are still out there."

"How sure are you?"

"Fairly." I shrug because I'm making several assumptions. "There's no way to know for certain, but they're already past the time when they should begin collecting the girls."

My voice shakes nearly as much as my hands.

Time is the one resource we don't have enough of, and I need more of it.

THIRTEEN

Jinx

Too engrossed in what I'm thinking, I miss Forest coming up to stand behind me.

"What's going on, Jinx?" His words rumble deep in my chest.

"How long have you been standing there?" I twist and crane my neck to look up at him.

"Enough to want to know more." Forest's gruff replies no longer rub me wrong.

A brilliant individual, he's on the spectrum, and doesn't *people* well, which means he cuts through all the fluff normal conversation demands and gets straight to the point.

"Jinx found the next set of women slated for abduction," Wolfe answers for me.

As for me, my hand rests over my stomach as a sinking sensation fills me with dread.

If we're too late …

"Mitz!" Forest bellows, and the room stills.

"Geez Louise, Forest, no need to bring the roof down." Mitzy's crystal clear, high-pitched voice pierces the quiet. "What have I told you about using your indoor voice?"

A wounded expression fills Forest's face. "This is my indoor voice." His voice softens.

"Well, try your indoor, whisper-quiet voice." Mitzy pushes back from the table. "You scared the shit out of me."

"Sorry." Forest makes a conscious effort to decrease the volume of his voice, but it doesn't work.

"Whatever." Mitzy shakes her head. It's comical because her short pixie hair flies in a spiral around her head. "You going to spit it out?"

"What?" Forest looks confused.

"Whatever's so damn important you felt the need to scare me senseless."

"Now you're being melodramatic." The deep register of Forest's voice returns to normal volume, just shy of a shout.

"Just get on with it." Mitzy blows out a puff of air which makes her purple bangs bounce.

Forest grabs my tablet and reads off a very short list of names. "Julie Gant, Lori Black, Sybil Niles ..." He continues until he gets to the last name.

"What do you want me to do with those?"

"Track them down."

"Why?"

I speak for Forest, jumping into the conversation. "Because they haven't been taken yet." Everyone in the room looks at me. "I hope."

"If they haven't been taken ..." Wolfe backs me up. "We need to protect them." His gaze cuts to Max.

The two men stare at each other for a long beat, but then Max cuts the connection as I take in a breath.

"We could turn this to our advantage." Max's jaw bunches as he grits his teeth. "If we can get our hands on one of the abductors, or the handlers who take over from there ..."

"That's too risky." Sam props his elbows on the conference room table. "Our job is to keep those women safe, protect them, not use them as bait."

"He's only suggesting it might help." Wolfe defends his team leader. "We need leads."

"Wolfe's right." All eyes once again turn toward me. "Benefield's dead. Mitzy found the brokerage firm, but we still have no idea who stepped up and is running the whole operation." I swallow around the lump in my throat. "We need to know who those men work for."

Sam has a point. To get to the men responsible for abducting the girls—and through them to who's now in charge of the operation—we have to let the abduction play out. That's inherently risky, and while I believe each girl will be adequately protected, there's always a chance she could be taken out from under our watchful eye.

"We should at least consider it, before discarding it out of hand." Wolfe continues to support Max.

I love the way they back each other up, not only in the field, but everywhere. Their bond is something I'll never understand.

"Max has a point." CJ steps in, giving his two cents. "First off, we can't assume any of those girls are safe." He turns to Forest. "We can put a protection detail on them, but for how long? I don't like the idea of using those girls, especially without their consent, but there's something to be said about knowing more about who's in charge."

"Well, I don't know who's calling the shots, but it's no problem finding these women." Mitzy's fingertips tap furiously on the keyboard.

"Do you think they …" I choke on the words. It's been far too long since Benefield's death.

All that wasted time. If those women aren't safe, I'll never forgive myself for not figuring things out sooner.

Wolfe doesn't offer false hope, but what he gives is a million times better.

His silent presence grounds me. His affirmative touch settles my nerves. The way he gently, but firmly, grips my leg, forces the nervous bouncing of my left knee to stop. Then he drapes an arm around my shoulders and pulls me into his embrace.

He's not shy about the public display of affection, although I guess the cat's out of the bag. Everyone knows there's something between us, and the fact we haven't been at each other's throats speaks volumes about the shift between us.

"We'll find them." He places a soft kiss to the top of my head.

And I believe him.

I wriggle in my seat, trying to find a more comfortable position, as Mitzy tracks down those women. It seems to take forever, but these aren't criminals hiding their whereabouts. These are young women who, most likely, live on social media. It should be a short search on the web.

Just as these words fly through my mind, Mitzy is back on her feet. "I found Julie Gant. Student. UC Davis Veterinarian school. I'm calling her apartment now."

Mitzy's crystal clear voice rings through the air, bringing quiet to the room. She puts the call on speaker so we can all listen in. The ringing sound keeps me on pins and needles. After far too many rings, a woman answers.

"Hello?"

"Julie?"

"No, it's Mary."

"Oh, is Julie there?"

"She's in class. Can I take a message?"

"Her book somehow got mixed in with mine at the library. We've got that test coming up, and I didn't want her not to have it."

"Oh, I bet she's frantic."

"I bet. Do you know where she is? Still on campus?"

"Oh, you know Julie, she's at the coffee shop."

"Ah, yeah, I forgot about that." Mitzy pauses. "Look, I'm leaving campus. Can you give me her number? It'd be easier if I texted her and dropped it off."

"Sure thing." Mary rattles off Julie's number.

"Thanks so much. Bye-ee!" Mitzy hangs up and turns her attention back to the computer screen. "One down, five to go."

A few seconds later, Mitzy calls out. "And bam, there's Julie."

Mitzy pops up a map of the United States and quickly zooms in on Davis, California. I'm continually amazed by how easily Mitzy navigates the electronic world.

"As long as she has her phone—" Mitzy says, "—we can track her."

"I want eyes on her." Forest crosses his arms over his broad chest. "Jenny, get Charlie. I want her on Julie's protection detail ASAP."

Charlene, aka Charlie, is a bubbly blonde. Her youthful face is still young enough to pass as a college co-ed.

"Charlie's out of pocket," Jenny says. "She's got that wedding for her sister. Who else do we have?"

"Well, shoot." Mitzy purses her lips and scrunches her nose. "If I'd known that, I would've had one of the guys make that call. If Mary calls Julie, she'll be expecting a female, not a male, to be looking for her." Her attention shifts to Forest. "Speaking of, how are your Protectors coming along?"

"I've got two so far, and they're all set. Deputized and ready to go."

This is one fun fact I learned only after being hired by Guardian HRS. Forest needed a way for the Guardians to operate across the country without local law enforcement questioning their activities, and he found it. By deputizing the Guardians as US Marshals on special assignment, they're acting law enforcement officers.

"Well, this seems like the perfect kickoff for your new Guardian Protectors," Mitzy says. "You should be able to get one of them on-site in a couple of hours."

Forest's gaze cuts to Max. "I could really use Alpha Two in the lead. Any chance Knox will change his mind and take it?"

Wolfe sniffs beside me.

"I've asked, and he's not interested." Max's focus cuts to Wolfe.

His eyes tighten, a subtle gesture, to keep this quiet. Max returns his attention to Forest. "You or Sam can always ask again."

"Hmm." Forest scratches his beard. "CJ, you're filling in as acting lead until we get Knox to get his head out of his ass and step up. What else do you have, Mitz?"

"Working on it." Mitzy moves on to the next girl, only things aren't as good. Evidently, Lori Black is on a summer-long European adventure. "Gigi Malone is in the Bay Area. Started her surgical internship at UCSF. Now, where are the rest of you …"

Mitzy's voice trails off as the tapping of her keyboard speeds up like a runaway freight train. She calls out the status on the next two names, then silence falls as she searches for the last girl.

I clutch Wolfe's leg and chew on my thumb as my leg bounces in step with the fury of Mitzy's typing. We all wait for Mitzy to find the last girl, Rose Hunt.

Seconds pass. They turn into a minute while my heart rate spikes.

"Why is it taking so long?" I lean over and whisper softly in his ear. "She found the others in seconds."

A glance over at Mitzy shows her leaning in toward her computer screen, brows pinched, forehead furrowed, eyes squinting as she scans the screen.

"Mitz?" Forest's low rumble rolls through the room. He's a formidable man and I don't care what everyone says, he makes me nervous.

Taller than tall, broader than broad, he's an anomaly of human perfection. With his white-blond hair, he reminds me of Lily. She has the same coloring, although her eyes are golden rather than glacial pale like Forest's. He notices me staring and winks at me. It's funny how that small gesture humanizes him, making him appear less frightening.

"Houston, we have a problem." Mitzy leans back from her screen and runs her hands through her pixie-short hair.

"A problem? What does that mean?" I bounce to my feet and rush over to Mitzy. "Did you find her?"

It's a stupid question. If Mitzy found Rose, she would've rattled off her current status like she did with the other girls.

"Rose Hunt is a bank teller in New Orleans. She failed to show up to work today." Mitzy scrubs at her face. "It may not mean anything, but there's nothing in her employee files to indicate a pattern of being late. At least nothing documented. Her cell phone keeps going to voicemail, and she lives alone. I'm getting ahold of her building manager."

I can't breathe. I feel like someone slugged me in the gut. My fingers curl around the back of Mitzy's chair as I stagger and lurch. The floor shifts beneath me. Everything slows down around me as I fall.

My grip on Mitzy's chair slips. Spots swim in my vision, dancing in slow motion as blackness creeps inward. People speak. I know they're saying something, but the sound is muffled and indistinct.

There's only one thought in my head.

I took too long, and it's too late.

Rose has been taken.

"Give her space." Strong arms wrap around me, turning my fall into a gentle rise as I'm lifted and cradled in someone's arms. Once again, the world shifts, but this time I fly instead of fall. The most amazing scent floods my senses, and I can't help but breathe in deep. "Jinx? Can you hear me?"

The encroaching darkness narrows my vision down to a blurry point of light. My gentle flight comes to an end as I'm placed down on something hard. A hand cups the side of my face. A finger strokes the side of my cheek. Pillowy soft lips press gently against mine, a gentle touch. A reassuring touch. A touch I know well.

"Wolfe?" The blackness pulls back.

"Yes, luv, it's me. How do you feel?"

"What happened?" The blurriness fades.

"You fainted."

"No, I didn't." I blink, pushing the darkness away until my vision clears. "I don't faint." My chin firms and my back straightens.

"Okay, you don't faint. You crumpled."

"Crumpled?" My nose itches. "I did no such thing."

I bat away Wolfe's hands stroking through my hair, then realize everyone is staring at me. With a sniff, I scoot off the edge of the conference table and sway on my feet as the room swims around me. I reach behind me, stabilizing myself as the room spins.

"Luv, Mitzy's still looking. It doesn't mean anything yet."

Yet.

Doesn't matter to me. I feel my failure as it sinks in deep and wraps around my gut in a cold vice. I took too long to break the cipher. I took too long to decode the entries. If I'd only been faster, smarter, more focused, then maybe I could've saved Rose.

"At least we know where most of the girls are." Forest rocks back on his heels. Arms crossed over his broad chest, he gives me the once over. I shiver as his cold gaze sweeps over me from head to toe. "Mitzy's not done working her magic, Jinx. Give her time."

"I'll find Rose." Mitzy calls out, sounding confident, but it doesn't change the fact that my gut never lies.

Rose is lost to us.

"First order of business, we protect the girls, after that we'll focus back on this." Forest makes the decision, which sets our path.

"Roger Dodger." Mitzy buries her head in her work.

While Mitzy attempts to contact Rose Hunt, Forest barks orders.

"Send Brett to check on the girls who are local. Sawyer can hop on a flight and track down Lori Black. We're not taking chances." He places his hands behind his back, fingers locked tight, and resumes his pacing. "Jinx, how long was it from placing the order for the first girl to when the abductions occurred?"

It takes a moment before I register Forest's question is directed at me. I give a quick shake of my head and focus on my job—the one I'm failing at. As for an answer to his question, there's no need to check my notes. I know this by heart.

"Two months."

"All right. They're behind in fulfilling their orders. Not unexpected, considering Benefield's operation went up in flames. Someone picked up the pieces."

We all agree on that.

The girls the Guardians rescued in New Orleans were in

Benefield's ledger, yet their abduction happened after his death. There's no doubt the operation continues as strong as ever.

But who's pulling the strings?

And how can I figure that out?

There's got to be a way to fix this.

My father's words return to me. He held me with pride and spoke to my heart. *"Whenever you find yourself lost on a case, go back to the basics. That's your foundation. Use it."*

"And what are those?"

"Always follow the money."

I reach for Wolfe and squeeze his hand.

Mitzy will focus on finding Rose, which means no one is looking for the man in charge. If I can find him, find who took over Benefield's operation, then maybe I can find Rose. I pray she's okay and that she wasn't abducted. I pray any number of things, but I know. My hand presses against my belly and my fingers flutter over my skin. Deep down, I know she's been taken. Which means it's vital the Guardians protect those other girls.

"I know how to find them." I tug on Wolfe's sleeve.

He stands by my side, one brow arching as I pull him toward the door.

Forest is there again, pacing back and forth. This time it feels like a coincidence that he blocks my path. He pulls up short, almost like he doesn't see me. His pale eyes take me in from head to foot. I squint at him, once again struck by the similarities between him and Lily.

"Leaving?" His left brow wings up and his attention shifts from me to Wolfe. "This isn't the time for a bit of one on one …"

"Be very careful what comes out of your mouth." Wolfe steps in front of me, going toe-to-toe with the gentle giant. "Don't make assumptions. We're working, not fooling around."

"I only meant to say that we need all hands on deck. This isn't the time to *take a break*." Forest uses his fingers to make air quotes.

"If that's what you think, then I'm sorry to say, you're wrong. And we're still on the case. Jinx has something she wants to take a look at."

"And you can't do that here?"

"There are too many distractions in here." Finding and following a money trail takes intense focus, at least for me, and I can't do that in a crowded room. I firm my chin and roll my shoulders back. With Forest, I've come to learn it's best not to show weakness.

Which I don't.

Four things really. I need access to *Jacen*. It's the only way to find what I need and track it down with any semblance of speed. Right now, I need speed. I also need food and caffeine. Despite the need for speed, I need a break from the intensity of all of this even more.

I know how I work best, and it's not locked in a room for hours on end. What I really need is a breather. Then, I can hit it hard again.

As Wolfe has no idea what I have planned, his unwavering support makes my heart do that pitter-patter thing. Yet again, this is something I've never experienced. Other than Lily, I'm not used to someone else—aka a man—having my back.

"I know what I need, and I'm very good at my job. Right now, that's taking a break. Now, if you don't mind …"

To my surprise, Forest takes a step back. Bending softly at the waist, he gestures toward the door.

"By all means, lover boy, didn't mean to offend. But be careful." His arctic eyes harden. "Don't fuck this up."

"Wasn't planning on it." Wolfe gives my hand a little pull, and we escape outside the room.

Once in the hallway, I lean against the wall.

"Whew, I didn't think he was going to let us go." My head tips back, and I blow out a breath. It feels good getting out of that room.

"Forest is a lot of things, but he trusts his people. Although …" Wolfe glances over his shoulder. "I expected a bit more of a fight out of him."

"Well, we're free now."

"And what exactly are *we* working on?"

That exchange with Forest wasn't much, yet I feel as if we're getting away with something.

"I need you to dust off your intelligence hat and help me."

"I figured something like that, but what are we doing?"

"We're going back to basics."

"Which means?"

"Benefield was in fulfillment. He didn't take the orders or handle the cash transactions. We're going to track every penny, or *peso*, going into and out of Benefield's operation. Do that and we find who's really in charge."

Wolfe groans playfully.

This is Intelligence 101, and we've all spent far too much time mired in the weeds, chasing the transfer of cash. It's an ignominious task and often relegated to the most junior member of the team because it's incredibly tedious and boring.

But I love that he doesn't shy away from more work. It's well past midnight and neither of us will be getting any sleep. Now that we know there are girls in danger, none of us are taking breaks.

Well, I'm taking a teeny tiny break. I need an infusion of caffeine.

"Hold up, Jinx." Wolfe stops at an intersecting hallway. "This way."

"*Jacen* is this way." I need the computing power of Forest's supercomputer.

"Yes, but the coffee and doughnuts are this way."

I can't help but smile.

"You remembered." Warmth radiates outward from my heart. It's little things like this which matter.

"I'd say we could call out for pizza, but no one delivers this late at night. The coffee is good."

"I'll take it. How about the doughnuts?"

"Pre-packaged, powdered doughnuts, but it's the best we have." He grips my hand and gives it a little squeeze. A tiny thrill runs through me, loving the way my hand fits in his. "And the bathrooms are on the way. You'll get that pee break you were wanting."

Way to kill the mood. "Gee, you make it sound so glamorous." I roll my eyes and shake my head.

With that, we walk hand in hand to the cafeteria, where we raid the cupboards and devour coffee and doughnuts until we're stuffed to the gills.

Wolfe turns our late-night raid into a game, challenging me to a game of twenty questions where I plan to finally discover how old he was when he lost his virginity. It's the perfect break to reset my head. Taking time away from the job at hand bugs me, but I'm tired, frustrated, and overwhelmed. This is exactly the distraction I need before diving back in.

FOURTEEN

Wolfe

It's late, O-dark thirty, and I sit on a concrete floor in the cafeteria licking powdered sugar off my fingers. I'd rather be doing something else, like licking Jinx, but I'm not in a rush. I can wait.

Jinx gave me a look when I suggested playing twenty questions, but I can't think of a more effective way to get to know each other on a deeper level. Not to mention, she needs a break.

Tension furrows her brow, draws her shoulders up, and tightens her entire face. I make it my goal to get her to relax. I don't know about her, but I do my best work when I'm not stressed out.

"We've already established first kisses." I set our baseline.

I nudge Jinx's foot with mine, just a light tap because what I want is to maul her, and if I touch her any other way, that's exactly what will happen.

Keeping things professional in the workplace challenges my restraint, testing the limits of my resolve. I had no problems earlier because we were surrounded by the others.

Now?

All I want is to get my hands on her and slake my hunger. My need grows by the hour, and while date night is technically this evening, I have a feeling we'll have to postpone. Too much hangs in the balance.

"Yes, we did." She licks powdered sugar off her fingers while I suppress a needy moan. I can't wait to feel those sinful lips wrap around my cock. Jinx on her knees, her mouth on my cock, it ranks number one on my list of things I want to do with Jinx. Sure, I want to fuck her, but there's something about her on her knees that fuels my fantasies.

"Now we're going to delve deeper." I figure if I have to hold back on the physical side of our relationship, it's time to find out more about each other.

"Deeper?"

The way she says deeper makes my cock jerk and swell. I want deeper, harder, and faster. But I'm trying to control myself. Jinx doesn't make that easy.

"Yes, beyond first kisses."

I clear my throat, uncross my ankles, then cross them again. This time with the other foot on top. I take that moment to readjust things as my pants grow tighter by the second.

She looks over at me, another finger getting sucked on by those pillowy soft lips. Our gazes meet. She smiles, pops out her finger, then a slight flush turns her cheeks pink. Surely, she knows how she affects me.

Everything about Jinx turns me on.

"You mean your very precocious kindergarten years?" She places her hand over the back of mine.

The contact sends a jolt of energy shooting through me. I flip my hand over and thread our fingers together. Lifting her hand to my mouth, I barely move my lips across her knuckles.

Jinx's pupils dilate and her breaths flutter in her chest. Good to know I'm not the only one hanging on by a thread.

"That sloppy kiss turned me off girls for years." I scrunch up my nose, enjoying the playful back and forth between us.

"Such a shame, but your kisses are no longer sloppy." She leans her head against my shoulder and brings my hand to her mouth, where she repeats that tender kiss.

"They aren't?" I can't help but puff out my chest.

For the record, I'm an excellent kisser and an even better lover. It's not false male bravado. I've made it my life's work to learn how to please a woman. Guys like to brag about how many broads they've banged. I prefer to shower my lovers with back-to-back orgasms.

"Definitely not." Her lashes flutter, revealing her shy side.

As for shy, Jinx is definitely not shy about sex. To this day, I'm not sure who picked up who in Callie's bar. All I know is one moment we were talking and the next we were going at it, hot and heavy, in the bathroom. I actually have no idea why we didn't fuck then and there.

"How are my kissing skills?" A grin tugs at the corners of my lips. For some reason, I need to know what she thinks of my oral abilities.

"A perfect ten."

"Nice to know. Better than my nighttime performances, I see." I refer to the measly scores she gave me night after night as she watched me from her window.

The pink in her cheeks turns flame red. This is what I love about Jinx. She's aggressive when it comes to what she wants, but it's little things like that which make her blush.

"We already talked about that."

Don't I know it. She intentionally downgraded my skills, making me think I needed to step up my game. All along, I was batting a perfect 10.

Which isn't a problem.

I plan on a bit of payback.

"Ready to begin?" I shift to a more comfortable position.

This concrete is not comfortable, and I have no idea why we're sitting on the floor. Except, Jinx is the one who scooted down the wall first. I merely followed, completely entranced by my girl.

"Hit me." Jinx leans forward to grab another powdered doughnut.

"Best childhood memory?"

"Hmm ..." She leans back and closes her eyes. "I'd have to say it was going to the ice cream shop with my dad."

"Really?"

"Yeah, he had this '70 Barracuda convertible and was a total car fanatic. On Saturdays, he took Lily, Callie, and me to the car shows, which happened to be at an old mom and pop's burger place. We feasted on burgers, fries, and vanilla milkshakes. It was divine."

"Sounds amazing."

I'm happy to hear her childhood was a good one. Both she and Lily were abandoned at birth, adopted by the same parents, and seem to have grown up surrounded by love.

It's sad how many children don't get to enjoy lives filled with adoring parents who shower them with love.

"What about you?" She nibbles on the doughnut, which leaves powdered sugar on her lips.

I'm tempted to lean over and lick the white substance from her lips, but the pink tip of her tongue darts out and takes that joy away from me.

"Mine would be when we lived in Hawaii."

"You lived in Hawaii?"

"My father was stationed there. We spent our Saturdays at the beach, boogie boarding. Those are my best memories."

"I didn't know you lived in Hawaii."

There's a lot we don't know about each other.

"Dad was Navy. He's the reason I joined."

I still hold her hand. Stretching out my fingers, I straighten hers, then I cover her hand between both of mine.

Her fingers are slender. Her palm almost half the size of mine. It amazes me how tiny she is compared to me, and yet we're a perfect fit in every way. I can't believe she threw me down, not once, but twice. My girl is a she-devil in a fistfight. Full of liquid grace, she's a whirling dervish, no doubt lethal if that's what she desires.

I underestimated her abilities, judging her for her size rather than what she was capable of when pushed to fight.

"My dad was an intel guy like me, at least until I put in my application for SEAL training. He never understood why I did that."

"My dad worked with the NSA. He couldn't tell us what he did, but I'm pretty sure it was intel of some sort." She pops the last of the doughnut in her mouth while I hold back a groan.

This girl is killing me, making my mind spin and my body come alive. Will we ever get to the point where we're alone and I can finally get a taste of her?

It feels as if it's never going to happen.

"Ready for the next question?"

Despite my body's demands to move this along, I enjoy talking to Jinx.

"Ready, Freddy."

"Worst crime you've ever committed."

"Crime?"

"As a kid. I assume you aren't a criminal now since you used to work for the DEA."

"What was yours?"

"Oh no, you tell me yours, then I tell you mine. It's a lady's first kind of thing."

"Okay, I'll bite." She nibbles on her lower lip. "My worst crime had to be the Great Bubble Gum Heist."

"Bubble gum heist?"

"Yup. I'm the Bubble Gum Bandit."

"That's lame, but I'll bite. What did you do?"

"Well, I was five and I wanted the bubble gum at the checkout register. Dad said no, so I took it. He caught me with it in the parking lot and made me go back in the store and confess my crime."

"Oh wow. I bet that made an impact."

"Never stole again." Her eyes brighten with the memory. "What was yours?"

"I was seventeen, just got my motorcycle license, and was out for a ride. I may, or may not, have hit triple digits on the speedometer."

"May or may not?" She shakes her head. "That's lame."

"Speeding wasn't my crime."

"What was it then?"

"I ran from the cops."

"You're kidding?" She gives a little giggle, covering her mouth and peeking over her hand. "You got pulled over? I bet they yanked your license."

"They didn't."

"You talked your way out of it?"

"More like I ditched them."

"You ran from the cops?" Her eyes practically bug out of her face. "No way."

"Sure did, and since I was on a motorcycle, and really stupid with the speed, they couldn't catch me."

"Didn't they run the tag?"

"I may, or may not, have kind of covered it up."

"Damn, you were a bad boy. I bet the chicks ate that shit up."

"They did. Seventeen was a very good year."

"I bet it was. I have a feeling you were quite popular in high school."

"Not going to lie. I saw my fair share of action. School jock, smart kid, and these looks with this body." I wave my hand in front of my face and down my torso. "I was every high school cliché you can imagine. Locker room lover. Bleacher king. Took my dates to lookout point where we steamed up the windows every Friday and Saturday night."

"I bet you did." She gives me a long look.

For a second, I think she's going to make a comment about my high school exploits, but she surprises me.

"Next question, and I get to ask, which means you answer first." She pokes me in the arm, emphasizing her point.

"That's not how this game is played."

"Well, I'm not answering every question first. We'll trade off."

"Fine." I lift my hands in defeat. "Hit me."

"Strangest, or most unusual, place you've had sex."

"Going right for the good stuff, are we?"

"Definitely."

"Most unusual place was definitely the bike."

"You had sex on your motorcycle?"

"It sounded hot at the time but was a bit more complicated in practice. The angles didn't exactly line up well. But don't worry, I persevered."

"I'm sure you did."

"And you?"

"Mine's boring next to yours."

"You still have to answer the question."

"What if I don't want to? We should be allowed three passes."

"Seriously? You're not going to answer?"

"I'm taking a pass on that one." There's a wicked gleam in her eyes, which tells me I want to know her answer, but I'll wait and bide my time.

"Fine, I'll give you that pass." I tap my chin, pretending like I'm thinking hard about my next question. "I have a four-part question."

"Four parts? You only get one question."

"It is one question. It just comes in four parts."

"Fine." She blows out a puff of air. "Hit me."

"How old were you when you experienced your first crush? Was it Tommy in third grade?"

"No."

"Wait, I'm not done with my question."

"Go ahead."

"What was his or her name? And did you act on it?"

"Wow, hitting all the biggies at once."

"Yes, and I'm dying to know your answer. No passes on this one."

"I've got two left."

"Sure, but you can't use them back-to-back, so choose wisely."

"You're making this up on the fly." Her lower lip pushes out in a pout. It's cute as shit.

"And you're being evasive. What's your answer?"

"I was sixteen."

"Sixteen? Late bloomer?"

"I wasn't interested in boys. They were gangly and awkward."

"Not boys? What was her name?"

"I didn't say I liked girls. I just never crushed on boys."

"Name?"

"Mr. Tuttle."

"Mister?"

"He was my high school chemistry teacher." She nibbles on her lower lip and looks away.

She's hiding something.

"Crushing on your teacher. Naughty girl …"

"I totally crushed on him." Her grin is back. Yet again, I feel there's more there than she's telling me.

"And did you act on it?"

"I did."

"No elaboration?"

"Is that a question?"

"You can't leave me hanging like that. I need details."

"Answer the question first."

"Mine's easy and boring. First crush was in kindergarten. Her name was Susie, and you already know I acted on it. Now tell me about your chemistry teacher. What did you do?"

"I'm going to keep that one to myself for now. It's my turn for a question."

"Hit me." I'm too curious to stop.

"What's something you do in secret but would never admit to in public?"

"Now that's an easy one, and you already know the answer."

"I do?"

"Yes, luv. You most definitely do. Me working for a perfect 10 these past few weeks."

It takes a moment, but then her face turns the prettiest shade of pink.

"See." I nudge her shoulder. "Told you it was easy, and that kind of thing is definitely a between you and me only event."

"I've never done anything like that before." She peeks up at me.

"Watch a man masturbate?"

"Watch a man masturbate from my bedroom window while he's thinking about me. I'm not a voyeur like that."

"Luv, I can't wait to play out all the filthy fantasies that went through my head while doing that. But, yeah, that's definitely something I'd never admit to anyone but you."

If the guys ever found out about that, I'd die a thousand deaths and would never survive all the ribbing they'd give me.

"Have you always been an exhibitionist?"

"I wouldn't call myself that, but if you're asking if I've fucked in front of others, I have. It wasn't so much about exhibition as it was raging hormones. I'm not into that anymore. Worked it out of my system years ago. When we fuck, I'm not sharing that with anyone but you."

"Good to know, and thank you." She cocks her head. "I'm not into that, and watching you is probably the most adventurous thing I've done."

"I have a hard time believing that. You don't count making out in the bathroom of your friend's bar adventurous?"

"You probably think I'm easy."

"I think you're the kind of woman who goes after, and takes, what she wants. There's no shame in that. Although …"

"Although, what?"

"I'm not looking for casual sex." At least, I'm not anymore. I used to be the king of casual hookups, but I want more with Jinx. It's best to establish some ground rules before we go too far with this. "You're either with me, or you're not. I'm all about adventurous sex between consenting adults, but this isn't a one-and-done thing between us. If that's all you want, this is a good place to stop."

"Do I look like I want to stop?"

"Is it wrong of me to ask?"

There she goes again with the lip nibbling thing. It's sexy, but what I love best is when one of my comments catches her off guard. Jinx doesn't seem to me to be a woman who blushes, but she's done that several times around me.

"You are a very interesting man."

"How so?"

"I thought you were such a player that night after taking me to the bathroom, then going after that blonde."

"The blonde I *didn't* go after." I feel as if I need to reemphasize that point.

"I know you didn't. I made an assumption, but that's the point. I made you out to be this big player, banging one chick after the next. It was impossible to see you any other way, and then when I couldn't stop thinking about you, it drove me crazy."

"I'm glad we sorted all that out." I draw my legs up and hug my knees. "We should probably get back to work."

"Just a little longer?" She leans against me again, placing her head on my shoulder. "You smell good."

"You smell like heaven—and a bit of powdered sugar."

Jinx places her hand on my thigh and lifts up to brush her lips against mine. It's soft, sweet, sexy, and absolutely perfect.

"Thank you for this. I feel much better with a shot of caffeine and a chaser of sugar."

"Luv, you devoured nearly a pot of coffee."

"True." She squirms. "Probably need to make a pit stop before hitting up *Jacen*."

We clean up after ourselves and make one more pot of coffee. A yawn escapes me, and I rub at my eyes. Not a normal coffee drinker, I sip at my cup. Jinx sucks the coffee down like water and is wired, high on caffeine, as we make our way to the supercomputer, affectionately named *Jacen* by all.

FIFTEEN

Wolfe

I sit beside Jinx, acutely aware of her presence, and remind myself to focus on work.

Playtime will come later.

Hopefully.

"Okay, let me pull up what we have." Jinx grabs the files from Benefield's ledgers.

"What are we starting with? The last group of girls or the first entries?"

"We're not going to touch those."

"We're not?"

"Nope." Jinx flashes a grin, looking to all the world like a cat caught with a canary in its mouth.

"Then what are we looking at?"

"We're looking for construction expenses. Power, utilities. Fencing."

"Fencing?"

"Yeah, didn't Eve say the entire compound was surrounded by an electrified fence?"

"It is, or was."

Honestly, I don't know if the fencing is still up after our raid.

That operation turned into much more than we bargained for, requiring pooling Alpha, Bravo, and Charlie forces together. We expected resistance, but not the all-out firefight we ran up against.

The worst part about that raid was that we had to leave Max and Knox behind. We rescued over a dozen girls from the slave pens while Max, Knox, and Eve escaped into the rain forest surrounding the entire place.

"Well, it's a lot of fencing to maintain, and if electrified, the drain on the local power grid had to be intense. People like Benefield go to great lengths to encode their books but fail to hide their footprint on the world. I'm looking at the power grid and who paid that bill. We'll scour local contractors to see who supplied the fencing and follow that money. Eve said he kept monkeys, birds, and butterflies in cages. Someone had to feed those animals, and someone had to build the cages. We're going after it all."

"That's a lot of work."

"For us." Jinx makes a sweeping gesture toward the masterpiece which is JCN. "Not for *Jacen.*"

The hum of cooling fans drone in the background as the servers churn through 0's and 1's, spitting out data to those who ask. We have a lot to ask, but our queries will be but a blip for JCN's massive computing power.

"Where do you want me to begin?" I roll up my sleeves, eager to work.

It's been years since I've used this part of my brain. I'm used to the physical demands of being a Guardian and look forward to returning to my roots. Although, that may have more to do with working alongside Jinx than anything else.

While Jinx runs the data on the local power grid, I take a look into specialty foods for rare and exotic birds, monkeys, and butterflies. It feels like a waste of time, and after an hour of formulating the query for *Jacen*, I feel foolish enough to toss it in the trash and try another angle.

For some reason, I decide not to. Maybe I hate wasting all that time? Maybe, I'm simply sleep-deprived after pulling an all-nighter.

Whatever the reason, I submit my query and let *Jacen* do the heavy lifting it was designed to do.

"How's it going?" I spin around in my chair to face Jinx. She holds a cup of coffee in her hand and taps her foot.

"Slow." She slowly spins around. "How about you?"

"I may have wasted that last hour." I jab my thumb over my shoulder. "But I sent what I had to *Jacen*. He's crunching through it now."

"You never really know what to look for in cases like these."

A ping sounds behind me.

It's *Jacen's* notification it returned my query. I spin around as Jinx leans forward. Several entries fill my screen. Orders for birdseed and butterfly nectar. I guess the monkeys were fed locally sourced food, which makes sense. What I don't understand is the split delivery. Half the order went to Colombia, Benefield's place. The other half went to a warehouse in New Orleans.

I scratch my head and send commands to *Jacen*. The supercomputer will follow the shipment and see where it ends.

Jinx places her hands on my neck and leans over my shoulder. She reads the screen.

"M. Rossi?" She's close enough to feel the soft swell of her breast pressing against my back. I find heaven when her fingers dig into the tired muscles of my neck and shoulders, giving me a massage. She leans in toward my monitor. "I know that name." Her fist bangs on the desk.

"What do you mean you know it?"

"The Rossi's run one of the largest crime syndicates in the Northeast. We've had dealings with them before."

"We?"

"The DEA." Jinx corrects herself. "One of my earliest cases. I ran support intel on a drug bust."

A minute passes, then another, while Jinx peers at her screen. I lean back and rub my temples while pushing through my exhaustion. Unlike Jinx, I don't have a pot of coffee flowing through my veins.

Acutely aware of everything Jinx, the sudden quieting of her fidgeting and quick intake of breath tells me everything I need to know.

Jinx turns in her chair, mouth gaping, eyes wide, shock and elation at war to claim her expression.

"You found something, didn't you?"

"More than that." She swallows then takes in a deep breath. "I found the connection, and you'll never guess where it leads."

It could be anywhere, considering this group operates out of New Orleans, Cancun, and Colombia, I take a guess.

"New Orleans?"

"That warehouse belongs to the Belvedere." She swallows again. "And can you guess who runs the Belvedere?"

"The Rossi crime family?" I wing up a brow, curious, but interested in what she thinks.

"Do you know what else they run?"

My eyes grow wide as I delve into Belvedere's subsidiaries. Specifically, the mention of a cruise line catches my eye, but Jinx is a mile ahead of me.

"Wolfe, that cruise line ..." She's like a dog with a bone, gnawing her way to the truth.

"Yeah." My mouth is dry as I respond. "Belvedere runs the hospitality side of the cruise line, but the ships are owned by a subsidiary of ..."

"Deverough Shipping." It's all right there. Tracked down through butterfly nectar and exotic bird food.

"Home port, New Orleans. Destination ports include Cancun, Colombia ..." Her voice rises in inflection, like it's a question only she has the answer to. "Do you think that's a coincidence?"

A rhetorical question, I encourage her to continue thinking out loud. I need that. As a man caught between two worlds, I've embraced the physical demands of a Guardian while turning my back on more intellectually challenging pursuits.

This is what I love about Jinx. She balances me.

For too long, I've neglected this piece of myself. Not neglected. No, I love my job. I'm fucking great at what I do. All the Guardians are fierce warriors. I'm one of them. Braun doesn't mean we lack brains. It's merely an addition to our natural assets.

Jinx reminds me of the early dreams that lit a fire beneath my feet and set me on a path to go forth and conquer the world. I'm more than the muscle that gets things done. Like the rest of my team, the sum of the parts is greater than the whole.

"This isn't a coincidence." I agree with what she says. "I guess this answers the question as to whether Eve's dad is involved." Turning on the intelligence officer part of my brain, after such dormancy, doesn't come easily. But it does come. I slip into my old patterns as easily as taking the next breath.

"Maybe." She hesitates and glances at the screen. "I don't want to jump to any conclusions, but it certainly smells fishy."

I won't lie. It seems pretty cut and dry to me. I don't know what she's thinking, but I'll do what I can to tease through her thoughts. If Jinx is anything like me, the act of talking out loud helps to gel her thoughts. From the pinching of her lips to the furrowing of her brows, she needs a gentle nudge. I'm more than happy to provide that little push.

"What are you thinking?"

Where is your mind taking you, my precious Jinx?

"We busted their operation in New Orleans. That's not the first time the Guardians intercepted their product." She launches a soft lob, something to center her thoughts. Jinx isn't confident, but she believes in her gut. "Didn't Bravo team hit them at the docks?"

"They tried, but it was a trap. And it was in Cancun, not New Orleans."

"Okay, so the Guardians prevented the delivery of that one batch?"

"More than that. The girls Bravo team were sent in to save were placed on a different ship which left port hours earlier. We eventually did save those girls, but it was at sea."

"At sea?"

"In the middle of the Gulf. We HALO'd in and approached from the water. Climbed on board, freed the girls, and rescued them."

Her mouth gapes, and she shakes her head.

"What's wrong?"

"I'm sorry, I'm just impressed. You say it like it was nothing while I'm sitting here trying to figure out how all of that would work. How did you get twelve girls off a cargo container ship in the middle of the Gulf of Mexico?"

"We had two teams, twelve men for twelve women. We strapped them to our backs and rappelled over the side into our Zodiacs."

"I don't think I'll ever get used to that. It sounds like something out of a movie."

"I don't know about that, but that's the second group of women we saved. Then there were the ones at The Retreat when we stormed Benefield's fortress."

"I can't imagine how much that costs."

"The operation?" My brows tug together.

The Guardians are fortunate because we're backed by Forest and his sister, Skye. We have the best gear, cutting-edge tech, and near limitless resources.

"Not the operation. I know how that works. I was thinking about the girls."

"What do you mean?"

"Whoever was in charge of transporting those girls lost millions in revenue. Someone had to pay for that. We need to talk to Deverough."

"Why?"

"Because the cargo container ship belonged to him. If he lost those girls, that would amount to a huge loss for the Rossi family. I'm sure they weren't happy about that. In the DEA, I specialize in the structure of South American drug cartels. The Rossi's aren't that different. They would demand payment to cover the loss."

"And you think Deverough did that?"

"Didn't he pay thirty million in ransom demands for his daughter?"

"You think he used the kidnapping insurance to pay back a debt?"

"I'd have to look into it closer. But he lost at least two dozen girls because of the Guardians. Honestly, I'm surprised he's still breathing. That kind of screwup doesn't go over well, and …" Her voice trails off as her attention shifts back to the screen.

"And, what?" I lean forward, encouraging her to continue her train of thought.

"This is an assumption, and you know what I think about those, but what if they changed their operation as a result?"

"How so?"

"Shipping product via cargo container ship is no longer viable. Deverough cost them millions. I have no doubt Eve's ransom came as a result of that." Her lips press together. "I'm worried."

"About what?"

"I'm worried they've adapted."

"How so?"

"Guardian activities hit them where it hurts; their bottom line suffered. Whether the drugs, or the girls, they have no choice but to adapt and overcome." She glances up at me. "My bet is they're abandoning the cargo container ships."

Her statement guts me. We've rescued dozens of girls consigned to a life of sexual servitude, precisely through covert operations to free them.

"If they did, they likely abandoned Deverough and his ships as well." I can't see why they'd stay in business with Deverough after all of that. "Which begs the question of what are they using now?"

"That ship is a Deverough asset. Deverough is still working with them. He's too valuable for them to let him go. Once the Rossi's get their hands on someone, they never let them go." What she says is unsettling but makes sense."

Jinx blows out a breath. "The Rossi's own the Belvedere. They operate the hospitality services for C&C cruise line, but that's separate from the running of the actual ship. After what happened to Eve, why is he still involved in the trafficking of women?"

It's not an idle question. The Guardians have been wrestling with that for weeks.

Deverough smells like shit, but his actions confuse us. He left his daughter, his only child, in the hands of a monster, paying escalating ransom demands until it became clear Benefield never intended to return Eve. Desperation drove him to hire the Guardians to rescue her. It never sat well with any of us why he waited as long as he did.

But this feels like truth. It makes sense, and I think we might finally have what we need to get Deverough to open up and answer our questions. He sacrificed everything to rescue his daughter. We thought that spoke to a rift between Deverough and Benefield. What if that's not the case? What if the true rift is between Deverough and the Rossi crime family?

"Jinx, we need to bring this back to the others."

"Agreed, and I want a face-to-face with Deverough."

"He isn't spilling any secrets." I shake my head. "Griff hasn't been able to make Deverough sing."

"Deverough's hiding something."

"We all believe that, but he's not talking."

"He'll talk to me."

"Luv, Griff is amazing at his job, but he can't get Deverough to tell us anything."

We know he's dirty, or assume so, but he maintains his innocence. Nothing directly connects him to Benefield's operation. There's the fact his company owns the ships, but he claims no knowledge of the cargo containers transporting the girls. Which could very well be true. Tens of thousands of containers fill every vessel. There's no way for him to know what's in every container.

All our intel is circumstantial at best. We're making assumptions about the girls. Maybe he knew nothing about that side of the operation? Maybe he was only aware of the narcotics being shipped and delivered using his ships?

Is he telling the truth?

Is Deverough filthy as fuck? Or is he something else? Another victim?

It doesn't seem possible, but no man survives Griff's specialized skillset. They all crack. It's only a matter of time, but Deverough continues to plead his innocence.

Could Eve's father be what he says? A father desperate to free his daughter?

I'd love to believe it, but I don't trust Deverough. None of us do. That man has filth on him. It seeps from his pores.

"Why do you think Deverough will talk to you when he hasn't cracked for us."

"Griff's not the only one trained in interrogation techniques." She doesn't elaborate, and from the smile on her face, I'm not sure I want to ask. "Come on. Let's tell the others what we found."

During our walk back to the conference room, I mull over what we discussed. Like most things in the intelligence community, nothing is ever straightforward. We sift through facts until we find a link between them.

"I can't believe the purchase of butterfly nectar is what connected the dots. It's such an insignificant thing."

"There's always a connection." Jinx's step is light but determined.

"Wasn't expecting a link between Deverough, Benefield, and the Rossi's."

"I've learned to never be surprised with what I dig up. Chicago based, the Rossi crime family isn't known for human sex trafficking, or snuff films. They're heavily invested in the narcotic trade. That's a known fact."

"I assume they have their fingers in the usual places: garbage collection, construction, labor unions …"

"Ship workers and docks," Jinx adds. "With New Orleans being as big of a shipping hub as it is, I'm not surprised. They skim money off the top of every industry they touch. Gambling is there too."

She refers, of course, to the Belvedere, which operates a legitimate business where dirty money goes to get cleaned. As for the Belvedere, it's relatively new in NOLA. Opened its doors a little less than eight years ago.

I did a minor dive into their operations. No surprise, it's family run, but who's in charge came as a surprise. The Rossi's tend to be old school, which means patriarchal. Yet, the CEO in charge of hotel operations is a woman.

Maria Rossi is a Cornell University Hotel Business school graduate. She's also niece to the head of the Rossi family. In addition to her responsibilities at the Belvedere, she also runs the hotel operations of C&C Cruises.

C&C Cruises is a link between the Rossi's and Deverough. We need to delve into Deverough's business.

I pull to a halt. It takes Jinx two steps before she stops.

"What's up?" Her brow arches gracefully with her question.

"I'm going to make an assumption but hear me out." I know how Jinx feels about assumptions.

"Okay?"

"Those girls we rescued, the ones in New Orleans …"

"What about them?"

"There has to be some kind of staging area in New Orleans, a place where they keep them before locking them in a container for loading onto the *Lei'lani*. We need to go back and see if we can track where that container came from."

The *Lei'lani* is the name of the cargo container ship those girls were destined for. Alpha team rescued the girls while they were still on the dock waiting to be loaded onto the massive ship.

"I don't know if we'll be able to do that." Jinx pivots, turning back the way we came. She's already formulating the search parameters for *Jacen* to do exactly what we need. "We'd have to rely on road cams, tracking that container backward from the dock." Jinx thinks out loud while I nod my head. "Most of that footage isn't stored longer than a few days."

The traffic cams are a problem.

"What if they used the Belvedere? An outfit like that would keep recordings going back weeks, if not months."

"That could work. No one would think twice about a truck backing into their loading docks with a cargo container on its back. A hotel that size has deliveries virtually non-stop, coming and going at all hours of the day."

"It would be a blip in their operations." I lean against the wall and stare at the ceiling as I think things through. "But that's what makes it perfect for moving the girls."

"I agree." Jinx glances in the other direction, toward the conference room rather than back to *Jacen*. "Abduct them. Bring them to the Belvedere until all the girls are collected. Call in a truck with a shipping container on its back."

"Take them to the dock and load them onto a ship."

"It's an interesting theory." She pulls at her chin. "And simple."

"Simple is good." I agree.

She bites on her lower lip and glances at the ceiling. It's her way of thinking through a problem. "It's less than two miles from the docks. That makes it convenient as well."

"Agreed, and since we know they coordinated those abductions to occur within the same twenty-four-hour period, they would need a place to hold the girls before locking them in that cargo container."

"It's a stretch at best. A lot of assumptions."

"I know."

"There are numerous properties they could've used instead."

"Think about this." I wait for her to look at me. "If they're no longer utilizing cargo container ships because of Guardian activity, they have one more option left open to them."

Jinx sucks in a breath.

"C&C Cruises." Our gazes collide as we say exactly the same thing. "Now, that would be simple and convenient."

"We need to go back to New Orleans and have that chat with Carson Deverough."

I plant the best, and sloppiest, kiss on her lips, and I don't care that it's wet or sloppy.

Jinx and I make a fabulous team.

It's time to get to work.

SIXTEEN

Wolfe

Jinx mentioned her surprise at how fast the Guardians move. She has no idea how quickly we spin up our missions, but she's learning.

Forest doesn't believe in wasting time. Sam orchestrates the Guardian and technical teams like a master conductor, seamlessly integrating the needs of both arms of Guardian HRS. CJ barks orders that we, the *Guardians*, obey, jumping before he can take a breath or formulate his thoughts. Mitzy's team, as chaotic and disorganized as they seem on the outside, always get it together in record time.

I don't get the tech guys. How do they function without order or a clear leader? Mitzy's technically in charge of the tech team, but her leadership skills are practically nonexistent. Nevertheless, it works for them.

Simply put, we're an organization bound together by a common goal. It's not a job. Not for any of us. It's a calling.

We live and breathe our motto: to rescue those who've been taken.

Within an hour of returning to the main conference room, and reporting what we found, Jinx and myself, along with the rest of

Alpha team, Mitzy and her tech team, Lily—because she demands a spot on the mission—and Eve who convinces Max she needs to come because we're questioning her father again—all pile into the company jet.

"I'm surprised Eve is here." Jinx leans close, keeping her voice low. "Is it true she hasn't spoken to her father since before her abduction?"

"That's true."

"How can that be?"

"Max."

"Huh?"

"He tied her to him with a ring, and she moved in with him after her rescue. I'm surprised she wants to see her father, although I doubt Max will allow it."

"He can't keep her from her father." Jinx's protective instincts rage, but I place my hand over hers.

"Be careful putting yourself between Max and Eve. His heart is in the right place." I try to explain it, at least how I understand things.

"I suppose."

"He's protective when it comes to Eve." I feel him. Running through his veins is the need to protect the one he loves. "Once Deverough gives us what we need, I'm sure there will be no problem with Eve having a face-to-face with her father."

"I can't imagine how she must feel." Jinx rubs the side of her arm. "If I thought my father bartered my freedom as part of some business deal, I'd never want to see him again."

"Copy that." I lean back and pinch the bridge of my nose. "Regardless of why she's here, I'm afraid she's either not going to find the answers she needs, or those answers will be more than she can bear."

"I can't imagine living through something like that." Jinx leans into the aisle, peering forward three rows where Max sits with Eve. "Although …"

"Although, what?"

"Just thinking out loud." She does that thing with her nose, scrunching it up, which tells me she's thinking up something.

"I need more than that." I blow out a breath of frustration. "What are you planning?"

Jinx has something up her sleeve, and it kills me she's not sharing.

Sam and Forest give their go-ahead for Jinx to interrogate Deverough alone. I trust their instincts, even if I don't understand the why behind it. There's a reason behind that madness, but I've yet to be let in on whatever they're thinking.

It's one more reminder about how little I know about Jinx.

"I'm not telling you my secrets." Jinx flashes an impish grin as she hugs my arm and leans her head on my shoulder. She threads her fingers through mine, clasping our hands together.

This feels like something a couple would do, except I wish she'd trust me with one of her secrets. I'm not happy.

"The one thing we all agree on is Deverough is hiding something." I flip our hands over and bring the back of her hand to my mouth. Brushing my lips lightly against her knuckles makes her gasp. In response, my chest puffs out. The energy between us will be explosive if we ever get a moment to be alone.

We sit side by side, shoulder to shoulder, and lift the armrest separating our seats. Her thigh rests against mine. It's a comfortable familiarity we share, but I don't get why she thinks she'll be successful where Griff has failed.

The jet finishes taxiing. With a roar, we speed down the runway and are in the air, climbing to cruising altitude, headed for New Orleans.

Last time we descended on this city, it was Alpha team minus Max. We rented a small house for the five of us. Max didn't join that mission because he was still on medical hold from an injury and not cleared to operate. That house became exceedingly small when things ramped up, and Mitzy's team basically took over our quaint, but tiny, abode.

This time, we travel in style. Forest approved a stately mansion to house our tiny army of tech geniuses, Guardian men, and the women we love.

Axel and Griff crack up, thinking it hilarious Max, Knox, and I bring our women on a mission. Which leads to a heated argument between them, Jinx, and Lily who don't take well to Axel and Griff dismissing their roles. Things devolve further when Axel and Griff pronounce the rest of us as pussy-whipped.

Jinx and Lily aren't happy to be lumped in under girlfriend status, stating loud and clear their qualifications. They go further to say they could run this operation without the assistance of, and I quote, *the hired muscle without a neuron between them.*

Her words. Not mine.

A smile bounces on my lips remembering how the girls tore into Axel and Griff.

But damn if it doesn't make me chuckle. If any of us are pussy-whipped, it's Axel and Griff. They dote on their women and are inseparable when we're not on a mission. I never understood why that might be until I met Jinx.

The short truth is life's more fun with her around than when she's not.

Regardless, the "pussy-whipped" comment goes over like a load of bricks. Fortunately, or unfortunately, Jinx and Lily won't be staying at the palatial southern mansion Sam appropriated for our time in New Orleans. The two of them make it clear they'll be staying with Callie at Callie's bar. I hate hearing that, although I understand.

Jinx, Lily, and Callie grew up together, raised as sisters. When Jinx and Lily left the DEA to join the Guardians, they left Callie behind. I get wanting to spend time together, and I'm doing my damned best not to be jealous of Callie stealing Jinx from me.

It's important I support Jinx, and if she needs bonding time with Callie and Lily without me, then I need to be man enough to deal with it.

But I'm jealous as fuck.

I have a feeling much of our team's downtime will occur in Callie's bar. There's no way Knox and I will stay away. If we go,

Liam will follow. Griff and Axel will tuck tail and join us. Honestly, it's hilarious as fuck to watch the two of them get dressed down by Jinx and Lily.

Wish I recorded the whole thing.

The expressions on their faces were priceless.

As we climb to our cruising altitude, I settle in for the flight. Three hours after liftoff in California, we touch down in New Orleans. An hour later, we roll up to Rose Manor, a palatial southern estate, which will be our home away from home while in New Orleans.

Jinx and Lily travel with us to Rose Manor, but only to attend the pre-mission briefing. As the sun sets on the Mississippi delta, Knox and I stand on the steps of Rose Manor with our jaws dropping as we are politely, and firmly, disinvited.

"What do you mean we can't come?" Knox looks at Lily, confusion and irritation parading across his face.

"I told you, no boys." Lily's lilting voice lifts on the sultry evening breeze as the cicadas wake and fill the air with their deafening buzz.

"Who are you calling a boy?" Knox props his hands on his hips, scowling as the Uber driver pulls up the long, tree-covered drive.

"You call us girls." Lily props her hands on her hips. "So, we're calling you boys."

"That just sounds wrong," Knox grumbles as he shoves his hands deep in the pockets of his jeans. "Besides, it's not an insult to call a woman a girl."

"And I'm not using it as an insult when I say no boys are allowed. Get over yourself; it's just for tonight." Lily shoves Knox playfully.

"I don't trust you."

"You don't?" Lily pokes her finger in the middle of Knox's chest.

"No, you need supervision." His gaze includes Jinx, then he looks to me for support.

I lift my hands up and take a step back. This is not an argument I'm stepping into.

"Supervision?" Lily's temper flares.

"Damn straight." He takes a step toward his girl. "There will be rules if I'm not there."

"What do you have in mind?" Lily gives Knox a suggestive look.

Jinx and I exchange a look of our own. Jinx rolls her eyes while I cover my mouth and cough to hide my laugh. Lily and Knox definitely deserve each other.

"Do y'all need a bit of privacy?" Jinx covers her eyes but spreads her fingers, peeking through them. "Or should I grab a hose?"

"No need." Knox's words come out a growl. "No body shots allowed. No touching other men. No dancing. No grinding. No …"

"For the love of all that's holy." Lily closes the distance and plants her lips on Knox's mouth. "I won't do anything but talk to my girls."

"Callie owns a bar." Knox's shoulders roll back. "You're going to be in the thick of drunk assholes hoping to get lucky."

"Knox, stop it." Lily loops her arms over his shoulders. "I love you, and I promise I won't do anything I wouldn't do if you were standing right beside me. Do you trust me?"

Knox glances over at me, and I cover my mouth. Those are fighting words, and he better get it right.

"I trust you." Knox does the smart thing and gives in, but damn if I don't feel him. "But no body shots."

I'm with Knox. I'm not happy about Jinx leaving me behind either, especially since this is supposed to be our night together. Knox's comment about no body shots makes me laugh.

The night they met, Lily tricked Knox into a game of darts, which he summarily lost. She wiped the mat with him, humiliating him with her expert skill. Evidently, Lily used to play darts competitively on a national level.

The bet was he had to do whatever she said. Lily set Knox up on the bar, stripped down to his boxers, and offered him up for body shots to all the women in the bar. Liam and I documented the whole thing, getting stills and videos we continue to share on a regular basis. We randomly post pictures throughout Guardian HQ and attach them to corporate emails.

It's fun because it pisses Knox off.

"No body shots." Lily crosses her arms over her chest. "We're simply having a girls' night in. I promise to be very well behaved."

My eyes squint as I hold my tongue. I almost made the same mistake Knox did, assuming I'd go with Jinx to Callie's bar. She's been a bit standoffish since we landed. Which I don't get.

Tonight is supposed to be our night. Our reset where we erase our complicated beginning with all the misunderstandings and start over.

I assumed it would be the two of us, a short dinner to meet the technical requirements of a date, and then a very long night in bed. Not once did I think I'd be in NOLA, with Alpha team, and all of Mitzy's geeks, while Jinx ditches me for the night.

Instead of our date, an Uber driver comes to pick her up and take her away.

I don't like it.

Not one bit.

But if I want more than one night with Jinx, I need to show her that I trust her. I can't let jealously get the better of me.

I especially can't allow my emotions to ruin my headspace. We're on a mission. There's work to be done. Lives to save. My personal issues mean squat in comparison.

I need to focus on that rather than what Jinx might be doing later tonight without me.

At least, that's the lie I tell myself, trying to be noble and all that shit. The truth is I'm ready to throw one epic temper tantrum like a fucking child denied his tasty treat.

Fuck that shit. I'm a better man than that.

I watch Knox chase Lily down, jealousy gnawing at my gut, as he sweeps her off her feet and twirls her in the air. A cold lump forms in my throat.

When will I get that with Jinx?

I'm pissed and jealous of my friend as he mauls his fiancée in front of me.

Fuck Lily. Fuck Knox. I hate them both.

"Hey, I'm sorry." Jinx places her hand on my arm. "I hope you're not too upset about tonight?"

She asks as if it's a question.

As if I have a say.

Maybe that's what has me riled up. Jinx never asked what I wanted. She told me what she was going to do.

There are no good words to describe what I think about that.

But I'm not so far gone as to slip up and speak my mind.

No.

I don't do that.

I'm not that guy; the one who makes a scene because some chick stepped on his feelings.

I'm the bigger man, and I'm going to act like a fucking adult.

I don't look down at Jinx, at least, not until I can get the anger flowing through my veins to go away. I place my hand over hers, taking any contact I can get, and grab my emotions by the horn, wrestling them into submission.

"It's okay."

It's totally *not* okay.

She spins around until she faces me. "Are you sure?"

Nope.

I'm not sure at all.

In fact, I hate it.

But I affix a smile to my face and lie.

"Yeah, I'm cool. I'll catch you on the flip side." I kick at the dirt, as if Jinx's leaving doesn't gut me to the core. I want to be the most important person in her life.

Not Lily.

Not Callie.

Me.

Leaving me behind, especially on what's supposed to be our night, makes me feel as if I've made a massive error in judgment. Maybe all Jinx wants is something casual after all?

It's possible I got it wrong. It wouldn't be the first time I read the signals wrong, and I don't like that at all. That's not something I deal with well.

There's a reason I keep sex casual. I'm a fucking green-eyed monster when it comes to the women I care about.

As Knox buries Lily in kisses, I pivot and turn. Without another word, I leave Jinx as the driver of the Uber pulls to a stop. I don't look back. Instead, I head inside.

Mitzy's team is fast at work, taking up space, laying out miles of color-coded cable that makes me think of a clown throwing up all over the floor. While I work my way to the salon, I tell myself this means nothing. I'm such a fucking liar.

Max, Axel, Griff, and Liam sit around the bar. Sam and CJ join them. They sip at whiskey and glance at me as I stroll in like I don't have a care in the world.

Max takes one look at me, seeing straight through me, and pours a double shot of whiskey. "Looks like you need this." He pushes it across the bar.

I pound the shot, loving the burn flowing down my throat. Slamming the glass on the bar, I speak the only word left in me.

"Another."

I plan on getting royally shit-faced.

SEVENTEEN

Jinx

"WAS THAT WEIRD?" I CRANE MY NECK, LOOKING AT WOLFE through the rear window. He heads back to the majestic southern plantation-styled home and doesn't look back. "It felt weird."

"What?" Lily sits beside me with a breathy smile on her lips.

"Wolfe."

"What do you mean?" Her fingers flutter over her lips, most likely remembering that swoony kiss Knox laid on her before we hopped in the Uber.

I'm jealous of my sister. I'm jealous because I'm not entirely certain where Wolfe and I are as far as our relationship is concerned.

Like, are we in one?

Or are we simply messing around?

Scratching that itch?

Chasing tail?

"He's mad at me." I chew at my cuticles, feeling like I'm missing something.

"Mad? Why would he be mad? Did you see the way he looked at you?"

"No."

"Girl, he looked like he wanted to devour you."

"Well, he didn't maul me like Knox did you."

"It was just a kiss."

Lily turns around, glancing out the back window as our driver takes us down the stately drive.

Taking me away from Wolfe.

Unlike Wolfe, who practically ran inside, Knox stands in the driveway, eyes fixed to the car. Lily waves, and he waves back. Wolfe's nowhere to be found. I press against my sternum as pain spears through my heart.

"Is that why you keep touching your lips?" It's irrational, but I'm jealous of what Lily has with Knox.

"What can I say? He's a phenomenal kisser."

"Is that all?"

The tires crunch on the gravel-packed drive. On massive oaks stretch out their limbs, touching overhead. Hundreds of years old, Spanish moss dangles from their limbs where it sways gently on the late afternoon breeze.

"You're in a mood." She gives me a look. "Want to talk about it?"

"No."

"Liar. Come on, we've got thirty minutes. Tell me your problems. Spill your guts, girl." Lily's hard to resist when she gets demanding like that. It's the right amount of push I need.

"It's just …" I face forward and purse my lips. "He didn't kiss me."

"Maybe he didn't want to kiss you in front of everyone. Y'all haven't officially come out as a couple. Maybe he's waiting?"

"I don't think that's it. He's mad."

"Why would he be mad? I thought things were finally going well between the two of you. It's been nearly a week since you two tore shit up."

"Things are going really well." Too well, as a matter of fact. It's enough to make me want to take a step back. "Shit." I fist my hand and smack the side of my leg.

"Why are you hitting yourself?"

"Because." I lean back and tilt my head against the headrest as I stare at the headliner of the car. "I'm doing it again."

"Doing, what?"

"Sabotaging."

"Jinx, just spill already. I'm not in a mood for twenty questions. What's going on with you?"

"Remember what I said about starting over with Wolfe?"

"Yeah, your big *date night*." She uses her fingers, making quotes in the air. "Or should I say the night you both finally get your heads out of your asses and engage in some freaky animal sex. Honestly, I don't know why you've waited this long. Wolfe is nice on the eye, and I bet he's phenomenal in bed."

"Well, I wouldn't know."

I know Knox is good in bed. After their first time together, Lily went on and on about the multiple orgasms Knox bestowed on her. I always believed that to be an urban myth. Evidently, it's not, unless Lily's lying, which she totally wouldn't. Not to me, at least.

"And why is that?"

"Tonight was supposed to be date night." I press my lips together, frustrated with myself. "I'm supposed to be with him."

"Why didn't you say anything? We can turn around." Lily leans forward, ready to tap the Uber driver on the shoulder, but I grab her wrist.

"This is the only night we have to see Callie. It wouldn't be right to ditch."

"But you ditched Wolfe?"

"We'll have other nights."

"And that's what you're worried about? That he's pissed you walked out on your starting-over date night."

"That's exactly what I'm worried about." I nibble at my lower lip. "Was it wrong not to invite the guys?"

"It's been weeks since we've seen Callie. She's excited to see us. Knox and Wolfe are cool, but that's not what Callie's looking forward to. One night away from them shouldn't be the end of the world. Besides ..."

"Besides, what?"

"Tomorrow, we're back on the clock. Have you thought about how you're going to handle Deverough?"

"Actually, I have."

"Want to clue me in?"

"It's simple really. We're going to go in there, make demands he won't budge on, then we're going to hit him where it hurts."

"And where's that?"

"Eve says he's been trying to get ahold of her since she was rescued. She's been too pissed to speak to him, but she came on this trip."

"I see where you're going with that."

"I have a lot of questions for that man."

"I can't wait." Lily rubs her palms together. "And don't worry about Wolfe. One night away from you isn't the end of the world." She leans back. "I'm just thrilled you're no longer trying to rip each other's throats out. Looks like working together is good for you."

"It is, and it has been. He's smart. Smarter than I thought. Actually, all the Guardians are. I figured they were nothing more than the brute strength needed to get the job done, but they're more than that."

"At least you now have someone else to harass with your side hobby." Lily refers to my love for all things code. "I'm officially off the hook."

"You wish." I'll never let Lily off the hook. "It's cool that we have our secret code. Although, it seems it's required training in BUDS."

"I wonder how many of the Guardians remember enough about the Prisoner's code to be fluent in it?"

"It'll be fun to find out." I see lots of ways Lily and I can have fun with that. We created a couple of variations that will drive the guys nuts.

"You know, Callie will understand if you want to go back." Lily gives me an out, and she's right.

Callie will totally understand. She watched me drag Wolfe to the bathroom that first night. She also saw me lay him on his back when his team said I couldn't go with them to save Lily. If there's one thing Callie is good at, it's reading people.

She'd totally be fine with it.

But I'm not.

There's a small part of me that's totally chickenshit when it comes to being alone with Wolfe. Not that we haven't been alone most of this week working on Benefield's ledger, but that was work. Our date is going to be different.

We'll finally be crossing that last barrier between us. Maybe that's what's freaking me out. Casual sex is easy. It means nothing. Sex with Wolfe, however … Let's just say there will be nothing casual about it.

Which means, he'll have the power to hurt me for real. I scratch at my shoulder, fidgeting with everything that means.

It's sad to say, but for a woman in her mid-twenties, I've never been in a relationship.

I've had flings. More one-night stands than I'm willing to admit. I don't have enough fingers and toes to count all the men I've slept with.

There have been a small handful of guys I hung out with on a somewhat regular basis, but I dated none of them and kept them all at a safe distance.

I'm good with the physical side of a relationship. The emotional side?

Not so much. In fact, it makes me kind of queasy in the gut.

Maybe, I'm running from Wolfe?

Or maybe, I'm running from myself?

It fits.

It totally fits.

I hate that about myself. Why do relationships make me want to hightail it out of there and run for the hills?

It's not like I have a reason. I have loving parents, Lily and Callie, sisters who adore me. We were blessed with a great childhood. No troubled past. Well, no troubled past except for the whole being abandoned as a baby thing, but it's not like I remember any of that. No abusive relationships litter my past. My heart was never broken by a boy because I never let anyone get that close.

"Stop that." Lily lightly taps my arm.

"Stop, what?"

"Obsessing over whatever it is you're thinking about. If you're going to be like this all night, we're turning around so you and Wolfe can finally get your game on."

"You make it sound lame." I roll my eyes at her. "Get our game on? Seriously?"

"We're talking about sex, right?"

"I suppose."

"Well, if the sex is good enough, maybe you'll be too *lame* in the morning to walk straight. Get it?"

"Ha ha, not funny. Not everyone can have the kind of sex you and Knox have."

"When you've got it, you've got it." It's Lily's turn to roll her eyes at me. There's a smirk on her face, but it droops then falls away. "Wait a minute. We're not talking about sex, are we?" Lily leans in. "You like him." She states it as a fact, and that makes me squirm.

"I don't know." I rub at my arm, growing more uncomfortable by the minute.

"You do. You really like him." She pokes my arm. "That's why you're running."

"I'm not running."

"There's absolutely zero reason why you're here with me rather than with Wolfe."

"Callie's expecting us. She'll be heartbroken if I'm not there."

"Callie will be totally fine. It's not like we planned this trip. It's not like she can't live without us." Lily leans forward and taps the driver on the shoulder. "Um, can you turn around?"

"Lily." I grab her arm and yank it away from our poor driver's shoulder. "We're going to Callie's."

"No. I'm going to see Callie. You're going back."

A knot of fear coils in my gut. I punch my fist into my stomach, but it doesn't do any good. There's real fear there, and it's only going to get worse. Lily doesn't understand.

She doesn't get my fear.

But she's going to steamroll right on past it. Despite my protests, the driver makes a U-turn. Ten minutes later, I stand outside Rose Manor, mouth gaping as Lily leaves me. If I didn't love her, I'd take her out back and shoot her.

As for what to do next, I'm at a loss.

The sun dips toward the horizon, getting ready to disappear. As it nears the horizon, the buzzing of the cicadas intensifies. Tree frogs join in the chorus, adding their chirping to the evening melody. A soft breeze blows. It lifts my hair and blows it into my eyes. I sweep the stray strands off my face and tuck them behind my ear. That breeze brings the gentle scent of magnolias floating on air. It's barely there, nearly invisible unless I close my eyes and breathe in through my nose. I've always loved living in the South.

California is beautiful. The sweeping vistas out to sea never fail to steal my breath. It's hot, without the oppressive humidity of home, but that's why it doesn't feel like a home to me. It's as if California air is unsubstantial and not weighted down by decades of history.

I open my eyes and glance at the steps leading up to the house. I try to ignore the pit of fear gnawing at my gut, but it doesn't work.

I've spent hours upon hours alone with Wolfe this past week, working side by side as we decoded Benefield's cipher, translated the entries, and discovered a list of girls, young women, whose safety is at risk.

I wasn't a ball of nerves then. Hell, we kissed at work. We kissed more than once. Our chemistry simmers in the background, growing hot, cooling off, and rising to a simmer again as discoveries were made. One look at the front door, and I turn my back on it.

I'm not ready to face Wolfe.

I'm not ready to be alone with him.

Instead of heading inside, I brave the insect swarms and wander over to a hundred-year-old oak tree with branches that spread wide and dip toward the ground. A wooden swing dangles from one of those branches.

It draws me to it, and soon I find myself swinging gently under the boughs, no closer to figuring out whatever the hell is wrong with me than I was moments before.

My eyes close as my legs pump in and out. I'm not looking to swing high. All I want is a bit of motion to keep me from thinking too hard.

Several minutes later, a throat clears behind me, and my legs draw up beneath the swing. My fingers clench the rope, and I attempt to swallow past the sudden lump in my throat.

"I thought you were headed into town." Wolfe's deep baritone sweeps across my skin, tunnels along my nerves, and wraps itself around my heart.

Without my legs pumping the swing, it slows, and I let it come to a stop.

There's no need to turn around. Before he spoke, I knew it was him.

"Change in plans." I curl in my lower lip, nibbling at it with my teeth.

The last thing I'm going to tell him is that Lily turned the car around so he and I could have crazy wild monkey sex.

"What are you doing out here?" He moves behind me and gently pushes the swing. "What happened to girls' night out?"

I'd tell him to stop, but it feels safest if I remain in the swing.

"Thinking."

"About what?"

When I don't answer, Wolfe says nothing. He continues to push the swing while the silence between us lengthens. Overhead, the setting sun puts on a magnificent show, spilling umber orange and deep russet red across the heavens.

My grip tightens on the ropes holding the swing, and I realize he's no longer pushing.

I twist around only to find him walking away.

"Wolfe? Where are you going?"

He spins around, and rather than taking a step toward me, he takes a step back.

"Giving you space." His brows tug together as he drags his hand over his mouth and down his chin. "Things feel a bit off, and I don't want … Well, I figure maybe we played this wrong."

"What the hell does that mean?" Fire burns in my gut, and heat rises along the back of my neck.

"Only that I misread. Or misjudged." He holds his hands out, away from his body. "Either way …"

"No either way about it." Along with the heat at the back of my neck, warmth spreads across my cheeks. My anger stirs, and I get ready to unleash my rage.

Rage?

What the fuck is wrong with me? There's zero—absolutely zero —reason for me to be angry or upset.

My words make his entire body jerk. He peers at me, eyes narrow, pinched, and bearing far too much confusion.

"Please don't go." I stretch out my hand, pleading with him.

The man must think I'm a total head case. I see it in his eyes, a wariness that has never been there before. He rubs at the back of his neck and turns his attention to the sunset overhead. After a moment, a very long moment where I hold my breath, his attention shifts back to me.

"I'm not clear on what the problem is, or what kind of issue you have with me, but I know one thing."

"Wolfe …"

"Let me finish." He holds up a hand. "Distractions during a mission are a liability. They're dangerous, putting my team, and you, at risk. Maybe I pushed too hard. Maybe I misunderstood. Maybe things were different when it was just a tease."

"That's not what …"

His hand goes up again. "Maybe you're thinking about the mission, and this thing between us is distracting you. If you need to think. I accept that, and that's exactly what I'm going to do."

"What are you talking about?"

"I'm giving you space." He shrugs as if it means nothing to him.

As if I mean nothing to him.

With those words, Wolfe executes a precise about-face and

slowly walks away. His stride is determined, focused, and picking up speed as the distance between us grows.

I want to call out to him. I should go after him. I'm the one who turned this into something awkward. I'm such a fucking idiot.

But what do I do?

I stay in that damn swing, pumping my legs until I soar forward and fall back. Over and over and over, until it's pitch-black outside.

I've been lucky. It's not the season for mosquitos. If it was, they would suck me dry. As it is, I've been bitten only once, but I can only stay out here for so long.

At some point, I need to enter that house, find a bed, and … Shit.

I forgot all about the sleeping arrangements. Lily and I are supposed to be with Callie, spending the night there.

What am I going to do about a bed?

EIGHTEEN

Wolfe

I stopped drinking whiskey after the third shot. I won't be that guy who drinks because of a woman. My plan had been to wander outside, clear my head, and figure out why Jinx and I can't seem to get it together.

Honestly, I handled that wrong.

Lily and Jinx moved all the way across the country, with very little notice, to work for the Guardians. They didn't have a lot of time to say goodbye. It's normal for Jinx to want to spend a night with Callie.

Jinx, Lily, and Callie grew up as sisters. That's a special bond, and here I am swinging my dick and getting all butt hurt because Jinx didn't choose me.

I'm frustrated: sexually for sure, mentally exhausted from the long hours spent breaking and deciphering Benefield's ledgers. That leaves me emotionally in a weird space.

After leaving Jinx outside, I head back to the salon, pour another two fingers of whiskey, on the rocks, and spend the next two hours watching the ice melt as I swirl the amber liquid in the glass. Each time I bring the glass to my lips, I inhale the heady aroma of the whiskey. Then I set the glass down to stare at the massive front doors.

Two hours of sitting.

My seat in the salon, a large, overstuffed lounging chair, faces the foyer, and by extension, the front doors. The guys left me alone some while ago, and the house slowly shut down around me. Lights turned off and people headed upstairs to find their rooms for the night. Most are double-bunked. Axel and Griff share a room, but Max, Knox, and myself, all got private rooms.

Whoever decided on sleeping arrangements took into consideration who slept with whom, except I'm not sleeping with anyone. They simply assumed Jinx and I would share. Our room is not in the main house like the others. It sits over the carriage house, a private but modest suite.

It sucks that I'll have it all to myself.

Mitzy wanders through the foyer, head down, her face lit by the glow of the tablet she carries. She flicks off the light in the foyer, disappears from view, then reappears walking backward and craning her neck.

"Wolfe? Is that you?"

"It is." I lift my glass as if making a toast.

"What are you doing sitting in the dark?" Her brows scrunch up and she tucks the tablet under her arm.

"Sitting."

"Well, that's obvious." Her sarcastic reply is not unexpected. "Why are you sitting, in the dark, alone, with a glass of whiskey you haven't touched?"

"I'm touching it now." To prove my point, I lift the glass.

"Ha ha, smarty pants." She wanders in and leans against the doorframe. The tablet goes dark, and I realize I have been sitting in the dark. "What's up with you?"

"Nothing. Just not ready to hit the sack."

"I'm surprised the others aren't still here."

"Max and Eve went to bed early. Knox, Axel, and Griff went for a late run and headed up not too long ago to shower and settle in for the night. Why are you still up?"

"Checking on things." She gives a noncommittal shrug. "Talking to Noodles."

It's easy to forget Mitzy married the pianist of the mega rock band, Angel Fire. How does that work? Mitzy is high-strung most days, and from what I've heard, Noodles is totally Zen. How does that kind of dynamic work?

"Haven't you checked things a gazillion times already?" I shift in my seat, lift the whiskey to my lips and take another slow sip.

Damn, that's fine whiskey. Such a shame I ruined it by letting the ice melt.

Mitzy's OCD tendencies are legendary and well-earned. She's a compulsive freak, which means I have no doubt she'll still be double-checking things long into the night.

"Yeah, but you know me." She taps the tablet tucked under her arm for emphasis.

I can't help but smile. Despite the smarty pants comment, this almost feels like a normal conversation. I don't have many normal conversations with our brilliant tech lead. In fact, I don't know if I've had a conversation with her that was just the two of us. I do notice one thing. The normal bounce to her step and bubbly personality looks a little flat.

"Anything bothering you?" Not sure why I ask. I'm not looking to prolong our conversation, but maybe I need some human interaction, anything to take my mind off Jinx.

I feel a bit down and out myself.

What's that they say about misery loving company?

"There's always something on my mind, but not really." She lifts the tablet. "I just got off with Noodles. We spend more time apart than I want. The band's gearing up for another European tour, which means even less time together. I swear, we spend more time talking through the screen than we do in person. Anyhow, I figured it was time to head up and get some sleep. It's getting late. You going to tell me what's bothering you or pretend like everything's A-Okay?" she flips my question back on me.

"Just chilling."

"You sure about that?" Some of her snark returns. "Or does it maybe have something to do with Jinx swinging outside rather than cuddling with you in here?"

How the fuck does Mitzy always know everything about everyone?

I should say something sensitive about her and her rock star husband. Her sharp tongue took on a wistful tone when she spoke about him, and she clearly misses him. I'd say something, but I'm too wound up about Jinx.

Is she still really outside?

How long has it been?

Rhetorical question. There's no need to look at my watch.

I've felt every agonizing minute while sitting in here waiting for Jinx to come through those doors. I'd go after her, but there's a definite vibe between us that wasn't there before. If I push, I have a feeling it'll only push her away.

"I'm headed to bed soon." I pretend as if that's my plan. It's not, not by a long shot. "I'd say I have an early morning, but it doesn't look like there's much for the Guardians to do just yet." Our role is anticipated but not ironed out.

"I have a feeling there will be sooner than you think." Mitzy shifts her weight and pushes off the wall.

"How's that?"

"I keep going over what you and Jinx said about shifting gears."

"With the girls?"

"The girls and the narcotics. I'm looking into a few things as far as Deverough is concerned. Griff says the man is adamant he's not involved, but everything points to him."

"That man is dirty."

"Maybe."

"No maybe about it."

"Well, how about I agree based on how things look, but I'm not totally convinced. He's not dirty on purpose."

"How can you be 'not dirty on purpose?'" I lift my hands and use air quotes for emphasis. I don't care what Mitzy says; Deverough is rotten to the core. Whether he started out that way makes no difference now. He's walking filth, and the world will be a better place without him in it.

"Just something I'm looking into. You know his father died when Deverough was rather young. I mean, not young, young, but thirty years old. He inherited the family business and all that came with it."

"Meaning?"

"Meaning the Rossi family is involved."

"How?"

"All the usual ways organized crime gets involved in docks, shipping, and the transport of goods. I've been digging into Deverough's father and found some interesting things."

"Such as?"

"Gambling debts for one thing. Debts that magically disappeared a few years before his father's heart attack. I believe they strong-armed his father, forcing him to use his shipping assets to move their narcotics, and when his father died …"

"Deverough inherited his father's debt."

What Mitzy says has a certain ring of truth about it.

"Exactly." Mitzy places her finger on the tip of her nose. "One thing the Rossi's are well known for is taking good men and turning them dirty. There's a trail and a connection spanning decades. I just haven't had a chance to chase down all the leads."

"Does Jinx know about this?"

"No. I haven't told anyone." Mitzy cocks her head to the side. "Actually, you're the only one I've mentioned it to."

"Jinx needs to know about this when she speaks with Deverough."

"True, but …" Now, she taps the tip of her chin.

For some reason, that makes me sit up and take notice. Mitzy does nothing without reason. Those gears in her head churn nonstop, and I'm somewhere in that mix.

"But, what?" I clear my throat, not meaning for my voice to pitch that high.

"I have a better idea."

"What's that?" Now, my voice is in its proper, deeper register. Which is equally as awkward as that high-pitched tone.

Mitzy's playing with me. I know this, yet I'm trapped, firmly caught in the machinations of her phenomenal brain.

"Why don't you go with her?" The way Mitzy says it makes it seem as if tagging along with Jinx on her mission to make Deverough sing is like taking a walk in the park.

"Of course, I want to go with Jinx, but I've been disinvited along with the rest of the Guardian men." I blow out a frustrated breath. "I don't think Jinx will like that. She's adamant that she speaks with him alone." How many times has Jinx expressed that to me? A hundred? A thousand? Far too many times to disregard.

For whatever reason, she believes she'll have greater success with Deverough than Griff did. I'm not one to disagree, but I've seen Griff at work. The man can make a rock sing.

"Just tell her I said so." Mitzy states it as if it's no big deal.

"I think you should tell Jinx, not me." No way am I stepping in that shit. Jinx will be pissed, and she'll direct all that anger at me, the messenger.

I feel Jinx before I see her.

"Tell me what?"

A ripple of sensation races down my spine as Jinx's sultry voice floats through the air. It tunnels under my skin and settles in with a low buzzing sensation. The foyer is dark, the salon is darker still, but the moment Jinx enters that space, I feel her everywhere.

Fuck if that's not intense.

It's unsettling, that's what it is.

"Change in plans." Mitzy spins around, and while I can't see her expression, I feel the mischievous grin on her face as she speaks. "Wolfe will be accompanying you tomorrow."

"I go alone." Doesn't take Jinx but a millisecond to respond. Her abrupt reply cuts through me, stealing my breath.

Jinx isn't happy.

"Deverough is going to expect a Guardian, so it's not like it'll be a surprise. We're going to give him exactly what he wants. Wolfe goes." She pivots and winks at me.

"That's not what we agreed." Jinx folds her arms across her chest and cocks a hip out. All I see is her silhouette but feel every bite of her anger as it builds.

"Like I said, plans changed." Mitzy doesn't care about any of the subtext here. She continues on, steamrolling past Jinx's objections. "Wolfe will be Eve's bodyguard."

"How did you …" Jinx takes a step back.

"Wait, you're taking Eve? That's …" Wrong on so many levels, potentially dangerous, and makes no sense.

I must be doing something right because I blurt none of that out loud. Yes, I know Eve came because she wants to talk to her father, but that's supposed to be separate from the rest of this.

"I know everything. I know what you're planning, and I think it's brilliant. If Deverough doesn't crack, however, Wolfe will step up to bat."

"What does that mean?" Jinx's gaze shifts to me, and I can't help but feel guilty. About what, I'm not sure. Mitzy seems to be changing things up on the fly.

"Only that Wolfe can apply leverage you can't." Mitzy gives a little flounce as she pivots, shifting from me to Jinx.

"Griff hasn't been able to make Deverough crack." Jinx crosses her arms, which only draws my attention to her breasts. "Wolfe won't either. Which is exactly why you need me."

"Griff hasn't been able to pressure Deverough the way he'd like." I feel a need to defend his interrogation techniques.

The man can crack a stone and make it sing if that's what he wants. Since Deverough is a private citizen, and Griff hasn't been able to use his go-to techniques, things have been slow. I know for a fact Griff's frustrated.

I bite my lower lip and try to keep this professional. I'm not getting good vibes from Jinx. If anything, she's pissed and growing more so by the minute.

Jinx isn't happy with Mitzy messing with her plans. Why is it so important she do this herself? I'm on her side, not in competition with her.

Honestly, I'm growing more pissed off by the second.

Just perfect.

Jinx and I don't do angry and pissed off well together.

"Griff didn't have Deverough's daughter in the same room." Mitzy glances between the two of us, and I swear the gears in that brilliant head of hers spin. "Get some sleep. Both of you. Jinx, you're bunking in the carriage house with Wolfe. All the other beds are full. I'm sure that won't be a problem." She gives a little flick of her fingers. "Morning report is delayed. We meet at ten."

"Ten?" Jinx uncrosses her arms and takes a step forward. "We don't have the time to waste. I planned on being at Deverough's by eight."

"You go in hot-headed, and that costs us. We meet at ten to go over the plan of the day. This is one instance where the early bird doesn't get the worm. They simply get smacked on the head. Goodnight." Mitzy's gaze flicks to me. "Both of you. I'll catch you on the flip side." Mitzy disappears with a flick of her fingers.

We've been dismissed, and now Jinx's angry, I'm pissed, and we're terribly alone.

That's a recipe for disaster.

NINETEEN

Wolfe

I'VE NEVER FELT MORE UNCOMFORTABLE THAN I DO NOW, ESPECIALLY with Jinx glaring at me as if I'm at fault.

"I had nothing to do with that." I hold up my hands and take a step back, smoothing my voice as I brace for Jinx's fiery temper. "She just …"

"Steamrolled you? I know what she did. My question is why didn't you stop her?"

"Now, wait a minute." I take a step toward Jinx, defending myself.

"You don't trust a chick to do the job, do you? You think I need Guardian oversight?"

"Don't put words in my mouth. Mitzy said that. Not me. The last thing I think is that you need Guardian oversight. Don't turn this into something it isn't."

"Is that so?" She juts her chin out, growing more indignant with each passing second. "Because I didn't hear you say otherwise."

"You calling me a liar?" Heat rises in the back of my neck. My fingers flex, forming fists. Jinx can be pissed all she wants, but that doesn't give her the right to question my integrity. I shake out my fists. No matter how angry I become, I'll never hit a woman. I'll never hit Jinx.

"I'm simply stating a fact." Jinx's lips press into a tight line of fury and resentment.

"And what would that be?" I shift forward.

She needs to watch it because I stand by my word. No one question's my integrity.

"How typical this is." Jinx juts out her jaw, throwing a snit. "Men like you always think you can do things better than a woman. Frankly, it's tiring."

"You need to calm down." I'm too tired for this. Getting into a fight with Jinx tops my list of things I don't want to do.

"Calm down?" Jinx takes a few steps, closing the distance between us. Her entire body vibrates with rage. "In the entire history of mankind, men telling women to calm down has never once made things better. Don't feed me that shit; it's a sure-fire way to make things worse. And I don't need to calm the fuck down. I'm right, and you're a fucking bastard because you know it."

"A what!?" Tension fills my body as I become anything but calm. The kicker is I'm not angry. I'm not mad. Oh no, it's far worse than that. I'm fucking turned on and getting more so by the minute.

"You heard me." She takes a step toward me. "And here I thought …" Jinx makes a move to turn away.

"You thought, what?" I grab her arm, spinning her back toward me.

"I shouldn't have come back." Jinx yanks free and rubs at her arm. "I should've stayed with Lily and had that girls' night out."

"I didn't make you turn around."

"No, you didn't. Lily did."

And like that, her words hit me with the force of a sucker punch to the gut, stealing my breath. I thought Jinx came back for me. She didn't. Lily did.

Well, fuck that.

I put my barely touched glass of whiskey down on the table and do my best to take in long, slow breaths. Jinx's temper is on the rise, growing hotter by the second. I'm aroused, getting more so by the minute, which is becoming a problem with each passing second. Time to nip that in the bud. I need to keep my cool, or we'll once again be at each other's throats.

I pull in a calming breath. Or at least I try. All that does is draw Jinx's subtle fragrance deep into my lungs, where it makes my senses go wild. Amazing doesn't begin to describe Jinx's unique scent.

Why the anger?

I don't get it. It's almost as if she's doing everything in her power to sabotage our relationship, as if she's closed off to anything more than a casual hookup for sex.

That pisses me off even more. Which sends more blood to fill my engorged cock.

Angry. Hard. Aroused.

If she's not careful, I'm going to slam her against that wall and fuck the anger right out of her, and damned be the consequences. My fingers flex and curl as heat rises in the back of my neck.

She's not shy about what she wants. I felt that in the bathroom of Callie's bar, where Jinx clawed me and practically climbed my body. I should've fucked her then. If I had, I wouldn't be a seething mess of frustrated need right now.

I close the distance between us, noting how the pull of her breath intensifies. She takes a step back. I pivot, then take another step toward her, herding her where I want.

Jinx shifts back as I force her into the salon.

Her back connects with the doorframe. I stay on her, removing the space between us with each determined step. Her hands press against the immaculately restored wood behind her while I lean in close, sliding my hands around her waist and crowding her small frame.

Before she can speak, before she can spit out another obscenity, I slide my fingers into the back pockets of her jeans. This lets me squeeze her ass, letting her know I'm here. It also has the added benefit of tucking our hips together. No way she doesn't feel the hard length of my arousal.

"I'm not going to fight with you." I keep my tone level, calm. Inside, I'm a seething mess.

Her chocolate-brown eyes search my face. I don't see anger, but rather something much more concerning. She's flushed. Aroused.

Holy hell, that's hot.

"Fuck, Jinx, but you make my blood boil. If you need angry, fucked-up sex, we can do that. If you need to use me, we can do that too. But that's your choice. Not mine. That's not what I want."

I want forever with Jinx, and that doesn't happen if we fuck things up from the start.

She rocks her hips forward and pushes against my chest, trying to shove me away. Refusing to let me in.

"Let me go."

"That's easy; all you have to do is say no." I lean back, giving her space, but keep my hands right where they are. "Stop shutting me out. Let me in."

She pushes harder, confident and aggressive, as I continue to hold her tight, demanding and confident in my own right. She can easily spin out of the hold I have on her, but Jinx makes no move to be free of me. My fingers remain shoved down the back pockets of her jeans, but that's the extent of the hold I have on her.

"Let me go ..." She continues to resist, but there's a tremor in her voice, which stops my heart.

"Say the word, and I will." I walk a fine line, refusing to let her go, but something within me speaks a truth Jinx doesn't know about herself. "Answer one question, and I'll let you go."

"I don't need to answer jack shit." She pounds on my chest with her small fists.

In close quarters, I have the advantage. The only reason she beat me before was because I never got close enough to put my hands on her. She had the advantage of momentum. This close, the advantage is mine. Brute strength wins over momentum, and she knows it.

Up close, I take a moment to admire the delicate features of her face and her silky, olive skin. Her mouth makes me ache in the best possible way.

The way she presses her lips together, fueled by her anger, stirs the beast within me. I'm moments from losing my ever-loving mind and taking what I want, tasting and bruising her flesh as I sink into her wet heat.

Fire flashes in her eyes, challenging me to take, daring me to make the first move.

I shouldn't.

Lord, I shouldn't, but soon there will be no turning back.

"What are you afraid of?"

"Nothing." Jinx rises on tiptoe until our lips are kissably close, practically begging me to close the distance and take the kiss she won't complete.

Her temper sparks and heats the air between us.

Maybe it's the whiskey?

I wish I could blame it on my favorite drink, but my head is clear. I swallow hard, losing the war within me to retain control. The more fired up Jinx gets, the more aroused I become.

My dick, the fucker, is primed and ready, hard and eager to slam home. To rut and fuck like a goddamn animal.

The bold lines of her furrowed brow do nothing to calm me down. The madder she gets, the more I want to shake her, take her, and fuck some sense into that head of hers.

The air shudders between us, becoming a vibrating, seething, crackling mess of supercharged electricity filled with lust, want, and need.

"Liar." I hold her to me, caging her in, crowding her, forcing her back against the wall.

"Asshole." As the energy between us spikes, her expression hardens as her anger magnifies.

I feel her everywhere. Heat licking down my spine. Blood racing to my cock. My heart bangs away inside my chest, thundering with every breath. When I focus on her eyes, I tumble into their depths and drown in her fury.

A low growl rumbles in the back of my throat. I'm moments from losing control. Jinx matches the sound with an angry exhale. Her lids narrow and her eyes pinch in challenge. Tension builds in her body until she vibrates with righteous anger.

What the fuck is she doing to me?

I've never felt this gripping, overwhelming need to take a woman before. My reaction is compelling, overpowering, and inevitable. If this goes on much longer, I will reach the point of no return; a place where consent no longer matters.

"Let me go." She pounds her fist against my chest as I lean in.

Breath saws in and out of my lungs as my need rises and my control slips.

"Answer the fucking question." I stare at her, meeting her furious, white-hot gaze, while letting her know this is the line I draw in the sand. "Or say the word."

The heat of her gaze flares against my chest and burns indelibly into my soul. But if she wants me to let go, she'll have to answer the damn question.

I meet her turbulent gaze, giving nothing. I'm not backing down, and she's only just realizing I'm serious. The artery in her neck pulses as her nostrils flare.

I block her escape, using my size as a weapon.

Her scowl deepens. Her anger flares.

"Let me go." Jinx goes wild, thrashing in my grip. Fists pounding at my chest. She punches and kicks. She snarls and snaps.

"Holy fuck." I draw back when she bites me.

Jinx breaks free and bolts for the door. I'm on her before she can escape. Whirling her back around, I press her against the wall, and lean in.

"You fucking bit me."

Her nails dig into the skin of my forearms as I use the formidable power of my body to trap her within the cage of my arms. My thoughts spin down an inevitable spiral as blood pounds in my ears then heads straight for my cock.

I shift my position, knowing she'll bolt, but I'm ahead of her reactions. Before she can push off from the wall, I grab her by the throat. The fingers of my other hand twist in her hair. I press her against the wall, nearly lifting her off her feet.

I'm too far gone now.

Only the beast remains. No amount of fighting or screaming will stop this. Although, I take note of one important thing.

Jinx doesn't mutter a sound. She doesn't shout for help. If anything, her eyes widen and her pupils dilate. She's out of breath, panting hard, yet we've barely broken a sweat.

That comes next.

I haul her into the salon, kicking the door leading to the foyer closed. It shuts with a sense of finality, locking us inside where we're achingly alone. Jinx struggles to free herself, but she's caught in my grip. I move us into the middle of the room and wrestle her to the floor.

There I straddle her legs, making it impossible for her to move, and pin her arms over her head as I lean over her. She struggles beneath me, but it doesn't slow me down. I haven't broken a sweat, whereas she's out of breath and out of strength.

We stare at each other for the longest time, breaths panting, hearts pulsing, desire and need flowing through our veins.

"Last chance," I growl.

She will either answer my question, tell me no, or let this continue.

"Go to hell." She twists beneath me, struggling weakly.

We've gone a time or two on the mat. I know what she's capable of when she wants to win.

This isn't Jinx wanting to win.

TWENTY

Jinx

Holy hellfire, Wolfe's muscle-girded frame bears down on me.

He's heavy. Immovable. Aroused.

My pathetic thrashing only weakens me. I squirm and writhe beneath him until I gasp and surrender out of breath.

Not a bead of sweat mars his brow.

We've sparred before. Using momentum, I flipped him on his back. Wrestling in close quarters is not the same. I lose before I begin. There's simply no way to move his bulk.

He presses me against the hard floor, using his body as a weapon. The vice of his hand on my wrists immobilizes my hands over my head. Only my fingers move, scraping his knuckles, gouging skin. His other hand wraps around my throat, tightening until I can't breathe, then releasing so I can gasp and whimper beneath him.

His low grunts and controlled breathing piss me the fuck off. He's not even trying, whereas I'm struggling.

Damn, but he's magnificent. Fire and fury spark in his eyes as he looks down at me. Thunder rumbles in his throat as he demands I answer his stupid question. His strength, something I've always dismissed, is undeniable, irrefutable, and completely engaged with only one goal in mind.

To subdue me.

To fuck.

His hard gaze makes me suck in a breath, terrified and insanely aroused. Sparks fly between us. Those embers flare and smolder, further igniting my desire.

In my anger, something unexpected arises. Or rather, I shouldn't be surprised. Wolfe and I in a fight are incendiary, hot as sin, and sexually supercharge the air around us. His arousing musk floods my senses, making me wonder why I even bother to fight.

I want him to win.

Giving in to this man doesn't seem like such a bad idea, except for my wounded pride. I struggle and thrash, but he's all bulging biceps, sexy shoulders, rock-hard abs, and powerful thighs holding me down. I shift beneath him, and he eases some of the pressure on my chest.

"What are you afraid of?" He growls the words into the side of my neck while his nose runs across my skin. His lips follow, leaving a trail of fire in their wake. He nibbles at my earlobe and huffs softly in my ear. "Is this what you need, my fiery Jinx? Me forcing you? Dominating you."

Wolfe, in a state of male arousal, is nothing short of gorgeous. There's a viciousness flaring in his eyes, a promise he makes. It's as mesmerizing and terrifying as it is intoxicating and arousing.

He releases my neck and slides his hand down, forcing his way between my legs.

A moan slips past my lips as my back arches against him. I turn my head, refusing to look at him, but Wolfe doesn't allow that tiny escape.

"I'm going to fuck you. I'm going to slide right inside where I belong. I'm going to take what I want, and you're going to learn the truth."

I hold my breath and squeeze my eyes together. I know what he's going to say, and I don't want to hear it.

His hot tongue traces around the outer helix of my ear. He sucks in my earlobe and flicks his tongue against the sensitive tissues.

"Kick and scream, fight if you must, but you're mine. There's no stopping what's going to happen."

This is the closest we've ever been, physically at least. Sure, we've kissed. We've sparred. I tossed him to the mat, using skill and momentum to take him out rather than brute strength.

This—whatever this is—isn't something I can win. He'll either release me, or …

The tighter his grip becomes, the closer he comes, obliterating the space between us until his chest bears down on mine and his lips hover a hairsbreadth away.

"Last fucking chance." He gives me an out, honorable enough to release me if I demand it, only my body's gone haywire, reacting to his masculinity and virility on a level that transcends what's proper or right.

I want him to fuck me. I need him to take me.

As I fight, my fingernails dig into the back of his hand. One last chance, and I use my head, thinking to head-butt him, but he's prepared for that. His grip around my throat tightens, and his lips meet mine, forcing me back to the floor.

Carnal and animalistic, I'm reduced to a feral state. My desire turns wanton and needful as I squirm underneath his hard body and moan beneath the demands of his mouth.

Our intimate position entices and demands we travel only one path. With his lips crushed against mine, he reaches between us, yanking my shirt up. I reel beneath the heat of his kiss as his hand finds my breast and slips under the lacy fabric of my bra.

Just like the kiss, there's no gentle exploration, no reverent admiration. He mauls at me, broad thumb dragging over my peaked nipple and back again. Sparks of electricity shoot through me, zinging along my nerves, where they meet at my core and build.

Wolfe is nothing more than a beast with one singular destination in mind. While I reel beneath him, currents of electricity twine between our bodies. They wrap over and around us, tying us together.

My breaths come in short gasps punctuated by low whimpers and needy moans. This encourages him to continue. He manhandles my breast and invades my mouth with his tongue. The layers of sensation are too much.

Too complex.

Too perfectly imperfect.

Too beautifully brutal.

I shouldn't like this, but the more feral he turns, the more aroused I become.

"You have two options to stop this. Answer the question, or say no." He pinches my nipple, eliciting my first scream. My scream goes nowhere because he devours it with the press of his lips against mine.

"Fuck you." I squirm and buck, but it does no good. He's too heavy. Impossible to budge.

"With pleasure." The low, menacing growl sends a lick of pleasure shooting between my legs. I ache to feel him sliding in and out.

Filling me.

Fucking me.

His hand leaves my breast and heads for the waistband of my jeans. As he shifts his weight, I buck and kick, but he presses me back with the weight of his large frame.

I gulp for air beneath him as he shifts again and, this time, yanks my jeans down below my knees. He takes my panties with them, then shoves his fingers between my legs, finding me wet, aroused, and ready for what comes next.

His fingers slip and slide, then dive inside. Sparks of pleasure riot within me. My hips buck. My back bows. My breaths stutter and stop as I squeeze my eyes shut, then pick up again as his fingers move, pumping in and out.

"Fuck, you're wet for me."

"Bastard." I buck, kick, and growl, but all that does is turn his scowl into a roguish smirk.

While I stare at him, he reaches between us once again. After a bit of maneuvering, he manages to shove his pants down to his knees. The hard length of him presses against my inner thigh, hotter than hot, with the tip wet and weeping for me.

The heat of our bodies enflames me.

The intimacy of skin upon skin overwhelms me.

He exposes my vulnerabilities and reveals my insecurities, forcing me to face unpleasant truths.

With our clothing semi-removed, he forces my legs to part and notches himself between them. The heat of his cock pulses against my inner thigh as the tip presses against my outer folds.

Wolfe grabs for my breast again, pushing aside the lace cup of my bra. He finds my nipple and pinches between his thumb and forefinger until my back arches off the floor and another strangled scream is swallowed by the viciousness of Wolfe's kiss.

"Are you on the pill?" Low, throaty, and hoarse, I barely understand him, but I hear enough to nod.

The whole "I'm clean, you're clean" talk isn't necessary. As Guardian HRS employees, we're tested regularly, but pregnancy remains a risk. Fortunately, we're safe there as well.

"Last chance. If you don't want this, say no. I'll stop."

I don't want him to stop. With a whimper, I squeeze my eyes tight. It's the best answer I can give, and I hope he understands this is as close to a yes that I can get.

Wolfe shifts his weight and once again reaches between us. The head of his cock presses against my opening, and before I can take a breath, he slams inside.

The heat and the weight of his body returns as Wolfe makes me fly. He kisses me, tongue sweeping in, licking and lashing, claiming and dominating, as his body moves.

The kiss isn't a kiss.

It's something more.

It's passion, violence, and tenderness twisted and tormented into the most intense and brutal pleasure. As his body moves, fucking me with fury and anger, Wolfe assumes control and sends a message.

My body will cave to his demands, not the other way around.

I gulp for air as pleasure surges and builds within me. Subjected to his feral nature, my body responds and surrenders.

He releases my wrists to brace himself and change the angle of his thrusts. My hands fall to his shoulders, where I hang on and bury my screams against the muscles straining in his neck.

His breaths pulse in and out, keeping time with the force of his hips. One hand plays with my nipple, pinching until I squirm. His other arm braces him on the floor. Wolfe's tongue sweeps into my mouth, lashing and taking, pouring violence and anger into the kiss.

My nails dig into the muscles of his shoulders, gouging his skin, and I cling to him as he bites and licks, as he sucks and destroys. Wolfe's fury decimates the last of my resistance.

The only thing I can do is hang on as he commands my body to give in.

My breaths rise in a crescendo as his guttural growls join the thundering of my pulse pounding in my ears.

There's too much sensation. Too much to process. I'm locked in a world caught between deliciously depraved and sinfully perfect. It's an uncharted place in my mind, where my darkest desires bang away at the locks holding them in. My imagination soars as Wolfe steers me through and past my fears.

There is no fight. There is no fear.

In surrender, he sets me free.

Barely human sounds escape my lips as I jerk beneath him. I'm mindless, but freed to feel every sensation without fear, without judgment. I let go, and the low throbbing between my legs builds. It comes and goes, building, burning, until everything blurs together into one blinding pulse of pleasure so intense it overtakes everything.

I cry out and cling to Wolfe as he follows me over the edge, collapsing on top of me as our bodies grow limp. We float together in a sea of bliss.

But then Wolfe shifts.

Chilly air sweeps over my body as he stands and yanks up his jeans. I stare up at him, wide-eyed and surprised, suddenly worried by the darkness in his gaze.

His eyes simmer with residual lust, and his hard gaze rakes my body. A scowl steals across his face, settling in and making my pulse tick up a notch.

"Why do you only have sex with strangers?"

His question confuses me. I have no answer.

"Why do you refuse to let people in?" He yanks up the zipper of his pants.

Again, I have no words. I reach down, suddenly feeling self-conscious, and drag my panties and jeans back over my hips.

His scowl deepens, and I hate the expression claiming his face.

I see pain there. I see regret. A heavy lump forms in my throat. I try to swallow but find that impossible.

"I'm not here to hurt you." He points to the floor, where I lay. "I'm not here for gratuitous, meaningless sex. I'm definitely not here to undermine you or your work." His lips firm into a severe line as he tugs at his ear. "I'm here for us to be an us, but not if this is all you want."

"Wolfe ..." I sit up and draw my knees to my chest, rocking slowly on the floor.

"I'm not done." He cuts off anything I was going to say and continues, his tone turning hard and sharp. "Before this past week, you and I played a game. It was safe and fun. Deliciously dirty. Something special between the two of us. This past week, things changed. We spent time together, working side by side, and got to know each other on a different level. You let me kiss you, but the moment I got under your skin, you pushed me away. Rather than spending the night with me, you chose to spend it with your sisters. Why do you only have sex with strangers? Why are you running from me?" He fastens the buckle of his belt. "I'm going to ask you one more time ..."

No.

I don't want him to ask. I'm not going to answer.

"What are you afraid of?" He gives me a second, but when it's clear I won't be answering, he takes a step back.

"I'm not afraid." I'm terrified, though, and past tears.

I don't do relationships. I never have. I don't know how.

He shakes his head and takes another step from me. A deep breath makes his nostrils flare.

"Don't play games with me. Don't start arguments as an excuse to have angry sex with me. If you want things rough, we can do rough. If you need them soft, we can do that too. What's not going to happen is manipulating me into doing something that's not healthy for either of us. That's the first, and last time, that ever happens." He points to the floor, where he just fucked my brains out, emphasizing the point.

His breaths accelerate, and despite the dim lighting, his eyes narrow as my mouth gapes.

"There's a sofa in the apartment over the carriage house. I'll give you the bed."

"You don't need to do that." I don't understand. My fingers curl in frustration.

"Please try not to wake me when you go to bed." With that, he spins around.

As he opens the door leading into the foyer, he calls out over his shoulder.

"Thanks for the quick fuck." He pivots left and heads down the long hall leading to the kitchen while my heart breaks and tears swim in my vision.

TWENTY-ONE

Jinx

I SINK INTO AN OVERSTUFFED CHAIR IN THE SALON AND CRY. FOR how long is up for debate.

Time slows.

It races by.

I should get up and go to bed, but Wolfe will be there, waiting for me. I blow out a frustrated breath and swipe at my cheeks.

The tears come and go. Right now, they're gone, but heat pricks behind my lids.

Again.

"Well done, Jinx. You turned that into a fucked-up mess."

As I chastise myself for that unnerving exchange with Wolfe, his words settle in, taking up residence in my mind.

I have no reservations about putting myself out there. About fucking without regret. Casual sex is the beginning and end of all the relationships I *never* have.

No need to keep a man around, when I'm going to kick him out in the morning.

No need to exchange names when he'll be a forgotten memory the next day.

No need to allow emotions to cloud what is nothing more than a physical release.

I regret pushing Wolfe the way I did. Using him. Forcing him to take instead of give.

"Let me in." The hoarseness of Wolfe's plea makes me squirm.

"I let you in."

Lie.

My inner voice isn't going to let me get away with that. Working on the cipher and translations with Wolfe is exactly that—work. We still know essentially nothing about each other. Granted, the game of twenty questions shed some light on that. I feel like I know him a little better than before.

So, what's the deal?

That voice in my head needs to shut the fuck up. I want to figure this out, before heading to bed, but it's getting late. Or rather, it's becoming entirely too early. Dawn is not that far away.

What's funny is despite Mitzy's comment about a late start tomorrow, I always wake at the crack of dawn. It's in my nature to rise early. Tonight, I get no sleep. How can I knowing Wolfe is asleep on the couch?

Guilt rolls through me, an uncomfortable squirming mess of regret. I could have shared a bed with him and indulged in more vigorous sex.

But I fucked up.

He relegated himself to the couch, and I stay here where I listen to the clock on the mantle tick down the seconds until dawn. In between are far too many sobbing episodes.

I know why Wolfe did it; took the couch.

The two of us are incapable of sharing a bed without making use of *said* bed for activities other than sleeping. He was pretty damn clear about how things went down.

How I manipulated him.

How I used him.

How I forced him to fuck me.

I wish I could say he's wrong, but Wolfe hit that squarely on the head.

"Fuck!" I shout into the darkness, pissed at myself for making things weird between us.

Did I manipulate him?

Yes.

Did I use him?

Yes.

Do I regret it?

Absolutely.

My cheeks puff as I blow out a long, slow breath.

As for the sex, even though I pushed him to be rougher than he may have liked, it was pretty damn epic. His aggression and power sent me to a different place. A good place. An unexpected place.

Considering I have some experience when it comes to men, none of them performed at the level Wolfe did. He put his whole soul into fusing our bodies into one.

I can't even explain it to myself. Domination during sex is not my go-to thing. Like I've said a thousand times, sex is an itch I like to scratch. But Wolfe didn't simply have sex with me. We transcended base physical needs. He not only opened a door I didn't know was there, he carried me through it.

Then, he closed it.

He's right about one thing. I need to get into a better headspace with him. I need rough and angry sex with him because I'm not ready to handle intimacy.

I don't trust something like that.

Some might say that's lingering tragedy from being abandoned as a baby, but I challenge that assumption. My parents are the only parents I've ever known. They showered me with love and affection as a child. They still check in with me. I know what it means to be loved.

For some reason, I'm the problem. The moment a guy gets close, I walk away.

What I do, and how I act, makes sex impersonal. Or so I'd like to think.

Wolfe wants to know what I'm afraid of.

I'm afraid of taking the next step with him.

There, I admit it. That's the long, the short, the beginning, and the end. I'm a goddamn fucking chicken.

I should stand and do the chicken dance to make it official. What would Wolfe think if he saw me doing that?

A grin settles on my face. It would be pretty hysterical, but I'm not sure he's going to let me get away with a simple chicken dance. He's going to pry and ask, demanding answers to why I did what I did. He'll dig in deep, getting to the root of the matter, while I squirm beneath the interrogation.

This is a real problem for me.

I've never been in a relationship. I don't know how one works. I don't know how to act as one part of a couple. I find it intimidating and frightening. The whole idea of being with someone terrifies me.

I've always been just a *Me*.

Never part of an *Us*.

"Shit, what have I done?" I palm my face and slowly drag my hand down until I cover my mouth. Now, I have to apologize for acting like a total ass.

I'm not good with apologies either.

I'm not sure how long I sit in the salon. It was well past midnight when Wolfe fucked me. It's damn well past O-dark-thirty by now.

The entire house went to bed hours ago, yet I continue to sit in the salon. Despite the hour, moonlight spills through the massive windows and bathes the room in an otherworldly glow. If I sit by the window, there's enough light to read by but still dark enough to hide in.

There's barely enough light to make me feel a little less alone as I wallow in regret and my poor decisions. It's getting late enough that if I don't go to bed soon, the sun will rise and any chance for sleep will be gone. But I can't seem to muster up the energy to go to bed.

What do I want with Wolfe?

I can say, with absolute assurance, I'm not looking for casual sex —correction—I'm no longer looking for casual sex with him. That boat left a long time ago.

I lean back in the large, overstuffed chair, letting it swallow me whole, as I debate getting my ass up and to bed.

Five more minutes, and I will.

Fifteen minutes later, I move from that chair to one across the room next to the window where I can read by moonlight.

The salon is an interesting room. A place where the gentlemen retired after dinner for scotch and smoking cigars, it's lined with bookcases and some incredible finds. I keep my hands off the books that look old, not wanting to harm them, but grab classics like the Great Gatsby that everyone talks about, but I haven't read.

I'm at the end of the first chapter when motion in the grand foyer grabs my attention. Closing the book, I figure it's one of the techies. A cool group of people that I'm now a part of, they—or we —tend to be segregated into two camps. There are the midnight warriors and the early risers. The Guardians seem to have only one camp. They all get up at the ass-crack of dawn for early PT. They only sleep when the mission's done.

Now that I'm part of the technical team, Wolfe pokes fun at the rivalry between the two groups. There's something to be said there, but when the rubber meets the road, techies and Guardians have a healthy respect for one another.

I shift in my seat, and the person gasps.

"Hello?" The vaguely familiar voice calls out into the darkness. "Who's there?" The timid voice calls out again.

"It's Jinx."

"Oh, thank goodness." The slender figure enters the salon. "It's so dark in here."

"I guess I didn't notice." I peer through the dim light trying to figure out who I'm talking to. Fortunately, she approaches, and I match the voice with a face. "Hi, Eve."

"Hi." She gives a little finger wave in greeting. "Are you unable to sleep as well?"

"More like never went to bed."

"Why?"

"I was thinking about stuff." Stuff I don't want to think about. I turn my attention back to Eve, curious. "Why can't you sleep?"

"I haven't been here since—well, since before my …"

"Abduction?"

I know Eve's story, but I've never had a chance to sit down and talk to her about it. What she went through is unimaginable. What she had to do to survive is compelling. I'd like to think I would stand up for myself with the same grit and determination she demonstrated if something similar ever happened to me.

"Yeah."

This is the perfect opportunity to talk to her about her father and my plans.

"It must be hard for you."

"Well, this will be the first time I see my father since it happened. Well, if I see him. After everything everyone's saying, I don't know if I want to. I know Max doesn't want me to."

"But you're here. I suppose that means you want to."

"I don't know. I do, and I don't. A part of me wants to never see or speak to him again. Another part needs to know why he did what he did. I feel like I need to hear him tell me to my face."

"I can't begin to imagine what you must be going through." I pat the cushion of the couch beside me. "Want to talk about it?"

"Thanks." She crosses the threshold of the salon and, instead of sitting beside me, she wanders around the grand room. "Do you mind if I turn on one of the lights?"

"I guess I just got used to the darkness."

"Oh, I don't want to blind you."

"Turn that one on." I point to one of the lamps on a corner table. "It's not that bright."

She turns the light on and a soft glow fills that corner of the room. I close the Great Gatsby and set it to the side.

"If you need an ear, I'm already up."

"Max says you're going to talk to my dad tomorrow."

"Technically, tomorrow is already today." I'm not wearing a watch. "Any idea what time it is?"

"The clock in our room said a quarter to four."

"Wow." Have I really been stewing here for that long?

Granted, most of the house already went to sleep way before

Wolfe and I had sex, but I didn't realize I wasted that much time. Tomorrow is going to hurt if I don't get some kind of sleep.

"I want to see him, but I'm nervous. I figured I'd come to NOLA with the Guardians and see if I felt any different being in the same town." Eve finally wanders over and sits beside me.

She draws her feet up on the couch and hugs her knees, then stares at me for a moment. She's working up to talking to me, but since she's not ready, I wait her out.

Eventually, she'll get comfortable and work up the nerve to ask whatever's on her mind. With my silence either urging her on, or making her uncomfortable, Eve props her chin on her knees and blows out a breath.

"What can I do to help?" I throw her a bone, interested to see what she says.

"Max says you're going to talk to my dad?"

Me talking to her dad is no secret, although she phrases her words as a question.

"I am." My answer is short because I want her to steer this conversation. Not me.

"He says my dad isn't giving the Guardians the answers they need."

"That's my understanding." Again, I tender another short reply.

There's some kind of rift between Eve and her father, but I don't know if it's run-of-the-mill, parent-child, acting-out drama, or if there's an inciting event. That matters in how I handle my side of things.

Getting Deverough to tell me what I want hinges on the relationship between father and daughter. My gut tells me Deverough loves his daughter. He'll do anything to see her again.

He paid the escalating ransom demands, expecting Eve would be returned to him at the end. When that didn't happen, he made a bold move by involving the Guardians. That speaks volumes about where his loyalties lie. He's willing to put his daughter at risk—up to a point. He was willing to fight to get her back.

That line in the sand is something I intend to discover. Once I've done that, I'll use it to get him to tell me what I need to know.

"You think he'll talk to you?" She peers up at me, oddly hopeful.

That's not the expression I expect. I expect her to be more reticent. Time to explain my plan.

"I think he'll talk to you."

"Me?"

"Well, that's what I hope. I was going to talk to you about it in the morning, to be honest."

I haven't had a chance to bring Eve in on what I have planned, but I don't consider that an issue. All I need from Eve are her honest reactions. In this case, too much pre-planning is counterproductive.

"I don't know what I'm going to say when I see him." She blows out another breath and tugs her knees tight to her chest. "Part of me doesn't believe he did what they say he did. Another part of me does. We aren't exactly close."

"I'm sorry to hear that."

The rift between Eve and her father is well known, and if I'm to believe the commonly accepted train of events, Eve rebelled against her father's wishes and went to Cancun for spring break. While there, she was kidnapped.

It was either an unrelated event, or a well-planned kidnapping with the express purpose of moving over thirty million in cash. That's the value of the kidnapping policy Deverough took out on his daughter and then paid to Tomas Benefield.

"What do you need me to do?" She plays with her hair, twining a strand around her finger. Eve's on board, which makes the rest of this easier.

"Just be yourself."

"I don't understand."

"I plan on seeing what your father is willing to tell me on his own. With my DEA background, I can approach him from that angle rather than the one the Guardians are pursuing."

Deverough isn't talking about human sex trafficking. He's too terrified, but I believe I can get him to talk about the illegal transport of narcotics.

"You said you're not looking at it from the same angle as the Guardians. What does that mean?"

"Drugs." I thought the DEA reference was self-explanatory, but I guess not. "I'm going to approach him as a DEA agent. If I can get him to spill about the illegal transport of narcotics into the country, then the rest will be easier."

A frown fills her face. "I just can't believe the man I grew up with would be into stuff like that."

"Don't judge too quickly."

"Everyone else has."

"True. I believe we never know anyone's true motives, but by not cooperating, he's not doing himself any favors. What that tells me is whoever is behind the sex trafficking is holding something over his head."

"You mean me."

"While Benefield was alive, most definitely, but now that he's dead, and you're safe, everything shifted. I'm positive your father is working for a new boss. I don't need him to divulge anything about sex trafficking. What I need is for the threat of DEA involvement, such as seizures of his holdings, to get him to give me something, anything really, that I can follow. It always comes down to following the money."

"Following the money?"

"The money always tells a story, but with your dad, we're missing key information."

"And you think I can help?"

"If you're willing." This is the sketchy part, but there's no other alternative. I need her to make this work.

"When Max told me the Guardians were coming here, I needed to come. Max isn't happy about that. He says he can't keep me safe, and concentrate on work, but I want to look my father in the eye and have him tell me why he did what he did to me."

"I get that, but don't be too hard on him."

"Why not?"

"I'm not convinced he wasn't coerced."

"Really?"

"Are you familiar with the Rossi's?"

"I don't know who that is."

"They." When she continues to give me a blank stare, I elaborate. "The Rossi's are a crime family from Chicago. Think mafia."

"And they're involved in sex trafficking?"

"That and the importation and sale of illegal narcotics. I'm thinking that's where the connection comes in."

"If you say so." She doesn't look convinced.

I don't go into what I really think happened. I'm positive Carson Deverough inherited his father's debt with the Rossi's. Like they do every day, they took a good man and used him to further their interests.

"After I talk to your dad, if I'm not feeling like he's cooperating, I want to use you as leverage."

"Use me? How?"

"By offering up a meeting. Do you think you're ready to face him?"

"Not alone. And most definitely not with Max around. Every time my father's name is mentioned around him, he acts like he wants to kill him. I want to see my father. I need to hear what he has to say. If he put me in danger because of a drug deal, or if he's involved in trafficking women, I want to know."

"He may never confess to any of that."

"Perhaps, but at least I'll be able to look him in the eye. I'll know the truth."

And that's exactly what I'm hoping for. Eve's gut reaction to what her father has to say might be the key to figuring everything out.

"Sorry I didn't talk to you before about this. I plan on talking to him tomorrow and then offering up a conversation with you the day after."

"Technically, tomorrow is today." Eve throws my words right back at me with a wink.

I have a feeling we're going to become really good friends.

"So true." I stretch my arms overhead and stifle a yawn. "What do you say to some coffee and beignets?"

While I'm going to regret pulling an all-nighter before

interviewing Deverough, I've done it before. All I need is a stiff cup of coffee, or two or three, and the high that comes with the sugar rush of NOLA's best beignets.

"That sounds amazing." Eve glances at the foyer. "Should I tell Max?"

"Only if you want him to stop you."

"You know what?" Eve nibbles at her lower lip and takes in a deep breath.

"What?"

"I'm never going to have the kind of conversation with my dad I want if Max is around. If we slip out, no one will know until it's too late."

"Girl, I like your style. There's only one problem with that plan."

"What's that?"

"Uber doesn't come out here this late at night, or this early in the morning, and I don't have wheels."

"Well, I do."

"You do?"

"Heck ya. The last thing I want is to be stuck in a belle mansion with nothing to do all day long. Meeting with my dad is only one reason I came back. Granted, it's a big reason, but there are things I want to do."

"And you have a car?"

"I do."

"Girl, what are we waiting for? I need beignets and coffee stat."

"Let me grab my purse. Don't go anywhere."

Oh, there's no problem with me going anywhere. Putting a bit of distance between me and Wolfe is a good thing.

Not to mention, I don't want him tagging along. For that matter, I hope Eve is able to grab her purse without waking Max. If Max wakes, Alpha team will be all over us, protecting their women.

Mitzy wants Wolfe to come as protection for Eve, but I'm not anticipating any problems.

Deverough and I are going to have a nice, civilized chat. If he gives me what I want, I'll give him a conversation with his daughter.

But Eve and I need backup. Fortunately, I have Lily and our old team at the DEA.

While waiting for Eve to return, I send a few texts.

Like I told Wolfe, the money always tells a story. If I can get Deverough to cooperate with the promise of DEA protection—something I need to secure—getting the rest out of him isn't going to be hard.

It's going to be easy-peasy, like a walk in the park.

TWENTY-TWO

Wolfe

OUT THE BACK DOOR AND ACROSS THE DRIVE, I CLIMBED THE STAIRS
to the small apartment over the carriage house after fucking Jinx.
Once inside, I kicked off my boots, stripped out of my pants, and
grabbed a blanket and pillow off the bed.

The floor rattled as I stomped over to the couch. It's a foot too
short, or I'm a foot too long, but damn if I didn't cram myself in it.
With irritation surging in my veins, I punched the pillow and
covered myself with the blanket while waiting for sleep to overcome
me.

I stayed up, thinking about what happened with Jinx. That
wasn't how I envisioned our first time together. As an expert in
casual hookups, I know the drill forward and backward.

Find a chick. Talk her up. Fuck her. Leave her. Rinse and repeat.

With Jinx, I want more, but she doesn't.

She fabricated an argument and held me at arm's length while
forcing me to use her. Anger vibrates within me, thinking about it.
I'm ashamed by how that went down.

Granted, she didn't tell me to stop. She never said no. I gave her
multiple opportunities to call a stop. When I asked if she was on the

pill, I hoped she would say no. It was her last out. I wasn't packing condoms. I would've stopped.

But she said yes.

She wanted what happened, as rough as it was, but she wanted distant and emotionally disconnected as well. What she didn't want was a connection to me. With those troubled thoughts flowing through my mind, I tossed and turned until finally, thankfully, I drifted off to sleep.

I don't know if Jinx ever went to bed. What I do know are two important things. First, whoever the hell is pounding on the front door is courting death. Second, when I drag my sorry ass off the couch, the bed shows no signs of anyone sleeping in it.

Where the fuck is Jinx?

"Goddamn it, Wolfe, open the fuck up." My teammate, Liam, shouts at me from behind the door.

"Hold your goddamn horses."

Clearly, Jinx is not here, but that doesn't stop me from making a cursory pass of the small apartment. I check in the bathroom. I open the closet doors. As if she would be hiding in a closet. Fuck me if this isn't where my head is at. What the fuck am I doing looking for a chick in a closet?

I scrub my face with my palm. Is this how far I've fallen?

No denying the truth.

There's no sign of Jinx.

I hate to say it, but that was always a possibility. Maybe she felt bad about the angry-hate-sex and couldn't bring herself to sleep in the same room with me? Maybe she called a car and joined Lily and Callie in the French Quarter after all? Maybe she found somewhere else to crash?

Whatever she did, she's not with me.

That fucking pisses me off.

I head to the door and yank it open with a scowl firmly fixed on my face.

"What?" I bark at Liam and block the door.

I'm not up for a social call, especially at whatever fucking hour this is. A peek over his shoulder reveals a twilight-colored sky. Since

I saw the sun go down, I can only surmise this is the ass-crack of dawn.

"Good morning to you too, sunshine." Liam shoves past my blockade and saunters into my room like he owns the place. He tosses my pillow and blanket off the couch and glances in the bedroom and the bed no one slept in. "This is a story." He leans back with a smug smirk on his face.

"Fuck off."

"No fucking way. What happened? The bed's pristine and you slept on the couch." He gestures toward my pillow and blanket.

"And?" No way am I spilling to Liam.

"Where is she?" Bastard has to push. That's Liam, always shoving his nose where it doesn't belong.

I'm not in a good place to go down this path. Time to redirect.

"Why are you here?"

"To get your sorry ass out of bed, obviously." He looks at me with an innocent expression, only there's nothing innocent about it. Liam knows Jinx is supposed to be here. He also now knows she did not spend the night with me. His curiosity is not appreciated. "You need to get dressed, pronto."

"Why?"

"Emergency meeting."

"Mitzy said we were meeting at ten." I remember exactly what Mitzy said. No early morning meeting.

"Like I said, emergency meeting." He glances around the small apartment. "You going to tell me where she is? Or are we going to ignore the fact that bed hasn't been slept in and you slept on the couch?"

"Fuck if I know." I sniff my pits, making a snap decision about a shower, and stomp over to the bathroom. "Do I have time for a shower?"

"Make it Navy short." Liam plops down on my couch, looking all the world like he owns it. Navy short refers to the super short showers we were allowed while in the Navy.

Not a problem.

I turn on the shower, strip, hop in, suds up, and rinse all before the water gets warm. I'm in and out in less than three minutes. Two minutes later, I'm dressed and lacing my boots.

"Let's go." Striding past him, I'm out the door and headed down the stairs before he can get off my couch and follow me.

He catches up by the time I make it to the kitchen door. Nerves riot through me because I don't know if Jinx will be in there.

Do I act like nothing happened? Like I didn't fuck her and walk away? Or do I cozy up beside her, taking her hand in mine like we're a goddamn happy couple?

Fuck this shit.

I run my fingers through my hair, pissed at Jinx for making things weird.

Liam's on my heels as I move into the dining room.

Like most of the surviving southern plantation homes, Rose Manor was built ostentatiously to impress all those who entered. The dining room holds a table built to seat two dozen comfortably. Guardian HRS has the entire team, nearly thirty of us, gathered in the room, and there's still space left over.

A large monitor sits at the far end of the room. Six photos are displayed. I don't know the girls by sight, but I recognize their names: Rose Hunt, Julie Gant, Lori Black, Sybil Niles, Gigi Malone, and Myra Goldstein.

Most of Alpha team is present, but Max and Knox are notably absent. I join Axel and Griff, who stand to the side. They're doing a so-so job of holding up the wall, so I go to help them out. It seems like a safe place to be. Both of them stare at the chaos of our technical team, who swarms the other side of the dining room.

"What the fuck is happening?" I keep my voice low.

"Don't know." Griff shrugs. "Haven't started yet. Although, I'm thinking it has to do with them." He points toward the photos of six young women.

Doesn't take a rocket scientist to figure that out.

An unsettled feeling swims in my gut. The need to do something is nearly overwhelming and this standing around is for the birds. The spot between my shoulder blades itches like a motherfucker.

Griff gives Liam a once over, then turns his attention to me. "Do you know where Jinx is?"

"Fuck if I know."

I thought she might be here. Evidently, I'm wrong. Seems I'm wrong about a lot of things.

"I have a feeling this will, in part, be about her." Griff gives a snort and leans his head against the wall. He looks up at the ceiling, tuning out our tech colleagues, who scurry about setting up monitors and other devices.

"Really? Why would you say that?"

What does he know about Jinx that I don't?

"Not just Jinx." Axel kicks off the wall and shifts to stand beside Griff. The four of us form a mini-circle, heads tucked close. "Eve's missing too."

"What?" An unsettled feeling overcomes me.

Missing?

"What do you mean Eve's missing too?" Liam closes in, bumping shoulders with me. "Is that why Max isn't here?" Come to think of it, Knox is MIA as well.

They aren't the only ones not in attendance. All the higher-ups are missing. Forest, Sam, CJ, and Mitzy are notably absent. For an emergency meeting, why aren't they here?

"I don't know about Eve, but Lily went to the French Quarter to see Callie. I'm sure she was planning on spending the night. Don't see why that would bother Knox." I scratch my head trying to figure out what's going on.

"Heard Jinx didn't go." Axel looks at me. "Heard she came back."

How did he hear that? The only one who knew Jinx was here last night is Mitzy.

"She went and came back." Liam answers for me, filling in the blanks.

I see mischief scrawled all over his face, and I'm not having any of it. I'm not in the mood for any of his comments, especially if they have anything to do with Jinx.

"Don't." I practically growl at Liam and shove him back a step.

"Jinx came back?" Axel tugs on his ear. "This doesn't make sense."

"Why wouldn't it?" I struggle to make sense of what's happening.

"If Jinx came back, why isn't she here?" Axel glances around the dining room, as if doing that for a third, fourth, and fifth time will magically make Jinx appear.

Now, if that isn't a loaded question. I'm not one to fuck and tell, but my team needs to know what happened. They'll rib me about it in private but will keep it under wraps in public. They'll never breathe a word of it where Jinx can hear. I rub at the back of my neck, deciding how much to tell them.

"By itself, Jinx being gone doesn't trouble me." I lower my voice and lean in. Axel, Griff, and Liam tuck in close. "Not after the way we left things last night."

"What happened?" Axel glances over my shoulder, looking for anyone standing too close. He gets this is an Alpha team need-to-know conversation.

"I'm not sure." I feel like an idiot admitting this, but it's easiest to just spit it out and move on. "We fucked."

"About damn time." Liam blows out a breath and holds out a hand. "I believe I win."

"You fuckers bet on it?" I look at them and make a show of rolling my eyes.

Of course, they bet on it. That's what Alpha team does. We bet on anything and everything.

"Damn straight we did." Liam holds his palm out and flicks his fingers while Griff fishes out four buttons from his jean pocket. The buttons disappear and Liam turns his attention back to me. "So you finally hooked up. How does that explain Jinx not being here? And if you fucked, it wasn't in bed, because no one slept in that."

"Huh?" Griff's brows tuck together.

"Found this idiot camped out on the couch." Liam hooks a thumb in my direction.

"No, you didn't. You pounded on the door, and I answered. I wasn't on the couch."

"Okay, technically that happened, but the blanket and pillow don't lie. Wolfe slept on the couch, and no one slept in the bed." Liam glances over our shoulders, checking out the rest of the room. "Jinx wasn't there."

Other than Alpha team, the rest of those gathered are from the technical team. They hover on one side of the room while we occupy the other side. Guardians and techies rarely intermingle.

"How does this explain where Jinx is? And for that matter, what happened to Eve?" Axel is still trying to figure that out.

"I can take a stab at that." I blow out a breath, not thrilled with admitting any of this. "Shit between me and Jinx was—rough." That's as close to the truth as I'll get with the guys. "I don't know if she's angry about what happened or not."

"What the fuck does that mean? You didn't ..." Griff puffs out his chest and gives me a look like he's about to rip off my head. "What reason would she have to be angry? You didn't force ..." Griff's muscles flex, getting ready to pound me to the ground.

"Shit, it was nothing like that." I pause, thinking it kind of was exactly like that. As for knock-out, drag-out fights, Jinx and I are known for our explosive arguments. The whole team has been witness to most of them. "Honestly, I don't know what the fuck happened. I don't know if she's angry with me or if I left her on Cloud Nine."

"Oh, one of your Wolfe specials?" Liam's humor keeps things light. He jabs his elbow into my gut, ribbing me.

I appreciate Liam stepping in. He takes away the edge of what I said, giving me a chance to defend myself and explain what happened.

Griff's all for having fun, but he won't stand for anyone using, or abusing, a woman.

I'm still not sure which of those I did. Did I use Jinx? Did I cross the line and abuse her? Or did she use me?

The sex was rough, but I asked. I gave her several chances to tell me to go to hell. I gave her what she needed in the moment. But I did use force to take her.

Technically, I did, but she consented.

Fuck if I know what happened.

Does she regret what we did?

Is that why she never came to bed? Even to sleep in the bed without me while I camped out on the couch? My whole body aches from that small assed couch.

Fuck, I don't do relationships precisely because of this shit. They become twisted and complicated too easily. But damn if I don't want complicated with Jinx.

My nerves fire more and more as the seconds pass. I shouldn't have had sex with her last night. She wasn't in the right frame of mind. I should've backed off and approached her later when we both had time to cool off.

Shit.

Where is she?

Is she safe?

My gut clenches with fear for her safety. If anything happens to Jinx, I'll never forgive myself. If she ran after what happened in the salon, and that put her into a dangerous scenario, simply thinking about it makes me want to puke.

My thoughts spin in a downward spiral, growing more macabre with each passing moment. Jinx can take care of herself. I know this, but damn if I don't want to be by her side. A team of two is far better than a team of one.

How many times has that been drilled into my head?

The one thing we all learn during BUDS is no matter how strong you are, eventually, everyone needs someone to lean on.

We all need a buddy watching our six.

I want to be that for Jinx.

As for what's happening right now?

Why have we been called to an emergency meeting? Where are our leads? The absence of Sam, CJ, and Mitzy says they've got their heads together dealing with a crisis.

We're gathered to get our marching orders once they figure out our course of action. The longer we wait for them to appear, the more nervous I become.

And where the fuck are Max and Knox? Why aren't they here?

Because Eve and Lily are missing along with Jinx, asshole. Put one and two together.

Fuck that inner voice. It's annoying as hell.

Back to Jinx, and what I may, or may not, have done. I remain confused. If there's one thing I'm good at, it's pleasing a woman. I'm the one who taught Knox all about the multiple-O. I didn't get to do that with Jinx, but I will if she ever gives me the opportunity.

Fuck.

The best fucking word on the planet.

Fuck. Fuck. Fuck. Fuck.

This is all fucked up. Griff stares at me, waiting for me to absolve him of responsibility. Otherwise, he'll pound me to the ground for taking advantage of a woman.

"I didn't force her. Jinx enjoyed herself, it was just—rough."

"Rough?" Liam's brow wings up, concerned. He knows me the best out of the rest of the team. The subtext is not lost of him.

"Rougher than I'd like."

"So, what's the hang-up?" Griff's not relinquishing his role as protector.

"It's more the way I left her." My gut wants me to look away, stare at my feet and hide, but fuck that shit. I look Griff straight in the eye, owning what happened.

"What do you mean by left her?" Axel looks confused.

"Meaning I literally left her on the floor."

"You had sex and then ditched?" Griff shakes his head. "Bro, that's uncool."

"That's not what happened." I continue to defend myself.

"Okay, then what exactly happened? How did you leave her? And why were you sleeping on the couch?"

"That's complicated and remains between me and her. All I know is she never made it to the room."

"Wait a second." Liam takes a step back. "You left her? Left her where? Where exactly did you fuck her?" He looks at the long table and points at it. Then he mouths silently, *"In here?"*

"No. Not here." I slug him in the arm.

"Then where?" Liam continues to push.

"I'm not giving you a play-by-play. Suffice it to say it happened."

There's zero chance Liam will let that go. He will right now, but the bastard will bring it up later.

"It's more the way I walked out at the end of it."

Thinking back, I should've hung around. Walking out could've pissed her off and kept her from joining me at the carriage house.

In my defense, I figured she might have gone to Mitzy and bunked with her. That doesn't explain Eve's disappearance, although I have an idea about that. Jinx made it exceptionally clear what she thought about Mitzy assigning me to oversee her interrogation of Deverough.

Which is precisely where Jinx and Eve will be. Lily too. She and Jinx are thick as thieves. Not to mention, they've worked together before in the DEA.

I knock the back of my skull against the wall and close my eyes while I slowly count to ten. Once done, I look at my team.

If I know my girl, and I think I do, we're going to find Lily in the middle of it too.

Jinx and Lily can take care of themselves. I don't know Eve that well, except she has no formal training other than what Max might be teaching her. The idea of the three of them confronting Deverough, without a team of Guardians backing them up, sits like a cold, hard lump in my gut.

We still don't know where Deverough stands. Is he dirty? Or simply a victim of circumstance? Either way, it makes my gut churn.

I turn my attention to the screen at the far end of the dining hall with its six photographs.

"What's up with that?"

"That is our current objective." The low rolling thunder of Forest Summers's voice brings the entire room to a standstill.

He enters the room with Sam, CJ, and Mitzy in tow. Standing behind them are the two missing members of our team. Max glances over at the four of us, and his gaze pegs on me. His eyes narrow, and his jaw bunches. I don't know what the fuck he's pissed about, but I have nothing to do with it.

"What the fuck does that mean?" It's unusual for me to step out of place, but I'm not happy with the vibe Max and Knox throw in my direction. I'm feeling all kinds of out of sorts right now. Like I'm missing pertinent information.

"We lost them." Sam addresses the room. "Finding, and rescuing, these women are priority number one."

Mitzy located all the women on that list yesterday. How can they be lost?

I exchange a look with Liam and ask the question on everyone's mind. "What the fuck does that mean?"

TWENTY-THREE

Jinx

After making a quick call to my old boss, Eve and I hook up with Lily and Callie for beignets and coffee. With my lack of sleep, I down three cups and would go for a fourth if not for exceeding the capacity of my bladder.

We drop Callie off back at her bar, then meet up with Harry Sheldon and what remains of our old team. Our team was massacred down at the docks. Only three of us survived. Lucas and Mateo are recovering from their injuries and aren't yet back on active service. We were there to stop a shipment of drugs entering the country. What we found was a shipment of young women slated for the slave trade. That was the first time we ran into the organization that is Guardian HRS.

Harry is itching for revenge against the Rossi family, who we now know were involved in both the drug shipment and the kidnapping of a dozen women.

"How are the Guardians treating the two of you?" Our old boss hugs us both, then proffers his hand to Eve. "Nice to make your acquaintance, Miss Deverough. Have Jinx and Lily briefed you on what we plan?"

"Yes and no." I step in and answer because Eve shows all the signs of being overwhelmed.

I need her to do her part, which is simple really. All she needs to do is wait in the wings. If Deverough gives me what I want, then we, meaning Lily and Harry, coordinate a meeting someplace public with Eve and her father.

"I wasn't sure what you might be able to do for Deverough, and I didn't want to promise Eve something I couldn't deliver."

There's no helping it. The DEA sings in my blood. Now that I'm back on my home turf, it's kind of weird being back. My gut says I still work for Harry. My head says the Guardians are my new home.

It's a bit off-putting, to be honest.

"Full witness protection, providing he agrees to testify in court, and only if he has actionable information that leads to an arrest." Harry states it in terms that are easy to digest. There's a whole lot more involved than that, but we'll get to that later.

"What does full protection mean?" Eve places a shaky hand on my arm. "If he does that, won't that …" She chokes up but manages to find her voice after a ragged inhale. "Won't he be a target?"

"I'm not going to lie, Miss Deverough, anyone who becomes an informant for the DEA, especially when it involves a major player like the Rossi's, incurs a certain risk. A risk we mitigate by placing them in witness protection. I'm glad you're here. We have a moment to explain what that might look like, but if he gives Jinx what she needs, what we all need, and agrees to meet with you, it's likely it'll be the last time you see your father."

"I won't be able to see him?" Eve gasps and takes a step back. It's an unconscious reaction but telling. "The last time?"

I should've prepared her for this possibility, but I didn't want to speak about something that might not happen.

"Sadly, no. Or at least, not until the trial, and even then, it's safest for our informants to continue leading their new lives with their new identities. Those who want to harm him, looking for payback, will be looking at all his close contacts to find him."

"And this is the only way?" Eve steadies her breath. Yet again, showing her strength. She doesn't like what might happen, but she's going to deal with it.

"It is." Harry takes in a deep breath. "I wanted to prepare you. There's a very good chance you'll be saying goodbye to your father."

"For how long?"

"Forever, love."

Eve's face pales, and she blinks in disbelief. I give her props. She doesn't argue, complain, or beg. The news hits her hard. She reacts. Then she moves on.

I shouldn't be surprised, especially considering what she went through to survive her kidnapping. The girl has a major pair of balls, that's for sure.

It also helps to have Harry here to walk Eve through it. I love how he speaks to the families of those who help us. He's got a nice, easy cadence to his voice. It's soothing and gives a sense that everything will be all right.

He never lies. He doesn't sugarcoat. What he does is deliver bad news in the best way possible.

Eve has the next couple of hours to contemplate what may be her very last words to her father.

After talking to Eve, Harry turns his attention back to me.

"Now, tell me your plan."

For the next thirty minutes, I explain my thoughts and how I intend to direct my questions. Harry offers a few pointers. We go through everything one last time.

Lily sits with Eve, hugging her while Harry and I hammer out last-minute details. The paper napkin Harry gave Eve with her cup of coffee is a shredded mess by the time we're done talking, and the sun is barely above the horizon.

Harry asks why I don't want to wait. I tell him about the Guardians wanting to run shotgun on my operation. That's all I need to say. Harry understands.

Time is of the essence. Once my absence is noticed, Eve's as well, there's no doubt the Guardians of Alpha team will come looking.

A few minutes later, I stand at the base of Deverough's building, a glass and metal structure standing alongside some of New Orleans' most historic buildings. It's an odd contrast of old and new, but that's what New Orleans is famous for.

I've been here once before. It was the night Lily was taken.

They took her from Callie's bar, tying her and Callie to chairs. I barely got there in time to save Callie. I almost saved Lily but wasn't fast enough. The rest of that night is still a blur.

Alpha team arrived en-mass, with CJ and Max in tow. Somehow, they tracked the men who took Lily using traffic cams. I strong-armed my way into going with them. It was the first time I threw Wolfe to the floor. We came to this building to catch a helicopter to the *USS Charles Sexton* and eventually rescued Lily.

Harry and I debate whether I do this alone or with a couple of DEA agents backing me up. In the end, we opt for just me.

As I walk through the revolving glass doors, the immensity of the foyer gives me pause. The ceiling soars upward several stories, turning the foyer into a galleria. Light, soothing jazz music pipes in from hidden speakers. The sultry sound combines with the soft rushing of water from not one but three waterfalls.

Without breaking a stride, I march up to the receptionist. This is my first hurdle and the easiest. The receptionist greets me with a smile.

"Welcome, how may I help you?" Her cheery disposition is a facade.

Her entire purpose is to act as gatekeeper, keeping people like me out. Her presence also tells me what we already know.

Deverough is in his office.

He's been under DEA surveillance since the day the Guardians blew into our lives. They ruined that narcotics case we were working, an event that resulted in an ambush and the murder of most of our team. It was a bad day for the DEA, but the Guardians saved a dozen girls in the process, girls whose names are imprinted in my mind after decoding Benefield's ledger.

"I'm here to see Carson Deverough." I flash her a bright smile.

She pretends to look at her computer screen, but this girl knows I have no business being here at this hour asking to see Carson Deverough. Regardless, we're going to play this game.

"I'm sorry, but he's not in his office." She glances up at me and gives an apologetic smile.

This is when I'm supposed to turn around and leave in defeat. Only, that's not happening.

"He's in his office, and he's going to want to see me."

"I'm sorry, but without an appointment, I can't let you up." I get another look, but she gives in too easily. She also confirms what I already know. Deverough is, in fact, in his office.

"You might want to call and tell him I'm here." I place my hand on the counter and drum my fingers on the expensive marble.

"I'm sorry, but I can't do that." She firms her voice, but the girl's got nothing on me.

I point to the phone. "Call him."

"Miss …" Her finger goes to the silent buzzer that alerts security.

"It's about his daughter."

It's a bit of a stretch assuming she knows anything about Deverough's daughter, but the kidnapping of the shipping mogul's daughter made national news.

Instead of responding, her attention flicks to her computer screen. Her eyes widen as she reads what's on the screen, then she looks back at me. "Mr. Deverough will see you, Miss …"

"Thank you." I don't give her my name. We no longer need to exchange pleasantries.

I do find it curious, although I'm not surprised, that Deverough pays attention to who asks to see him. The receptionist escorts me to a bank of elevators, swipes her keycard, and presses the up button.

She waits with me for the elevator car to arrive. When the doors open, she leans in and gives another swipe of her card. She pushes the top button, and without another word exchanged, I ride alone to the top of the building.

Carson Deverough meets me at the elevator. "Where's my daughter?"

No preamble. No "Who are you?" He cuts right to the chase. Not that I don't get it.

The last time he saw Eve was prior to her abduction. The only photos he received after that were proof of life photographs Benefield sent prior to each escalating ransom demand. After her rescue, Eve accompanied Max to California, headquarters of Guardian HRS.

I breeze past him without saying a word and walk toward the floor-to-ceiling glass windows overlooking the city of New Orleans. The sun barely crests the horizon. It casts a swath of pastel pinks, yellows, greens, and blues across the sky.

With my feet planted firmly, shoulder-width apart, I clasp my hands behind my back and continue to face away from Deverough.

"Your daughter is well."

"Is she here? Can I speak to her?"

"That depends on how our conversation goes." I spin around and move over to a set of sofas facing each other. Maintaining my view, because, let's face it, New Orleans at sunrise is magnificent to behold, I take a seat.

"What does that mean?" His fingers flutter over the seam of his pants as he closes the distance and sits opposite me.

For a shipping mogul, I expect more resistance from him. The man sitting across from me slumps his shoulders, drags his feet, picks at nonexistent lint on his trousers, and can barely maintain eye contact.

Beyond the outward signs of his discomfort, however, I see the strong and powerful man he once was. He's been stripped of that and reduced to what I see before me now.

"I have a few questions. If you answer to my satisfaction, we'll talk about your daughter."

"I'm not answering any questions, and you can't keep me from Evie."

"I want you to reconsider your decision."

"Who do you work for? Are you with the Guardians? Because I told them all I can."

"The answer to that is yes and no."

"What does that mean?"

"I'm speaking to you today on behalf of the DEA, but I am affiliated with the Guardians."

"The DEA?" His brows knit together.

This is the part where I stretch the truth and embellish the rest. I need him to flip and become a witness. "It's our understanding your father incurred sizable debts when he was alive. Debts owed to the Rossi family that he paid back by agreeing to ship narcotics into the country."

The muscles of Deverough's jaw twitch, and I smile. It's a small tell, but I hit a home run with that assumption. Generally, I don't begin interrogations with assumptions. If wrong, it immediately puts me at a disadvantage. The key to success is to establish power early, display credibility, and tender an appealing solution.

I've got the balance of power down pat.

Deverough is gun shy, probably from the directness of Griff's questioning.

Griff is formidable when he smiles and downright terrifying when questioning prisoners. I haven't seen him in action, but I've heard the stories.

This is where I pivot. I'll use Griff's strong-arm tactics to my advantage, becoming the good cop to Griff's bad cop.

"Before my current job with the Guardians, I worked for the DEA and continue to consult with them on the cases I was actively investigating. I come to you with an offer you need to accept."

"I don't know how I can help you."

"I assume you're aware Benefield is dead?"

Deverough sits on the couch and rocks forward and back. He rubs the palms of his hands over the tops of his knees and down his thighs. It's such a rhythmic motion; I have a feeling he's not aware he does it. I scrutinize everything he does.

Assumptions are never the friend of a field agent and definitely never the friend of an intelligence agent. Sometimes, however, we're forced to make certain assumptions. In this case, my assumption works in my favor.

"I had heard rumors." He sits back in relief.

"I can confirm, without a doubt, that Tomas Benefield was killed during the rescue of your daughter, but the drug shipments continue."

I'm not here to address Deverough's involvement in the transport of women overseas. At least, not if I want to turn him into a DEA informant. The rest of that information will follow with time as Deverough offers it on his own for special consideration.

"He's dead then?"

"Yes, but I'm not here to discuss Tomas Benefield. I'm here to discuss your dealings with the Rossi family."

"Tomas is a Rossi, or was." Deverough gives a shake of his head as Benefield's death settles in. "The narcotics ran through him."

"Narcotics flowed through him to your ships, which brought the product into the country. The women moved the opposite direction."

Deverough hangs his head and stares at his knees for several beats too long. That's the best admission of guilt I'll ever get, but again, that's not why I'm here.

"Mr. Deverough, your daughter remains under the protection of Guardian Hostage Rescue Specialists. Until we confirm her safety is guaranteed, that's where she'll remain."

"I have a right to see my daughter. You can't keep me from her."

"I'm not the one keeping you from your daughter. Eve is not interested in a meeting."

"I don't believe you."

"Well, to be completely honest, she is willing to talk to you, but there's a condition."

"I don't care what that is. I need to see my daughter. I need to know she's okay."

"You left your daughter with a monster for months, Mr. Deverough. I'm certain we can say she will never be okay. That kind of trauma tends to stick with a person for life. Fortunately, Guardian HRS has the facilities, people, and programs to help her heal."

"How is she doing?"

"Like I said, it's a process."

"What do I have to do to see my daughter? Is she here? In New Orleans?"

"I can answer your questions, but first, we need to discuss terms."

"Terms? What does that mean?"

"The DEA is building a case against the Rossi crime family. To make it stick, we need your cooperation."

"How?"

"Your testimony for one thing."

"I'm a dead man if I do that." He shakes his head. "What else?"

"That's the offer."

"You might as well shoot me right now." Deverough crosses his arms and closes me out.

"About that …"

TWENTY-FOUR

Jinx

Deverough is scared. There's no way he'll agree if he thinks his life, or Eve's, will be put at risk. This is where I dig deep and give him the carrot.

"The offer doesn't come without protection." This is where I reel him in.

He already said he's willing to do whatever it takes to see his daughter again.

"There's no way you can protect me."

"Hear me out." I pause, waiting for him to acquiesce. Deverough gives the tiniest of nods.

"The DEA requires your testimony regarding how the Rossi's use your ships to transport narcotics into the country. In return, you'll be placed into witness protection until the trial. At trial, your testimony will be taken remotely. There will be no personal risk on your part."

"And afterward? You don't turn on the Rossi's. Not if you want to live."

"How deep are your dealings with them?"

"What do you mean?"

"How involved are you?"

His response tells me many things. The longer he delays in giving it says much. Deverough is holding back. He'll admit to being strong-armed into moving Rossi narcotics, but he won't admit to the other bit. I almost feel sorry for him, but I play his game.

All I need is for him to flip, and we've got him. Just like the Rossi's placed pressure on him to transport their narcotics, and then coerced him to provide transportation for the women robbed of their freedom, the DEA will do that same.

One step at a time.

"Involved enough to know better than to become an informant to any law enforcement agency."

"We're asking for you to be a witness, not an informant."

"What's the difference?"

"For starters, you probably won't die as a witness."

He asks for the difference because he's trying to reclaim some of the power between us. The man knows the difference between an informant and a witness, he's simply stalling. I glance at my watch and stand.

"My offer is only good for the next ten minutes."

"What?"

"You heard me. The offer is this, you agree to testify against the Rossi family and provide pertinent information to build the case. The DEA will place you in witness protection until the trial, and you will remain in witness protection after the trial concludes. Agree to those terms, and we'll grant you fifteen minutes to say goodbye to your daughter."

"That's outrageous."

"Eight minutes remaining." I glance at my watch, pretending to count the minutes.

There is no time limit, except I'm eager to close the deal before Wolfe realizes I'm gone and sends all of Guardian HRS out looking for me.

I need this to work.

I need the win.

Probably more for myself than to prove anything to Wolfe.

"Mr. Deverough, this is a generous offer, and the moment I walk out, you won't receive another like it. The Rossi's will continue to push you. Eventually, the DEA will build a case around you, and you'll be the one doing jail time. No need for me to elaborate how a man like you will fare in prison."

"When would I see Evie?" His knee bounces, and his shoulders slump. This once proud man looks broken beyond repair.

I give myself a high five because he caved after applying minimal pressure. Not that I deserve all the credit. Griff definitely softened the man before I came along.

"You can see her now. Do I need to explain how this will work?"

"Will I have time to put things in order?"

"You'll meet with your daughter then go immediately into witness protection. As you can imagine, we can't afford any leaks as to where you are or what's happening."

"But my business affairs?"

"You will have a representative selected to operate on your behalf, but you will be literally walking away. Any ties are potential leaks."

"I understand." He draws his hand down his face and cups his jaw. "There's something I need to give Evie." He checks the clock on his desk. "Can I have five minutes?"

"I caution you against sending anything out of this room, electronic or otherwise. There can be nothing to trace your movements."

"It's not a message, but rather files she should have."

I tug on my ear, debating. Nearly every person moved into witness protection has that *one* thing they need to do. It almost always compromises their safety, leaving a trail of breadcrumbs behind them.

"I'll download whatever you need. I can't emphasize enough how important it is that you send no communications at this time."

"Okay." He moves to his desk and opens a drawer. Deverough pulls out a thumb drive and hands it to me. "I'll walk you through it."

I give him more than five minutes. I download innocuous files I'll personally go through, looking for anything suspect. Then I spend another ten minutes getting him ready to meet Eve, going over protocol and what to expect.

"You understand you won't have a private conversation with Eve."

"I understand. I just want to see her one more time. How do you think Evie will take it?"

"She already understands."

"All of it?"

"What she needs to know." I gather up the thumb drive and place it in my back pocket. "Are you ready?"

"No." He gives a defeated shrug. "But I suppose it's time."

I head over to the private elevator and press the button. Deverough stands beside me, hands shoved deep into his pants. He rocks back on his heels and blows out a breath.

"You know, I never thought this would be my life."

"I can imagine."

"I didn't know what my father was doing. After his death, a representative of the Rossi's met with me. He laid everything out then asked for a small favor."

"That's all it takes." It's how the Rossi's dig in their claws.

"I know." He dips his head and stares at the floor. "One favor turned into another. Before I knew it, instead of using my ships to transport narcotics, they were moving women."

"You knew then?"

"Not at first. I tried to keep myself out of it. But, by then, they amassed enough to blackmail me. That was the end of it for me."

"I do believe in second chances, Mr. Deverough. You never really know what the future holds. This, at least, is behind you."

"Not exactly behind, is it? I still have to testify."

"Yes, and agents will be up here momentarily to gather and protect what they can. I have your access keys." I pat my front pocket where a second thumb drive holds all his business passwords.

"And where will we meet Evie?"

"She's with a friend of mine in the French Quarter. Public places are best for this. Lots of eyes."

"I understand."

The elevator opens. We step in. He pushes the button for the lobby.

Once downstairs, he straightens his spine, rolls back his shoulders, and puts a smile on his face. He practically beams at the receptionist as we breeze by her desk.

"I'm out for the morning, Sydney, and not expecting any more visitors. Have a nice day."

"Of course, Mr. Deverough, and you too." Sydney gives me a long look.

I can only imagine what's going through her mind. That's a gossip train that left the building the moment I mentioned my business has to do with Deverough's daughter.

That can work to our advantage.

We're met outside by a black town car. I hold the door while Deverough climbs in. Harry reaches between the seats from the passenger side and extends his hand. "Mr. Deverough, I'm Harry, the lead agent in your case. Has Jinx briefed you on what to expect?"

"She has."

"Do you have any questions?" Harry asks.

"None that matter." Deverough rubs his palms over his knees, moving his hands nervously up and down his thighs. The man's a nervous wreck. Not that I blame him.

During the half-hour drive through traffic, we slowly wind our way toward the French Quarter, where Lily and Callie wait with Eve. I send Lily a text. She'll move Eve to the center square where we've arranged for their meeting to take place.

Deverough leans forward, neck craned as he tries to spot his daughter. We picked their meeting place with great care; something to give them privacy while keeping an eye on them the entire time. As I explained earlier, they won't be left alone. Anything he might say to Eve is something the DEA might need later on.

The moment Deverough spots Eve, his entire body goes stiff. He tugs in a deep breath and pulls on his tie, loosening it. More wiping of the hands on his trousers. The driver pulls to a stop next to the curb. Harry gets out and holds the door for Deverough. I climb out my side and catch Lily's eye.

We debated whether to include Harry but decided it was for the best. His face is recognizable, but then so is mine, and Lily's for that matter.

This isn't our first witness protection induction. We know the drill. I give Lily a sign telling her everything is good to go. Lily nudges Eve, who doesn't notice we've arrived. Eve jumps, then stands beside Lily, who grabs hold of Eve's elbow.

We need them to meet exactly where Lily stands.

Harry and I bracket Deverough, each of us grasping his upper arms. With each step, his anxiety builds. We get to within five feet. Lily releases her hold on Eve. Harry and I let Deverough go.

Lily moves a short distance away, where she's joined by Harry. I glance over my shoulder, checking the area behind me, and move two steps to the left.

Eve and her father don't move for what seems like forever. I'm concerned they're not going to say anything when all of a sudden, Eve launches into her father's arms with a sob. He wraps his arms around her and runs his fingers through her hair.

I take another step back, giving them what little privacy I can. The hug goes on for a while, and I shift forward, intent on breaking them apart, but there's no need. Eve takes her father's hand and leads him back to the bench.

We're surrounded by people. It's officially early morning rather than the ass-crack of dawn, which means the tourists are out in force. Ready to get in the sights before the oppressive heat and humidity chases them back indoors.

With my head on a swivel, I continually scan the crowd, looking for threats. Eve sits with her father. They hold hands. She smiles, and he bows his head. The crowd continues on, oblivious to this last meeting of father and daughter.

It's almost time.

I check in with Harry, who gives a nod. On his signal, I move in.

"Mr. Deverough, it's time to go."

The agony in his expression is something I'll never forget. He leans in, kisses Eve on the side of her cheek, then grips her hands. When he stands, motion in my peripheral vision whips my head around.

A block away, the crowd parts. Smack dab in the middle, six, overly large, overly pissed looking men march toward me.

Shit.

Not now.

"Mr. Deverough." I firm my voice, needing to get him moving. Needing to place enough distance between him and Eve.

He smiles at his daughter, then lets her go.

Deverough pivots.

He takes two steps.

A shot rings out.

The concussive boom sends the crowd scurrying off the street, ducking as they race for cover. Random people in the crowd shout out. Screams from women fill the air. Parents grab children, carrying them in their arms, or dragging them as they run.

"*Shooter!*" Several in the crowd cry out, intensifying the fear.

Wolfe and his team break into a sprint, running toward danger rather than away.

I hold out my hand—as if that can stop the Guardians—while Eve's scream pierces the air. Deverough claps a hand over his chest. Blood seeps through his shirt: a direct hit to his heart. He looks at me as he falls.

"Get down!" Wolfe leaps across the last few feet separating us. Somehow, he manages to un-holster his weapon as he drags me down to the ground. Kneeling over me, he searches for a gunman he'll never find.

"Get off!" I growl at him and push, but he doesn't budge.

Knox goes for Lily, covering her the same way as Wolfe, meaning he pins her to the ground. Like Wolfe, he too sweeps the scene, eyes sighted down the barrel of his weapon, searching. Max runs to Eve, kneeling down beside her as she cries over the crumpled form of her father. Sirens sound in the distance as the last few pedestrians scramble to safety.

We're soon left with just the ten of us. Axel, Griff, and Liam surround us, weapons drawn, heads on a swivel. Knox protects Lily. Wolfe digs his knee into the small of my back, plastering me on the ground. Max holds Eve as she rocks over the still form of her father. The crowd is gone. Two police cars, an ambulance, and two fire trucks pull up right beside us.

The EMT's jump out of the ambulance, unload the stretcher, and go to the still form of Deverough. They do a quick set of vitals, place an IV in his arm, load him on a stretcher, and attach one of those new robotic CPR machines. It starts pumping on his chest as they load him into the back of the ambulance.

Eve's desperate cries ring out as they close the doors on the ambulance and drive away. Harry deals with the cops. No doubt this will make the evening news, as well as getting splattered all over social media. Many of those in the crowd stopped running long enough to get everything on film. No doubt they're editing and uploading as I remain sprawled on the ground.

"For the love of God, get off of me." I smack my fist against Wolfe's leg, then all of a sudden, he lifts me off the ground and sets me not so gently on my feet.

Wolfe drags me to the nearest building and shoves me through the front door. A quick look outside shows Lily and Eve receiving the same bodily treatment. As Knox and Max drag Lily and Eve to safety, Axel, Griff, and Liam hold up the rear. Harry follows beside them but pauses to speak to the police.

The moment Wolfe lets me go, I punch him in the gut.

"Oomph!" He lets out a breath as I rear back to punch again. "I wouldn't do that."

He gives me a look, and I know I've lost my opportunity. He tenses his abs, making them rock hard. The only thing I'll do is hurt myself.

"What the hell are you doing here?" I poke him in the chest, not that it does anything to make him budge.

"I might ask you the same." He towers over me and crowds my space, forcing me back until my heels hit the wall. I glance around his massive form and catch the terrified gazes of those sheltering inside.

I have words for Wolfe, but those will come later.

Harry comes into the building. "Jinx, are you okay?"

"I am." I step around Wolfe, much to his displeasure.

"What happened to Deverough?" Wolfe barges into my case, demanding answers.

"Doesn't look good." Harry gives Wolfe the eye, then turns his attention to me. "Since our witness appears to be deceased, excuse me while I fill out a mile of red tape. Nice to see you again, Jinx. Make sure you follow up with that other matter."

"Absolutely, sir." Can't help it. Harry has been my boss for years. The 'sir' simply rolls off my tongue.

Harry makes his exit, leaving Lily and me to deal with six seething Guardians. Well, five actually. Max holds Eve in his arms as she sobs. He's in comfort mode.

Wolfe gives me the I'm-two-seconds-from-ripping-you-a-new-asshole look. That's followed by thirty minutes of stony silence as the men of Alpha team take the three of us back to Rose Manor.

TWENTY-FIVE

Wolfe

OF ALL THE STUPID ASSHOLE MOVES, I NEVER WOULD'VE PUT JINX IN the role of town idiot.

I shield her with my body while my teammates attempt to locate the shooter, then hustle her inside, under cover.

If I didn't show up when I did, would she still be standing there? It's like she put out a sign calling out *Shoot me next!*

What part of getting to cover in an active shooter real-life scenario does she not understand?

The ride back is made in tense silence. I hold my tongue because the things I want to say to Jinx will ruin any chance we have as a couple.

If we're still a couple.

Max and Knox take the lead car. Eve and Lily join them, which leaves Axel, Griff, and Liam to ride with me and Jinx. My teammates aren't thrilled with squishing together in the back seat, but there's no way I'll maintain my cool if Jinx's hot body is pressed against mine for the drive back to home base.

As soon as the door closes, I lay into Jinx, not giving a fuck my buddies have front and center seats to another one of our arguments.

"What the ever-loving fuck? What the hell got into your brain going off like that?"

"I didn't go off."

"The hell you didn't." I grip the steering wheel tight enough I'm afraid I might rip it off the steering column. "What you did—running off." It's hard to glare at her as I navigate through the congested streets of downtown, but I do my best.

"I didn't run off."

"Then what the fuck are we calling it?"

"You're such an ass."

"And you're such a …"

"Wolfe …" Liam's calm voice calls out from the back seat. He's sandwiched between Axel and Griff. "Maybe you don't complete that sentence. I don't know about Tweedle Dee and Tweedle Dum here, but I'm not ready for World War III."

"No." Jinx twists toward me. "I want to hear what he was going to say."

"No, you don't." Griff shakes his head and stares out the window. "I can say with absolute certainty that nobody in this car wants to hear what he was going to say."

Jinx folds her arms over her chest and gives a derisive snort. "For the record, I didn't run off."

"Really?" I can't believe she lies to my face. "Isn't that what you do? You run?"

"Now wait just one minute. That's not …" Jinx's face turns red as her anger rises.

"Speaking for the peanut gallery here." Axel pipes up. "If y'all are going to rip each other's heads off, I respectfully request you let the three of us out of the car."

"Nobody is ripping anything off anyone." Jinx stares forward, unwilling to look me in the eye. "Wolfe's simply being a Grade-A prime asshole."

"Nice." I can't believe I held back from calling her a bitch.

"Good to know." Liam leans forward, putting his head between our shoulders. "How about the two of you calm the fuck down."

"Fuck you!" Jinx and I say it at the same time.

I can't help the smile tugging at the corner of my mouth as I remember what Jinx said to me earlier when I told her to calm down. *In the history of mankind …*

A glance over at Jinx reveals the same grin filling her face.

And just like that, the tension between us evaporates. A tiny giggle escapes Jinx, and I can't help but laugh. Liam leans back, wedging his broad shoulders between Axel and Griff.

"And that's how it's done." He puts his hands out, palms up. "Pay up."

Both Axel and Griff fish out a raggedy button each and plop it into Liam's palms.

"You bet on that?" I glance in the rearview mirror and catch Liam's eye.

"I bet that I could break up your argument, and I did."

"Ass—"

"—Hole." Jinx finishes my sentence then looks at me. "I'm just going to state this for the record."

"You are, are you?"

"Yes, and I have Liam, Axel, and Griff as witnesses."

"Witnesses to what?"

"That assumptions are a bitch. You're going to regret making the ones you did."

"What are you talking about?"

"I'm talking about the assumption you made back there and continue making here."

"Ain't no assumptions being made. You were in the middle of an active shooting, standing around like an idiot with your thumb up your butt."

"You know we're not supposed to use that word anymore." She's still in a snit, but at least we're talking.

I'll take that over another knock-down-drag-out fight.

"What word?" I jerk the wheel, oversteering, after drifting into the lane beside us.

"Idiot. It's the same with retard. It's demeaning, many would say vulgar, and no longer acceptable."

"You're correcting my grammar?"

"Technically, she's correcting your vocabulary." Liam quips from the back seat.

"Shut up, fuzz ball." I give Liam a stern look he's going to ignore. When he rolls his eyes at me, I give him the finger. "I didn't realize that was on the list."

"Well, now you know." Jinx sits back looking pleased as punch correcting my uninformed use of words. "And I wasn't standing around like an idiot with my thumb up my butt."

"You're not supposed to use that word."

"Technically, I'm only repeating what you said." She shifts in her seat, pulling the shoulder harness down and away from her neck.

I point to the post next to her. "There's an adjustment for that."

"What?"

"For the seatbelt, so it doesn't choke you."

Hey, I'm a progressive guy. I'm all for equality and all that shit, but sometimes I find it difficult to keep up. At least I can still insult the guys, and none of them take offense. Although, idiot is one word I'm putting on the sidelines.

Jinx adjusts the shoulder position of her seatbelt and stares out the front window, looking much more comfortable. We ride in silence for a few minutes. I'm about to open my mouth when Jinx speaks.

"For the record, I wasn't standing like an …"

"Idiot?"

"No. We're not using that word. All I'm saying is what you saw isn't what happened."

"Seems like we were walking toward you when a shooter started taking potshots at the crowd. Managed to kill our only lead. That's a pretty fucking epic fuck-up."

She rolls her eyes. "What you heard was a DEA agent taking a shot at a witness going into witness protection. There was no bullet."

"Come again?"

"You heard me."

"But Eve …"

"Eve doesn't know. We need the reactions of family members to be as authentic as possible. Deverough agreed to be a witness against the Rossi's. If he went into the witness protection program, they would find him. They always do. If he's dead, they won't bother looking. I plan on telling Eve as soon as possible."

"Damn, that's cold," Axel mumbles under his breath from the back. "She was distraught."

"She knew what was happening." Jinx pulls the visor down in front of her and checks her hair, combing her fingers through the long dark strands.

"That her dad was going to get shot in front of her?" From the tone of Griff's voice, he's not happy.

"She didn't know that part, but she knew her father was going into witness protection. We gave her time to say goodbye." Jinx flips up the mirror and leaves the visor down.

"That's really fucked up, Jinx." My fingers clench around the steering wheel. "So not cool."

"What's not cool is her father being executed for real. Right now, the Rossi's are learning about his death. They're going to see the evidence of it splattered all across the news and social media. They have no reason to go looking for a dead man. It's the only way to keep him safe. We talked about this."

"We? Who's we?"

"Me, Lily, and Harry."

"Harry?" I can't believe the words coming out of her mouth. "He's not even a member of Guardian HRS."

"So? Harry is an amazing boss. This isn't his first rodeo. Everything is going according to plan."

"And what are they going to say to those EMTs? Or the hospital?"

"The EMTs are DEA plants. Deverough is dead as far as the rest of the world is concerned." She examines her cuticles then brings her finger to her mouth.

"Right, and dead means he's no longer of use to us." Griff utters a rumbling dissent. "He is our key to tracking down those girls."

"What girls?" Jinx's body tenses, suddenly on full alert.

"The ones that went missing."

"What girls are you talking about?" She looks to me, confused.

"The last six girls in Benefield's ledgers," I explain. "Sometime in the last twenty-four hours they were abducted. The shipment is going forward, and now that you took Deverough out of the equation, that makes finding, and rescuing them, damn near impossible."

"No it doesn't." She nibbles on her lower lip. "Deverough isn't personally involved in any of the shipments. Whether it be narcotics or women."

"And how do you know this?"

"Because he told me."

"The man's a criminal." Griff says with a snort. "You can't trust a word out of his mouth."

"Maybe, but that doesn't mean he's not trustworthy." Jinx shifts in her seat.

"What the fuck?" Griff's curse is echoed by Axel.

"That man's filth." Axel taps on the window, obviously not pleased.

"He's not an inherently evil man. The Rossi's used him, tying him to their organization one small job at a time until there was no escape. Regardless, he's not personally involved in any of it. His company is simply the conduit."

"And how does that help us? Forest mobilized the entire team early this morning. It's a total clusterfuck there right now as Mitzy tries to figure out how to intercept that shipment."

Beside me, Jinx presses her lips together. She blows out a breath and fishes into her pocket, where she pulls out a USB drive. "I think this is going to help."

"What's that?"

"The key codes to everything Deverough has access to. In addition, I installed a small program that opens up his entire system to Guardian HRS. You may think I went off the rails, but if you had any faith in me at all, you'd know I'd never do anything to jeopardize Guardian HRS operations."

With that said, she turns away and remains silent for the remainder of the drive. Each time I look in the rearview mirror, Liam gestures to me, encouraging me to talk to Jinx.

I don't.

I don't because I have no idea what to say. She violated standard Guardian operating procedures going rogue. Even if she enlisted the aid of her DEA friends, that kind of shit requires approval. She put her entire job with the Guardians at risk.

That's what I'm pissed about. If Mitzy fires her ass, and Mitzy has every reason to do so, I lose Jinx. She'll move back here, and that leaves me where?

Fuck if I know.

I remember Knox debating this very thing. He was willing to leave the Guardians and become a bouncer if it meant staying close to his girl. Is that what I'm going to do? Will I need to leave the Guardians to stay with Jinx?

No fucking way in hell is that happening. First off, Jinx's talents are sorely underutilized within the bureaucracy of the DEA. She's a Guardian HRS asset. If they don't keep her, I'll leave, but I'll fight for her to stay. Not that I'm all that, but operatives like me are few and far between. My position will be filled. My spot as a SEAL filled the day I left the Navy, but that doesn't mean I'm replaceable.

Fuck, why didn't Jinx tell me what she planned? I could've been beside her, watching her six. I know I'm not supposed to use words like retard and idiot. I'm still navigating my way around those, but one thing I know for certain. What she did, going out without backup, was dumb as fuck. One of the things I love about her is that she's confident. It's also one of the things that gives me the most grief.

She doesn't ask for help when she needs it.

There's no reason Jinx can't kick my ass. She's done it more times than I'm willing to admit. She's sharp as a tack, a brilliant operative. What she did with those ledgers is nothing short of brilliant. I've seen her skill with a weapon. Whether a sidearm or scoped rifle, her aim is scary accurate. There's no reason she can't be a Guardian, except she made the choice to stay with the techies.

She belongs with Guardian HRS, but I swear if she ever goes off script like that again, I'm going to bend her over my knee and paddle her ass until she can't sit for a week.

And fuck whatever socially acceptable rule it is that I'm breaking. It is what it is, and I'm done apologizing for wanting to keep my woman safe. I'd do the same to Liam if he did the same, ripping him a new asshole until he couldn't shit straight. Jinx is no different when it comes to work.

That means my expectations are no different. She gets no slack because she's a woman. Equality means equality, and that means we're a fucking team.

"This is the first, and last time, you leave me out." My words come out an angry growl, but I need Jinx to know exactly how I feel. "I don't care what hair-brained scheme you have or what bug crawls up your butt, you never go off-script without me. You got me?"

The guys in the back go stone cold.

Jinx takes in a breath and bites her lower lip. She says nothing, but her silence says it all.

And that's how we communicate.

Now, to make sure she doesn't lose her job after this epic fuck-up.

I swear I'm either going to kill Jinx or marry her ass.

One or the other, it needs to be done.

Twenty tense moments later and the tires crunch along the gravel drive leading up to Rose Manor. The stately estate greets us with a welcoming committee.

Forest, Sam, CJ, and Mitzy stand on the top steps as I pull the car around. I come to a stop and slam the gear shift into park, then gesture outside. Max and Knox, with Eve and Lily, roll up in the car behind us.

"It's your funeral." I point to the scowls on our leaders' faces.

"Don't be a fucking ass." Jinx gives me a look, but I simply shrug.

Griff chuckles behind me, doing a piss-poor job of hiding his amusement. Axel opens his door, exits the car, and stretches as Liam piles out behind him. Our team is tight, and we're used to close quarters and uncomfortable situations, but I don't think we've encountered anything as uncomfortable as that drive back.

Before I can talk to Jinx, she jumps out and rushes over to the other car. Max helps Eve out of the car, eager to shelter and protect his woman, but Jinx blows through. I swear she's a force of nature; like a hurricane, she's unstoppable and inescapable.

Jinx grasps Eve. Their foreheads touch. The power of Jinx's words falling over Eve is a palpable thing. It's like watching a train wreck. I can't look away and wait for the crash.

Eve's body tenses. Jinx says something. Eve's head pops up, surprise and disbelief scrawled over her features. Jinx says something else. She grasps Eve and pulls her into a hug. More words are exchanged, words impossible to read from this distance, but the emotion is clear. Eve slumps and covers her face. Her entire body shakes.

Max grasps Eve. Supports her. Then Eve looks at Jinx. She asks a question. Jinx answers. Eve spins around and throws her arms around Max's neck.

I don't know what they say, but the context is clear.

Jinx reveals what she and her DEA crew subjected Eve to: the agonizing loss of a parent that is nothing but a ruse.

Eve clutches Max. Cries in his arms. But then she turns around. Her arms go around Jinx, and more words are exchanged.

Meanwhile, I sit in the car.

Watching.

Separated from the action.

I've never felt so alone.

I exit the car and make my way up the steps. CJ slaps my back. Somehow, he's already been briefed. No doubt Max called in during the drive.

"Good job."

I don't tell CJ there's nothing good about this job. The Guardians did nothing other than provide eye candy for the hundreds of civilians eager to post their most exciting moment to social media.

It's a fucking shitstorm.

And Jinx is at the center of it all.

TWENTY-SIX

Jinx

Harry and I discussed whether to tell Eve. In Deverough's case, leaving him among the living presents too great of a security risk. In the last minutes before Deverough and I headed down from his office, I briefed him on what he could expect.

During the drive to meet Eve, we kitted Deverough out with a specialized vest, complete with remotely activated blood bags. When our man fired a blank round into the crowd, the blood bag, which was primed to explode, delivered enough force to make a person jump.

Which is exactly what Deverough did.

On cue, he clutched his chest and fell to the ground, exactly as we prepped him.

To anyone not in on the subterfuge, it looked like the bullet hit him over his heart. Deverough jerks, a tiny hole forms over the miniature blast cap, the blood releases, and he falls to the ground.

To the world, Deverough is dead.

An ambulance, with our men prepositioned a few blocks away, allows the emergency response time to be as organic as possible. The fire and rescue responses are real, responding via actual 9-1-1 calls to the scene.

All in all, the entire thing goes off without a hitch.

Textbook perfect.

So why is Wolfe pissed at me?

He stalks up the steps and disappears inside Rose Manor while I explain to Eve what happened and why. The girl is justifiably traumatized. Now she's in shock as her brain attempts to process what she saw with what she now knows.

"Battle room!" An ear-piercing whistle grabs our attention. CJ stands at the top of the steps leading up to Rose Manor and gestures for us to file inside.

"Battle room?" I glance over at Liam. "What does that mean?"

"Battle room is what we call the briefing room when we shift from training drills to working an active hostage rescue mission." He places his hand over mine and moves us inside.

"Those girls are supposed to be safe."

Mitzy sent the new Protectors to be their personal protection specialists until we can figure out how the entire operation works.

"Evidently, they got to them first," Liam confirms what I don't want to hear.

"How can that be?" I clasp my hand over my mouth.

"That's what we're getting ready to find out."

"How did we know?"

"Brett, the Protector sent to watch over Julie Gant, discovered her missing. Sawyer also called in. Lori Black is MIA. Sawyer's on a plane back from Madrid, no doubt, headed here."

"And the others? How sure is Mitzy that they've all been taken?"

"I can't believe we decoded the list, and hours later, the girls were taken." I crane my neck to take in Liam as a shiver rushes down my spine. I'm not a fan of coincidences.

Liam and I double-time it up the steps. Axel and Griff are three steps ahead. Knox and Lily are right behind, jogging, while Eve and Max follow at a much slower pace. Their heads are together, talking softly to each other.

The shock of her father's fictitious death is going to be hard to shake. I regret it happened the way it did, but honest, unscripted reactions are what make the illusion of death real. Those details are often the difference between life and death for the witness.

If the Rossi's don't believe the social media blitz happening out there in the cyber world, Deverough is as good as dead. The rest of his new identity and movement into the witness protection program is streamlined and incredibly efficient. Later on, I'll check in with Eve. Right now, I join my contemporaries on the right-hand side of the dining room. There are more of us than there are Guardians, which makes our side of the room crowded compared to theirs.

I want to shift sides and stand beside Wolfe, but he doesn't look at me. The few times I try to catch his eye, he turns away.

He's pissed, but I explained what happened, and why. It felt as if we reconnected there for a moment, dispelling the lingering tension when Liam won his second bet.

As for now, we stand on opposite sides of the room. Alpha team leans against the wall, looking nearly identical with arms crossed over their chests and scowls fixed to their faces.

Mitzy is at the head of the table. Forest paces back and forth behind her. His brow furrows, and tension bunches in his shoulders. Every now and again, he stops behind Mitzy to peer over her shoulder. This inevitably results in her shooing him away.

CJ is the last to enter after rounding the rest of us up. He stands at the foot of the table while the rest of us wait to begin.

The energy in here spirals upward. We all feel it. From the nervous coughs, to throats being cleared, we shift from foot to foot like we all have ants in our pants.

"Mitzy, you want me to start, or are you ready?" CJ's deep voice brings calm to the room.

"You start." Mitzy answers without looking away from her screen. Her fingers fly over the keys as her eyes dart around the screen.

"This is the situation—" CJ begins the briefing. "Brett was sent to protect Julie Gant at UC Davis. Upon his arrival, she was not in the class she was supposed to be in. He called her roommate, who told him Julie mentioned going home with a headache. He met the roommate at the apartment. The door had been kicked in."

Someone gasps near me.

"Brett found a hastily scratched note kicked under the sofa."

"What was on the note?" Max takes a step off the wall.

"Men at the door. Breaking in. I'm scared. Tell my mom I love her." CJ points to the screen with a picture of the note. "Brett found that after a brief search. Whoever took Julie tossed her phone on the floor. Probably so we couldn't follow her. We believe they sedated her."

"Why?" I join Max in taking a step off the wall. "Why would you think that?"

"Because ..." Mitzy clicks something on the display in front of her. The massive computer screen mounted to the wall behind her flickers. On the screen, over half a dozen cameras record various angles of the apartment complex where Julie lives. "As you can see, there is no evidence of her leaving her apartment complex."

"No video near her door?" Wolfe's brows tug together.

For the first time since I stepped in the room, he glances at me.

"I wish." The video reverses then speeds up. "I pulled all video from the past twenty-four hours."

We watch college-aged kids loaded down with backpacks as they climb on their bikes and leave for morning classes and return during breaks. I forgot how eco-green the UC Davis campus is, prioritizing bicycles over cars.

"Here." Mitzy points at the screen. "See this van?" She taps the screen as three men climb out. One of them shoulders what looks to be an empty duffel bag. "The men enter the apartment complex and then ..." She pivots back to her screen. The image on the main display fast forwards then stops when the same three men exit the apartment complex.

This time, the large duffel bag is full. One of the men opens the side door to the van while the one carrying the duffel drops it in the back of the van. From the way it moves, or doesn't move, there's something heavy inside.

"That is Julie Gant." Mitzy taps the screen. "I'd bet my life on it."

"The bag isn't moving." I take a few steps toward the screen, trying to get a better look. This involves weaving in-between my fellow techies, who are more than happy to let me pass. "That's why you think they drugged her."

"That's my thought," CJ responds from the other side of the room. "Mitzy, you care to take it from here?"

"Yes." The screen flickers, and a series of credit card transactions appears. "These are the credit card receipts of Lori Black. If you remember, she's on a summer holiday in Europe. There's a steady stream of credit card transactions that suddenly stop."

"Yeah, but look at the times." I join Mitzy at the front of the room. "The last charge is at nine p.m. local time. She could simply be asleep."

"That's what I thought, but it doesn't match with her normal pattern." Mitzy points to several entries over a span of days. "Lori is a party girl. She likes to stay out late at the clubs. The last charges on her credit cards are generally between one and three in the morning."

"It's still an assumption." I'm not arguing with Mitzy, just going with my gut. In our line of work, assumptions truly do make an ass out of us if we're not careful.

"That's what I thought, too." Mitzy puts another photo on the screen. "I tapped into her phone's GPS. Lori's supposed to be in Madrid."

Mitzy joins up the various locations where she pings the phone in chronological order. True to what she said previously, Lori spends most of her nights in nightclubs, arriving to her hotel between one and three in the morning.

"Why the big jump here?" I point to the last dot. No longer in Spain, Lori's phone pings in London. It's the last location of the phone.

"That's Heathrow, the private side of the airport." Mitzy taps on the screen again, enlarging the image. "My assumption, and I know how you feel about those, is this is where they discovered and dropped her phone. There's no activity on her credit cards the four hours prior, and I called the hotel in Madrid. She didn't check out, and all her belongings are inside."

"Well, shit." I blow out a breath and scratch my head. "And the others?"

"Sybil Niles is currently completing an internship for her Hotel Management degree at the Belvedere. I poked around, and guess who didn't show up for work today?"

"Sybil Niles." Liam kicks off from the wall. "She's a student at Cornell's Hotel School."

"That's correct," Mitzy says. "She's on a summer internship, and you'll never guess who her friend is?"

"Who?" I'm curious.

"Maria Rossi, general manager of the Belvedere. From what I've been able to find out, Maria secured Sybil's internship."

"Shit." I scrub my face, shocked at the connection.

"It doesn't make sense for Sybil to be taken if Maria is her friend." Wolfe shakes his head.

I agree with Wolfe, but something is there. I feel it.

"No way to know. Could be true and unrelated." I take in a deep breath, processing everything Mitzy shows us. Before we can rescue the girls, we need more information.

"Huh?" Wolfe glances at me. "What the fuck does that mean?"

"Only that it could be true that Sybil's doing an internship at the Belvedere and also true that Maria helped her secure the internship, but that doesn't mean there's a connection to her abduction."

"Looks pretty connected to me." Wolfe isn't letting it go.

Not that I disagree. They could very well be related, but it feels wrong. Too neat and tidy.

"I wouldn't bet on that. The Belvedere operates as a legitimate business. Sure, there's more going on beneath the surface, but the best front is a front that looks and acts exactly like what it's supposed to be. In this case, an upscale casino."

"Fine, but don't forget about who runs operations." Wolfe's argumentative, but I don't mind. His words aren't directed at me. Like everyone in this room, he works through the problem by talking out loud.

I glance over at Wolfe wishing things between us were smoother. I can remain professional and work alongside him in my role as tech support, but damn if I don't want more.

Right now, I feel disconnected.

He's not happy with how things went last night, and he sure as shit isn't happy about the whole Deverough thing.

The thing is, only one of those two things is my fault. What happened to Deverough needed to happen. What I did to Wolfe last night in the salon, pushing him the way I did, requires a conversation I don't want to initiate.

However, it needs to be done. Is it bad I hope throwing ourselves into this case means we won't need to talk about it?

"What about the other girls?" Max stretches his neck. "Did we locate all of them?"

"I'm working on it." Mitzy chews at her bottom lip. "After Brett checked in, I sent him to Napa. Myra Goldstein is a student at the CIA." Mitzy holds up a hand, stalling any replies. "Before anyone asks, that is the Culinary Institute of America and not the Central Intelligence Agency."

She gives all of us a stern look, telling us she's not in the mood for cutting up. Regardless, there are a few snickers from those around me. The CIA is pretty damn cool. It's on my list of things to do once I get a moment off from work. Part of me was hoping to make it a weekend getaway; steal away with Wolfe over a long weekend where we could spend time as a couple.

Although, I'm not really sure where we stand at the moment.

"Julie Gant is missing." CJ ticks off his fingers. "Lori Black is too. Sybil Niles is doing an internship at the Belvedere. She failed to show up this morning." CJ rocks back on his heels and stares at the ceiling. "We're missing updates on Rose, Gigi, and Myra."

"Nada. Dead silent on Rose." Mitzy rubs at the back of her neck. She closes her eyes and rolls her shoulders, stretching from hours hunched over a computer. "Brett is checking on Myra. I hope to have confirmation within the hour."

"That leaves—Gigi Malone." CJ folds his arms across his chest. "What do we have on her?"

"Excuse me." A timid voice calls out from the hallway.

Everyone turns at the sound. Eve stands in the doorway, one foot in and one foot out of the room. Max moves, magnetically drawn to his woman.

"What's wrong?" He reaches for her several steps away, and she glides into his arms.

"Nothing's wrong." She holds up a thumb drive. "I think you need this. My father gave it to me."

My brows pinch together. Where did she get that?

Rule number one of transitioning a witness into witness protection is keep them from touching anything electronic. No footprints. No fingerprints. Nothing that can hint at what's happening.

My lips press into a hard line. I'd go to Eve and snatch that thumb drive out of her hand, but I have to walk across the conference table to get to her. Conflict brews within me. Harry needs whatever is on that thumb drive for damage control.

What the hell was Deverough thinking giving that to Eve?

CJ takes the thumb drive from Eve and passes it to one of my colleagues, who passes it to the guy beside him, who passes it down. I shift position as it comes my way. As soon as it's within my grasp, I grab it. Mitzy holds out a hand, then arches a brow when I don't give it to her.

"I have to get this to Harry. It's important for damage control. The DEA needs this."

"We need it." Mitzy glares and gives a flick of her fingers.

"No."

TWENTY-SEVEN

Wolfe

THE FIRST THOUGHT THAT GOES THROUGH MY MIND IS: WHAT THE fuck is Jinx doing?

No? She told Mitzy no?

Her lips press together. Her breathing changes. Her shoulders snap back, and her spine stiffens. This is not going to be pretty.

I can't turn away as the muscles of her shoulders bunch. I can't un-see the way her fingers flex and tighten as she clenches the thumb drive. I can't un-hear the hitching of her breath, as if she's about ready to blurt out something she knows she's going to regret.

I read my girl like a goddamn book, and it's a shitshow in the making.

I know that page.

I know it too damn well.

Jinx is the kind of person who digs in. Even if she's wrong. Hell, especially when she's wrong. There's a chip on her shoulder, the product of a lifetime of competing in a man's world.

It's fucking toxic.

I'm about ready to storm over there, give her a piece of my mind, and knock some sense into that head of hers, but I don't. Me rushing in to save the day isn't what Jinx needs. She needs me to believe in her—to stand by her side—but if Jinx wants to sabotage her career, there's jack shit I can do about it. I desperately want to save her from herself.

If I could—if it were up to me—I'd toss her over my shoulder and carry her out of the room before she explodes and ruins her future with Guardian HRS.

"Jinx?" Mitzy's hand is out, wanting the thumb drive, but Jinx takes a step back. Her fingers tighten, and her scowl deepens.

"I need to speak to my boss." Jinx reaches for her phone.

"I'm your boss." Mitzy's sharp retort snaps Jinx's spine.

Jinx glances around the room, looking to me first, but this is a sticky situation. The moment Jinx signed her name to Guardian HRS's charter, she stopped working for the DEA.

I return her stare, narrowing my eyes, and give a little flick toward Mitzy, silently urging Jinx to get the goddamn message and hand over that thumb drive.

Mitzy opens her mouth to snap at Jinx, but Forest's deep bass rumble rolls through the room. It booms like thunder, vibrating beneath my skin.

"Everyone out." He points to the door as the tech team scrambles to empty the room.

Eve takes a step back.

"Not you." Forest points at Eve. "You stay."

Eve's face pales, and she huddles in Max's embrace, shaking like a leaf beneath Forest's fury.

My teammates don't move. We're doing an excellent job holding up this wall and will continue to do so until expressly ordered to leave. Which means CJ dismisses us, or Sam tells us to take a hike. We take our orders from them.

Not Forest.

Forest created Guardian HRS, but Sam runs it. We follow the chain of command, and Forest isn't in that chain.

The room empties as the techies scurry out of sight, leaving Eve trembling in Max's arms by the door. Jinx stands her ground at the front of the room. A scowl firmly fixed on her face. Lily leans against Knox. His arm drapes casually over her shoulder like he doesn't have a care in the world.

Jinx and Mitzy continue their epic stare down. Mitzy's a crazy lunatic, but damn if she doesn't fight fire with fire. I take bets on which one of them wins that staring contest.

The room empties of everyone except for Alpha team, CJ and Sam, Jinx and Lily, and finally Mitzy and Forest. And of course, there's Eve.

"Close the doors." Forest issues orders. He may not be technically in charge, but his word carries weight.

CJ leaps to shut the doors to the dining room. The moment he does, Jinx's phone rings. She reaches for her phone but stops when Forest's low growl makes the air rumble.

"I have to get it." Jinx glances at the screen. Her thumb moves to accept the call.

"Not until we sort this out." Forest snaps his fingers. "Give it to me."

"Not until I speak to Harry." Jinx shakes her head and takes a step back.

Damn, she's hot when ferociously fierce. My cock takes notice and I count to three. A woody is not what I need right now. Three slow breaths in, and I'm back in control. My cock needs to stand down, but damn if it doesn't love a fiery Jinx.

"Harry can wait." Sam places a buffer between Jinx and Forest's menacing standoff.

"You don't understand. Witness protection protocol ..." Jinx's voice cracks a little. Irritation flickers in her gaze, annoyed with herself for betraying any weakness.

It's all I can do not to rush to her side. The urge to protect and defend my woman isn't something I can control. It's instinctual.

Primal.

She's a part of me now.

Even if there are things between us left unresolved.

"Your witness protection protocol is busted." Forest takes a step toward Jinx. "Everyone in this room knows Deverough is, in fact, not dead. Whatever conversation you need to have with Harry can wait. That train left the building. Protocol or no protocol."

"You don't understand." Her voice strengthens and she shifts her weight onto the balls of her feet. She's glorious when defending her views. "This jeopardizes everything."

"Every person in this room knows. The rest were excused. They will only know what the press releases. I don't need to stress time is of the essence. We have two girls confirmed missing."

Jinx's phone goes silent. The caller, Harry, gives up.

Mitzy's attention shifts from Jinx to her computer screen.

I called that one right. Jinx is as fierce as they come. I had no doubt she'd win that little stare down.

"Three." Mitzy purses her lips. "There are three confirmed missing."

"Three?" Sam presses the heel of his palm to his forehead. "This is fucked."

"Brett sent me a text." Mitzy looks up from her screen. "Myra is missing. Didn't show up for class. Signs of forced entry at her apartment."

"Well shit." Sam drags his hand down his face. "We're not losing these girls. Jinx, I get you're conflicted between protecting a DEA witness, but if there's anything on that thumb drive of use to the Guardians, we don't have time to dick around."

Jinx's phone rings again.

She glances down. "That's Harry. Whatever it is, it's important."

"Take the call, but give the thumb drive to Mitzy." Sam issues a direct order. The force of his command makes my skin draw tight.

The surest path to expulsion from Guardian HRS employment is to disobey a direct order. Sam won't dick around. Forest is technically the lead figure of Guardian HRS, but Sam is where the rubber meets the road.

Irritation and stubbornness flicker across Jinx's features. When she looks in my direction, I make a show of cutting my gaze to Mitzy, urging her to comply with the direct order.

She needs to decide. She's either with us, or she's not.

Jinx follows my gaze. Her shoulders slump as she blows out a breath. Slowly, she hands the thumb drive to Mitzy. Then she puts the phone to her ear.

"What's up, Harry?" A moment of silence passes. Jinx's eyes widen and her jaw gapes. "You're outside?"

The entire room grows silent as we focus in on Jinx.

"Shit, Harry …" Her hand shakes as she runs her fingers through her hair. "Okay, okay … Listen, come around to the carriage house. I'll open the garage. We can talk in there." Another pause. "Yes, it's private—it's secure." More silence. "Copy that."

Jinx ends the call and tucks her phone into her back pocket. Instead of looking at Mitzy, or Sam, her attention focuses in on me. Her eyes plead for support.

"What was that about?" I ask the question on everyone's mind.

"Mitzy," Jinx gives a flick of her fingers, "I need that thumb drive now and a secure computer to open it on. Something not connected to any Guardian systems."

"This is a secure computer." Much of Mitzy's annoyance remains. "My firewalls are impenetrable."

"I need a mobile computer and you need to give that back." Jinx is being evasive, but it's not hard to figure out why.

I know exactly what's happening. I may not give my blind support, but now that I've figured it out, I do what I can to stand by my woman.

"Mitz, give her a mobile computer." I push off from the wall. "Griff, you're going to want to join us."

Griff gives me a look like I've lost my mind.

"And where the hell do you think you're going?" Max's low growl stops me in my tracks.

"If Harry is here, he brought Deverough." I point at Jinx. "If Deverough's here, he wants to speak to Jinx. I'm pretty damn sure it has to do with the six missing girls." I push past Max, shouldering him out of the way. "Jinx did what Griff could not."

"And what's that?" Griff joins me, arms crossed, temper flaring. His left brow arches in challenge.

"I reminded him that he's a father." Jinx answers for herself. "But that doesn't mean the Rossi's didn't sink their claws in deep."

She holds out her hand. "I followed witness protection protocol. He didn't touch his phone, his computer, or even a pen to leave a note. Wherever he got that, it was planted ahead of time. Which means …"

Mitzy hands over the thumb drive like it's a hot potato. She pushes out of her chair and goes to a stack of computers propped up in a corner of the room. It doesn't take long for her to dig through the stack before handing Jinx a beat-up dinosaur of a computer.

"No Wi-Fi. No connection. All standard firewalls installed." Mitzy passes the laptop to Jinx.

"Mitz, you're good with this?" Forest Summers comes to stand behind Mitzy.

The difference in their relative sizes is comical at best. The top of her head barely comes up to the middle of Forest's chest, and that's being generous.

"I am." Mitzy's eyes narrow. "We'll call everyone back in, start planning. Talk to him. Do whatever it was you did before. We need him."

"I will." Jinx pivots and makes a beeline for the door. I'm right on her heels.

Jinx

THE INFORMATION TRAPPED IN DEVEROUGH'S HEAD MIGHT BE THE one thing that brings the Rossi crime family to justice. From what he admitted to me, he's been helping the Rossi's move drugs since he took over his father's business decades ago. With that came the debts his father owed the Rossi's.

When the trafficking of helpless women and children began is anyone's guess. Not that that matters.

"What's our game plan?" Wolfe walks beside me.

"I don't know. Bringing Deverough to Rose Manor is a major violation of protocol. It sacrifices his safety, and there's one reason Harry would do that."

"What's that?"

"Like me, his loyalties are divided."

I crossed a line withholding information for the benefit of the DEA. My loyalty may be in question, but I know men like Deverough. I know how he thinks.

"Deverough or Harry?"

"Deverough is a survivor. He'll do whatever it takes to save his despicable ass. Now that he's seen what's possible with witness protection, he wants more."

"More?"

"Yes. Our conversation gave him a window to see through to the other side of witness protection, to the life he might one day live if all goes according to plan. He imagines a life free of coercion. Free of corruption. He sees a chance for redemption. Forgiveness from his daughter and some small part in her life. The only thing I believe about Deverough is that he loves his daughter." I grip Wolfe's arm. "He's second-guessing everything."

"What does that mean?"

"The information on that thumb drive contains one of two things: information vital to our case, or it's a weapon. I think it's a weapon, something the Rossi's gave him."

"But coming here carries significant risk, exposing Deverough's death as the lie it is. If the Rossi's get a whiff he remains among the living, they'll never stop looking for him."

"I know, which is why we need to talk to him. Why would he risk everything now? It doesn't make sense."

One of the many things I learned from my father is honorable men are corruptible. No matter the morals, the faith, or the values a man holds dear, there's always a way to turn anyone. Find the right person, press on the right pain point; that's how you turn a man from good to bad.

Harry risks blowing the case that will likely make his career. It's no small thing.

Mitzy hands me a laptop.

The itching sensation on my scalp tells me to proceed with extreme caution. Deverough could've loaded vital intelligence on that thumb drive, or it could be a Trojan Horse primed to wreak havoc on any computer system it encounters. Mitzy understands how dangerous it might be.

Wolfe follows me into the hallway as we silently walk to the carriage house. A black SUV waits outside, exhaust huffing into the air as the engine chugs along. Blacked-out windows prevent us from seeing inside. I can't even make out the driver.

Right on our heels are the rest of Alpha team. First is Griff. He passes me with something that's either a scowl or a look of the deepest appreciation. It's hard to tell with him.

He's proud of his interrogation techniques. From what I've heard among the guys, and from what's whispered in the halls at Guardian HQ, his success rate is nearly perfect.

Wolfe gets the garage doors open. The SUV slowly rolls inside. Tires crunch over the gravel drive. It comes to a stop while Axel and Griff close the garage doors. The engine turns off while I head for the door leading into the carriage house, or rather the stairs that lead up to the small apartment sitting over the garage.

I was supposed to stay there with Wolfe last night. Instead, I ran. I'm not proud of that, but I honestly don't think we'd be here right now if I'd done anything else.

The only reason Deverough cracked is because I remind him of his daughter. We look nothing like each other. Our coloring is different, but our builds are the same, and we're nearly the same age.

Griff tried to break a criminal. I appealed to the father inside.

Sometimes that switch in perspective is all it takes.

Axel and Griff stand at the back of the SUV, arms tucked behind their backs as they assume the position of parade rest. Liam moves to the side of the car, blocking the driver and back passenger doors. Knox and Max circle around to the other side. Griff gives me a look.

"We doing this here or inside?"

"Up to you." I'm willing to take pointers from an expert.

"This is your shitshow. You call the shots."

My eyes pinch, and I want to give him a piece of my mind, but I don't. This isn't about us. This is work.

I consider for a moment how to let this play out. It would be much easier to talk in the apartment upstairs, but there are windows up there. I could draw the drapes, but I'm not risking it.

"We do it here." I glance around the small garage.

The carriage house was designed over a hundred years ago, built to accommodate two carriages, a true luxury at the time. That makes it somewhat cramped inside with a full-sized SUV and six overly large men.

Lily would normally be by my side, but I have a feeling she stayed behind with Eve and the others. I'm kind of surprised CJ and Sam don't join us, but I'm guessing they're doing exactly what Mitzy said. They brought the techies back inside and are beginning strategy sessions.

Max raps on the back-passenger window. The sudden sound makes me jump. The window rolls down, and I crane my neck.

This conversation would be much easier without the Guardians present, but I know why they're here. I pushed too hard back there. Alpha team isn't here to oversee my conversation with Deverough. They're watching me.

"We'll talk here. It's the only secure space. Too many windows upstairs and too many people at the main house."

The tension in Harry's face eases when he sees me. Not that he couldn't see me before, but the question of who's in charge is answered, and he's comfortable dealing with me.

The back door opens, and Harry steps out of the car. He gestures for Deverough to get out. Expensive leather squeaks as Deverough slides over the seat. Then his tall frame slowly unfolds as he exits the vehicle. Griff catches his attention first. Deverough's face pales, and he visibly swallows.

It's a weird reaction watching the confident man show weakness. Considering most men who find themselves on the wrong side of Griff's interrogations shit their pants, Deverough is holding up just fine.

Thankfully, Griff stays where he is. Axel shifts a little to the right, so the two of them cover the entirety of the garage door. Wolfe and Liam stay on the driver's side. Max and Knox move to either side of me, bracketing me between them.

Deverough takes in each of the Guardians, measuring his mettle against battle-hardened men. He stands straighter and takes in a breath. Not that it helps. His fingers fiddle with the seam of his pants as he turns his attention to me.

"Mr. Deverough, I wasn't expecting to see you again." I hold the thumb drive Eve gave me, twirling it between my fingers. I make a show of lifting the thumb drive up to my face, where I examine it closely. "I must say, I'm curious. Why did you give this to Eve?"

I slowly tuck the thumb drive into the tiny front pocket of my jeans, taking my time. I lift my gaze and meet his with an arched brow.

That will be the extent of my questioning, for now.

Silence stretches. Deverough's gaze darts around the dimly lit garage. He coughs as dust rises from the dirt floor. A single incandescent bulb slowly swings overhead, bathing us in a warm, yellow glow.

He swallows and clears his throat. When he looks back at me, a soft smile curves my lips, and I greet him with a warm expression.

Waiting.

Silently.

He clears his throat again and wets his lips. "Is Eve here?"

"You know I can't answer that. You're risking much coming here. Not that I'd let you see her if she was." I cock my head to the right, waiting for him to give me an indication of why he's here.

Harry doesn't say a word. He leans against the SUV, adjusts his tie, then folds his arms over his chest. I don't need Harry to say anything. He's so far out of bounds bringing Deverough here, instead of to the first of many safe houses, that nothing needs to be said.

I reach inside that tiny, useless pocket and withdraw the thumb drive. I take half a step forward and hold it out, offering it to him.

"Give my regards to the Rossi's."

Deverough's face pales.

When he doesn't take the thumb drive, I take another step, closing the distance between us. I make a show of reaching for his hand. My fingers tighten around his wrist as I shove the thumb drive into his palm and physically fold his fingers over it.

"I thought you were a better man." Slowly, I shake my head, really feeding him a heaping dose of disappointment. Unlike earlier, there's no anger. I truly am disappointed.

"You don't understand." His voice cracks. "They're going to kill Eve if I don't …"

"Excuse me?" Max closes the distance between him and Deverough in two steps.

He grabs Deverough by the wrist, spins the man around, and pins him face-first against the SUV. He holds Deverough in an arm lock, placing his wrist high on his back, which places strain on the shoulder joint.

Deverough cries out and tries to twist into a less painful position. It doesn't work. Max holds pressure and increases it until Deverough weeps.

"What do you mean they're going to kill Eve?"

"That's what they told me. They said if I was ever taken, I was to hand that over as evidence."

"It's a Trojan horse." I'm not impressed. It's far too obvious, which makes me wonder what I'm missing.

I don't expect the Rossi's to be particularly tech-savvy, but I'm not going to risk Eve's life based on an assumption. With the dinosaur laptop, I'll be able to download whatever is on that drive and figure out what it contains. That, however, is a full-time job, and I'm already busy.

"Yes." Deverough cries out as Max tweaks his arm upward. He rises up on his toes, as if that will relieve any of the pressure.

"What was your game plan? The whole point of faking your death is to avoid things like that. Eve should be safe."

Deverough's not the first witness to sabotage his safety because of threats levied against his family. It's one of the reasons why there are protocols in place, especially for those witnesses considered high-value targets. A faked, highly publicized death is the only way to ensure any leverage placed on the witness is rendered ineffective.

Dead men can't deliver Trojan horses.

Deverough fucked himself.

But I'm going to un-fuck his colossal screwup. Eve turned over the thumb drive, but there will be no evidence that it's missing. Right now, officers are combing through Deverough's office. It's standard procedure.

"Where did you get this?" I prop a hand on my hip.

"You don't understand. If that doesn't …"

"For fuck's sake, shut up." I hate dealing with idiots. "All the Rossi's know right now is that Eve came to town. When they dig, they're going to find out she spent the night with her newest friend, Lily, down in the French Quarter. There's plenty of proof of the four of us enjoying beignets and coffee. Just a bunch of girls having a good time. But if you don't tell me where you hid this, I can't put it back. If I don't put it back, the Rossi's are going to discover it's missing when they search your office. If that happens, they'll know someone spooked you. Instead of thinking I came to your office to reunite you and your daughter, they're going to go down a whole other path. I don't need to tell you we don't want that."

"I was only trying to keep Eve safe."

"Well, you're a fucking idiot. We do things a certain way because it works. It doesn't arouse suspicion. Now, tell me where you hid this." I practically shove the thumb drive into his face.

"There's a plant on the window behind my desk. A bonsai tree. I kept it there." Deverough's lower lip trembles.

"Any particular orientation you used?" I can't believe his stupidity.

"What?"

"It's best that we put it back exactly as it was." I hate explaining the obvious.

"I don't know. I just dropped it in." His voice shifts to a higher register.

"We need to get this back to Deverough's office ASAP." I remove the thumb drive from his face and hand it to Axel.

"Copy that." Axel shoves it in his back pocket and looks to Griff.

"We've got this, Axel." Griff pats his friend on the back. "Take that to Sam. He'll see that it gets to where it needs to go."

"On it." Axel glances over at Deverough, a torn expression on his face.

I get it. He doesn't want to leave. In a moment, I'm going to roll up my sleeves and show Griff how I work. Torture isn't always about tearing a man down physically. Sometimes, all it takes is a softly spoken word and a touch of kindness.

I place my hand over Max's and give a little tug.

Max isn't happy, but he releases Deverough. It's more of a shove. Deverough slams against the SUV. Max takes five steps back, muttering under his breath about all the ways he wants Deverough to suffer.

Deverough spins around and rubs at his shoulder.

"Now…" I cock my head to the side and smooth out my expression.

I approach Deverough and cup the side of his face. He flinches, and I draw back.

"Imagine how Eve felt when they took her. When they locked her in that shipping container for days? She suffered. She begged. Imagine what might have happened if they mistakenly put her in the other truck."

Deverough's legs give way. He slumps to the ground, and I follow him down.

"You know what happened to those girls. You know how they died. Terrified. Alone. They died, suffering horribly. Imagine your daughter standing in that line. Waiting for her turn to die." I reach out again and wipe away his tears. "You can stop this. This senseless trade of innocent girls. Those who were put in the same truck as your daughter have been wiped from existence. No one knows where they are. What depredations they suffer. That could've been Eve."

He chokes out a sob.

"Now—Carson." My thumb wipes away his tears as I force him to look at me. "Tell me about the girls."

"W-wh-what g-girls?" His body twitches. His breaths heave. His eyes spill a river of tears.

I lean in and place my lips by his ear.

"The ones who were taken."

TWENTY-NINE

Wolfe

I'VE WATCHED GRIFF MAKE GROWN MEN CRY. I'VE SEEN HIM INSTILL so much fear; men lost control of all bodily functions, urinating and defecating as they begged for the torture to end. I've seen strong men crumble. I've seen them give in. I've seen Griff extract their darkest secrets.

What I've never seen is a man brought to his knees by kindness and compassion.

Watching Jinx at work can only be described as mesmerizing. I don't hear whatever it is she whispers in his ear, but it doesn't matter.

Jinx gestures for Max and Knox to join her. They rush forward and take a knee as Deverough tells us everything. As his secrets spill, Jinx falls back. Her knees draw up to her chest. Her arms wrap around her shins. She props her chin on her knees.

I don't know if anyone else sees it, but my Jinx teeters on a precipice. She's barely holding herself together, rocking ever so slowly on the ground.

"The women will be collected at the Belvedere …" Deverough's confession is detailed. Too detailed. "They'll be moved out from there." Deverough walks us through each step of the operation.

Which leaves us with three opportunities to rescue the victims. If we're not too late, there's a chance we can take them back from the Belvedere. If not there, we're looking at boarding the cruise ship while at sea.

That's operationally more complicated, but tactically may be a better option. The Belvedere is likely guarded by scores of Rossi-employed muscle. The C&C cruise ship, Caviar Dreams, will have armed guards, but since it operates as a luxury cruise line, there will be far fewer security on board, but a whole lot of civilians.

The final option will be when the ship docks in Colombia. Knowing how Mitzy, CJ, and Sam think, they'll bring in several Guardian teams to cover each possibility. Since we're on-site, Alpha will either take the Belvedere or Caviar Dreams.

"Has Caviar Dreams left dock?" Mitzy would already know this, but I do not. I turn my attention to Deverough. If the girls have already been loaded, that brings us down to two possibilities.

"Today." Deverough confirms what I fear, but I'm already processing how that changes the operation.

"Where will we find them?" Max keeps his voice level, barely holding back his rage.

It's a good thing Max takes over the interrogation because I don't think Griff would be able to keep his hands off Deverough. He stays back, however, because whatever Jinx did to get Deverough talking opened up the floodgates. Griff won't interfere with that.

"Crew quarters."

"How are they hiding six women in crew quarters?"

"Just the three," Deverough speaks without emotion. His flat affect and distant gaze are inhuman.

A sudden chill rushes down my spine.

"What do you mean *just the three*?" Knox breathes in through his nose, a slow, deep inhale, then breathes out just as slow. "Why split them up like that?"

I know what he's doing because I'm doing it too. It's a technique used to calm down. Like now, when all I see is red and the urge to smash in Deverough's face nearly overwhelms me. Whatever answer Deverough gives, I already know I don't want to hear it.

"Those are the ones for Mr. X."

"Mr. X." Knox's left eyebrow lifts. "Three are for him?" Knox is on his game. He leaves his question open-ended, encouraging Deverough to fill in the gaps.

"Those are the ones ..." Deverough's voice falters.

"The ones who, what?" Max hops back in, urging Deverough to continue that train of thought, but Deverough bites his lip and shakes his head.

Jinx answers instead. "Those are the ones loaded into the other truck, aren't they?"

Deverough's chin snaps up, eyes wide, mouth gaping. His expression says it all.

"Like they did with Eve, half are loaded into one truck. The others go to die. That's what he means. Those are the three slated for slaughter." Jinx rubs at her arms as she scoots back, placing distance between herself and Deverough.

"Yes." Deverough's voice is so low, I barely hear it, but he confirms what Jinx says.

"Tell me, was Eve's placement a lucky break?" Jinx's eyes narrow into thin slits. "When they kidnapped Eve, did they know which truck to put her in? Or was it luck that she didn't die for Mr. X's pleasure?"

Deverough gulps. He doesn't answer out loud, but there's the slightest shake of his head.

"Did Benefield tell you he had your daughter, or did you plan her abduction in advance to clean that money?"

He refuses to meet her eye.

"Answer me!" Jinx's shout startles me. "Which was it?"

Deverough mumbles something unintelligible. Jinx closes in on him, grabs his chin and pinches his cheeks. She slams the back of his head against the car. "Which one was it?"

"We pl-planned it." Deverough's head drops. His shoulders slump.

"You don't deserve to live." Jinx releases him, shoving him against the SUV.

She takes a step back, folding her arms in front of her chest.

Only because I'm acutely attuned to all things Jinx, do I see the way her hands tremble. She's fierce but moments from falling apart.

Max and Knox take over as Deverough spews more filth. He tells us about how the orders were taken, how they were fulfilled, and how the women were transported in the cargo containers. Then he details the adjustments made after Alpha team rescued the last batch on the dock not too long ago.

Jinx's old boss, Harry, looks on with a murderous glare. I can only imagine what's going through his mind as his expert witness, promised immunity in exchange for testimony, turns out to be one of the major players.

Deverough is one smart motherfucker. Protected from the consequences of his actions, he doesn't hold back. As sickening as it is to hear his filth, it's a major break for Guardian HRS. We now know where the women are, how they're being held, and that's enough to get started.

Jinx rubs at her arms and takes two shaky steps back. I move in behind her and place my hand on her shoulder. I give a tiny squeeze, letting her know I'm here. It's not much, but it's enough. She lifts her hand and places it over mine.

My nerves settle with that tiny act. All is well with the world. Jinx is mine.

Griff remains stock still. He doesn't move from his post by the garage door. The muscles of his jaw bounce, the only outward sign he's moments from losing control. It surprises me he hasn't launched himself at Deverough, pounding the cretin into the ground where he belongs.

I've thought about it a dozen times in the past five minutes. Deverough deserves far worse than an ass kicking. He deserves to suffer. But he won't. Immunity protects him.

From the expressions on everyone's faces, it's on all our minds. Sitting in the balance, however, is the information Deverough gives that will save lives. I have to focus on the positive, or none of this makes sense.

As for Jinx, my woman is fierce. She's seen some of the worst humanity has to offer in her job as a DEA intelligence officer, but this is the first time she's been on the front lines of the despicable world of sex trafficking the Guardians exist within.

It's different. It's a whole other ballgame.

A single tear trickles down her face. She swipes at it and takes in a shuddering breath as her body begins to shake. Not sure whether she'll get mad at me for getting her out of this place, I make a decision I hope I won't regret. While Max, Knox, Liam, and Griff put Deverough to the question, I get Jinx out of there.

"Come. They've got it from here." I wrap my arm around her waist and escort her toward the door leading up to the small apartment above us.

For once, she doesn't struggle. She doesn't fight. Jinx doesn't snap or tell me to stop. She leans against me as I walk her out of that garage and take her upstairs. She says nothing as I take a seat on the couch and guide her down to sit beside me.

She lays her head against my shoulder. One breath in, and a sob slips out. Her body shakes as she shamelessly wipes at the tears falling freely down her cheeks now that we're alone.

"I wanted to believe he was forced." She speaks so softly, I have to strain to hear. "What am I going to tell Eve?"

"Max will take care of Eve. That's not on you to tell her what happened down there."

"But …"

"Max will find a way to tell her."

"I just can't believe …"

"It's a shock to us all." I only say that because I'm trying to comfort her, but the reality is we all suspected Deverough was dirtier than he seemed.

Now we know.

He transported drugs. He transported women. He knowingly sent women to their deaths. The man is a monster through and through.

I tug Jinx tight to my chest and kiss the crown of her head. How long we sit like this, I have no idea, but a knock at the door draws my attention. Liam steps in. He clutches his hands in front of him.

"Hey, the guys are done. Is there anything ..." In an uncharacteristic display of emotion, Liam chokes up.

"Luv, do you want to speak to Deverough before he goes?" I brush back the hair from her face, loving the way the silky strands slide through my fingers.

"No." She swipes at her cheeks and stirs in my arms.

Jinx sits up. She draws in a deep breath, then she crawls out of my lap.

"You sure?"

"If I never see that man again, it will be too soon. Let Harry have him." She shakes her head. "I wanted to believe he was a good man, that he was forced to transport those girls. It didn't bother me that he shipped narcotics. Not that it's without harm, but it's a distant harm. Those victims have some degree of choice, at least in the beginning. But he knew about the girls. He knew about the girls slated for execution. The man didn't even flinch." Jinx scrubs her face and blinks away the tears. Her eyes are bloodshot and puffy. She sniffs as she looks up at the ceiling. "I fucked up. I fucked up big time."

I rush to her side. "What you did was incredible. We got what we needed. Now we know exactly what to do. If it wasn't for you, those girls would be lost like all the others."

"I meant my job. There's no way I'll recover from what I did."

"Oh, luv, you have no idea what amazing people you work with."

"I want to be a part of this mission."

"I'm sure Mitzy is already lining up your to-do list."

"You don't understand." Jinx places her hand on my arm. "I want to be *a part* of this mission. I want to go as an operative."

And just like that, she steals my breath. It's a sucker punch to the gut, but far worse, I don't know how to respond.

I don't know how Knox does it. Lily is training to be a Guardian. That girl is a ball of spitfire and will be a fabulous addition to Delta team when the time comes.

In my opinion, Jinx is light years ahead of Lily when it comes to close-quarters combat. However, the thought of her in harm's way makes me want to puke.

Fortunately, that's not my decision to make which means I'm not the one to tell Jinx she must sit on the sidelines. I get to support her without fear.

Liam clears his throat, reminding us he's still in the room.

"Um, sorry to break this up, but if Harry can take Deverough, we need to join the others. We're officially on the clock now. The mission is a go."

"Give us five."

"Wolfe …" Liam reminds me of my priorities.

Unfortunately, he's wrong. My place is with Jinx, and she's in no position to walk back into the battle room.

"We'll be there in five." I look to my buddy. "I promise."

"Okay then." With that, Liam leaves us alone.

Jinx scrubs at her face, making her cheeks redder and her puffy eyes more swollen than they already are.

"I'm okay."

"We can take five minutes. Nothing is going to happen in five minutes." I fold her into my embrace. "You did good."

"I disobeyed orders. You were right. My priorities were out of line."

"You did what you thought was right, and everything worked out in the end."

"Only because I'm lucky. I should've never …"

"Stop that." I dip down, getting eye level with her. "What's done is done. We have what we need to rescue those girls. Now go in there, wash up, and take a breather." I release her, but Jinx doesn't move.

Instead, she leans into me and hugs me tight.

"You're the absolute best." She looks up and smiles. "You know that, don't you?"

"Careful with the compliments. They'll go to my head."

Her gaze flicks downward, and I huff out a laugh.

"Not that head, my fiery Jinx." I make a show of following the direction of her gaze, which makes Jinx laugh. The low, sultry sound is the best sound in the world. It sinks beneath my skin, where it curls around my heart and settles in.

"I guess it's true what they say." She playfully slaps at my chest.

"What's that?"

"That men have sex on the brain 24/7."

"Luv, we have it on the brain 24/7/365. All day. Every day. And all the moments in between." I spin her around and give her ass a light tap. "Now, go wash that face. Collect your thoughts. We have a mission to plan."

This time, Jinx does as I say. She takes far longer than I anticipate, which leads me to pace in the small apartment. Which makes me think about how we're going to come at this mission.

Boarding trawlers and cargo container ships are all in a day's work, but we've never boarded a cruise ship. It's a totally different animal. I need to make sure Jinx stays in her support role because there's no way I'll stay focused if I have to worry about her safety.

THIRTY

Jinx

THE BATTLE ROOM.

When I think about the name, I see it all in capital letters.

This is my first official battle room with the Guardians. It's the first time I truly feel like a member of the team.

It's been some time since Lily and I relocated from New Orleans to Guardian HQ on the California coastline. We've been busy orientating, training, and getting into our groove, but this is the first active hostage rescue mission since we joined.

Our orientation is nearly complete. I participated in a few intelligence gathering events, most notable being the work I did on Benefield's cipher, which is why we're all here in New Orleans.

Lily is still in the middle of her orientation, learning how the Guardians train, work, and operate as a team. Her DEA background correlates with joining Delta team, which specializes in FBI hostage rescues within the United States.

My mind is literally blown by the speed and efficiency with which the Guardians move. In less than twenty minutes, Sam calls in several favors.

An ex-military helicopter pilot is en route to transport the boarding party to a US Coast Guard Cutter. The *USS Charles Sexton* is the same ship that helped us rescue Lily when she was taken, and it's the same female pilot who lifted us off Deverough's rooftop and flew us to the *USS Charles Sexton.*

It's kind of badass because both the pilot and captain are female.

Chicks Rule.

I feel like that should be my slogan.

Which is why my fingers curl into fists, and I'm about ready to stomp my foot.

"What do you mean I can't go?" My question is a thinly veiled demand because there's no reason I can't go. "You're short on operatives."

"Because, you're not a Guardian," Mitzy answers, although my comment was directed at CJ.

"The amount of team training required to operate *on* a Guardian team isn't something that just happens," CJ explains why I can't join one of his teams. "Simply put, you're a liability."

A liability?

I take a step forward. "That's not a good enough reason." It's the best reason in the world, but I'm not done pleading my case. "I'm no stranger to that kind of teamwork." I shift my attention to CJ. "You know what I say makes sense."

"Jinx …" Wolfe's low warning tone only stokes my anger. He grabs my arm, trying to get me to take a step back, but I'm not having it.

"Let me go." I rip my arm out of his grip. "You have two objectives: the Belvedere and Caviar Dreams. You have six Guardians. Seven if you count Lily." There's been some talk about deploying Lily, but none about me. "It makes perfect sense. Put me in. You'll have eight operatives, two teams of four."

Or a team of six for the ship and two to focus on the Belvedere. If all six on Alpha team are needed for that extraction, I'm certain Lily and I can figure out how to free the three women still trapped somewhere within the bowels of the Belvedere.

"Jinx, you're simply not familiar with how our teams operate.

That alone disqualifies you." CJ digs in, not giving an inch. "We don't have time for this."

"If it's about …"

He holds up a hand, silencing me. "It has nothing to do with being a woman. Don't even bring that into this conversation."

I was totally going to bring that into this little back and forth. CJ's damn perceptive, for a man.

Although, I can't really argue that he's sexist. The lead operative for Delta team is female. Charlie, aka Charlene, is also female, and soon Lily will join their team.

This has nothing to do with discrimination and everything to do with exactly what Mitzy and CJ said. I've never trained with the Guardians. That makes me a liability.

But it's not like I'm asking to go on the mission to rescue the hostages on Caviar Dreams. I'm merely suggesting I can be useful here on the ground.

Why is no one listening to me?

Heat rises on the back of my neck, and I'm seconds from totally blowing my cool and losing it.

"We have—" I glance at the wall clock and do some quick mental math, "twenty minutes until the helicopter lands. You know I'm right."

There's no way I'm letting this go.

"We still need to gear up." Max blows out his breath. From the way his fingers drum on the tabletop, he's eager to get going.

I'm slowing him down.

"You can do that in your sleep. How long will it take you? Five minutes?" In this, he can't blow smoke up my ass.

One of the things I've learned is how little time it takes for the Guardians to prep for a mission. Especially when all their gear sits in six neat piles in the main living room. The first thing the Guardians did when we moved in was make that room their personal bullpen.

"Running an op like this isn't the same as what you're used to with the DEA," Axel chimes in, adding a useless opinion.

I'm not going to argue that point. One of the reasons the

Guardians are as lethal and efficient as they are is specifically because of the way they train as a team. It's an amalgamation of what they learned in the military, as part of a special forces team, and what they've added to as Guardians.

It is different, but not so much that I'm a complete liability. Besides, they're door kickers. Brute strength combined with efficient teamwork is a Guardian's major selling point.

What they don't have is experience working undercover. Granted, Max and Knox went undercover at Benefield's estate, but that's not what the Guardians do best. They know it, and I know it.

"How different can it be?" I look to Lily, hoping for support.

Lily and I talk all the time, trading stories about our experiences with the Guardians. It's different. I get that it's different. But talking to Lily night after night, I feel like I know what to expect and how to adapt.

"Jinx can do it." Lily doesn't balk at backing me up. "And what she says makes sense."

"I *can* do this." I feel like it needs to be said again and barely refrain from stamping my foot like a toddler throwing a tantrum. "I may not have been trained by you, but I'm a fully trained DEA operative. I know all about busting down doors and taking out the bad guys. Rescuing hostages is new for me, but I know when to shoot, when to hold my fire, how to clear a room, and how to cover a teammate. I'm not saying I should be on the team boarding Caviar Dreams, but I can handle the Belvedere. I've done it before." I turn to Lily. "Just ask Lily."

"Jinx is right." Lily's gaze cuts to Knox, who's trying to get her not to plead my case. She may sleep in his bed, but Lily is my sister by another mother. We share a history he can't touch. No way will Lily leave me high and dry. "What's needed at the Belvedere isn't much different from many of the operations we were involved with while working for the DEA, and to be honest, we don't need a big team." She looks to me. "Jinx and I can do it ourselves if you need all of Alpha on Caviar Dreams."

"No way are the two of you going alone." Knox's face turns beet red. He's not happy about Lily operating and especially unhappy about not being there to protect her. He makes that clear as day. In the past, he's also mentioned how distracting it would be to do a mission with her.

Honestly, I agree with him on that. A distracted Guardian is a liability.

"And are y'all forgetting the day we met?" I turn to Wolfe and prop my fists on my hips.

No need to go over that again. I laid him flat on his back when he told me I couldn't go with him and his team to rescue Lily. Granted, it wasn't technically the day I met Wolfe, Liam, or Knox, but it was the first time I met the others. "You let me go with you then." I forced them to take me. "And I didn't get in your way. I followed orders."

Wolfe might argue that I didn't do anything. They basically carried me around like a sack of potatoes. Max assigned Wolfe to watch over me, and all I did was hang out on the *USS Charles Sexton* while they boarded the boat carrying Lily and eventually rescued her. It was a bit more complicated than that, but close enough.

I restate my point, pounding my fist on the table for emphasis.

I went with them.

I know how to support a team.

"You can't send everyone to Caviar Dreams." I turn back to Sam, knowing he's the one I must convince. "Deverough said three of the girls are headed to Colombia. The others are still at the Belvedere. If we don't move on both places simultaneously, we'll lose the other girls." I look at the stony expressions of those gathered.

Convincing them is like moving a mountain. The resistance is mind-boggling.

And Wolfe?

The man stands with his arms crossed over his chest, doing nothing to support me. Out of all of them, he knows what I'm capable of physically. When not arguing, he works with me during sparring practice. They all do.

The first job I was given when they hired me was to teach my unique fighting style to the different members of the Guardian teams.

I know how to fight. I know how to shoot. My sharpshooting skills are nothing compared to Axel, the team's sniper, but I can sink my bullets into the center mass of a moving target. My skills are not in question.

"Come on." I turn my attention to CJ. "You know I'm right. Put four men on Caviar Dreams, then put two on the Belvedere with Lily and me in support. It makes sense. It's a hotel. A casino. We go in as couples having fun for the night. Work our way behind the scenes. Find the girls. Smuggle them out. Hell, we can Uber there if transport is an issue."

It's not. The Uber comment is just to piss them off.

CJ and Sam exchange a look. Max coughs into his fist. He's been silent during my entire tirade.

"You know I'm right." I'm going to plead my case until they physically kick me out of the battle room. "You need two teams of six, and you have one. Then there's Lily and me. That's eight qualified operatives. Lily and I have experience working undercover with the DEA. Not to mention, we trained together. We know how the other person thinks. If you do nothing at all with the Belvedere, send me and Lily. We know how to work together, and we're not afraid to go in alone. Send Alpha team to Caviar Dreams if you must, but Lily and I will rescue the other three women."

If they don't listen to reason, I'm done. I'll walk out the front door and rescue those women myself.

That hits a nerve. I swear I've never seen grown men pucker their assholes at the same time. They don't like what I say because they know I'm right. What they need to get past is their chauvinistic attitudes that tells them not to put a woman in danger.

They're great guys, but their alpha ass-hole-ry has a habit of getting in the way. I place my hand on Wolfe's arm and look up at him.

"I can do this." I hate that I have to beg for permission to save three innocent lives. "Don't you have any faith in me?"

Wolfe's entire body tenses. "Luv, it's not about faith. It's about …"

"I know we can do this." I cut him off before he says something we're both going to regret. "I wish you believed in me."

Okay, that comment may not have been fair, but I can't help getting that dig in.

Deep down, Wolfe's faith in my abilities is unshakable. He knows what I'm capable of as I've proven myself over and over again. I put him in a difficult position, forcing him to balance his loyalties to his team against his loyalty to me.

"Look, I get that you're not convinced. Call Harry if you need proof." I speak to the room, taking some of the pressure off Wolfe. "Granted, I've never worked without a full team of backup on standby, but I've been in some pretty sketchy situations before. I handled myself well. Lily did too. With the information Deverough gave us, we know exactly where we need to go and exactly how to get out of there."

Honestly, now that I've really thought about it, and argued until my face is blue, there's no way in hell they're keeping me from doing what's right. Losing those three women is the wrong thing to do. There's just no excuse.

Like Lily, I'm still new to the team. The tech team doesn't *need* me to carry out this mission. I'm extra, which means nothing is keeping them from diverting my talents.

"You might as well give in." Liam's words come as a complete surprise.

Out of everyone gathered, he's not where I expect support to come from. I expect that from Wolfe, but I'm not getting it from him.

"And how exactly do you see that working out?" Knox gives a shake of his head.

"Easy," Liam explains. "You, Max, Axel, and Griff take Caviar Dreams. Brett is en route. Sawyer is too. They both touch down within the hour. Let them fill out Alpha team. Wolfe and I go with Lily and Jinx. Jinx has a great idea about the whole couple thing, unless you have a problem lending me Lily for the night?"

Knox's face turns red. "Keep your hands off my woman."

"To make it look real, there will be touching." Liam gives one of the biggest smirks I've seen in my life. "If you're super nice, I'll keep the kissing to a minimum."

"Why you …" Knox nearly launches himself across the table to get to Liam but stops when Sam claps his hands together. The whole room quiets. I swear I can hear a pin drop.

"Stop. We don't have time for this." Sam takes in a deep breath. "As much as I hate to admit it, Jinx makes some good points."

I knew it. I want to cheer but keep a lid on it until Sam finishes his thought.

"I can do this." I smile at Sam. "You won't regret it."

He's got the final say. Convincing the others is more for show than anything else.

"As soon as they get wind we rescued the girls on Caviar Dreams, they're going to move the ones still at the Belvedere. So, this is what we're going to do."

As Sam breaks things down, basically spitting out my ideas, a single raggedy button bounces on the dining table. It's joined by another, and then another. Soon, it's raining buttons and laughter follows.

"What's going on?" I look around the room at the Guardians and the techies who tossed well over two dozen buttons on the table. Buttons are an Alpha team thing, but there are buttons raining down from both sides of the table.

The corner of Wolfe's mouth tics up into a smirk, and he winks at me. He leans in, gathering all the buttons into a pile. Those that bounced off the table are picked up and added to the growing pile.

"I don't get it." I get the button thing. It's this weird thing Alpha team does when they bet. But there are far more than six buttons on that table. "You bet?"

I glance around the room, finding smiles and smirks on nearly every face. Wolfe scoops up the buttons.

"What's this for?"

"Welcome to Guardian HRS, my fiery Jinx. I just won my bet."

"And what did you bet?"

"I'll tell you later." He winks at me again, then shoves the buttons into the front pocket of his jeans. "Looks like we need to get dressed." He turns and offers me his arm.

Liam laughs and saunters over to Knox. He gives a little bow. "May I borrow your woman for the evening?"

"If you kiss her, I'm going to kill you." Knox shakes his finger in Liam's face.

Liam doesn't blink. He simply sticks out his elbow and waits for Lily to take his arm.

"Don't worry, I promise no tongue." She lifts up on tiptoe to kiss Knox.

Knox's eyes widen and he takes a step back. With her lilting laughter filling the room, Lily grabs Liam's arm, and they march out. Wolfe steers me through the room. The moment we hit the doorway leading out, the entire room bursts into laughter.

I thought no one was listening to me, but I was wrong about that.

"I thought you didn't have my back."

"I'll always have your back." Wolfe places his free hand over mine, patting it lightly. "Besides, we already talked about it."

"When?" I glance back over my shoulder. "You haven't left my side since Deverough ..."

"Luv, you're not the only one with a secret code. The guys and I were talking all about it while you were making your case."

"You should've told me. You let me ... I must've looked like an idiot."

He stops, spins me around until I face him, then stares deeply into my eyes. "We're not supposed to use that word, luv, and you're fucking hot when you're mad." He reaches down between us, shamelessly hiding the proof of exactly how I make him feel.

I nibble my lower lip and take in a deep breath.

"Well, I feel like I should be pissed at you for doing that to me, but I'm not. Do you haze all the new hires?"

"Only the ones I want to fuck, and that wasn't us hazing you." He cups the side of my face. "That was us welcoming you into the fold. Now, let's get dressed."

"I don't have anything to wear." A cocktail dress was not on the list when I packed for this mission.

"Mitzy got what you need."

"How the hell did she do that? We just found out about …"

Wolfe places his finger over my mouth. "We call it Mitzy Magic. It's best not to ask too many questions about how that girl gets stuff done." With that, Wolfe leans down and brushes his lips against mine.

For a kiss that's barely a kiss, my toes curl, and my heart takes flight.

THIRTY-ONE

Jinx

THE SCARLET COCKTAIL DRESS IS THE PERFECT COMPLEMENT TO MY olive skin and dark hair. It's skintight, hot as sin, and totally inappropriate for an operation. The red, over-the-knee boots are not what I would pair with the dress, but I admire the thought put into them.

Running around in five-inch heels is impractical. The wide heel on the boots compensates for that disadvantage. As for where to put my weapon, Wolfe hands me twin knives to tuck into the boots, and there's a strap for a small tranquilizer gun. In my micro purse, I carry a Mitzy special cell phone and a lock picking kit.

Wolfe dresses in a black suit with a tie matching the shade of my dress. He, too, carries a tranq gun, along with his sidearm.

"Damn, but you clean up well." My entire body engages in the act of checking him out: heart palpitations, dry mouth, and that fluttering in my belly. He's definitely a triple threat.

"Wow." His mouth drops.

"What?"

"That shouldn't be legal."

"What shouldn't?"

"How hot you look in that dress. I want to rip it off and do filthy things to your body." His gaze heats.

A quick look at the clock tells me we don't have time for any fun stuff.

Maybe.

I glide across the room and wrap my arms around him. Wolfe towers over me. All it takes is one look, and his gaze heats.

"You are a goddess in that dress. Every man is going to have his eyes on you."

I walk my fingers up his crisply pressed shirt and tug on his tie.

"That works for me. If everyone's looking at me, they won't notice the muscle standing by my side."

"Is that all I am to you?" He hugs me tight, and there's no mistaking the hard length of him pressing against my belly. "Muscle?"

"I like this muscle best." My hand slips between us, heading down until I cup his very hard cock. It twitches, and Wolfe groans.

"Now, that's not fair." His lips part and his tongue darts out to wet his lips. "I'm going to do very bad things to you when this mission is done."

"How bad?"

"Sinfully bad." He places his hand over mine, pulling it off the hard shaft.

I lick my lips as an idea comes to mind.

I owe Wolfe an apology, and I know the perfect way to tell him I'm sorry.

Before I have time to act on that, Wolfe leans down and kisses me. I moan as our lips press together. Our tongues glide against each other, and I loop my hands around his neck. The kiss is a dance that can only be described as sinfully smoldering and righteously perfect.

Wolfe puts the entirety of his soul into kissing me. I feel it in the thundering of my heart and in the sparks of electricity dancing across my skin.

This kiss feels different from all the rest. It's intimate and carnal, devoted and reverent. It's triumphant and magnificent. It's all-consuming, and I'm frantic for more. It steals my breath and burns me from the inside out.

Our bodies press together, and I can't help but thrust my hips, needing more contact. Wolfe's breathing changes, growing hoarse and needful with every punishing lash of his tongue as he devours my mouth.

"Fuck, what you do to me should be illegal." He pulls away with a groan and tugs at his tie as he tries to regain control.

"What you do for me ..." I glance toward the door leading out of our room. "What you did for me back there. I don't deserve you."

"Luv, I pray each day that I somehow find a way to deserve you, but if we don't hurry up ..."

I bite at my lower lip and peek up at him. There's no way we're making it out of here without taking the edge off.

He places the tips of his fingers beneath my chin and forces me to look at him.

"What the hell just went through that mind of yours?"

I can't help but smile and press my lips together. It's a good thing I haven't finished my makeup. At least I won't need to reapply my lipstick.

"Do you know what I fantasized about all those nights you stripped for me?"

"No, but I'm curious?" He releases my chin. His hand sweeps down my neck, raising goose bumps as his fingers flutter over my skin. His hand settles at the tip of my shoulder.

I reach between us and tug on his belt. "Do you want me to tell you, or show you?"

"Luv, we have a mission to prep."

I cup his groin, letting my fingers explore the long, hard length of him.

"Seems like the best prep is to take care of this. Wouldn't want you to be unfocused now, would we?" My fingers curl around his shaft. I grip him solidly and work his buckle with one hand.

As I fumble, Wolfe groans and reaches between us, taking care of the belt, the button, and the zipper of his pants. He shamelessly shoves his pants down mid-thigh, baring himself to me. The muscles of his thighs tremble and his voice strains.

"You're killing me." His hand slips off my shoulder to cup my breast. His thumb brushes over my peaked nipple, and it's my turn to moan. "What went through your mind?"

With my eyes on him, I lower to my knees. I bite my lower lip as his thick musk floods my senses. My gaze shifts to his cock then bounces back to meet his eyes.

The heat of his stare sends a shiver racing down my spine. The energy between us heats my skin, lighting up my nerve endings making my entire body go haywire.

"I thought what a shame that you had to take care of things yourself all those nights. I watched from my bedroom, wanting to be there. With you."

His cock jerks as more blood rushes in, engorging the ropy veins and turning him as hard as steel. The tip of his cock weeps, and a bead of pre-cum urges me to hurry up.

"Fuck, Jinx, the sight of you on your knees is exactly what went through my mind those nights."

I take in a breath and surrender to the moment.

"Show me."

"What?" Smooth, deep, delicious, and sinful, the texture of his voice feels like velvet skating across my skin.

"Show me what you fantasized about."

"Fucking your mouth isn't the only thing I fantasized about." He shifts half a step toward me and fists his cock. "You have no idea what filthy things went through my mind."

Watching Wolfe all those nights messed a bit with my head. He never held back, showing me night after night how much he wanted me. I have a feeling sex with Wolfe will never be predictable. Heat snakes through my body, coiling deep within me as I wonder what it might be like.

I want him with an irrational hunger.

"Show me." It's odd, but I'm a tiny bit scared.

My breathy words, rather than encouraging him, force him to take a step back. My brows draw together until I realize why.

Time for damage control.

"About the other night …" His hand shakes with the grip he has on his cock. "I shouldn't have pushed. It was wrong to make you …"

"The other night was my fault. I shouldn't have forced you the way I did."

"Then why did you …?"

"I don't know. I was scared. Maybe?" I shrug, not sure myself. "I don't really know why. I wanted you but didn't want to want you as much as I did. Pushing you—it took the responsibility off me. Does that make sense?"

"Tell me you want this." He slowly strokes his cock. "I'm not going to force it."

"More than I can say." I reach for his hand and fold my fingers around his. "I want this. Show me how you fantasized about me."

Wolfe reaches for my hair, fisting it at my nape. He shifts forward and slides his hand down to the root of his cock. He's a big man with an even bigger cock. I remember struggling to take him in my mouth back in Callie's bar, but he already knows that.

His lips press together as he places the tip on my lips.

"Open for me." His expression darkens. His voice rolls through me, primal, raw, and eager to fuck.

I open for him. His fingers fist my hair, and Wolfe pushes his way inside.

My jaw opens as he buries his cock in my mouth. His low groan sends licks of pleasure down my spine, and he continues to feed me his cock until he meets resistance. His knuckles press against my lips, and he holds there. Legs shaking. Breaths tugging.

"Fuck, that feels so good."

When I look up at him, his head tips back and all I can see is the strain in the muscles of his neck as he takes a moment to collect himself.

"I thought about fucking your mouth, my fiery Jinx. Choking you as I punished you for teasing me night after night."

I'd say something, but that's not possible right now.

His fist tightens further in my hair, and then Wolfe pulls out. It's agonizingly slow, and lord have mercy if he doesn't shove right back inside.

When Wolfe takes, he takes with ruthless aggression, merciless with the need to plunge his cock deep into my mouth. He groans with pleasure as I struggle to suck and lick, determined to make this something he'll never forget.

Wolfe becomes something else as he fucks my mouth. Unapologetic and raw, he's heat and virility, power and aggression. He plunders and claims with singular focus as he destroys everything I know about giving head.

And that's exactly what I'm not doing.

I'm not giving.

He's taking.

And he does it without remorse, fucking with anger and passion, love and heat. Each time he plunges deep, licks of pleasure burst and spark within me. Each time he pulls out, an aching emptiness fills me. Then he shoves forward again, fueling the fire burning within and through me.

My insides heat. My skin tightens. My mind scrambles with too much sensation. It's impossible to process what's happening.

I simply exist.

There's nothing soft about this, but his brutality, while rough, is also restrained. It shakes me all the way down to my core. The faster he moves, the more sparks flare within me, turning that burn into a firestorm of need.

Wolfe falters above me. He starts to pull out, but I grasp his ass and give a shake of my head.

This is for him, me fulfilling his fantasies night after night. A low moan escapes him, and everything changes. No longer animalistic and raw, he begins to rock into me. It's nearly reverent as the pace slows and I somehow take him deeper.

Wolfe doesn't exactly chase his release as much as move relentlessly toward it. He releases the grip at my nape and slowly strokes my hair until his legs tremble and his breaths surge.

My breasts tingle with a rush of heat and my pussy throbs with a low, needy ache. My chest feels like it's splintering open, cracking in half, laying my heart bare before him. Wolfe's body trembles as his release crashes upon him.

I swallow and gasp for breath as he pulls out. I lean back, sitting on my heels.

He stoops down and gathers me in his arms, fingers combing through my hair, as he kisses along my jawline and finds my mouth.

"You're an amazing woman, constantly surprising me."

My lips are raw and a bit bruised, but I don't care.

"I'm sorry about the other night."

"No need to ..."

"No, let me finish." I give a shake of my head. "I've never dated. Like—never. Sex never meant anything to me. It was simply a physical urge I took care of, but you terrify me. The way you make me feel is something I've never experienced. Anger is my defense, and I used it against you. I'm sorry about that. I never meant to make you feel like I used you, or that I made you do something you weren't comfortable with."

"Luv, I like my sex in all flavors. Soft and gentle. Hard and fast. Rough and dirty; the dirtier the better." He sweeps a strand of hair off my face and tucks it behind my ear. "For me, sex is a playground."

"A playground?"

"Yes, luv, it's the only place where adults get to cut loose and play." His fingers trail along my jaw and sweep down my throat. There, he lets his fingers dig in, reminiscent of when he choked me in the salon.

"Play?"

"It's where we explore our darkness." He leans in and whispers in my ear. "Where we fuck without regret. No remorse." His tongue sweeps around the outer helix of my ear. "It's where we make love, slow and gentle, sweet and tender. It's where we can be whatever we want to be and do whatever we want to do. It's where we can take what we need and give what we want: hard, fast, and ruthless. I think you and I just needed to get over that hump and cross that line together. If I thought you really didn't want it, or that I was forcing you in anyway, I wouldn't have fucked you like I did. But now, we've crossed that line. It's behind us now. We can be whatever we want to be. We can do whatever we want to do. Fantasies are meant to be fulfilled."

"You're an incredible man."

"And you're pretty damn awesome." He shifts back and pulls up his pants. "And we're officially late." Wolfe glances at his watch and a grin fills his face. "Although, I don't regret it one bit."

He reaches down to help me to my feet. I fold into his embrace, loving the way he smells. Then we break apart and I tug my skintight dress back into place. Walking hand in hand, we find Liam and Lily waiting on us in the foyer.

"What took you so long?" Lily blows out a frustrated breath.

Liam and Wolfe exchange a look. They say nothing, but the corners of Liam's mouth tip into a grin.

"Come on. It's time to get to work." Liam rolls his eyes, and that smirk gets bigger.

"What about the others?" Wolfe asks Liam about the rest of their team.

"Ariel Black just picked them up. They'll be in position within ninety minutes. Which means we need to catch up."

Liam opens the door. He gestures for Lily to head outside. I follow behind Lily with Wolfe's on my heels. I swear Liam thumps Wolfe on the back. I can't help my own smile from filling my face.

Outside, Lily drags me ahead of the men. A black limousine waits for us. The driver opens the door and Lily and I scoot in.

"Why were you late?" she whispers.

"Why do you think?" I arch a brow and press my lips together as Wolfe steps up to the door.

Lily grasps my hands and gives a little squeal. "I knew it. I knew the two of you would …"

"Would, what?" Wolfe slips into the car and slides in next to me.

"Nothing." Lily turns toward me with an excited grin.

Liam joins us and there's a bit of rearranging while the men settle in.

"Now that you've taken the edge off, let's discuss how this is going down." Liam taps his ear, activating his comm link. "Check your comms."

I haven't inserted my earpiece and do that now as Liam and Wolfe perform their communication checks. The car slowly rolls down the tree-lined drive as I try not to squirm in my seat. I don't need anyone noticing how nervous I feel. Not after I insisted I be allowed to participate in this case.

Wolfe makes that nearly impossible. He places his hand on my knee and slowly moves his hand up, teasing me with the sweep of his fingers up my thigh. Have I said how incredibly short my skirt is?

It takes forty minutes to work our way through traffic, but soon we pull up to the Belvedere, two couples looking for a bit of fun on the town. I take out my camera, hand it to one of the valets standing around, and have him take our picture.

Lily and I pose, lifting on tiptoe to kiss our men on the cheek. Lily and I give girly squeals as we walk down the red carpet, ready for action.

Wolfe and Liam exchange expressions with the valets, shrugging at our antics, then jog to catch up. Wolfe wraps an arm around me, while Liam pulls Lily to his side.

We enter the Belvedere with comm links active and hidden surveillance tech woven into the fabric of our clothes, the men's watches, and our jewelry. The large emerald around my neck is an infrared camera. Once we sneak into the employee-only areas, we'll use that, along with other bits of Mitzy Magic, to track down and rescue three traumatized women.

This is what the Guardians do. We rescue those who've been taken. I love this job.

Wolfe

We enter the Belvedere looking as normal as we can but draw the attention of all those around us. Lily looks phenomenal in her little black dress and cute combat boots. The black is perfect against her ivory skin and white-blonde hair.

I don't know how Knox let her out of his sight. There's no way I'd let Jinx go out looking like that without me by her side. It says much about the trust Knox has in Liam, but despite his Hollywood looks and whoring ways, Liam is protective of those he considers family.

As for Jinx, that sprayed-on red dress hugs all her curves. I protectively shelter her, tugging her tight to my side, and every man who dares to check her out gets a scowl from me.

After experiencing her amazing oral skills, I'm dying to get her alone and rip that dress off for good. There are several fantasies I can't wait to play out. I'm thinking the dirtier the better is a good place to start.

Until then, I remind myself we're on a mission.

As for our mission, the pin on my tie is a tiny camera, enhanced with Mitzy Magic. Through it, Mitzy directs us through the crowded casino with all of its flashing lights, and incessant ringing of the slot machines. There's already an evening crowd, which will grow merrier and poorer as the booze flows and their wallets empty.

Liam and I stop at the slot machines, letting the girls play a few rounds. Jinx loses ten bucks in less than five minutes. Lily scores a hundred. The girls make a show of it, jumping up and down, turning every eye.

Mitzy directs us through the gaming floor with laser-focused intensity. We stop to hang around a craps table, pretending to be interested in playing. However, Jinx tugs on my arm, begging me to follow her to one of the bars. She responds to Mitzy's direction, pulling us deeper into the bowels of the Belvedere.

We play up our roles; two couples looking for fun.

I allow my hand to drop down to Jinx's ass, where I give it a good squeeze, or light tap, depending on my mood. Jinx hangs on my arm, laughing and having a good time. I twirl her into my embrace over and over, letting the public display get dirtier and dirtier. My kisses last longer and our hips grind. Jinx's hip grinding action grows bolder and bolder, which I'm totally cool with, and on cue.

Liam and Lily follow us around, not nearly as handsy as I am with Jinx, but they're having fun. Liam loops his arm around Lily's shoulder and tugs her in close. She places her hand on his chest, shamelessly feeling him up. Liam keeps his word to Knox. There's no lip action, but it's clear he and Lily are together for those who watch us.

And we're definitely being watched.

Overhead, hundreds of cameras record everything. Mitzy's got that covered as well, or will.

We make our way to an employee access door. I put Jinx's back to the wall and prop my hand beside her head. Leaning in, I kiss and grope while we wait for an employee to come through the door.

It takes longer than it should, which means I get to kiss Jinx as much as I like. While we make a spectacle of ourselves, Mitzy works in the background with the techies to loop video footage they'll insert into the security feeds.

Objective Alpha: make a scene. Objective Bravo: get close enough to the security room for her stuff to do its magic.

"Get a room." Mitzy's voice crackles in my ear as Jinx and I get busy with some tongue action. I can't help but laugh. *"The loop's ready. Just need …"*

As she speaks, the door opens and two cocktail waitresses enter the gaming floor. From the smiles on their faces and their eager eyes, I suspect they're beginning their shifts. In another eight to ten hours, they won't look so perky.

Lily, who's closest to the door, holds out her purse as the door swings shut, propping it open.

"Objective Bravo achieved." I communicate our progress. Bravo checkpoint is to gain access to the employee-only halls.

We wait on Mitzy.

She takes point on our mission while CJ and Sam focus on the rest of Alpha team's mission.

"And go!" Mitzy gives us the go-ahead.

Jinx and I take no time slipping through that door. She pulls me after her, looking exactly like a horny chick eager to get fucked.

Other than security watching overhead, the hallways are deserted. Mitzy figures we've got three to eight minutes before they send a team out to set us straight. Lily and Liam remain behind, guarding the door while we *"get busy."*

If confronted, they have a script to follow. All Jinx and I need to do is stay put until Mitzy tells us we're good to go.

We don't go far. Jinx pulls me along, turning a corner and then another until we locate a janitorial closet.

"Passing Charlie."

"Copy that." Mitzy confirms our position. On the other side of the wall are the servers for the security system. Mitzy will remotely hack into them while Jinx and I make out.

It's kind of cool, and weird at the same time.

Biting her lip, Jinx grabs my tie, and without missing a beat, yanks me into the janitorial closet, practically mauling me as our lips lock.

Controlled remotely by Mitzy, the cell phone in my back pocket and the one in Jinx's very tiny purse, get to work.

Always willing to kiss my girl, I wrap her in my arms and lock my lips to hers. She punches playfully at my chest.

"Hang on."

Reluctantly, I release her. Jinx opens her purse and pulls out her cell phone. With a quick look around, she kicks it under the mop bucket. Smart girl. If we're caught before Mitzy's done, Jinx's phone will finish the job.

I pull her against me. "You make me ache for you in the worst possible way." I lean back and give her a look. "I owe you an orgasm."

"Eww, gross." Mitzy pipes in through the comms. *"You do realize I can hear everything you say and do. Cut back on the heavy breathing."*

"We need to make this as realistic as possible. You may want to turn down the volume."

"Don't you want to know when security is getting close?"

"Not really." I'd turn off my comms if I could, but that's not possible.

Jinx glances up at me. There's nothing but sin in her eyes. She places her hands on my shoulders and lifts up on tiptoe to whisper into my ear.

"We never did get to fuck in that bathroom. A janitor's closet is a close second."

I pull back, eyes wide. "You're not serious, are you?"

I'm all for fucking in unusual places, but we're technically on duty.

"I wish I was." Jinx's smile droops.

The reason why we're here is the worst cold shower in the world. My erect and eager cock slowly deflates.

Damn, if that's not a buzzkill.

A quick check of my watch reveals three minutes have passed. Jinx and I kind of stand there, staring at each other, instead of going at it hot and heavy.

"Security blew by," Lily calls out a warning.

"Damn, they're faster than I thought." I glance at the door, debating how sturdy the sink on the wall is. "Come here."

Quickly, I unfasten my belt, undo the fly, and push my pants down to my thighs. I grab Jinx and lift her onto the sink. She doesn't miss a beat, wrapping her arms around me as I wedge my hips between her legs.

I grip her hips and nuzzle her neck as I rock forward and back. It's a bit discombobulating, pretend fucking with a half-erect cock, but I do my best. Jinx wraps her legs around me, crossing her ankles over my ass. She yanks one of the straps off her shoulder to expose her nipple. Arching her back, she writhes as I bend down, taking her tit into my mouth.

The door behind us shudders, but I locked it.

"Open up in there."

Jinx cries out. She's pretty damn good at faking an orgasm. Not sure what to think about that.

More pounding.

"Open the door!"

The door shakes as security slams into it. Jinx's cries escalate. Really playing it up.

"Just a minute." I call out while Jinx moans and shouts.

"Yes, baby! Yes!"

The doorknob twitches.

More pounding.

Jinx completes her orgasmic performance and gives a salacious wink.

My turn.

Only, I don't get to finish, which is probably a good thing. I'm not as good of an actor as Jinx, and definitely not while under pressure.

The door gives way, opening with a crash. Two burly security guards crowd the doorway as I glance over my shoulder. Jinx gives a little squeak. I pull back and hastily pull up my pants while Jinx jumps off the sink.

With no shame, she readjusts her dress. Jinx pulls the shoulder strap slowly, while the men stare at her exposed tit. I kind of want to pop them in the nose for staring, but I'm too busy putting my pants back together.

"Hi, boys." Jinx gives a little wiggle as she pulls the hem of her skirt back down. "We were just having a bit of harmless fun."

"Guests are not allowed back here." The guy in front tries to keep his expression stern, professional, but I see it in his eyes. This is not what he was expecting to find. He can barely look Jinx in the eye.

The guy behind him taps him on the shoulder. "Come on, Gus. They're just having a bit of fun."

"They can have *fun* somewhere else." Gus takes a step back and waves us out of the small janitorial closet. "Come on."

I have no idea if Mitzy finished what she needed, but Jinx's phone is well hidden for the time being. I'm not keen on leaving it behind, though, and continue to stall.

"We're not in trouble, are we?" Jinx pauses by the door. Her lashes flutter as she looks at Gus. "It was a dare. You know how it is? Just a bit of fun? My friend and I kind of have this list. We call it our Dare list and well ..." Her gaze flicks back inside the closet. "She dared me. Please tell me we're not in trouble." She places her hand on Gus's chest. "It won't happen again."

"Rules say we gotta take you in." Gus remains steadfast.

"Take me in?" Her hands fly to her cheeks, and damn if there's not the tiniest tear getting ready to fall. "Please don't do that. I'm ... we're really, really sorry. Can't we just get back to our friends? I swear this will never happen again." She nibbles on her lip.

"Come on, you two." The guard with Gus takes a step back. "Let's get you back to the casino."

"Chuck, that's not protocol." Gus isn't having it.

"Weren't you young once?" Chuck checks out the tiny closet. "Out of everything we see, this is nothing but some harmless fun."

"Yes." Jinx puts her hand on Chuck's arm while I try to appear appropriately chastised.

This is so not the way I operate, but I have a feeling Jinx will have better luck getting us out of this with nothing but a warning. She's also doing a great job at stalling.

I cock my head, waiting on Mitzy to report in.

"Come on, sweetie," I say. "We should probably go."

"Yes." Jinx gives Chuck's arm a little squeeze. "Thank you."

She steps out into the hallway and turns the wrong way. Just then, Mitzy's voice crackles through the comms.

"Objective Charlie complete."

"Luv, where's your purse?" I glance at Jinx, looking her over.

"Oh." She spins around and bats her lashes at Chuck. "I left my purse in there."

She points, but when she moves to get it, Gus pushes her aside and leans into the closet himself.

"It's bright red, matches my dress. You should be … Oh!" Gus hands over her purse. Jinx takes it from him, immediately opens the small purse, and glances inside. "Um, I don't see my phone. It must've fallen out. Can you …" She looks expectantly at Gus.

While Chuck stands guard over me in the hall, Gus gets on hands and knees to look for Jinx's phone. It takes less than a minute before he hands it over to Jinx.

She's fucking gorgeous when she smiles, and Gus totally falls for her charms.

"Thank you, so much. I don't know what I would've done." She tucks her phone into her tiny purse and looks at me. "I'm totally getting Lily back after this."

I hold out my hand. "Come on, luv, we've bothered these men long enough." I point the correct way down the hall. "This way?"

"You got it." Chuck gestures for us to lead the way.

He and Gus trail behind us until we reach the doors we entered through. Gus holds the door open as Jinx steps through.

"I'm so going to kill you!" Jinx screeches at Lily. "We got caught." The girls hug as Gus and Chuck look on. "They were going to take us in, but Gus here is a total sweetie, letting us off the hook." Jinx gives a little wave, wriggling her fingers at Gus and Chuck.

"A dare's a dare." Lily slides right into character. "Um, thank you for not locking up my friend."

The way the two of them work seamlessly together is fun to watch. It's obvious they've done similar things in the past. I can't wait for Jinx to spill all her filthy secrets.

Before Gus and Chuck leave, Jinx gives each of them a peck on the cheek. "Thanks for being so cool about this."

Chuck laughs, and there's even the tiniest smile on Gus's gruff mug. The two of them leave us with a warning, then depart. We're lucky they don't kick us out of the establishment. It was always a possibility, but clearly, they couldn't say no to Jinx. I appreciate the difficulty in that.

"Now, how about drinks?" Lily grabs Liam's arm and drags him away. "I hear this place has the most amazing rooftop bar with an awesome view."

Jinx and I follow behind Lily and Liam. Liam and I scan the crowd, heads on a swivel, looking for threats. But there's nothing to worry about. Soon, we ride a massive glass elevator to the top of the building. There's a lot of traffic up and down these elevators, which will work in our favor.

"Checkpoint Delta achieved." We reach our next objective of the night.

"Copy that. Head over to the southern corner. You'll see a maintenance hatch which leads down to the HVAC floor."

Deverough said the women are being held in a secure room located beneath the rooftop bar. This mission is different from our other ops. It's more casual and lacks that sense of imminent danger I associate with an active operation. The undercover vibe isn't my strongest suit, but Jinx and Lily are completely at home. I'm reminded they were trained as undercover operatives with the DEA.

Did Max and Knox feel the same way when they infiltrated Benefield's establishment? Max acted the part of a wealthy buyer with Knox as his bodyguard. They went into that mission unarmed. At least I have a sidearm and a dart gun.

It still feels weird.

Decked out in my black tactical gear and armed to the teeth,

I'm used to capitalizing on the cover of darkness to achieve my objectives. Executing an op in a suit, with only a tranq gun and my sidearm, feels weirder than weird.

And we haven't gotten to the oddest part of this crazy mission. My eyes practically bugged out of my head when Sam and Mitzy came up with the idea. Honestly, I don't see how they can pull it off.

Hopefully, Mitzy gains control of the security system soon, as I'm not keen on spending too much time up on this roof.

THIRTY-THREE

Wolfe

We head over to the southwest corner of the roof and commandeer a table next to the maintenance hatch. It's a bit out of the way of the main press of the crowd.

Liam heads for the bar, doing exactly what anyone would expect. Our tiny ensemble is still under scrutiny by Belvedere security.

That will soon change.

There are far more important things to occupy their time than watching our sex-capades.

With limited personnel, and two simultaneous missions to run, Mitzy came up with a creative and brilliant solution for our extraction plan—if she can pull it off. If not, we're fucked.

Since our arrival, bits and pieces of that plan are being set in motion. While Liam gets our drinks, Mitzy walks us through the next stage of our operation.

Behind me is an access door for the HVAC units, which fill up the floor beneath us.

As the evening wears on, the crowd grows. The music thumps. The dance floor pulses. The air supercharges with the energy of over a hundred people partying it up on the rooftop.

Liam and I scan the crowd, looking for threats, finding none. Everyone here is up for a good time. And in a town like New Orleans, anything is possible.

"T-minus ten. You guys ready?"

I look to Lily, Liam, and Jinx. They return three affirmatives. Lily casts her gaze across the crowded dance floor. More people spill out of the glass elevators and join the crowd.

We wait for Mitzy's signal.

Things become a bit more organized within the crowd. People cluster together and form lines. It doesn't take long for the entire dance floor to turn into a massive line dance. More people arrive via the elevators. The crowd spills off the dance floor, moving out toward where we sit. Soon, there are people all around us, shielding us from prying eyes.

"T-minus five-four-three-two …" As Mitzy counts us down, Lily and Jinx shift in their seats. Someone reaches out from the crowd; it's one of our techies. He hands Liam a duffel bag. Liam slings the bag over his shoulder as the access door remotely unlocks. *"One."*

We move to the door. I hold it open as the three of them slip inside and follow behind. We move according to directions as Mitzy guides us through a maze of machinery until we reach another door.

"How much farther?" I keep my voice low, vocalizing just loud enough for Mitzy to hear.

"Take the stairwell down one flight." There's a pause, then she's back online. *"When you exit, take an immediate right. Expect two guards on the door."* She fails to mention whether there are any more inside.

"Copy that." I wave to the others.

"You have to take them out from a distance."

"On it." Liam pulls out a dart gun from his boot. Jinx does the same. We're all equipped with standard sidearms, but the darts are what we need. We're not here to kill. That results in red tape, which is difficult to wade through, and despite being deputized US Marshalls, we try to keep our body counts to a minimum.

"I don't have to tell you what will happen if those guards get the word out."

"We're on it."

Liam places his hand on the door leading to the stairwell. He pushes it open as I go in first. Sweeping the stairwell, I take two steps in as Jinx and Lily fall in behind me. I'm on point. Liam takes the rear.

We slowly work our way down and pause on the next landing.

"In position," I report to Mitzy.

"Hold." Silence crackles over the comm channel as we wait for Mitzy to scan the hallway. *"All clear. Confirmed. Two at the door."*

"Copy that."

I've never worked with a female in the field before, but I've seen Lily in action and seen Jinx fight. The only thing I worry about is hesitation on their part. In this line of work, there's no room for that.

Liam carries the duffel bag. It crosses over his chest and hangs on his back. He gives me a nod, telling me he's ready. His aim will be true. Mine too. All we need is one dart to hit the guards. That's enough sedative to knock them out. But just in case, we carry four darts each.

"I'll take the right. You take the left."

I slowly move us into position, following commands given by Mitzy, who has eyes on every square inch of the building. As we move through, she erases our presence, looping the various camera angles as required.

I hold up my fist.

Everyone checks their dart gun. Three fingers up, I count us down.

Three-two-one.

As a group, we step out into the open. It takes a moment for the men to notice. Their shock delays their reactions, which is exactly what we need. Carbon dioxide cartridges whiz and pop, sending our darts flying.

Mitzy assures us there's enough sedative in the darts to take the men down. Our darts fly true. The men jerk with the impact, then fall, knocked out cold before they hit the floor.

We're on the move, reloading the darts, rushing now. Time is of the essence. In this, Mitzy has no opportunity to loop the camera. We work on borrowed time.

At the door, we don't bother checking the lock. Mitzy's remote access works like a charm, but I hold up my fist again. Rushing now could prove fatal. We don't know who's behind that door.

Liam and I look at each other, counting down, silently, from three to one. On one, we kick down the door. He sweeps right. I sweep left. Jinx and Lily follow us in.

Liam takes out one guard. I take out another. We expect no more than two, but there are six inside. The remaining four men rise from a game of cards. They reach for their shoulder holsters. Lily and Jinx fire their tranq guns. The darts fly true.

Four men are down. Two are on their feet.

They rush me and Liam, completely ignoring the girls.

Jinx moves into action, flowing in a sinuous acrobatic attack. She sweeps out her leg, tripping the man going for Liam. Then follows with an elbow strike to his back. Capoeira is an artistic fighting style, conveying lethal power with incredible beauty. There's a force and rhythm to the way she dodges, jumps, and kicks.

My tranq gun is empty after taking down one of the four men. Liam's is as well. With Jinx and Lily engaging the other man, I brace for impact as the man charging me dips his head. Like a bull, he tries to ram me, grappling with me as he takes me to the ground. Anticipating his attack, I spin to the side and use his momentum to take him down to the ground.

I give Liam enough time, if not to reload his tranq gun, to at least pull one of his darts free. Liam slides to his knees as my opponent falls to the ground. His arm goes up, then slams the tip of the dart into the side of the man's neck.

The man jerks then stills.

Immediately, I glance up, worried about the girls. Not that there's anything to be worried about. Jinx stands over the still body of the fourth man. Like Liam, Lily drove a dart home.

All four men are down and out.

"Strong work." I stretch my neck and glance around. There's no sign of our hostages, but two doors lead out of the room. I give a short prayer there are no other guards in here with us.

"Where are the girls?" Jinx scans the room, brows tugged tight.

"Check that door." I give a jerk of my chin in the direction of one of two doors leading out of the room. I reload my tranq gun with a third dart. The others do the same. I head to the left while Jinx moves right. Lily and Liam cover the four men we neutralized.

The room I check out is a bathroom and empty.

"Found them," Jinx calls out from the other room.

Liam yanks the duffel bag off his shoulder and tosses it on the table. He yanks open the zipper and pulls out a stack of bright orange shirts with garish *Be Happy* smiley faces on them. They're obnoxious and painful to look at, which is why everyone will be looking at them. Again, I shake my head, wondering what the fuck Mitzy's thinking.

Regardless, I grab the shirts and head into the room with Jinx.

Jinx kneels beside three women who relax when Jinx pulls out a lock pick kit from her tiny purse. They finally understand we're here to rescue them rather than something worse. It doesn't take but a minute for Jinx to remove the cuffs and chains from the women.

They cower when I enter the room.

Well fuck.

Not that it's any surprise. All the men they've seen, at least recently, abducted and held them prisoner in this room. They stripped the women down to their shirts and panties, no doubt to reduce any chances they may have if they dared to escape.

"He's with me." Jinx soothes the women as she reaches a hand out to me. With a little flick of her fingers, she tells me to give her the shirts. "He just looks scary as shit, but he's a real softy beneath that wolfish mug. My name's Jinx, Jinx Freeman. What's yours?"

One of the girls sniffs and wipes at her face. "Rose. Rose Hunt."

"Julie Gant." Julie sucks in a deep breath, trying to be strong, but a sob escapes her. "Are you here to rescue us?"

"That's the plan." I should let Jinx handle things, but we're wasting precious seconds.

"It's nice to meet you, Rose." Jinx hands over one of the shirts.

"I know it looks funny, but you have to trust me. And, yes, we're Guardians. We're going to rescue you."

It's not necessary for Jinx to ask the girls their names. We all know them on sight. In addition to Rose, there's the missing vet school student, Julie Gant, and Lori Black, our missing international traveler.

Jinx hands each of the girls a shirt to wear. The women are filthy. They have no pants or shoes, which complicates things, but we'll make it work.

When Jinx stands and pulls the garish orange shirt over her head, there's no reason to worry. The shirt hangs down nearly to her knees.

"Come on. We don't have much time." Lily is right beside Jinx. She, too, pulls one of the shirts over her head.

Lily reaches for Lori Black and helps the girl to stand. Still in shock, Lori needs help putting on the shirt.

"We need to move." Liam comes up behind me and whispers in my ear.

"Copy that." I glance over at Jinx. "Ten seconds." I don't want to freak the girls out, but if we don't hurry it up, no one is getting out of here.

"Gotcha." Jinx finishes helping Rose Hunt with the orange monstrosity while Lily moves on to Julie Gant.

A smirk lifts the corner of my mouth as I look at the five women in identical *Be Happy* orange shirts. The eyes of the smiley face sit right over their boobs. I don't think Mitzy took that into consideration when she hatched this crazy plan.

I shrug into my shirt and reload my tranq gun. We all carry sidearms, but those are to be used only if absolutely necessary. The last thing we need is an exchange of gunfire.

"Wolfe ..." Jinx turns her attention to the women's bare feet then glances at me.

"We need to move." Those bare feet are a liability. "Nothing to do about that."

I move out of the room. Liam watches over our sleeping guards. Between Jinx and Lily, they manage to get the women up on their feet. All three tug at the offensive orange, but they're up and moving.

I stand by the door leading out and wait for Jinx and Lily to bring the girls. Liam will take the rear as I lead our procession to safety. Jinx holds hands with Rose. Lily has Julie and Lori.

"Mitzy?" I listen for Mitzy to tell me what's happening on the other side of the door.

"All clear, but you'll have company if you don't move now."

"Which direction? Up or down?" This is the sketchy part of the plan, but I trust my team.

"Back to the roof."

"So, we're really doing this?"

"Trust me."

I shake my head but trust Mitzy. This is definitely not a stealth night mission.

"I'll take point. Liam, you're in the rear. Lily and Jinx ..."

"We know." Jinx gives Rose's hand a squeeze. "Stay right by my side."

"I'm scared." Rose sniffs, but her eyes are sharp. Focused.

A quick glance at Lori and Julie reveals the same. As traumatized as these women are, they're strong where it counts. Which is exactly what they need to survive this trauma.

Once again, I count us down. I enter the hall, sweeping left then right. Moving back toward the stairwell, I keep my eyes focused forward while Liam checks our six.

The women surprise me. There are tears. Sniffles. But they keep it together. Damn strong women.

The shirts hang to their knees. Their hair leaves something to be desired, but like their lack of footwear, there's not much we can do about that.

It's comical watching all five women swallowed up in bright orange shirts. Liam and I wear the same shirts, but they're normal sized on us.

We make it to the stairwell free and clear. I head up. The girls follow. Jinx whispers something to them. I don't turn around. My focus is on what's ahead. Once we're all inside the stairwell, Liam uses the strap of the duffel bag to tie the door closed. It won't hold beneath a determined attack, but it will buy us time. He tucks seven white masks under his arm.

We race up the stairs and head back into the machine room. This time, I don't need Mitzy to guide me through. I follow the path we took until we're at the service door where we first entered.

Placing my ear to the door, the deep thumping bass is accompanied by stomping and clapping. I ease the door open and stare in awe.

"Fucking amazing."

The entire dance floor is covered with a flash mob, all with identical orange shirts, with that goofy white smiley face and white masks. They're dancing to the song "Happy" by Pharrell Williams, clapping and stomping along to the music.

THIRTY-FOUR

Wolfe

THE DANCE FLOOR IS A SEA OF ORANGE, THE PERFECT PLACE TO LOSE three women within a crowd.

"Hang on." Liam pulls us up short and passes out white plastic masks. "Put these on."

We put on the masks. Immediately, I don't like them as they interfere with my peripheral vision, but I trust the madness.

"We're ready." We do a quick reshuffling. I take Rose's hand. Liam grabs Julie. Jinx and Lily put Lori between them. With each woman attached to a member of our team, we're ready.

"This next bit is the tricky part." I keep my voice as low as I can but have to speak loud enough to hear over the music. "We need to make it across that dance floor to where the elevators are."

"But ..." All the color drains out of Rose's face. "Won't they ..."

"You look the same as everyone else out there, which is why this may be hard for you."

Rose gulps but gives a shaky nod.

"What's that?" Lori leans forward; at least I think it's her since she's sandwiched between Jinx and Lily.

"We have to move across the dance floor," Jinx explains. "The moves are easy, and it's okay to mess up. Most of those people are. Just stay with us, and we'll work our way to the other side."

Yes, that is what this operation comes down to, dancing across a crowded dance floor. Definitely not stealthy ops.

"If you like this, you're going to love what's downstairs." Mitzy chuckles in my ear.

No doubt I will, but first, we need to make it across the dance floor. On the other side, the elevator doors open, and half a dozen security guards pour out.

"Time to move." I grip Rose's hand and lead her onto the dance floor. We move right into the dance. I gotta give Rose props for being as light on her feet as she is.

All around us, people bump to the music, doing the same dance. The steps are basic, and I move right in line. Liam follows with Julie; the man is fucking Fred Astaire. Who knew he had those kinds of moves? Jinx and Lily are right there with us. Lori struggles with the dance but keeps moving as Jinx and Lily pull her along.

As the guards circle the periphery, we move down the line. Right as we get to the edge, all the phones around us suddenly sound off. The crowd gives a shout and moves en-mass for the bank of elevators right in front of us. Built for large crowds, each elevator holds over a score of people. We push in, keeping our group together and staying in the center, where we hide in plain sight.

The doors close us in, and we begin the long drop to the lobby. In our favor is that this is a dedicated elevator. There are no stops between the roof and the lobby.

I try to maintain my cool but not knowing what we're going to face downstairs makes my nerves buzz and vibrate. The doors could open to a contingent of security guards, weapons raised. That will lead to whole-scale panic as everyone around us loses their ever-loving minds. Of course, there is another option. The elevator can simply open, disgorging its occupants to the busy casino floor.

Those inside our elevator vibrate with the energy, which comes from being in the middle of a flash mob. Everyone wears a mask. Most are plain white like the ones we wear. But some are different.

Some take off the masks, not liking the reduced vision or maybe the added heat.

"This is so cool!" The guy beside me bounces on his heels, clasping his hands together. "I've never done this before. Have you?"

"Flash mob virgin." I keep my voice low, interested, but not enough to say more.

"It's going viral." He shows me a video on his phone. Hundreds of people in orange dancing on the rooftop. "Ten thousand views and climbing."

I'm used to highly focused stealth ops. Each move calculated in advance. This kind of mayhem is far outside my comfort zone, but it works.

Damn if it doesn't work.

The express elevator slows and comes to a stop. I grasp Rose's hand and give her a squeeze of encouragement. When the doors open, it takes a minute to fully process what I see.

The casino floor is a sea of orange shirts. "Happy" blares through the speakers. And the best part is the crowd moves en-mass toward the exit.

Liam shakes his head, as amused as I am by the brilliance of this plan. It's actually tons of fun, and while I don't forget my mission objective, for the first time in my career, I'm having one hell of a time.

We exit the elevator, and with everyone else, we merge into the crowd. We don't rush but keep pace with those around us.

Before I know it, we're outside. The street fills with people, and that stupid song blares over loudspeakers. Hundreds of people are cutting it up.

All in orange.

All with nearly identical masks.

All of them doing that funky dance.

"Cross the street. Head left. You'll see our van." Mitzy delivers her last instructions.

I lead my team through the crowd slowly so as not to attract unwanted attention while frustrated security guards scan the crowd. We come upon an unobtrusive gray van. The door opens, and CJ waves us forward. He steps back to the passenger seat, ushering us inside.

Lily and Jinx help Lori into the van, then climb in themselves. Liam helps Julie in next, then takes a step back, guarding my six while I get Rose in the van.

We did it. We fucking did it.

I hop inside, then look out at the street, waiting for Liam to join me.

Liam stands with his back to me, hands in the air.

Standing in front of him, a raven-haired beauty holds a Colt .45.

"Where the fuck is Sybil?" She presses the muzzle of her weapon against Liam's chest. "Where is she?"

"Whoa, hold up." Liam tries to play it cool. "Calm down."

Jinx and I exchange a look. Jinx's words return to me, and I cringe. In the history of the world, those words have never once calmed anyone down.

It takes but a second to assess the situation. This woman is very familiar with her weapon. She holds it like it's a part of her person. She's skilled and trained. The thumb safety is off, which means Liam will be in a world of hurt if she pulls the trigger.

"I am calm." She leans forward, keeping tight contact between the muzzle of the gun and Liam's chest.

If there weren't five women in the van with me, I'd grab her wrist and twist it while applying pressure to her nerve. Like me, Liam wears a plate beneath his suit. The kick of the bullet will concuss his lungs, bruise his heart, and take his breath, but it won't kill him.

Maybe.

But that isn't the worst of our problems.

Scanning over the crowd, a dozen or more security guards push through the crowd. They make a beeline for the van, which means this is officially a Whiskey Tango Foxtrot situation.

"Maria Rossi?" Jinx leans forward, peering over Liam's shoulder.

"Who are you?" Maria cries out. "And where the fuck is Sybil?"

Jinx holds up her hands. Unlike me and Liam, she's not wearing a chest plate. Jinx catches sight of the men pushing through the crowd and nibbles at her lower lip.

"Maria, you need to pay attention. We don't have much time." Jinx lowers her hands and leans closer to Maria. "Sybil isn't here. She's not one of the three we rescued, but we know where she is." Jinx looks up, following the path of the men.

"Where is she?" Maria is seconds from shooting Liam.

"We have a team headed to a cruise ship named Caviar Dreams where Sybil is being held captive." I exchange a look with Jinx. "We can explain, but we have to move."

"No one is going anywhere." Maria looks over her shoulder, searching for the men. It's exactly what I hoped would happen.

Liam immediately reacts.

He grabs the muzzle of the gun and rips it out of Maria's grip. She looks at him, disbelief in her face, but Liam's not done. He grabs Maria and bodily pulls her into the van. She lands on top of him.

The men close in and draw weapons.

"For the love of ..." The moment Liam's feet are inside the van, I slam the door shut and shout. "Go!"

The van lurches forward, moving faster than I would think possible with the crowd. People scatter, and we speed into the breach.

Liam spins Maria to her back, then straddles her hips, gaining control.

She pummels his chest and tries to knee him in the groin. Liam takes her wrists and pins them overhead. He turns his head, and damn if the bastard doesn't have a cheeky grin plastered all over his face.

"What the hell is going on?" Mitzy's voice crackles in our earpieces.

"We've got a bit of a SNAFU." I glance at Liam.

He leans down, his face hovering inches from Maria's stormy expression.

"Now, aren't you a pretty thing." Liam's husky laugh earns him a head butt.

Maria smacks him in the forehead. Liam loses his grip on her wrists. She reaches up and gives a karate chop to the side of Liam's neck. His lids pull back, and he sucks in a breath. Maria rocks her hips. Her knee lifts and slams home.

Liam grunts as her knee rams right into his balls.

"Fuckin' A." Liam rolls to the side, curling into the fetal position. He covers his nuts and huffs in pain.

"Maria!" Jinx moves forward, places a hand on Maria's arm.

I'm not sure what happens because it occurs in the blink of an eye, but Maria grabs hold of Jinx's wrist and manages to flip Jinx to her back.

"Okay, that's enough." I level the Colt .45 on Maria. "Everyone, take a time out."

Jinx coughs and rolls to her side. She takes to her knees and holds out a hand. "We're the good guys."

With her own weapon pointed at her head, I finally get Maria's attention. "Looks like we're having a failure to communicate. As for your friend, we have a team on the way to rescue her. As to why you're here, I need an answer right now."

Maria blows at her hair, puffing it out of her eyes. "Where the hell is my friend?" She shifts away from Liam, giving him a look, then she takes in the three women huddled in the rear. "Someone better start telling me what's going on, or I swear ..." Maria shows no fear with the Colt .45 leveled at her.

"What?" Liam pushes off the floor and spins to a sitting position. "You gonna knee me in the nuts again?"

"If that's what it takes." Maria glances between me and Jinx, then sees Lily and CJ. "Who are you?"

"I told you." I put on the safety and lower the gun, showing good faith. "We're the good guys."

"I thought ..." She looks to the women huddled in the back of the van. "Are they who they say they are?"

Julie wipes her tear-streaked face. "I don't know who they are, but they saved us."

"Saved you? I thought they were kidnapping you..." Maria suddenly grows quiet. She takes in a deep breath and turns her attention back to me. "I thought you were taking them where you took Sybil."

"You did not just kidnap Maria Rossi?" Mitzy cuts through the chatter. *"Please tell me you didn't kidnap her."*

"Can't do that."

"Can't do what?"

"Well fuck." There's a bit of a pause. *"CJ, open a private channel. We need damage control. Under no circumstances do you bring them here. I'm sending out another car. This is totally fucked up."*

I couldn't agree more.

While CJ and Mitzy conduct a meeting of the minds, Jinx and Lily take care of the girls. They cry. They can't believe they're finally safe. They're in shock and in need of medical attention.

What they don't know is the men who put in the orders for their personal slaves are still out there, and the operation who promised to deliver them will do anything to get them back.

These girls—these women—are far from safe.

And I've got one massive problem. Maria's words sink in, and I turn to her.

"You knew about the girls." I don't ask because I already know the answer. "You knew they were kidnapped?"

Maria slides back and crosses her arms over her chest. Her answer is a furious glare.

"You knew they were holding these women, and you did nothing to help them?" Liam shakes his head. "Of all the cold-hearted …"

"Don't bother finishing that sentence," she says. "What was I going to do? Walk in there and set them free? That's not how things work."

"And exactly how do things work?" Liam's voice heats. "Ever think to call the cops?"

"The cops?" Maria's harsh laugh is like dragging fingernails down a chalkboard. "Most of them are bought and paid for, so no, I didn't go to the cops."

"You sat there and did nothing." The look on Liam's face is full of disgust.

"You have no idea what it means to live in my world. Take your judgment and shove it up your ass." She's a ball of spitfire, that's for sure.

Liam better watch out, or he'll get burned.

I clear my throat, needing to cut through the tension. "We have a problem." I stare at her. "You need to fix it."

"Me?"

"Yes, you." I hook a thumb over my shoulder. "Those men following you, are they a part of your security detail?"

"My security detail?" She rolls her eyes. "More like my protection detail."

"That's kind of the same thing, sweetheart." Liam rubs at his neck where she karate chopped him.

"No. It's totally different." She crosses her arms but doesn't elaborate. "One keeps me safe. One keeps me a prisoner in my own home."

I'm kind of interested in how they're different because I agree with Liam.

"From their viewpoint, it looks like we abducted you. We don't need that kind of heat breathing down our necks from the Rossi's."

"What are you going to do? Pump me full of lead and drop my body in a dark alley?" Maria responds with an arrogant lifting of her brow. Her comment isn't aimed at me.

"You're lucky I don't spin you around and paddle your ass," Liam shoots back, getting in another dig. "You're so damn worried about Sybil, but do nothing …"

"I wasn't doing nothing. I was watching that room. Waiting to see what was happening. A few hours ago, they took Sybil and two other women from that room. I tried following them but lost them. Then I saw the four of you. When you took them out …"

She followed us. Smart girl and crazy skills. I didn't think anyone would be able to follow us through that crazy flash mob Mitzy created.

"You figured pointing a gun at my chest, demanding to know where your friend is, was going to work?" He gives a dramatic eye roll. "You're fucking crazy."

"Children!" My shout makes the two of them shut up. "We have a serious situation on our hands. The Rossi's have two reasons to come after us."

"Two?" Liam dismisses my comment.

"Yes, we took their property and kidnapped their fucking princess."

"Princess?" Maria snorts with indignation. "I'm more of a pawn to be used and discarded as my uncle sees fit. I don't know what kind of books you've been reading, but I'm not a fucking princess. If you think I mean anything to my uncle, think again."

"I don't care what you mean to him. That's irrelevant. What matters is we took something that belongs to him. Instead of slipping in and out, we now have you to deal with." I level a hard stare at her, satisfied when she gulps. "Nobody was supposed to see us with the girls. I'm going to ask you again, were those men your personal security detail or are they …"

"Maria—" Jinx's smooth voice lends a bit of calm to the situation. "This is really important. Were those men following you or us?"

"They're my personal security detail. Their sole job is to watch over me. They weren't following you, if that's what you're worried about." She rolls her shoulders back and answers me directly. "When I ran outside, they followed. I ditch them all the time. It's nothing."

"Well, it's something to us."

"Fuck." Liam runs a hand through his hair. He must be feeling better because he's moving around again and no longer protecting his balls. "Do we stop and dump her?"

"Dump me?" Maria's eyes widen.

"It's too late for that." I glance at the back of the van. Jinx and Lily are doing their best to soothe our rescues and explain what's going on.

CJ finishes his conversation with Mitzy. "Miss Rossi?"

"Yes?" Her sharp retort is defiance-fueled spite, and it's getting on my nerves.

"Yeah, you need a good swat on that ass of yours and soap to wash out your mouth." Liam shifts position. "That's what you need."

"Shut up." Maria practically spits the words at Liam.

"Miss Rossi, my name is CJ, and you present a significant problem. Despite my colleague's misgivings, a longer conversation is in order. But first, we need to do two things."

"What?" Her flippant reply brings a roguish grin to Liam's face.

I can't tell if Liam wants to kick Maria to the curb or jump her bones. Knowing Liam, it's probably a little bit of both.

"We need to blindfold you and—I'm sorry—but we need to bind your hands."

"You're taking me as a hostage, then." Maria gives a dramatic eye roll. "Just perfect, perfectly predictable. I'm not one of the bad guys, in case you haven't figured that out."

"Understood, but take a look at it from our perspective. Following a conversation in much more comfortable surroundings, we'll figure out how to fix this for all involved."

"Fix? By blindfolding me? Like that instills trust."

"Frankly, princess, we don't give a damn. It's that, or we dump your ass." Liam leans in, crowding Maria's space until she falls back with a catch in her breath.

"Stop terrorizing the poor girl." Jinx places her hand on Liam's chest and pushes him back.

"Maria, I know it sounds bad, but it's for the safety of these girls and the safety of your friend. I know we're not making it easy for you to trust us, especially with this Neanderthal," Jinx pushes Liam again, "but if you can please be patient with us ..."

After a bit of back and forth, Maria finally relents to CJ's demands. She does it only because he promises to reunite her with Sybil.

Not knowing how that mission is going, I hope Max and the rest of the team don't encounter any issues. Unlike us, who are literally bringing the enemy into our camp.

Granted, she's now hooded, bound, and gagged.

Liam had far too much fun with that. I can't help but chuckle watching him with Maria. I don't know if he wants to strangle her or fuck her. Maybe he wants to do both. As someone who had a rocky start with my girl, I totally get it.

We ditch Maria's phone, tossing it in the river as the van drives over a bridge. Less than an hour later, we're back beneath the carriage house.

Forest Summers, and his sister, Skye, are there to greet our rescues. Skye didn't fly down with the rest of us, but once the possibility of a rescue became certain, she and her medical team hopped on the private jet and flew down to New Orleans.

The girls go with Skye. Lily joins them. Jinx stays with me, CJ, and Liam. We're joined a few minutes later by Sam, who questions Maria. I wait five minutes before tapping CJ on the arm.

"If we're no longer necessary, do you mind if we take five?"

"You're good. Great mission. Solid extraction." CJ speaks in clipped tones, keeping his voice low while Sam and Liam continue their interrogation.

"Don't know about the great mission part, but it went. That's for sure."

"The extraction was solid. You did a great job. We'll find a way to deal with this mess."

"It's a total shitshow, isn't it?"

Maria sits on an uncomfortable wooden chair. Liam stands behind her, holding her down by the shoulders, while Sam fires off a barrage of questions.

All I want is to take Jinx away from this mess. As if she senses my thoughts, she squeezes my hand.

"I'm not sure it's as bad as it seems." CJ glances over at Maria. "We might be able to turn this to our advantage."

"Seriously?" Jinx speaks up.

"I hope so." CJ taps me on the arm. "You're good to go. The rest of the night is yours. We debrief in the morning."

"How did it go with Max and the others?"

"Mission success."

"So, Sybil is …?" Maria perks up.

"Safe, traumatized, a bit beat up, still in shock." His attention turns to Maria. "We're still deciding whether to use her as leverage or not."

"I'm not sure what your read is on Maria, but my gut says she's our ticket into Rossi dealings." CJ didn't ask for my two cents, but I give it to him, regardless.

"Agree, but until we understand her loyalties, she's a liability."

"Don't disagree with that."

While I'm curious as to how Maria noticed us, followed us out of the hotel and through the crowd, I'm not curious enough that I feel a need to stick around for the questioning. I tug Jinx to my side and kiss the top of her head.

"Do you want to hang around, or …"

"How about we head upstairs? I don't know about you, but I can definitely use a shower." Jinx's low, sultry laugh is all the encouragement I need.

I practically drag her upstairs, where I lock the door behind us, pull her into my embrace, and whisper in her ear.

"I can think of several filthy things we can do before that shower." I nibble softly on her earlobe and love the hitch in her breathing.

"Show me." Jinx reaches down and grabs the hem of the horrid orange shirt. She pulls it up and over her head, revealing that skintight red dress.

My cock takes notice, standing at attention and demanding that I remove that dress. I'm more than happy to oblige.

THIRTY-FIVE

Jinx

"Take that dress off before I rip it off your body." Wolfe's husky tone sends licks of pleasure shooting through my body.

"Bossy much?" I playfully push him away, cock a hip forward, and arch my brow. I love our little back and forth.

"You have no idea." Wolfe prowls toward me.

When I take a step back, he closes the distance. When I take a second step, he launches at me with heat and fury, a virile male with only one objective in mind.

Me.

I suck in a breath and try to find the zipper to the dress, but Wolfe's faster. The poor dress doesn't stand a chance. The seams rip as he tears at the fabric. It flutters to the floor where it lands in surrender.

He scoops me into his arms, looks at me with a roguish grin, then he flips me over his shoulder and smacks my ass as he carries me to bed.

A bed which, as yet, has not been slept in.

Wolfe tosses me down, where I bounce a tiny bit. Then he's on me. The heat of his body covers mine. It steals my breath and makes my heart race.

There's no gentleness as he claims my lips, taking what he desires. The man is unstoppable. He's determined. Like the dress, my panties fare no better. He hooks a finger under the lacy fabric and rips them from my body.

I've slept with a lot of men, but none have ever taken and claimed me like Wolfe. He's relentless, determined, and engages in a savage battle to lay claim to my body.

He pulls at his clothes, fighting against the multiple layers with a growl until he stands naked in front of me.

"Last chance to say no." He fists his cock, stroking slowly as his teeth clench.

"I say yes."

Yes, to whatever he wants. It's my forever answer for the man I love. And as he stares at me with heat and desire simmering in his gaze, an answering heat builds in my blood. My nerve endings come alive, sizzling with the supercharged air crackling between us.

He leans over me, and a moan escapes my mouth as the heat of his body sets mine aflame. He makes me crave everything about him. His touch sparks desires I'm almost too afraid to face, but in his arms, I feel no shame.

The chemistry between us is as explosive as our anger. We fight tooth and nail, going round and round each other, neither of us giving in until skin touches skin.

Then everything changes in an instant.

The man is unstoppable. His single-minded quest to drown me in pleasure begins with a kiss to my neck. It travels to my breasts, where he teases and torments. It sinks deep to my core as he kisses my navel and seems to stop. When a frustrated groan escapes me, he moves down to my hip, frustrating me further.

When the urge to scream overwhelms me, Wolfe dips his head down between my legs. The first lick sends me flying. The second lifts me to dizzying heights. I cry out when his sinful mouth moves away but then groan with delicious pleasure with the invasion of his cock.

The cadence of his strokes starts out strangely slow as he rocks in and out. Wolfe nips at my earlobe and flutters barely-there kisses along my neck. The dragging pull of his cock in and out makes my body shake and quiver as he rocks into me. It's nearly reverent, spiritual; the joining of our bodies changes everything between us.

My legs tremble as my pleasure grows. He catches a rhythm, moving faster, plunging deeper. His easy breaths turn rough and ragged, frenzied as his cock seems to swell within me, growing harder, longer, impossibly thicker.

The pleasure is nearly painful, it's so intense, but I'm past caring. My fingernails dig into the muscles of his back as Wolfe takes us up and over the edge. His legs tremble, and his chest heaves as his release overcomes him. I fly in a tangle of limbs, blissfully sedated and wonderfully fucked.

"I think I've died and gone to heaven."

"Luv, I've barely begun." Wolfe shifts and does things to my body no man has ever done.

I come on his cock. I come on his hand. I come on his face. Wolfe uses fingers and tongue to make me come and come again. Lily brags about the multiple-Os Knox lavishes on her. He's got nothing on Wolfe.

I fly and soar in Wolfe's embrace as wave after wave of bliss rolls through me. When I don't think I can come again, Wolfe shows me how wrong I am.

When I need a break, Wolfe shakes the foundations of my world. He takes me into the darkness and through to the other side, where he delves deep into the hidden recesses of my mind, pulling forth my darkest desires and making them come alive.

When I do finally beg for the pleasure to stop, I turn the tables on Wolfe. Two can play at that game, and I show him how formidable I can be.

Sometime well past O-dark thirty, we take that shower, and he fucks me one last time. Then we crawl into bed and into each other's arms. Sleep overtakes us until morning where we do it all again.

Four orgasms later and out of breath, I cover my face with my forearm.

"We need to get out of bed."

"No, we don't."

"But the debrief ..."

"Can wait." Wolfe rolls on top of me, somehow hard and erect, ready for another round. There's a glimmer in his eyes, something devilishly dirty. "How do you feel about blindfolds and cuffs?"

Sex is the playground of adults, and I can't think of a better play partner in the world.

"For you?"

It takes a second, the slightest pause, then Wolfe rolls me to my stomach and takes me again. With the sheets a twisted mess, we lose track of time. Noon comes and goes. By dinnertime, hunger draws us from bed.

"Are we going to be in trouble for missing the debrief?" I'm a little worried about doing anything wrong. The mission went well, but there was still that moment when my loyalties came into question. I've got a lot to prove to the Guardians, and I'm up for the task.

I couldn't imagine a better job than the one I have now.

"We're not going to be in trouble."

"How can you be so sure?"

"Because no one's come knocking on our door." He glances at the door, and my gaze follows. "Shower. Dress. Then we see what's going on."

"Or ... we can stay in bed?" As tired as I am, I'm not quite willing to share Wolfe with the rest of the world. Right now, there's just the two of us, and I'd like to keep it that way for a little bit longer.

Wolfe spins around, a wicked gleam in his eye. "I like the sound of that."

I give a little squeak as he launches himself at the bed. The moment he lands, a sharp pounding on the door turns my head.

"You've got to be kidding." I huff with disappointment, too eager to try the blindfold again.

"Wolfe! Jinx! We need you in the battle room."

The battle room? I mouth the words, looking to Wolfe confused. "I thought we only used that word when spinning up a mission."

"We do." Wolfe scrambles out of bed and runs to the door. "What's going on?"

"We have a situation." The voice behind the door belongs to Max, Alpha team's leader. "Get your ass down here immediately."

"Um—okay. I'll be just a minute."

"You've got five." Max thumps on the door. "And bring Jinx. We need her."

"Copy that." Wolfe turns around, and a grin fills his face. "How quick can you take a shower?"

"As fast as I must."

"Come on, then. You're one of us now. Time waits for no man."

"And no woman."

I race to the shower, knowing it'll take me longer than Wolfe. He's in and out in less than two minutes. I take five and struggle to dress while Wolfe waits impatiently.

We fly down the stairs and cross the short distance to the kitchen. He holds the door open and we hustle to the dining room where absolute chaos reigns.

"What the—"

"—Fuck?"

We complete each other's sentences now, no longer at odds. Wolfe is mine, and I am his. I've never dated before. I've never had a boyfriend. What I found instead is the man who will stand by me through thick and thin. I found the other half of my soul.

"Jinx!" Mitzy calls out from the front of the room. "I need you, stat!"

"Gotta go. The boss is calling." I squeeze Wolfe's hand then let go.

Mitzy draws me into chaos as Max gestures for Wolfe to join the rest of Alpha team.

"What's going on?" I glance around, trying to figure out where the fire is, but nothing's jumping out at me.

"Just another day in the office." Mitzy's reply is clipped and short.

When I look around the room, my heart swells with joy. This is my home. Wolfe catches my eye and winks at me.

He's my heart, my soul. He's the man I love, and I can't wait to start our life together.

We're going to do great things.

I hope you enjoyed Wolfe and Jinx's story.

I certainly did, which is why I wrote the short novella of their wedding. Join Jinx and Lily as they fly to Vegas for a bachelorette party and one EPIC surprise!
You can grab your copy by clicking the link below.

Get my Copy of Guardian Christmas in Vegas.

Alpha Team isn't done. We've got one more book in the series and there's still a villain to catch.
Read on as the Guardians face off against the Rossi crime syndicate.
Grab your copy of Rescuing Maria Today!

THIRTY-SIX

Maria

SNEAK PEEK OF THE FIRST CHAPTER IN RESCUING
MARIA

I RACE AFTER THE TWO COUPLES WHO TAKE THE THREE CAPTIVE women out of my hotel, herding them like animals. The group's hard to follow, considering the entire street basically exploded in one massive flash mob.

All around me that damn "Happy" song blares overhead. Hundreds of people in bright orange shirts, with the same dorky white smiley face on the front, kick up their heels, doing the same damn dance. The white masks over everyone's faces makes it that much harder to follow my quarry.

The only reason I don't lose them is because the two men stick head and shoulders above the crowd, and the three women they herd are barefoot. They push the women through the excited crowd, arrowing directly toward a nondescript van. As they near it, the side door slides open. A man leans out and waves vigorously for them to hurry up.

One of the women wearing combat boots jumps in. She helps the barefoot women into the van. The last woman disappears inside. I yank out my Colt .45 and close the distance.

Nearly there.

The first man climbs inside. The second gets ready to follow. He turns his back to me, but I'm right there.

"Don't move." My voice isn't nearly as firm as I'd like, but he gets the message. The barrel of my weapon presses against his spine. He holds his hands up, then slowly turns around.

My gun waivers when the tall, freakishly handsome, Hollywood heartthrob turns and gives me a look. He's amused and not one bit concerned my gun points at his chest.

Holy hotness and Hollywood gorgeous, like, shoot-me-dead-and-stick-a-fork-in-me-I'm-done kind of H-O-T, hot.

Let's say that again.

He's fucking HAWT!

The deadly combination of surfer blond hair, mischievous eyes, and a body ripped right off a blockbuster movie poster, are a triple threat weakening my knees and stirring up wicked fantasies.

The Colt .45 wobbles in my grip.

Which is totally not good.

I'm trying to be a fucking badass. Instead, I drool at the mouth.

Focus!

Yeah, yeah, I'll focus when I'm dead.

Midnight blue eyes. Strong jaw. Taller than tall.

He's Adonis come to life. I don't know who Adonis is, except he's who everyone refers to when they say a man's body is chiseled out of stone. Maybe it's marble? What do I know?

Seriously, this guy can't be the real deal. I want to run my hands up and down his body, indulging sinful fantasies. Yet here I am, muzzle of my Colt .45 pressed against his chest, safety off, and my finger hovering over the trigger. My intent is clear.

"Where the fuck is Sybil?" My voice comes out steady, which is a surprise considering how off kilter I feel.

The anger simmering in his eyes is a challenge.

There's no backing down.

No fear.

He stares at me with lethal promise boiling within him, ready to stomp on me like an irritating bug and put me in my place. Like how dare I draw a weapon on him?

I have an answer for that.

He took my bestie and I want her back.

How does someone do that? Stare with such power? His confidence overwhelms me. Fuck, it's overpowering. Intoxicating.

Seductive. Sexy. Sin on a stick.

He hijacks my thoughts, mainlines my body's reactions, and turns them down a deliciously dark path.

Good thing, I'm the one with the gun.

I tighten my grip. Firm my resolve. I remind myself I'm here to rescue my best friend. My sister from another mother, Sybil was taken and these sad sacks are involved.

I know it.

And I'm going to make them give her back.

Despite his holy hotness factor, I focus. I press the muzzle of my gun, pushing harder against the man's chest.

"Where is she?" My voice comes out a low growl.

The Belvedere's annual charity auction is tonight. Sybil was supposed to meet me several hours ago. Last I saw her, she was on her way to the beauty salon for a half day indulgence of manicure, pedicure, facials, massage; basically all the things.

I texted. I called.

Sybil did not text me back.

She did not call back.

That never happens.

What did I do?

I overreacted.

"Whoa, hold up and calm down." The guy looks down at his chest, totally chill. Which pisses me off.

Hello? I'm pointing a gun at you.

"I am calm." Leaning forward, I hold the muzzle tight against his chest.

"Maria Rossi?" One of the women inside the van leans forward. Her brows pinch together then shift over my head to the crazy flash mob behind me.

"Who are you? How do you know my name? And where the fuck is Sybil?"

The woman holds up her hands. Once again, her attention shifts to the crowd behind me. She nibbles at her lower lip, then speaks.

"Maria, you need to pay attention. We don't have much time. Sybil isn't here. She's not one of the three we rescued, but we know where she is."

"Where is she?" I'm moments from shooting Hollywood Heartthrob in front of me.

"We can explain, but we have to move." The other man speaks up. He wears the same silly shirt as everyone else, an obnoxious orange with a white smiley face on it. He exchanges a look with the woman who spoke to me.

The entire flash mob behind me gyrates to the music in the same damn shirt. Only instead of trying to escape in a van like these assholes, the crowd dances to the music blaring up and down the street. There are hundreds of crazy people kicking up their feet.

I barely followed this group out of the lobby of the Belvedere and through the crowd.

But I did. I'm tenacious and protect my family.

Sybil is missing and I'll do whatever it takes to find her.

"No one is going anywhere." I glance over my shoulder, checking on my security detail. I ditched them to race after these assholes. But they're tenacious assholes too. My uncle charged them with keeping me safe and they don't want to piss off my uncle.

Fuckers follow me everywhere.

Honestly, they're a pain in the ass. The moment I took over as the Belvedere's CEO, my uncle insisted on the protective detail. They hound my every move. There to keep me safe. What they're really doing is preventing me from looking too hard into what my uncle is doing right under my nose.

For the first time ever, the monkeys assigned to protect me might actually do something worthwhile. I glance over my shoulder to track their progress. My protection detail double-times it to my position. They're still some distance off.

The moment I do, I regret it.

Hollywood Heartthrob grabs the muzzle of my Colt .45 and

rips the gun out of my grip. My mouth gapes, shocked by how easily he disarmed me, but he's not done. He grabs me and yanks me inside the van.

I land right on top of him.

A girlish screech escapes me.

"Go!" He yanks his feet inside the van.

The other man, the one who spoke earlier, pulls the sliding door shut. The van lurches forward, moving fast, with me trapped inside of it.

Hollywood spins me to my back, then straddles my hips. He's got the upper hand and he knows it. A cocky smirk fills his expression. I want to rip the look right off his face.

No one manhandles me like that and gets away with it.

I pummel his chest, beating him with my fists. Goddamn that hurts. His chest is wrapped in one of those bullet proof vests.

Fuck me.

But my actions distract him enough for me to lift my knee. I intend to ram it into his family jewels, but the bastard takes my wrists and pins them over my head.

Fucker.

"We've got a bit of a SNAFU." The man who slammed the door shut gives me the eye, like I'm some kind of puzzle he needs to sort out.

"Now aren't you a pretty thing?" Hollywood leans down until our faces are a breath apart.

His breath smells minty and his husky laugh should be illegal. Damn if it's not sexy like every other part of him. Doesn't mean I'm going to give him a pass.

With my hands pinned over my head and his powerful legs straddling me, I don't like my position. He can do anything to me and there's precious little I can do to fight back. Since he's stupid enough to lean forward, I do the only thing I can think of to fight back. I'm not completely defenseless. I head butt the sexy heartthrob.

Crack!

Pain becomes my universe and dark spots dance in front of my eyes. I blink, trying to clear my vision.

"Fuckin' A." He loses the grip on my wrists, which frees me to karate chop the side of his neck. From the way he sucks in a breath, that hurt.

Score one for me.

And I'm not done.

I rock my hips, giving me room to move. Given room to move, my knee lifts and I slam it home. Score two for me. Got his head and scored a direct hit to his nuts.

He grunts and rolls to the side, curling into fetal position as he huffs in pain.

"Maria!" The woman who seems to know exactly who I am moves forward and restrains my arm.

I was going to punch Hollywood's lights out and don't appreciate her stopping me. Using one of many of my defensive moves, I grab the chick's wrist and flip her onto her back. For the first time in my life, all that training in martial arts actually serves a purpose.

"Okay, that's enough." The man who shut the door aims my gun at my head. "Everyone take a time out."

"We're the good guys." The woman coughs and rolls to her side.

The man with my gun gives it a little shake. I puff at the hair which always seems to fall into my face and scoot backward.

"Where the hell is my friend?" I give Hollywood a look then peer into the back of the van.

Three frightened woman stare back at me. They cling to each other, huddling tight, shaking, with tears streaming down their faces.

"Looks like we're having a failure to communicate." The man gives a little shake of my gun. "As for your friend, we have a team on the way to rescue her. As to why you're here, I need an answer right now."

I'm not ready to answer his questions, not when I have so many of my own. I firm my chin and deepen my voice, trying to take back control.

"Where the hell is my friend?" I look at everyone in the van.

From the three women huddled in the back who look more relieved than scared, to the two men and two women staring at me, I'm having a really hard time sorting out what the hell I'm seeing.

There are two others in here with us. People I've ignored thus far; the driver and the man sitting in the passenger seat.

"Someone better start telling me what's going on, or I swear…" I stare at the man holding my Colt .45. What the hell am I going to do? I'm disarmed, trapped, and out-manned.

One against at least six.

I don't count the three women cowering in the back.

"Swear what?" Hollywood is no longer bent over double. "You gonna knee me in the nuts again?"

I got his attention. My kneecap still stings from slamming it into his groin. He's going to have bruised nuts for days. Gingerly, I feel my forehead where a lump is forming. I'm going to have one epic headache after this.

"Maybe." I wrap my arms around myself. "If that's what it takes."

When my father was alive, he insisted I take martial arts. I wanted to learn to dance and do cheer school. Despite my protests, I learned how to defend myself and handle a gun. I'm proficient with most handguns and know several ways to incapacitate a man with nothing but my hands. A knee to the groin is but one of the tools in my arsenal.

With what I'm learning about my family at the Belvedere, my father's insistence that I learn self-defense makes much more sense. And by learning, I'm referring to the past few hours since Sybil's disappearance. She's not the only thing I've lost tonight.

"Who are you?" I have questions that need immediate answers.

The man with my gun makes a show of lowering it. I feel marginally better not having my gun aimed directly between my eyes.

"I told you," he says. "We're the good guys."

"That's debatable." I turn my attention to the three people in this van who I trust to tell me the truth. I look to the women huddled in the back. "Are they who they say they are?"

"I don't know who they are, but they saved us." One of the women wipes at her tear-streaked face.

Okay, maybe they are the good guys. It's still not enough. Sybil is still missing.

"I thought they were kidnapping you…" My attention shifts to the man holding my gun. "I thought you were taking them where you took Sybil."

The man stares at me, then cocks his head. He places a finger to his ear then speaks. "Can't do that."

"Can't do what?" His response makes no sense, but then I see the earpiece.

Belvedere security wear something similar, hooking them up to the security suite where every square inch of the Belvedere is highly monitored. Well, almost every square inch. There's the whole twenty-fifth floor.

The van rocks as it navigates through the congested streets. There are no windows, which makes me queasy.

The man gives me one hell of a look. "You knew about the girls. You knew they were kidnapped?"

I slide back and glare at him. How dare he accuse me?

"You knew they were holding these women and you did nothing to help them?" Hollywood turns his magnetic blue eyes on me and shakes his head. His angry stare sends currents of electricity shooting into the air. "Of all the cold-hearted…"

The fine hairs on my arms lift as the air sizzles between us. Holy hotness, if that's not a superpower, I don't know what is.

"Don't bother finishing that sentence." It pisses me off for him to think that, let alone say it. The problem is he speaks the truth. "What was I going to do? Walk in there and set them free? That's not how things work."

Not to mention, I've been expressly forbidden from accessing that particular floor. Marco's orders are not questioned, and me being as new as I am to my position, the last person I want to piss off is my uncle.

Now that I'm suspicious about what exactly the family business might be, questioning anything can be downright dangerous.

Lethal comes to mind.

"And exactly how does it work?" He leans in, closing the distance between us. "Ever think to call the cops?"

I'm smarter than that. Not to mention the Chief of Police was recently at a meeting hosted by Marco at the Belvedere. I may be slow at putting two and two together, but I'm not dumb.

My entire life is a sham. I thought my family was in the hotel business. There are side businesses my cousins are in charge of; things like managing dock workers at port and the family's import and export company.

My eyes and ears are now open. No longer sheltered and innocent, the truths I've discovered about my family are uncomfortable and dangerous.

I don't know if Marco ever intended for me to know any of this, but he's a smart man. The questions I've asked, and the answers I've been given, don't match up.

I'm part of a crime family, a spoiled princess who until very recently has been completely and totally oblivious about everything.

I hate that the most.

And I don't know what to do about it.

I've never felt this lost in my life, and the one person I can count on is missing.

Please keep Sybil safe for me.

I lift up a prayer for my friend, terrified for her safety.

Returning my attention to the man in front of me, I straighten my spine and firm my chin. I'm ready to go to war to save Sybil and I'm going to need allies. But I don't know if I'm with friends or foe.

If these people are who they say they are, then maybe they didn't take Sybil. Someone in my family is responsible for that. Someone with access to the twenty-fifth floor.

They'd better watch out, because I'm coming for them. I'm no longer a sweet and innocent thing too stupid to see the forest for the trees.

Read on as the Guardians face off against the Rossi crime syndicate.
Grab your copy of Rescuing Maria Today!

ELLZ BELLZ

ELLIE'S FACEBOOK READER GROUP

If you are interested in joining the ELLZ BELLZ, Ellie's Facebook reader group, we'd love to have you.

Join Ellie's ELLZ BELLZ.
The ELLZ BELLZ Facebook Reader Group

Sign up for Ellie's Newsletter.
Elliemasters.com/newslettersignup

Also by Ellie Masters

The LIGHTER SIDE

Ellie Masters is the lighter side of the Jet & Ellie Masters writing duo! You will find Contemporary Romance, Military Romance, Romantic Suspense, Billionaire Romance, and Rock Star Romance in Ellie's Works.

YOU CAN FIND ELLIE'S BOOKS HERE:

ELLIEMASTERS.COM/BOOKS

Military Romance

Guardian Hostage Rescue Specialists

Rescuing Melissa

(Get a FREE copy of Rescuing Melissa

when you join Ellie's Newsletter)

Alpha Team

Rescuing Zoe

Rescuing Moira

Rescuing Eve

Rescuing Lily

Rescuing Jinx

Rescuing Maria

Bravo Team

Rescuing Angie

Rescuing Isabelle

Rescuing Carmen

Military Romance

Guardian Personal Protection Specialists

Sybil's Protector

Lyra's Protector

The One I Want Series

(Small Town, Military Heroes)

By Jet & Ellie Masters

EACH BOOK IN THIS SERIES CAN BE READ AS A STANDALONE AND IS ABOUT A DIFFERENT COUPLE WITH AN HEA.

Saving Ariel

Saving Brie

Saving Cate

Saving Dani

Saving Jen

Saving Abby

Rockstar Romance

The Angel Fire Rock Romance Series

EACH BOOK IN THIS SERIES CAN BE READ AS A STANDALONE AND IS ABOUT A DIFFERENT COUPLE WITH AN HEA. IT IS RECOMMENDED THEY ARE READ IN ORDER.

Ashes to New (prequel)

Heart's Insanity (book 1)

Heart's Desire (book 2)

Heart's Collide (book 3)

Hearts Divided (book 4)

Hearts Entwined (book5)

Forest's FALL (book 6)

Hearts The Last Beat (book7)

Contemporary Romance

Firestorm

(Kristy Bromberg's Everyday Heroes World)

Billionaire Romance

Billionaire Boys Club

Hawke

Richard

Brody

Contemporary Romance

Cocky Captain

(Vi Keeland & Penelope Ward's Cocky Hero World)

Romantic Suspense

Each book is a standalone novel.

The Starling

~AND~

Science Fiction

Ellie Masters writing as L.A. Warren

Vendel Rising: a Science Fiction Serialized Novel

About the Author

Ellie Masters is a USA Today Bestselling author and Amazon Top 15 Author who writes Angsty, Steamy, Heart-Stopping, Pulse-Pounding, Can't-Stop-Reading Romantic Suspense. In addition, she's a wife, military mom, doctor, and retired Colonel. She writes romantic suspense filled with all your sexy, swoon-worthy alpha men. Her writing will tug at your heartstrings and leave your heart racing.

Born in the South, raised under the Hawaiian sun, Ellie has traveled the globe while in service to her country. The love of her life, her amazing husband, is her number one fan and biggest supporter. And yes! He's read every word she's written.

She has lived all over the United States—east, west, north, south and central—but grew up under the Hawaiian sun. She's also been privileged to have lived overseas, experiencing other cultures and making lifelong friends. Now, Ellie is proud to call herself a Southern transplant, learning to say y'all and "bless her heart" with the best of them. She lives with her beloved husband, two children who refuse to flee the nest, and four fur-babies; three cats who rule the household, and a dog who wants nothing other than for the cats to be his best friends. The cats have a different opinion regarding this matter.

Ellie's favorite way to spend an evening is curled up on a couch, laptop in place, watching a fire, drinking a good wine, and bringing forth all the characters from her mind to the page and hopefully into the hearts of her readers.

FOR MORE INFORMATION

elliemasters.com

- facebook.com/elliemastersromance
- twitter.com/Ellie__Masters
- instagram.com/ellie_masters
- bookbub.com/authors/ellie-masters
- goodreads.com/Ellie_Masters

Connect with Ellie Masters

Website:
elliemasters.com
Amazon Author Page:
elliemasters.com/amazon
Facebook:
elliemasters.com/Facebook
Goodreads:
elliemasters.com/Goodreads
Instagram:
elliemasters.com/Instagram

Final Thoughts

I hope you enjoyed this book as much as I enjoyed writing it. If you enjoyed reading this story, please consider leaving a review on Amazon and Goodreads, and please let other people know. A sentence is all it takes. Friend recommendations are the strongest catalyst for readers' purchase decisions! And I'd love to be able to continue bringing the characters and stories from My-Mind-to-the-Page.

Second, call or e-mail a friend and tell them about this book. If you really want them to read it, gift it to them. If you prefer digital friends, please use the "Recommend" feature of Goodreads to spread the word.

Or visit my blog https://elliemasters.com, where you can find out more about my writing process and personal life.

Come visit The EDGE: Dark Discussions where we'll have a chance to talk about my works, their creation, and maybe what the future has in store for my writing.

Facebook Reader Group: Ellz Bellz

Thank you so much for your support!

Love,

Ellie

Dedication

This book is dedicated to you, my reader. Thank you for spending a few hours of your time with me. I wouldn't be able to write without you to cheer me on. Your wonderful words, your support, and your willingness to join me on this journey is a gift beyond measure.

Whether this is the first book of mine you've read, or if you've been with me since the very beginning, thank you for believing in me as I bring these characters 'from my mind to the page and into your hearts.'

Love,
Ellie

THE END

Please consider leaving a review

I HOPE YOU ENJOYED THIS BOOK AS MUCH AS I ENJOYED WRITING IT. If you like this book, please leave a review. I love reviews. I love reading your reviews, and they help other readers decide if this book is worth their time and money. I hope you think it is and decide to share this story with others. A sentence is all it takes. Thank you in advance!

CLICK ON THE LINK BELOW TO LEAVE YOUR REVIEW
Goodreads
Amazon
Bookbub